HERO'S LUST

Everyone in Crescent C. the town, most of all Red Norton. Red's an ace reporter, sure, but he's living in the mayor's side pocket. What the Mayor wants, he gets. And right now he wants Red to write up his new Medical Center. The Mayor needs a pitch, and finds it in tubercular Ann Porter, who is scheduled for an upcoming operation. Her story sells a lot of papers, and puts a face to the Mayor's pet project. Red didn't figure on falling in love with the kid, but now he's involved. And with the Mayor making some new demands, Red is about to find out just how rotten the town really is—the hard way.

THE MAN I KILLED

When Lew Ross was young, he got into a fight and killed a man, then fled the scene. Haunted by this event throughout his life, he finds himself back in that same town again, at the same club where it all happened. Except that now the place is a nightclub. And this is where he meets Kitty, one of the hostesses, and her slick boss, Marty Evans, who has a proposition for Ross—pick up a delivery from a local rival, and join his crew. Evans even loans him a gun for protection. Trouble is, the pick up is a set up, and Ross is the fall guy. Now he's in a squeeze play between a scheming D.A., an honest cop, and Evans' thugs. And then there's Kitty...

HOUSE OF EVIL

Nina Valjean needs a fix or she wouldn't have agreed to see Smith again. Smith is one of the sick ones, but sometimes a girl can't afford to be picky. Still, she's got a bad feeling about this time. The next day, Roman Laird lets himself into his out-of-town fiancée's apartment, and finds Valjean's nude, strangled body. Things haven't been good between he and Joyce for a while, but finding a body in her place is just crazy. Trying to protect her, Laird tracks the dead woman to a seedy bar called The Red Parrot, which is how he meets an exotic dancer named Cecille Merrill. But all this time, Smith is out there, watching him—ready to kill again.

"This is political noir on the local level, the personal level, a hard-fought, hard-scrabble novel." —Gary Lovisi on *Hero's Lust*

"Big city corruption in a fictitious city… The book is tough, realistic (for the time) and well-written." —Dan Roberts on *Hero's Lust*

"The story centers on a man who returns to the town where he got away with murder 10 years previous, only to get framed for a new murder that he didn't commit. The plot is ingenious, the writing crisp, and the action relentless." —Dan Roberts on *The Man I Killed*

"A noir classic, dark and foreboding and very violent." —Dan Roberts on *House of Evil*

"Reading these books are like watching late night film noir on late night TV with the lights out." —Rick Ollerman

"*Hero's Lust* is really a punch in the gut!" —James Reasoner, *Rough Edges*

A TRIO OF LIONS:

Hero's Lust
by Kermit Jaediker

The Man I Killed
by Shel Walker

House of Evil
by Clayre and Michel Lipman

Stark House Press • Eureka California

HERO'S LUST / THE MAN I KILLED / HOUSE OF EVIL

Published by Stark House Press
1315 H Street
Eureka, CA 95501
griffinskye3@sbcglobal.net
www.starkhousepress.com

ISBN-13: 978-1-944520-02-1

Book design by Mark Shepard, SHEPGRAPHICS.COM

First Stark House Press Edition: July 2016

FIRST EDITION

7

Hero's Lust & two other
Top Crime Noir Sleepers!
an introduction by Gary Lovisi

11

Lion Books: The Best
of the 1950s PBO Noir
By Dan Roberts

19

Hero's Lust
by Kermit Jaediker

127

The Man I Killed
by Shel Walker

215

House of Evil
by Clayre and Michel Lipman

301

Bibliographies

Hero's Lust & two other Top Crime Noir Sleepers!

an introduction by Gary Lovisi

Lion Books in the 1950s was a mini-powerhouse of hard-boiled and noir paperback original crime fiction. They published just over 200 books in their main series, mostly crime and westerns—but even their western novels were brutal, hard-boiled, violent noir. Their crime novels were something much more—even better—with stories that went far beyond anything anyone else was publishing at the time. The Lion series is loaded with unrelenting noir crime masterpieces, and some real sleepers for readers and collectors.

Lion Books originally published 10 of the intense crime noirs of Jim Thompson, who has become a legend today—including his most famous crime novel, *The Killer Inside Me*. They published hard-hitting original crime noirs that have become modern classics by such greats as Robert Bloch, Day Keene, David Goodis, Richard Matheson, David Karp, Richard S. Prather and Don Tracy.

Arnold Hano was responsible for obtaining most of the books. He became editor of Lion Books in 1950. It was said he furnished outlines of exactly what he wanted to see from some writers (such as Thompson), and they followed his directions, but in their own way. He also published crime novels written by prisoners and also new Black writers, with work from the slush pile. He had a very good eye for quality.

However, Lion also published a lot of books by writers most people never heard of even back then—writers whose names have been sadly forgotten today. While the author's names may have been forgotten, their books and stories have not, and many of these books have taken on a life of their own in the hearts of collectors, readers and crime noir aficionados the world over. These are the kind of books knowing readers rave about to each other in their most private moments when talking obscure hard crime noir favorites.

The three novels that make up this new Stark House volume offer some of the best examples of that unique fiction Lion Books was so famous for. Greg Shepard, editor of Stark House, has chosen three winners—all mini masterpieces. These are obscure novels—real sleepers in the parlance of true aficionados who love nothing more than to discover a great lost work and share it with others. In this book you will embark upon a new and mysterious excursion into the darkest pit of noir desperation, crime and corruption, three novels you will not soon forget.

In these three novels: *Hero's Lust* by Kermit Jaediker (1953)—followed by two equally hard-hitting novels—*The Man I Killed* by Shel Walker (1952, pseudonym of crime writer Walt Sheldon); and *House of Evil* by Clayre and Michel Lipman (their only novel, 1954), you will make for some very pleasant discoveries.

I don't know much about Kermit Jaediker, who wrote the lead novel in this book, but he is said to have been an early Golden Age comics writer and cartoonist. *Hero's Lust* is his only paperback original. While he only wrote two novels, he sure knew a lot about the inner workings of corruption and politics and he takes the reader on a full-face nose-dive into the charnel pit of these evil influences. I believe Jaediker even invented a medical scam in this novel I'd never heard of before—ghost doctors! I won't go into the details here, I'll let the hero of this novel explain it to you. You will be amazed!

Red Norton is the hero of Jaediker's novel, a two-bit reporter for the *Courier* of Crescent City who plays ball with the crooked mayor and his criminal gang. Mayor Gowan pulls all the strings and controls everyone and everything, but he has a soft spot for Red, and takes him under his wing. From this privileged position, Red sees just what the mayor's corrupt tentacles have done to his city, the people, and himself, but he is ensnared deeply in the trap and he doesn't care so long as he gets his pile—and he does. A more accurate title for this book might have been *Heel's Lust*, because Red is certainly a full-fledged heel, but just when things seem to be going great for Red, a dame is thrown into the mix to complicate his life.

Ann Porter is a sweet gal, young and cute and Red can't help but be interested, but she's got TB. Ann has been carefully chosen by the mayor to be the focus of a newspaper story by Red promoting the mayor's new Medical Center—and the mayor and his administration, of course. Ann is sent there to get the lung operation that will cure her. The Medical Center is the gleaming gem in all the mayor's dirty rotten schemes, it is the one thing in his life he has created that is not touched by graft and corruption—as far as he knows. It has one of the best surgeons in the city, Dr. Winston, who will perform the operation to save Ann's life. Red falls hard for Ann.

Things start going downhill when Red is approached by a friend who is an honest newspaperman from a rival paper. Bernstein believes Red still has some principles left, and seeks to recruit him into a scheme to get the goods on Mayor Gowan and bring down his administration, and the corruption it fosters. Meanwhile, Red is falling in love with Ann, so he considers working for Bernie, but he is no sucker. Red knows that Mayor Gowan has all the answers and he has Red firmly under his thumb.

Mayor Gowan rules by fear and intimidation and with bribes, but when that doesn't work he has a select group of men willing to do what needs to be done. Hartung, his police captain bodyguard, is a vicious thug who likes to catch rats, douse them with gasoline, and then set them ablaze for fun. He does the violent work and likes it. Murphy, is a brutal louse whose advice for any problem is to get rid of the problem. Then there's Frankie, a weasel set-up man who Red mistakenly trusts. The mayor also has actual gangsters on the payroll like Mike Calitorcio, which means he has eyes everywhere and on everyone. Red feels trapped and he knows it.

The battle between the Mayor and Bernstein causes Red to fall smack in the middle of their dangerous war. This sample from page 39 will give you an idea of just how trapped Red feels:

The Mayor and Bernie. It's their fight. It's their fight, but you're in the middle, a nut caught in the jaws of the biggest nutcracker ever made. When those big shining jaws come together, they could crack your shoulder blades and the bones of your arms and the bones of your hands, until you couldn't wash them of anything, and the bones of your thighs and legs and ribs, and then the jaws would slide up to your skull and slowly, surely, with a loud crunching sound, they would crack the bony white walls of your skull and suddenly the walls would cave in, crunching into sharp white splinters....

Well, you can see Red Norton is in deep trouble, with a dame he loves, and the strangling noose of corruption breathing hard down his neck. This is political noir on the local level, the personal level, a hard-fought, hard-scrabble novel of the way life really was back then—and still is today. It's a timeless story. The names have been changed, but the same type of corruption goes on and on.

I'm not going to get deeper into the plot of this novel, as that would spoil the story for you, but let me just say that there are a lot of twists and turns in this story and what happens in the end will be totally unexpected. You're in for a fine ride—and that's just the first novel in this exciting three novel package of classic Lion Books noir masterpieces. These are great powerful stories you can now resurrect by just turning this page as you begin read-

ing. I envy your discovery of these forgotten sleepers for the first time.
You're in for a real treat. Enjoy!

Gary Lovisi
Brooklyn, New York
March, 2016

GARY LOVISI is a crime author, who sells, collects, and writes about rare
and vintage paperbacks. Under his Gryphon Books imprint, he publishes
Paperback Parade, the world's leading magazine on collectable paperbacks
of all kinds, which is now in full color. You can find out more about him
or his work at his website: www.gryphonbooks.com or on Facebook.

Lion Books: The Best of the 1950s PBO Noir
By Dan Roberts

During the 1940s and well into the 1950s, many of the major U.S. paperback publishing houses (Pocket Book. Avon, Dell, Ace, Popular Library, Gold Medal, Bantam, and Signet) were engaged in high stakes one-upmanship to establish supremacy in the newly emerging and highly competitive paperback publishing field. Pocket Books was publishing a plethora of literary titles; Avon and Popular Library were concentrating on sensational cover art rather than literary merit; Dell was successfully exploiting its "mapback" format; Fawcett Gold Medal was successfully paying authors up front for novels that became some of the first paperback originals (PBOs); Bantam and Signet were featuring a "classic" look to their cover art and design; and Ace was publishing its distinctive "Ace Doubles" (two complete novels in one volume for $.35, only $.10 more than the $.25 charged by other houses for single titles). Meanwhile, other companies were forming to compete with these giants of the industry Firms such as Bartholomew House, Graphic, HandiBooks, Novel Library, Hillman, Zenith, and Quick Reader, to name a few, entered the fray in the late 1940s, but virtually none of them survived for more than a few years.

Another rival publishing house that didn't survive for very long was Lion Books, which was in business for only nine years, from 1949 to 1957. Although it didn't sustain the company in the long run, Lion Books had one thing going for it that none of its rivals except Gold Medal had: it published some of the best noir novels of the time as paperback originals (PBOs). Nearly one-third of Lion's 233 offerings in its initial series can be characterized as noir fiction PBOs and a large number of these titles are highly prized by today's collectors of such fiction. Stellar writers such as Jim Thompson, David Goodis, Day Keene, Richard Matheson, David Karp, and Robert Bloch all had PBOs published by Lion. Several PBO "sleepers" have also been discovered in recent years among Lion's initial series, including Paul Meskil's *Sin Pit*, G. H. Otis's *Bourbon Street*, Bruce Elliott's *One is a Lonely Number*, and Linton Baldwin's *Sinner's Game*. There are other sleepers in the series.

At the time of publication, of course, few of these writers had any reputation at all and for the most part they were completely unknown (with the possible exception of David Goodis, who was appreciated in some literary circles in France during his lifetime and Robert Bloch, who was rapidly gaining a solid reputation through some of his short story publications). Lion also published a large number of top notch noir reprints that first appeared as hardbacks in the 20s, 30s, and 40s, but this article focuses only on the noir titles published by Lion as PBOs. It may not be going too far out on a limb to say that the very best noir fiction at mid-twentieth century, hardback or paperback, was being produced by Lion Books over a period of just a few short years.

ENTER MARTIN GOODMAN

Lion Books was founded in 1949 by Martin Goodman, a somewhat mysterious figure who had been publishing pulps, magazines, and comics under a wide variety of corporate names since the early 1930s. Among his corporate entities was Timely Comics, which by 1960 would evolve into Marvel Comics. In 1932 Goodman founded Western Fiction Publishing, and his first two publications under this corporate entity were *Western Supernovel Magazine* and *Complete Western Book Magazine*. But even before Western Fiction Publishing was formed, Goodman had created a loosely-organized entity known as Red Circle to refer generically to his group of pulp and magazine publishing ventures. Distinguished by a red disk surrounded by a black ring bearing the phrase *"A Red Circle Magazine,"* the logo appeared on publications only intermittently, apparently only when someone remembered to include it on the cover. Other pulps published by Goodman included *All Star Adventure Fiction, Mystery Tale, Real Sports, Star Detective, Marvel Science Stories*, and *Ka-Zar*.

By 1939, the comic medium was rapidly gaining momentum and soon became hugely popular. Goodman wasted no time in entering this field, test-marketing in October 1939 a comic entitled *Marvel Comics #1*, in which the superheroes the Human Torch and the Sub-Mariner were introduced. The initial print run of 80,000 copies quickly sold out, as did a second print run of 800,000 copies! (Compare this with the miniscule print run of only 2,000 copies when Pocket Books' Robert deGraff test-marketed Pearl S. Buck's *The Good Earth* in paperback form a year earlier in November 1938!) Timely Comics was then formed to serve as Goodman's umbrella for his rapidly expanding comic book division.

As the popularity of pulp magazines started to wane in the late 40s, Goodman formed a magazine division called Magazine Management Company which published men's magazines such as *For Men Only, Male*, and *Stag* as well as more "mainstream" magazines such as *Popular Digest* and *Movie World* well into the 1950s. Another division established by Goodman published small-format "girly" digests such as *Breezy, Gaze, Gee-Whiz, Focus, Photo, Joker, Stare, Eye* and *Snappy*. Goodman also formed a new comics corporation, Seaboard Periodicals, that published under a new Atlas imprint. Many of the Atlas digests familiar to paperback and digest collectors were published under this imprint.

By the time Goodman decided to branch into the 10-year-old paperback field in the late 1940s with Lion Books, he was undeniably a major figure in New York publishing circles, creating, buying and selling publishing companies in the pulp, comic, and magazine fields seemingly as the mood suited him.

His biggest money-maker by far, however, was Marvel Comics, which he sold in 1968 to the Perfect Film and Chemical Corporation (a rather unlikely firm known for film processing and mail order drug sales) and retired to Florida, where he died in 1992.

THE BIRTH OF LION BOOKS

Lion Books began publication in November 1949 in a rather unusual way: the first seven Lions, as well as Nos. 12 and 13, weren't Lions at all. Rather, they were Red Circle Books that featured the red circle colophon that adorned many of the Goodman empire's magazines and pulps. Red Circle No. 1 is a rather non-descript non-pictorial self-help book entitled *Sex Life and You*. Red Circle Nos. 7 (Elliot Storm's *Hot Date*) and 13 (Anthony Scott's *Carnival Love*) are both Brett Halliday a.k.a. Davis Dresser re-titled pseudonymous reprints. The rest of the Red Circles are primarily inconsequential "potboiler" reprints. The first Lion is actually No. 8 in the series, a reprint of Edward Anderson's *Hungry Men*. Numbers 9, 10, and 11 also bear the distinctive "roaring lion" colophon, but inexplicably, Nos. 12 and 13 revert back to the red circle colophon. Interestingly, the title and indicia pages of Red Circle No. 12 (Token West's *Why Get Married?*) indicate the book is a Lion Book, complete with the distinctive "roaring lion" colophon as a counterpoint to the Red Circle logo on both the front and back covers. From No. 14 on, all Lion Books are bona fide Lions, with the "roaring lion" finally established as the company's colophon. Goodman rather belatedly adopted a slogan that appeared on all Lion Books starting with No. 134 (*Colorado Creek*, by E. E. Halleran): "... Better Books for Everybody." Between 1949 and 1952, four or five titles were issued each month, then six titles were issued each month in 1953 and 1954; the final titles were released in 1955, with the last being No. 233. Thus, the initial Lion series consists of Nos 1-7 (Red Circle), Nos. 8-11 (Lion), Nos. 12 and 13 (Red Circle), and Nos. 14-233 (Lion).

A second series of Lion Books was begun in 1954. Books in this series were referred to as either Lion Library or Lion Books, with either an "LL" or "LB" prefix. At least three different colophons were used in this second series, none of which resembles the colophon for the first series. Two-thirds of the offerings in this series are reprints of first edition hardback books not appearing in the initial series, and there are a handful of similar reprints of titles that first appeared in the first series. About 35 of the Lion Library books are PBOs, and some, but not many, can be considered noir. Jim Thompson's *The Kill-Off* is probably the most significant noir PBO in the Lion Library series. The last book in the series is numbered 175, but because some numbers were not assigned books, there are only about 165 books total. While all 233 books in the initial series were "short form" paperbacks (i.e. where the long axis measures 6.25 inches in length), the Lion Library series mixed and matched the book lengths between the short form and the "long form" (i.e. the now-standard 7.25 inch length).

The company never seemed to settle down into a stable New York City address. The address for the early titles of the initial series was listed simply as the Empire State Building, New York City but, after brief sojourns at 350 Fifth Avenue and 270 Park Avenue in 1952, the company moved into offices at 655 Madison Avenue in 1954. The general patterning of publication followed by the company in the early days was to publish one western, two suspense, crime, or detective (i.e. noir) novels, one or two "straight" novels that stressed emotional or sexual themes, and one title of an entirely different sort such as non-fiction, science fiction, religion, or an anthology. Lion Books was one of the first "mainstream" paperback houses to publish homosexual literature (e.g. No. 24, a reprint of Andre Tellier's *Twilight Men*).

In the beginning, Lion Books paid writers $1,500 for a novel, and in the end, $2,000. Authors received payment in two installments, one upon receipt of 10,000 words or three chapters and an outline, and the last payment upon completion of the book. At the same time, rival Gold Medal was paying a penny a copy based on the anticipated print run, and paying the entire amount up front. Thus, if the print run was expected to be 300,000, the author would receive $3,000 up front. Although many of Lion's writers enjoyed writing for Lion's editor Arnold Hano several, including David Goodis, Richard Matheson, Jim Thompson, and Day Keene ultimately defected to Gold Medal.

It is interesting to note that Lion granted copyright rights for PBO titles in almost all cases to the author, with only a handful retained by Lion. Curiously, virtually all PBOs are also published "by arrangement with" one of a myriad of publishing companies (e.g. Non-Pareil Publishing Corp., Prime Publications, Inc., Postal Publications, Inc., Bard Publishing Corp., among a great many). Since there are so many companies, it seems that a big part of Goodman's business strategy was setting up fictitious corporations, probably for tax purposes.

ENTER ARNOLD

More so than Martin Goodman, Arnold Hano was responsible for the cutting edge noir PBOs that Lion Books became known for. Hano was hired by Goodman as editor-in-chief in 1950 after Hano had had a two-year stint as editor at Bantam. He came to Lion with a large "backlog" of manuscripts that Bantam declined to publish, and Goodman gave Hano the green light to publish them. Hano essentially published books that he liked, and he was totally unaware that his taste in contemporary fiction would one day as a whole be recognized as some of the greatest noir ever written, all published under his editorship at Lion Books.

Hano's editorial practice frequently was to pre-determine the desired type of story and even the plot and cast about for an author to write it. Hano and his assistant Jim Bryans had considerable freedom as to what to publish and it was in fact Bryans who came up with the plot and story line for Jim Thompson's magnum opus *The Killer Inside Me* (No. 99). Not surprisingly, the company's best seller was a novel of crime and passion, No. 54, reprinted as No. 101, *Joy Street* by Clifton Cuthbert. It is Cuthbert's first novel, originally published in hardback in 1933 by William Godwin, Inc. and the only book in Lion's first series to be reprinted with a different stock number. But with the stranglehold competition being applied by Gold Medal, by 1956, Lion's title production began to tail off, with a high of 61 in 1954, dropping off to 43 in 1956 and 21 in 1957, at which point, the firm was purchased by New American Library. After the publication by NAL under its Signet imprint of a few titles previously under contract to Lion (Jim Thompson's *Wild Town*, Signet No. 1461 was one of these), Lion Books was relegated to the ever-growing trash heap of defunct paperback publishing houses.

COVER ART AND ARTISTS

Cover art on Lion Books' first series was for the most part exceptional. Because there were so many noir novels published by Lion, both PBOs and reprints, the cover art tended toward the dark and brooding, usually featuring a tension-filled scene of at least one man and one woman in a dingy hotel room or a trash-littered streetscape. While the precise nature of the tension is not known to the viewer, the artist makes it perfectly clear that all is not right among the protagonists. The overarching tenor and tone of many of Lion Books' covers is one of unmitigated despair.

The roster of artists who painted covers for Lion is a virtual Who's Who of American paperback illustrators of the period, and included such talents as Harry Schaare, Robert Skemp, Herman Bischoff, Bob Doares, Julian Paul, Victor Prezio, Mort Kunstler, George Gross, Arthur Sussman, Lou Marchetti, Mitchell Hooks, Clark Hulings, Robert Schulz, and John Leone, each of whom did multiple covers for Lion. The incomparable Robert Maguire, Norman Saunders, Rudolph Belarski, Rafael DeSoto, Earle Bergey, and Robert Stanley (with a rare signature visible on No. 10, *Canyon Hell* a western by Peter Dawson) also did at least one cover each for Lion. Unfortunately, Lion did not do a good job at crediting the cover artists; with the exception of the first 40 or so titles in the initial series, where the artist is credited on the back cover, we have to rely on deciphering signatures on the covers themselves. In a great many cases, the signature has been cropped or otherwise is not visible at all, making absolute identity of the cover artist difficult.

COVER BLURBS

Lion Books had, without a doubt, some of the best cover blurbs in the industry. If the purpose of the cover blurb was to work in tandem with the cover art to entice the newsstand browser to part with a quarter for the book, Lion titles should have sold out nearly every time. How could an enthusiastic reader possibly pass on *"A Loot Mad Thug Takes New Orleans Apart"*? Or how about *"She Taunted a Dope-Fiend Killer"*? Or this one: *"He Prowled the Bowels of a Florida Brothel."* Illicit sex, murder, corruption, juvenile delinquency, alcoholism, and/or drug addiction seem to be the themes that recur the most in Lion's cover blurbs and, of course, in the stories themselves. Because of the similarity of many of the blurbs— *"TNT Blonde,"* for example, shows up several times—it is likely that the blurbs were created by one person, or more than one person who had the same gift for the outré.

NOIR: A DEFINITION

In this article I use the term noir in its broadest sense, perhaps expressed best by Arnold Hano as "black suspense." While the compound term crime noir is probably used more often, black or dark suspense needn't always have a crime associated with it. But given that noir fiction expresses the deepest desires and passions of fundamentally bad, dark people, crime, particularly murder, is normally a central element of noir writing. With or without a crime element, in this definition, noir must also be set in contemporary, or just recently past, settings, thereby precluding the inclusion of historical novels, westerns, romances, or science fiction.

(Excerpted from the pages of *Paperback Parade* #86, June 2014, and reprinted with the kind permission of editor Gary Lovisi.)

DANIEL G. ROBERTS was born October 12, 1947 and passed away on May 24, 2014. Dan was a renown archaeologist whose work in that field won him many awards. In the rare book world, he was a fan, collector, and scholar whose contributions of information on rare books, collectable authors and cover artists appeared in many publications. He was especially knowledgeable in the field of vintage paperbacks and had built up a world-class collection of books and original art. He was always happy to share his vast knowledge on books with others, and 'talking books' with Dan was always a joy and inspiration.

Hero's Lust
by Kermit Jaediker

Chapter 1

Red opened his eyes and looked around. Mrs. Kelty was sound asleep. She was sleeping face down. The cover had rolled off her and her slip had hiked up, offering a nice unobstructed vista of her back. Her skin was smooth and white and she had a pretty good fanny for a woman past forty. He gave it a playful swat and she stirred but stayed asleep. Mrs. Kelty was the Party's woman leader of the Second Ward, where Red was born and raised, and there was a time when she wouldn't give him a tumble. That was before he landed his assignment at the Hall. Covering the Hall for the *Courier* made him something of a bigshot.

Gazing at her smooth, well-rounded figure, Red began getting ideas, but the phone rang. He reached out and grabbed it and growled "Hello," and Murphy's high-pitched voice squirted into his ear, like a streak of ice water fired from a water pistol. "You red-headed bastard. You still in the hay?"

"Oh. Hello, Murph."

"Hello, nuts. Come on down the Hall. The Mayor wants to see you."

"Anything big?"

"You'll find out when you get down here." Murphy hung up. He never said goodbye on a phone. He just told you what he wanted to tell you and then hung up.

Red looked at Mrs. Kelty, who was still sleeping despite the phone, and then with a sigh he got out of bed and pulled on a pair of shorts and put on his socks and shoes and pants and went to the bathroom. He gave himself a fast shave. He got a clean shirt and put it on, and a tie, and then he put on his jacket. He put on the blue Stetson. He went over to the bed and kissed Mrs. Kelty on the back of the neck. He gave the back of her neck a little nip and she woke up and said, "For Chrissakes, Red," and he grinned. He said, "I've got to beat it, Mary," and she grumbled, "Good riddance," and he said, "I got to go down the Hall. The Mayor wants me."

She turned around at that. She was only one step removed from a ward heel and the Mayor was like God to her. "What's he want to see you about?"

"I don't know."

"Why so mysterious?"

"I don't know. You know I'd tell you if I knew."

She got a big kick out of some of the things he told her, things that went on behind the door marked "Mayor's Office." He never told her anything important, just trivial gossip, but she ate it up. It made her feel she was in on the big stuff, that she was a sharer somehow in secrets and intrigues that affected the fate of the city, the state itself.

She said, "You want me to fix you some breakfast?"

"I haven't time. You going to hang around?"

"I can't, Red. We got a ladies' auxiliary luncheon at the club and I have to give the girls a pep talk."

"Okay. Goodbye, Mary."

"Goodbye, Red. Give me a ring the end of the week."

She took a look at the clock to make sure the alarm was set for whatever time she wanted to get up and she went back to sleep and he went out. He pressed the button of the self-service elevator and it came up and he boarded it and went down, smoothly. Some joint. The rent was one-fifty a month for two rooms and a kitchenette, but it was worth it. Air conditioning. Maid service. Gardens all around the building. Nice. It sure was a long way from the Second Ward. He sure had traveled a long way. And by accident. It was just an accident that he hadn't wound up like the other guys, a cop like McCabe or a strongarm like Frankie Collins or a heist guy like Ownie Welch, who had burned in the chair at State Prison.

An accident. He'd been in the right place at just the right time. He could see it now almost as clear as if it had been yesterday. It was one of the biggest yesterdays in his life. He'd been a kid of sixteen then, peddling papers around Courier Square. Besides selling papers around the square, he delivered them to the three Crescent City newspaper offices. He'd gone to the *Courier* one night, to deliver the *Advertiser* and the *Journal* and the papers from Jeff City, and he had walked into a first class row. The lobster trick copy boy was having a row with the night editor. Red didn't recall just what the argument was about. All he remembered was that the copy boy told the night editor to go crap in his hat. Then the kid had walked out. The editor had looked around and there was Red—Johnny-on-the-spot.

Red had quit school in the seventh grade, but he wasn't dumb. When there was nothing doing around the *Courier* office, he fooled around with the typewriter. He learned how to type pretty fast with two fingers and he learned how to write a story. By the time he was nineteen he was out covering a beat. Covering a beat paid him thirty a week, but he managed to pick up some side dough. All the ward clubs were willing to pay to get a paragraph or two in the paper. Red didn't invent the racket. The reporter he succeeded showed him the racket.

And Bernstein showed him something about writing. Bernstein was on rewrite. Red's vocabulary was limited but he found out from Bernstein that you could get by with even a small vocabulary, if you put the words you knew in the right spot. He wrote crudely but with feeling. He developed a knack for human interest. They finally put Red on general assignment. It was a big promotion but Red didn't turn handsprings over it. He lost all the side dough he'd picked up from the clubs. Even the raise the *Courier* gave him didn't make up for the side dough.

Then one day Old Man Gardner, who covered the Hall for the *Courier*, dropped dead and Red was assigned to take his place and the side dough he'd picked up on the beat was peanuts to what he eventually got at the Hall. He was put on the payroll of the Department of Works, under a phony name. Forty smackers a week to start, but now it was a hundred. Even Dawson and Giotti, who had covered the Hall for years, didn't get that much from the Hall. They got half that. That was because Red was in. The Mayor liked him. They talked the same language. They both came from the Second Ward. Red was the only one around the Hall who dared talk back to the Mayor. The Mayor got a big bang out of it. Murphy, the Deputy Mayor, was always warning Red, "Take it easy. Don't go too far." But Red kept talking back and the Mayor let him get away with it.

Sitting pretty, that's what I am, Red thought as he got into his 1953 convertible. Plenty of dough. A nice flat uptown. A swell car. Plenty of dames. He could get younger women than Mrs. Kelty, and he did, but she had something. She had meaning. When he was sixteen, seventeen, hanging around the Second Ward Club, chasing cans of beer for the older guys around the club, he used to see her, nights the ladies' auxiliary met. She was a committeewoman then. She'd just become a widow. What a widow! The best fanny in the ward. It used to drive him nuts, watching it. But he couldn't get a piece of it, not till he landed the job at the Hall.

He always thought of her as "Mrs." Kelty. That's what he used to call her when he was a kid. You couldn't call her that now, not when you were making love to her. Only a jerk would call a woman Missus when he was making love to her. But Red always thought of her as Mrs. Kelty and he liked to think of her that way. Mrs. Kelty, the piece he once couldn't have.

Yes, he'd traveled a long way, fast. Not as long as the Mayor had traveled, but far enough for him. If it would only stay this way. Just as far as this and no farther. An election sheet on a building caught Red's eye. VOTE FUSION. BRING CLEAN GOVERNMENT BACK TO CRESCENT CITY. The dirty blue-nose hypocrites. Clean Government, bull. Just a bunch of outers trying to climb in. When you were out and wanted in, you'd promise anything, the world. Low taxes. No graft. No rackets. Nothing but heaven. Vote for us and we'll give you heaven.

Who did they think they were kidding?

Red smiled ruefully. A lot of people. Too damn many people. That louse Shea. He was the Kidder-in-Chief. But he was good, you had to hand it to him. He had a thin, dark, good-looking face. He had dash. Those trenchcoats, they gave him dash. Like something out of a mick revolution. But he didn't wear the trenchcoats for looks. When the hoods came to splatter him with eggs at the street meetings, Shea would button up his trenchcoat and let 'em splatter. When it was over, he'd go home and hang the egg-splattered trenchcoat up to dry. And the next time he spoke at a street meeting, he'd wear a new trenchcoat. But he didn't throw the old coat away. He'd hang the old one on a pole behind him, a pole specially built on his speaker's platform. And the people would look at it, yellow with dried eggs, and they'd think: *This guy Shea's got guts. He's okay.* He sure was pulling crowds. Even with the hoods attacking the crowds, the people came.

He might win. There was another thing in his favor. There were no more paper ballots. Wonderful thing, paper ballots. You could take a ballot made of paper and toss it into the City Hall furnace. You couldn't do that with a voting machine.

He might win. Murphy had said so and when Murphy said that much, it was bad. And if he won, what? No more check from the Hall. No more fancy apartment. I'd be lucky to hold my job. At the Hall, anyway. The *Courier* would have to transfer me to a new beat. I'd be no good to the *Courier* there. *Mayor* Shea wouldn't give me the right time. Giotti and Dawson and I would be out, in the cold, a big freeze. Well, one thing, the papers couldn't fire us. The papers were in just as deep as us. Even deeper. The city paid the papers a million a year in legal advertising, job printing. The reporters played ball and the papers played ball. No. They'd never fire us. But we'd be out at the Hall.

Nuts. Shea won't win. He can't win, even with voting machines. He had organization against him, the finest organization in the U.S.A. You can't beat organization.

Chapter 2

Red went into the Mayor's office. There were about half a dozen people in the anteroom, mostly ward heelers, looking for favors, looking for something. One of the heelers said, "Hello, Red, lookin' for a scoop?" and Red said, "I'm lookin' for a drink," and they all laughed. He went over to the cop standing at the brass gate in front of the Mayor's door, and the cop opened the gate and Red passed through it and opened the Mayor's door.

The Mayor was standing, smiling at Murphy. When the Mayor saw Red, he winked and nodded at Murphy. Murphy was a little man with a pot-belly and an ulcer. He had three phones on his desk and he could use them

all simultaneously. Right now he was using two of them. He said into one
that if those lousy election buttons weren't delivered by the end of the week
then the contract was off. He'd get the buttons from some other lousy button maker. Before the button maker could reply, Murphy shifted to the
other phone and asked to speak to the Governor. Then he shifted back to
the button maker. He said he didn't give a damn how much the button
maker had contributed to the campaign; he wanted those buttons by the
end of the week—or else.

He spoke into the other phone. He said, "Hi, Gov." He asked the Governor what he was going to talk about at the Wyandotte beefsteak tonight
and the Governor said something and Murphy said, "Kill it. We wantcha
to talk about the Medical Center. We'll send you the dope." There was a
pause, then Murphy's voice shot up. "I don't give a damn if you had ten
speeches prepared. It's got to be the Medical Center!" He hung up. Then
he hung up on the button maker. Then he dialed a number and made another phone call.

"I don't know how the little bastard does it," the Mayor said to Red. The
Mayor was a tall man, six feet three, and spare. He was bald, except for
a black fringe of hair. His Florida tan was still on him. His face was getting wrinkled. The Crescent City papers were under orders never to take
any photographs of him close up. The only closeups they ever published
were pictures of him taken fifteen years ago. He was a nice guy, the
Mayor, but vain as hell.

The Mayor said, "How come you're so late?"

"I overslept," said Red.

"Who with?"

Red grinned. He said, "What's the big story Murphy called me about?"

"We'll wait till he gets off the phone. He makes too goddam much noise.
Want a drink?"

"Sure."

The Mayor nodded toward his desk. There was a small liquor cabinet
built into it, but you'd never suspect it. He'd had the cabinet built specially
in case any of the church crowd dropped in. Red took out a bottle of bourbon and a glass and poured a shot. He didn't pour anything for the
Mayor. The Mayor never drank.

The Mayor took a leather case out of his pocket and opened it and took
out a custom-built cigar, thick and long. Red smiled inwardly. Murphy
smoked cigars, too. He smoked two sets of cigars. One set, small ones, he
smoked in public. The other set, long ones, he smoked in secret. One night,
while at a party in the Mayor's flat, Murphy had gotten high and confided
his secret to Red. Murphy had taken out a leather case, just like the
Mayor's, but longer, and opened it and taken out a cigar, just like the

Mayor's, but longer and fatter. "This is three inches longer than the Boss's," Murphy had told Red. "Only don't you tell him about it." Drunk as Murphy was, he didn't dare smoke it in front of the Mayor.

The Mayor puffed on his long cigar, that was not quite as long as Murphy's secret cigars, and Red had another drink and finally Murphy finished with the phones and came over and Red poured him a double bourbon.

"Now here's the setup," the Mayor said. "We're gonna go all out on the Medical Center. It's gonna be the chief plank of our platform. I didn't wanna drag the hospital into a lousy election campaign, but after thinkin' things over, I decided we'd better."

"It's about time," said Red.

The Medical Center was the Organization's crowning glory, but for some wacky reason the Mayor had laid off it. He was crazy about the Medical Center, that was it. Building it was the one non-political act of his entire career. The Mayor had been thinking of the Second Ward when he built it, not the ward clubs, but the people. He was really crazy about it. There was graft all over, but not in the Medical Center. The Mayor wouldn't let anyone pull a racket there. He had told Red, and Red believed him, that if he caught anyone pulling a racket there, he'd brain him. A real wack over it. He went to the hospital every day, spent two or three hours there, looking around, shooting the breeze with the doctors, giving a lot of advice, making a pest of himself. He'd be the first to tell you what a pest he was. It was the same when they put the Center up. He went to the site every day and watched the steam shovels digging and the girders rising and spoke to the steam shovel men, full of advice. He kept revising the plans until he had the architects half nuts.

Red said, "Where do I come in?"

"You're gonna do a series on it," said the Mayor. "An article a day. Each article about a different hospital building."

"Not a bad idea," Red said. "Only I did it when the hospital opened."

"That's eight months ago."

"It's old, Boss, old."

"There's plenty new stuff. They got new equipment, a new research lab. And then there's that new wing to the maternity hospital they're buildin'. Lots of new stuff."

"Okay," Red said, resignedly.

"Don't like it, huh?"

"Frankly, it stinks."

"*You* got any ideas?"

"Not yet. You just sprung this on me."

"Have another drink."

Red poured another glass.

Murphy said, "I know what." Red and the Mayor looked at him. "We'll need Kraus for this," Murphy said. Kraus headed the third ticket in the Mayoralty race. He actually headed a paper organization. It was called the Independent Party and it had been organized by the Mayor himself, secretly, of course, to take votes away from Shea's Fusion outfit.

"Go ahead," said the Mayor.

"We'll get Kraus to attack the Medical Center," said Murphy. "Say it's a waste of dough. Say the poor are just a bunch of lazy slobs who won't work and pay their own hospital bills like decent, respectable citizens. If that don't burn the people up, nothin' will."

"I don't want any crap about wastin' dough," the Mayor said. "We get enough of that crap tossed at us now."

"I've got it," Red said. "I'll do a series, but not on the hospital—"

"Great!" said the Mayor sarcastically. "You're a genius."

"I mean it won't be on the hospital directly. It'll be about a guy."

"Who?" asked Murphy. "Jesus?"

"A guy. Any old guy. Someone sick. A blow-by-blow story of one guy's life in the Medical Center. Everything that happens to him from the minute he enters. How he feels, leaving his home, the wife and kids. What he eats. The lousy-tasting medicine he drinks. The operation he has to face. How he feels just before he's wheeled into the operating room—"

"That's enough," said the Mayor.

Red's face fell. "Don't you like it?"

"Of course I do," said the Mayor. "It's terrific."

"Yeah," said Murphy. "Terrific."

The Mayor glared at Murphy. "Well, what are you standin' there for? Get on the phone. Call Doc Stevens. Tell him what we want. A guy—"

"No," said Red, getting another idea. "Not a guy. A dame. Pretty. Stacked."

"Always thinkin' of the same thing," said the Mayor.

"A dame is always better than a guy," said Red.

Murphy headed for his desk. The Mayor said, "Wait a minute, Murph." He said to Red, "Suppose this dame croaks on us?"

"As long as she croaks after Election, it's okay."

The Mayor stared at the floor, snapping his fingers. "What's a good disease? Somethin' safe."

"How about appendicitis?" suggested Murphy.

"Too safe," said Red. "This babe has to be sick. Really sick, so the pinheads reading the story will have something to think about."

"Go ahead," said the Mayor. "Call Doc Stevens."

Murphy phoned the Medical Center. He turned to the Mayor. "Doc's out playin' golf. He won't be back till five."

"The dirty bastard," said the Mayor. "Here I give him the biggest Medical Center in the world to play with and he's out playin' golf!" He turned to Red. "I'll see Doc at five and have him get busy on it. You coverin' the Wyandotte beefsteak tonight?"

"I'd cover it even if you weren't speaking at it," Red said.

"They certainly give you a wonderful beefsteak," Murphy said longingly. He had an ulcer and couldn't touch beefsteak.

"I'm skipping lunch," Red said. "I always starve myself before I go to the Wyandotte."

"Well," said the Mayor, "I'll tell you what Doc says when I see you tonight."

"I just thought of somethin'," Murphy said. "You'd better watch out with this sick dame story, Boss. Red's liable to make a pass at her."

Red and the Mayor laughed. Red said, "I like mine healthy."

"I can see where some of them nurses are gonna get a lot of wear and tear," Murphy said, shaking his head.

Chapter 3

Red went out and had coffee and a couple of eggs, to keep him going till the Wyandotte racket, and then he went back to the Hall, up to the press room. Dawson and Giotti were playing rummy. Dawson was a tall slight man with horn-rimmed glasses and bitter eyes and dissatisfied lips. Giotti was a large heavy man, friendly, nice. Red liked Giotti but he couldn't bear Dawson. Dawson had learned somehow that Red's check from the Hall was twice as big as the check he got or Giotti got and he had told Giotti. Giotti didn't mind it a bit, or at least he didn't act as though he minded. But Dawson did. Every now and then he got off a crack about Red's check. Red never said much in front of him. Dawson was a bag-carrier. He'd carry tales back on his own mother if it would help him. Red said things right to the Mayor's face and that was all right, because it was to his face, but Red never said anything behind the Mayor's back. Not in earshot of Dawson.

Dawson said, "What's going on at the Mayor's office?"

"Nothing," said Red.

"Murphy phoned before. He was anxious to get you. Very anxious."

"He was born anxious," said Red.

Dawson said, "Hear about your old pal?" He was mixing the cards when he said it and was looking at them, but Red sensed some inward eye of Dawson's was watching him.

"Which pal?" asked Red.

"Bernstein. He *was* a pal of yours, wasn't he?"

Red went tight inside. He said, his voice tight, "What did you hear about him?"

"He just got a job across the river. The *Ajax Post.*" Dawson's lips twisted, as though their bitterness was more than he could endure. "City Editor, no less. He must have given them an awful line to land a job like that."

"A smart guy, Bernstein," said Giotti, "but he can't hold his liquor."

He sure couldn't. Two years ago, at a Press Club dinner, he got so high on five martinis that he climbed on a table and gave an imitation of the Mayor delivering a speech. With gestures. It was wonderful. The Press Club almost died laughing.

But there was no laughing next day, not for Bernstein. Someone tipped off the Mayor. Good old knife-slinging Dawson. That wasn't just a suspicion. Murphy himself told Red it was Dawson. The Mayor phoned the *Courier* and the *Courier* told Bernstein he was through. He hit the other two papers in town for jobs, but they gave him a fast brushoff.

Red was with a blonde the night of the Press Club shindig and he didn't know what happened until early next morning when the Mayor sent for him. He told Red what Bernie had done and asked Red what he thought about it. Red prided himself for talking back to the Mayor, but he didn't talk back that time. The Mayor was raging. If there was one thing he couldn't stand, it was ridicule. Red said Bernstein was a dirty louse and when the Mayor disclosed he had had Bernstein fired, Red said the louse had only gotten what he deserved. Red didn't really feel that way about Bernie, but he said it. He had to, to get off the hook.

From then on, he steered clear of Bernie. Every newspaperman in town did. The guy was poison.

A few weeks later Red heard that Bernie was broke. He had sought work on almost every paper in the state, but his luck was running against him—his luck and Mayor Gowan. The majority of newspapers in the state were friendly to the Mayor—his power reached beyond Crescent City— and they wanted no part of Bernie. The other papers just didn't have any jobs open at the time. To complicate matters, Bernie's wife was going to become a mother in less than a month.

When Red learned how things were with Bernie, the only ready cash he had was $80. He was always throwing his money away, on women, liquor, horses. He put the arm on Murphy for another thirty, not telling Murphy, of course, what he wanted the money for. He got an envelope and with a pen carefully printed Bernstein's name and address on it, to hide his handwriting. He kept $5 of the $115 for himself, to carry him until payday, and stuffed the rest into the envelope and mailed it. No note accompanied the money. Red didn't dare write a note. The Hall could easily intercept mail and frequently did. The postmaster of Crescent City owed his job to Mayor Gowan.

Shortly after that Bernstein blew town. There was a rumor he had gone east. Red didn't hear from him for nearly a year. Then one day Red received a letter with a Boston postmark. The letter, handprinted like Red's envelope, consisted of one word: "*Thanks.*" It bore no signature. It didn't have to. Clipped to it were a $100 bill and a ten-spot.

And now, thought Red, he was back, just across the river, with a big job on a good newspaper. Red was glad. Bernie was a swell guy, even if he couldn't hold his liquor.

Dawson said, "Funny Bernstein didn't let you know he was in Ajax. You were such good friends."

"We *were.*"

Red thought: I ought to paste him. I ought to haul off and hit him, with the glasses on, drive those horn rims right into his skull. He'd look nice that way. Like a guy from Mars.

And then he thought: I ought to paste myself. I'm just as bad as Dawson. Worse. Dawson turned Bernstein in, but I let him down. Me. His pal. That one hundred bucks I sent him doesn't wash me clean. I let him down. I ought to paste myself. I ought to take Dawson's glasses off his nose and put them on my nose and haul off and drive those horn rims of his into my skull. The red-headed man from Mars.

Chapter 4

Red got off the bus. He always went to the Wyandotte racket by bus. Last time he used his car to go to the Wyandotte, it had gotten all banged up, paint scraped, tires ripped, windows broken. The Wyandotte was in the Third Ward and the Third Ward kids were just like the kids in the old Second. Stick a new car under their noses and they couldn't resist.

There was a line a block long outside the Wyandotte clubhouse. Red went past the line, saying hello now and then to someone he recognized, and went up the stairs. The Undertaker was at the door, shaking hands. The Undertaker was Joe Terry, the Third Ward leader. He wasn't really an undertaker. He sold real estate. But he looked like an undertaker. He had a long, thin, gray face and the same sad smile that all undertakers had. Red shook hands with him and went in and checked his hat and topcoat and made his way into the big dining hall.

There was a dais, with a long white-clothed table for the guests of honor, and around this, in the shape of a huge horseshoe, were row on row of picnic tables, bare of cloth. The place, which could hold a thousand men, was almost full. With the exception of the Mayor and the Deputy Mayor, all the guests of honor were present, the Governor, the City Commissioners, a couple of judges, Mike Calitorcio, the stevedore, who ran the waterfront rackets, and Jerry O'Neill, the union boss, who helped Mike run the waterfront rackets. Just in front of the dais was a press table at which Dawson and Giotti were already seated, but Red had no intention of sitting with Dawson. He was going to enjoy himself.

Someone tapped him on the shoulder and he turned. It was Frankie Collins. Frankie said, "How are you, Red?" and Red said, "Fine, Frankie. How's it with you?" and Frankie said, "Okay. Sittin' anywheres in particular?" and Red said, "No. Come on. Let's find a seat." They found seats and sat down and Frankie opened a gold cigarette case and held it out and Red took a cigarette. There was a big monogrammed "C" on it.

Frankie had big gray eyes soft as a woman's with long black lashes and he looked at you softly and talked softly, but he was no swish. He was a strongarm man and something more. If you got ideas looking at his eyes, then look at his hands. They were hands no longer. They were fists. Iron jaws had smashed all the bones of his fingers and gnarled the fingers and the constant bunching of his hands for action had gnarled them a little more, until he never quite was able to hold them open. It was a wonder he could get his thick, bent forefinger inside a trigger guard, but he could.

He was on one of the Election Day flying squads. The squads rolled out in big Cadillacs with stolen plates that couldn't be traced and toured the polls. Most of the men on the squads lugged baseball bats, or rubber hose borrowed from the cops, but Frankie used only the equipment nature had given him, his fists. The squads didn't bother people who year in, year out, had voted against the Party. Their meat was the people who were in the Party and were, according to report, turning against it. They never had to slug more than one turncoat at a polling place. Just make an example, that was all. One man with his nose flattened and a bleeding black hole where his front teeth were and a big shoeprint across his face—that was all that was needed.

Between elections, Frankie's talents were employed on bookies who held back on the kick, rank-and-file unionists who organized movements to oust their leaders, people who welched on loans, on bets. Now and then he got a gun job. He was picked up several times, in Miami, New York, Chicago, and questioned about gun killings. But they never pinned a killing on him. The only rap they ever pinned on him was carrying a concealed weapon.

Red asked, "How's your old lady?" and Frankie's eyes got even softer and he said, "Fine. I been sendin' her to Hot Springs every year and her rheumatism is practically gone. How's your father?"

Red grinned. "Still not workin'."

"He livin' with you?"

"No. He can't shake the Second Ward."

"It was like that with my old lady, too, but she finally had to leave because of the rheumatism. Them Second Ward fogs from the river don't do anybody good, even without rheumatics."

"What a dump," Red said.

"But we had a lot of fun. Remember us playin' the hook and hidin' out in the syrup tunnels down at the old sugar house?"

"Do I remember?" Red smiled reminiscently. "First time I got laid was in one of those tunnels. She was a honey, too. Fifteen years old, but built like a brick privy."

"Ah," said Frankie. "Here come the eats. I ain't eaten since this morning."

"I know," said Red. "Nobody does when they go to the Wyandotte. The best beefsteak in the world."

All over the hall now waiters were carrying trays loaded with white-crowned pitchers of beer and long platters with thin red slices of beefsteak piled on them, and tiny sausages, wrapped in crisp bacon and pierced with toothpicks. The platters banged on the tables and the guests shoveled the meat into their paper plates and then they shoveled the meat into their gaping mouths. There were no potatoes and there would be no dessert, but neither was required. For hour after hour there would be beefsteak, tender as the tenderest filet mignon, oozing with salty blood-juice, and the tiny sausages, jacketed with bacon, and long cold draughts of beer to wash them down. The tab for the meal was ten dollars a head. A restaurant would have charged you twenty at least. The food was purchased wholesale and there was no profit involved. When Red first started on a beat, he had been assigned, among other things, to cover the weekly Rotary luncheon. The men who belonged to Rotary were the topcream of the city's industry, the heads of the steel mills and the chemical plants that stunk up the river and the five railroads that had terminals in Crescent City. They wore three-button Brooks Brothers suits and quiet ties and they lived in the country, far from the mills and the stunk-up river, but the food they ate at their weekly luncheon Red wouldn't toss to a dog. Fruit cocktail out of a can for a starter and then a small piece of roast chicken, with canned peas on the side, and a half ball of mashed potatoes that you could knock off at a gulp and a small ball of vanilla ice cream, and all the water you could drink. No wonder those bastards had labor trouble. Of course, it was luncheon fare, but even at the annual banquet of the Chamber of Commerce, which was run by the same crowd, you got the same thing, only a little more chicken and two balls of ice cream. For good solid food that was joy to a man's tongue and throat and filled his belly and that he could feel dissolving into his blood, becoming a part of him, racing through him, there was nothing like a Party beefsteak, any Party beefsteak. The Wyandotte simply topped the others in quantity.

At the Rotary luncheons, the entertainment, if you could call it that, consisted of everyone singing "Let Me Call You Sweetheart" and "Just a Song at Twilight" and "God Bless America." Here only one guy sung—a pro. He wasn't a great singer but he wasn't bad. He was an Irish tenor with a liquor-mottled face that had once been handsome and a patent leather haircomb and a slight liquor husk in his throat, but the songs he sang had a pull, a tug, "Mother Macree" and "My Wild Irish Rose" and "When Irish Eyes Are Smiling" and the more *you* drank the better *he* sang and the greater the tug of the far off homeland that some here had seen but that most had not but that most had heard of, drunk in with the milk they had sucked from the big juicy breasts of their mothers.

The tenor, because *paisans* were here, took a shot at opera, and Mike Calitrinio, who was as round as he was high and who had been knocking off one double shot after another from a bottle of whiskey, staggered to his feet and joined in the opera, and the crowd laughed and clapped ironically.

The tenor finished and Mike finished a couple of notes behind him and the tenor bowed to him, kidding, and Mike bowed back, not kidding, and fell back into his chair and the tenor started telling some off-color jokes that Red had heard five years ago. Red and Frankie got up and went to the toilet. They had had four or five beers and they would have plenty more, but Red wouldn't get drunk on it. Beer never made Red drunk when he was eating a big meal. All it did was make him go to the john.

When Red and Frankie got back, the tenor was seated at the table of the guests of honor, swigging Calitrinio's whiskey, and J. Harlow Barton, the Commissioner of Finance, was making the opening speech of the evening. Barton was a short spectacled man with a mouthful of big teeth. He was a high muckamuck in the Masons and he drew a big Protestant vote. Unlike most of the men on the City Commission, he really knew his stuff, finance. He was talking finance now, how sound the city treasury had become since the Gowan administration had taken over and how if the state courts would stop knuckling down to the railroads, one of these days the city would collect from the railroads the $20,000,000 that the roads owed in back taxes, and then the city could reduce its taxes.

Red grinned. The railroads would never pay that twenty million. The biggest of them, the G. R. & W., had on its payroll none other than the Governor, as "counsel" at fifty Gs a year. The Mayor himself had gotten the Governor the job. But nobody on the outside knew that. The Governor never argued a case for the G. R. & W., or prepared a brief. He just collected his fifty thousand a year and kicked in most of it to the Mayor. Every election year the Mayor attacked the G. R. & W. in the newspapers and on the radio, and denounced the state courts for not making the railroads pay their back taxes, but behind the scenes he told the judges of the state courts, the ones he controlled, to forget the twenty million.

Barton plunged into the budget, and the crowd half-listened. They weren't interested in budgets, statistics. They were interested in beefsteak.

Suddenly someone yelled, "Here comes the Mayor!" and the faces of the crowd jerked toward the entrance, a thousand faces jerked by strings, and the crowd came to its feet and shouted. Barton, utterly forgotten, drowned out, stood there on the dais, grinning a sickly grin. He should have been used to it by now. It was an old routine for the Mayor to come in, smack in the middle of Barton's speech. A good gimmick. Barton's spiel always rocked the people to sleep and when the Mayor made his sudden, late entrance, it was like a brass band crashing suddenly into music, on a quiet street, at three o'clock in the morning.

Smiling and nodding, the Mayor, accompanied by Murphy and the Undertaker and led by half a dozen cops, moved down the middle aisle. When he had ascended the dais, he raised his hands and clasped them, like a champ fighter accepting the applause of his fans. The photographers raised their cameras and the Mayor and Murphy and the Undertaker struck poses and the photographers' bulbs flashed and flashed until the Mayor got tired of it and said, smiling but with a snap in his words, "That's enough," and the photographers obediently stopped. The Mayor sat down. He nodded at Barton. Barton finished his speech. Then, being m.c., he introduced the Governor.

The Governor had two stock speeches that the reporters called "File 158" and "File 280." They never failed to wow the crowds. Even in Republican Lincoln County, "File 158" and "File 280" were surefire hits. File 158 was all about a Union soldier in the Civil War who was carrying the Stars and Stripes and a bullet hit him and he stopped and tottered and the flag in his dying grasp lowered, but suddenly, out of the smoke and the din of the battle, leaped another Union soldier, "a slim and beardless youth," as the Governor put it, and seized the flag.

"The flag," the Governor would say, voice shaking, "never touched the ground!"

File 280 was about his first ride in an airliner, how the night was full of fog and the pilot couldn't see but there was the radio beam he traveled by. The beam said "dit-da-dit-da" when the plane was too far to the left of the runway it was heading for and "da-dit-da-dit" when the plane was too far to the right. When the plane was directly in the center of the beam, the sound the pilot heard was a steady "m-m-m-m-m-m." By sticking to that "m-m-m-m-m," he was able to land right on the target, without a bump. Well, the Governor would say, life was just like a radio beam. "Stay on the beam!" he would shout, winding up File 280.

Tonight he spoke about the Medical Center. He gave it the usual treatment, plenty of corn-juice, plenty of tears. The old son-of-a-bitch even cried himself. Red used to think he had an onion palmed in his hand, but Murphy, who always had the inside on such matters, swore he didn't.

He pictured the plight of the poor before the Medical Center was built. He spoke scathingly of the private hospitals where you could be dying and they would turn you away, unless you got up the required fee. He spoke of the old city hospital, before Mayor Gowan came into power. It was dirty, badly equipped, and the poor died there like flies. He told a story about a little tow-headed boy who was a talented violinist but very poor and had died there. When he described how the kid on his deathbed called for his violin and played one last song on it and then died, a budding genius who never flowered, his listeners blew their noses or coughed or wept outright into their beer. And then he told how the Mayor cleaned the hospital up, modernized it. And then he spoke of the hospital that succeeded it, the Mayor's dream hospital, the Medical Center, rising, like a fantasy into the clouds, beautiful and clean, a monument to the Mayor, a challenge to death and dirt and disease, a white and towering proclamation that all men were created equal.

It brought the house down. Frankie, shamefacedly drawing a hand across his moist eyes, said, "Geez, he can speak. He gives you a clutch. Here." And he grasped his throat with his huge battered fist that had sent many a man to the Medical Center and more than one man to his grave.

The next speaker and the last was the Mayor. It took guts to get up there, after a tear-jerker like the Governor's, and try to grip the crowd, but he had the guts and he had the power to grip it. He had, shortly after he was first elected Mayor, hired an expensive elocution teacher, and he used the gestures that the teacher had taught him, but clumsily, jerkily, as though somewhere along the line, in the middle of the course, he had said to hell with elocution. His English was fearful and his sentences sometimes had no ending, and sometimes the object of the sentence mysteriously became the subject and vice versa. He was a perfect setup for the mimicry that had exiled Bernie. And yet he had power. When he headed toward the climax of his speech, his sentences somehow got finished. They became short and staccato. The words had the punch of steel-jacketed machine gun bullets.

He laid off the Medical Center. The Governor had given them the sob stuff, the dream stuff. He gave them the stuff out of which a party was built, the earth-stuff, the pavement stuff of the wards. The heat was on, this election, as it had never been before, and only loyalty and organization could guarantee a victory. Every man in the Party had to stand up and be counted. There could be no cowards, no shirkers. Every committeeman present, and the place was full of them, must get out his allotment of votes. He knew the exact allotment for every single one of the seven hundred election districts in Crescent City and he called off the allotment in those districts that this year were doubtful. There should be no doubtful districts, he shouted. And if those districts failed to deliver, God help the men who ran them. In the districts that were not doubtful, there was a tendency to take things easy. There would be no such letup this May. Everyone in the Party strongholds must exercise his American, God-given right to vote for the Party. If a woman pleaded that she couldn't go to the polls, because she had six or seven kids and no one to take care of them, then the committeemen would have to take care of them.

The road ahead, the Mayor warned, was a hard one. The Party's enemies, the Sheas, the liars, were waging a murderous campaign of slander.

"They call your Mayor a grafter, but I challenge them to prove it!" he cried. "They call your Mayor, the Leader of your Party, a dictator, but they lie in their teeth!" He laughed harshly. He tapped himself on the chest with a long forefinger. "Me. A dictator. Me that has been for years a symbol of democracy! Where else but in these United States could a man like me— a man of the poor—climb so high! Could you do it in Russia?"

"No!" the crowd yelled back.

It went on, the same old words of election time, but freshened, filled as they were with the love of fight that made the old man young. You could say all you wanted about Mayor Gowan, but the old boy loved a fight. He took the old words and his love of battle gave them youth and zing, two thousand volts of youth zipping into your ears and down your spine.

He hit the climax with a roar and then he killed it and sat down. The crowd's ovation lasted fifteen minutes.

The tenor rose uncertainly to his feet. He would sing the Mayor's favorite song, "The Sidewalks of New York," and then the Mayor would leave. Red said goodbye to Frankie and got his hat and coat and went outside and presently the Mayor and Murphy came out. Red asked the Mayor how he had made out on the Medical Center deal.

"We got a dame," the Mayor said. "Right down your alley. Young. Pretty. A thirty-buck-a-week stenographer with TB."

"TB?" Red was crestfallen. "We've got to have an operation—something dramatic."

"This'll be dramatic. They're gonna cut away part of her lung." The Mayor smiled. "Before Election Day. And we won't have to worry about her croakin'. It ain't a dangerous operation, but it sounds dangerous. Just to play safe, I'm havin' the best man in the state cut her, Doctor Winston, the head of the TB hospital."

"When's she going to the Center?"

"Tomorrow morning. She wasn't to be admitted until next week, but we moved up the time so you could get a start on this thing."

"Is she going by ambulance?"

"No. You're takin' her there. Ten a.m. sharp." He handed Red a piece of paper with something typewritten on it. "Here's her name and address."

Red looked at it by the light of the street lamp. *Ann Porter, 430 South 15th Street.* He stuck it in his wallet.

"How soon can you start runnin' the series?" the Mayor asked.

"Figure next Monday at the earliest. That'll give me time to do a good solid job interviewing her and it'll give the *Courier* time to promote it. It's got to have a buildup."

The Mayor nodded. "You goin' home?"

"Yes."

"I'll give you a lift."

"It's two miles beyond your place."

"That's all right. There's something I wanted to ask you." They got into the Mayor's limousine. No kids ever fooled around with that car. Hartung, the Mayor's bodyguard, was inside, at the wheel. You never saw Hartung in the Mayor's office because having a bodyguard in sight of all the people who day in day out visited the Mayor might make a bad impression. But Hartung was always close by, in a small office next door. He was a captain of police—he still drew a captain's salary—but the only police work he did now was keep an eye on the Mayor. He was six feet tall and had a lot of fat on him but there was muscle under the blubber and he could move fast and sure as a cat. He was once regarded as the best dick in Homicide. They said he could make a wooden Indian talk. His idea of a good time was to ride with a crony of his, another cop, along the elevated highway, to the ramp that led down to the city dumps. The dumps were overrun with rats and every now and then one would come up the ramp. Soon as they spotted a rat coming up, Hartung and his pal would get out of the car and close in on it. When they had the rat cornered, Hartung, his hand gloved in tough leather, would seize it by the neck and hold it up while his friend soaked it with gasoline and then lit a match to it. Then Hartung would release it. He told Red there was no living thing on earth faster than a blazing rat running squealing to its death. It could even beat a jackrabbit.

Red always felt queer about shaking Hartung's hand, even though it was always gloved when he went rat-killing.

The limousine headed for the Hill. At the crest of the Hill, pale and slim and beautiful, like six beautiful dames, stood the skyscraper hospitals of the Medical Center, dominating the city.

The Mayor said, "I guess you heard about Bernstein."

Red replied quite casually. He had known the Mayor would mention Bernstein sooner or later. "You mean about him getting that soft touch in Ajax?"

"Yeah. Who told you?"

"The same guy who told you. Dawson."

"Never mind who told me. You gonna see him?"

"Me?"

"Yes. You."

"You know how I feel about him."

"Do I?"

"If you don't," said Red, "you ought to have your head examined."

He heard Murphy's shocked intake of breath.

The Mayor burst out laughing and slapped Red's thigh. "That's what I like about you, Red. You certainly got brass."

When he became serious, the Mayor said, "I can't understand that fellow Bernstein. I never done anything to him. Whenever he dropped down the Hall to see you, I always made him welcome. All of a sudden, for no reason at all, he gets up there at that dinner, before all them newspapermen, and makes a goddam fool outta me!"

"The jerk was drunk," said Murphy.

An alarm bell rang in Red's skull. That line of Murphy's was a trap. It was a cue for Red to agree: "That's right, Mayor, the jerk was drunk. He didn't know what he was doing." Just say that and then the Mayor would know Red didn't really hate Bernie, as he pretended.

Red said, "He was drunk, all right, but that doesn't let him out. He must have hated you a long time, Boss, but held it in, till he got the load on. All the load did was show him up in his true colors."

"You oughta be a psychologist, Red," said the Mayor. "Maybe you can tell me why he had it in for me."

"You're a big man, Boss." Red knew just when to be fresh and when to use soft-soap. "People get jealous of you. Especially smart people, like Bernstein. They're smart, but they're not smart enough, and when they see a man like you climb to the top, far above them, they burn up. It happens all the time."

"That's it, Red. You hit it right on the nose."

The car stopped at Red's corner and he got out and the Mayor said, "You got that girl's name and address?" and Red said, "In my pocket," and the Mayor said, "See you tomorrow," and the big car purred away and Red opened the gate between the high hedges that surrounded the gardens and headed for the canopied entrance of the apartment house. The doorman was gone. He knocked off at midnight. The gardens were like a small park,

with trees and benches and fountains. It was early spring and the grass of
the lawns had just begun to sprout and in the cool of the night, with the
thin layer of mist hanging over the grass, there was a nice, strong green
smell.

Something, a movement, caught Red's eye and he turned and saw a man
rising from a bench beneath a tree. The man was short and slim and
vaguely familiar. His hat brim was down and the collar of his topcoat was
up and his face was a mere shadow.

He called softly. "Red."

Red stopped and the man came over and raised his hat brim and the glow
from a window fell on his face.

It was Bernstein.

Chapter 5

Bernie was about 35, neatly put together, with a nice homely face and
small brown eyes, bright, like a monkey's, with smile lines at the corners.
He held out his hand and Red gripped it.

"Come on upstairs," said Red. Red was glad to see Bernie, but anxious
to get him upstairs. If some payroll boy came along, someone who recognized Bernie, Red's name would be mud. Half a dozen payroll boys lived
in the house. Bernie had never been here before, but they might have seen
him down at the Hall, in the old days, when he dropped in to visit Red.

Bernie knew the score. "Is there a back entrance?"

"Yes. It leads to the stairway. Nobody uses the stairway much except the
kids."

Bernie turned down his hat brim and they went around to the back entrance and climbed the stairs. They met no one.

They entered Red's apartment and Red put on the lights and Bernie
looked over the joint. You could see he was impressed.

"I've been here only four months," said Red. "Where did you get my address? The phone book?"

"You don't think I'd call the Hall?"

They took off their hats and coats. Red said, "How about a drink?"

"I haven't touched a drop in two years."

"I don't blame you," said Red. "How's Sylvia?"

"Fine."

"And Junior?"

Bernie showed him a snapshot. "The kid's lucky," Red said. "He looks
just like Sylvia."

Bernie grinned.

Neither mentioned the one hundred and ten bucks. There was no need
to.

Red poured himself a Scotch. "What's new?"

"I got a job last week on the *Ajax Post.* City editor."

Red played it dumb. "Congratulations. They put out a good sheet."

"I want to make it better."

"Don't try too hard. You'll rock the boat. No newspaper publisher likes
rocking the boat. He makes his dough—the hell with something new."

"It's not that way on the *Post.* They *want* me to rock the boat. They've
got eighty-five thousand circulation and they want it doubled."

"That's a big order."

"When I get through," said Bernie, "it'll be doubled."

"What are you gonna do? Give away five-dollar bills with every issue?"

"That wouldn't be a bad stunt. But I've got other ideas."

"Like what?" Red asked, more out of politeness than curiosity.

Bernie said nothing for a moment, just sat there, studying Red. Then he
said, "Red, how would you like to work for me?"

"I wouldn't mind, Bernie. I think you're a helluva newspaperman. But
I like my job. Good dough. A racket—"

"I know. You sit on your behind down at the Hall and get everything
handed to you on a platter. And the *Courier* pays you and the Hall pays
you."

Red gave him a look. "How do you know the Hall pays me?"

"You never told me. But you always lived that way. And now you're living even better."

Red said nothing.

"If you went to work for me," Bernie said, "you could still live in
style."

"Could I?"

"I think so. I'll give you two hundred a week."

"You must be out of your head," said Red. "Even in New York they don't
pay that kind of dough."

"Sometimes they do. Two hundred—on the line. How about it?"

"I don't know, Bernie. I got a pretty good setup here."

Bernie smiled thinly. "Apparently the Hall's paying inflation prices."

"Look. If you came up here to preach—"

"I came here to hire you. I'll make it two-fifty—take it or leave it."

"Two-fifty!" The cabbage Red made was good, but not that good.

"There's something more," Bernie said. "Something you'll never get
working on the *Courier.* Prestige. You might even win the Pulitzer."

Red laughed.

"I mean it. The Pulitzer."

"What for?"

"Before I tell you, I want it clearly understood: this is under the hat. If you're not interested, you forget everything I said."

"It's a promise," said Red.

"I'm going after Mayor Gowan," said Bernie. "I'm going to take the *Ajax Post* and beat his brains out with it."

There was a silence, thick and hard. Like a brick wall.

Red smiled crookedly. "You wouldn't be the first to go after him."

"I'm aware of that. The Garrett Committee went after him and the State Anti-Crime Committee went after him and the *Advertiser* went after him, but there was always a fix. There'll be no fix this time. *I'm* going after him."

"You're nuts. He's too big—"

"Not now, Red. The time's ripe. The city's changing, stirring. Even the river wards, where his machine is strongest, are stirring. There's a rebel movement heating up in the dockers' union and if it comes to a boil, he'll lose the river wards. Industry's fed up. One factory after another is moving elsewhere, because of the taxes. All he needs is a shove."

"For a guy who's been away two years, you know quite a bit."

"I've got a reporter digging here already. A damn good reporter. But I need you, Red. You're in. You've got the contacts. You know everyone in the machine. With you on my side, we can't miss. We'll send that thieving, no-good son-of-a-bitch where he belongs—to jail—for life!"

"Not me," said Red. "You can keep it."

"I'm giving you the chance of a lifetime—"

"He's my friend, Bernie—"

"Sure, he's your friend. As long as he can use you. The minute you become useless, he'll drop you like a red-hot penny!"

"Maybe you're right. But *I'm* not ratting on him."

"I'm not asking you to rat on him. I'm asking you to stop ratting on a lot of decent people who've been getting a rotten deal here for twenty years—"

Red sneered. "You mean Shea and his pals?"

"I mean Shea and the people he's fighting for—the thousands and thousands who've been cowering like a bunch of sheep while Gowan and his heelers and his gangsters stomped all over them."

"They're doin' all right."

"Wonderful. Wonderful. Slums all over. High taxes. Rackets. And a lovely Medical Center that a town twice the size of Crescent couldn't fill up. He's been sucking the public tit for twenty years and now he's through sucking. Even without you and me, they're going to throw him out, right on his big bald skull. They're no longer sheep. They're getting their courage back."

"They'll never beat him. Never."

"They'll do it May 6th. And when he goes down, Red, you'll go down with him. Everyone in the machine." With a swift motion, Bernie drew a finger across his throat. The gesture made the short hairs on the back of Red's neck crawl. He poured himself another slug of whiskey, a double slug this time.

"On the other hand," Bernie went on, "if you go to work for me, you'll escape the deluge, and you'll make a mint besides."

"Two-fifty is good money—but it's not a mint."

"You'll make more than that. For the duration of the campaign, you'll collect, not only from the *Post*, but the *Courier* as well. And City Hall, too."

"I don't get it."

"You'll work in the open for *them*. For us you'll work underground. You'll go about your business just as you do now, palsy-walsy with the Mayor, palsy-walsy with the heels. Slap 'em on the back. Give 'em the old handshake. And all the while you pump them—gently—and feed the material to us. No doubt you've got a wealth of material in your head right now, but I'll want more. Some stories will require careful checking. You may even have to bust into a desk or two. It'll be dangerous, Red—but it'll be worth it."

"Go on," said Red.

"We'll run the exposé under a phony byline. But when the payoff comes, the morning after Election, we'll plaster your name across Page One. You know what this town'll do? They'll tear down that stone monstrosity they call Justice outside City Hall and put up a statue to Red Norton." Bernie grinned. "On a horse, with a big sword in your mitt."

"I can just see it," said Red.

"All kidding aside, there's no telling how far you'll go. You'll be known all over the country. The magazines will beg you for stories. You'll clean up."

"You sure can do a snow job, Bernie."

"This isn't a snow job. It's the truth… well, what do you say?"

"I'd like to think it over," said Red. "This isn't one of those things you rush into."

Bernie looked disappointed, but he managed to smile. "All right. Can you let me know in a few days?"

"Yes?"

"You'll find me at the *Post* every weekday."

"I'm not going near the *Post*."

"Mister Gowan must have eyes everywhere."

"Damn near everywhere."

"Give me a buzz then."

"All right. But I'll stuff a handkerchief into the mouthpiece, and I'll talk in riddles. You'll have to figure it out somehow."

"You think my phone's tapped?"

"No. There's no reason yet. But I'm taking no chances…. How about a cup of coffee?"

"No, thanks." Bernie put on his hat and coat and raised the collar and turned down the hat brim and went over to the door. "Better see if anyone's in the hall."

Red looked outside. "Nobody."

"So long, Red."

"So long, Bernie."

Red stood there, listening, until Bernie's footfalls no longer could be heard. Then he shut the door and locked it and went over to the window and flipped open the slats of the Venetian blind and looked out and after awhile he saw Bernie, walking fast toward the gate. He was walking just like a thief. Red smiled. Good thing there was no cop around. He'd pick Bernie up on general principles.

Red lit a cigarette and went into the bedroom and took off his shirt. Something on the night table caught his eye. It was the phone. He looked away and then he looked back at it.

He went over to it. He picked it up and stuck his forefinger into one of the holes and gave the dial a spin. He spun the dial a second time and a third and if he spun it three more times he'd be talking to the Mayor, but suddenly, as though the tip of his finger had driven against the edge of a hidden razor blade, he pulled his finger out.

Leave it alone. Your name's not Dawson. Let it drop. This is the Mayor's business and Bernie's. Let 'em fight their feud without you. Wash your hands of it.

He took off his trousers and put them and his jacket on a hanger and hung the hanger in the closet. He had quite a wardrobe. He was quite a dresser. Every suit in the closet was custom-built, by the Mayor's own tailor. Red got a break on the price because the Mayor told the tailor to give Red a break. Even with the dough Red made, he'd never be able to afford that tailor.

Red slipped his compactly built body into pajamas and put out the light and hit the sack. He closed his eyes. But his mind kept its eyes open. They were open on Bernie and the Mayor. He tried to stop thinking of them. He tried to think of Mrs. Kelty, to picture her, nude, as though that image, excitingly warming, would melt away the cold hard faces of the Mayor and Bernie, but she refused to come to life. He tried thinking of other women, younger, slimmer, plumper, hotter-lipped, but could not form them. All he could form was their names, words. He passed down the line, one name after another, and then finally he came to a new name and that, because it was new, mysterious, its owner never seen, intrigued him.

Ann Porter, 430 South 15th Street. Ann. Nice name. Short and sweet. Wonder how she shaped up? Short or tall, blonde or brunette, sweet or salt? He liked dames with a tang of salt in them. We've got a date, Annie. You and me and the Medical Center.

What did a guy wear when he blind-dated a dame with TB?

Something dark, something quiet.

Hell, no. That would only make the poor dame feel worse.

Something snappy, that was it. The russet-brown job with the two vents in the back. She'd go for that. And the dark green hat. She'd go for that combo. But what good was it, her going for it? She was sick. TB. Can't do anything with her. Sick. Hell with her. Wash your hands of her? Of *her*? No. *Them*. The Mayor and Bernie. It's their fight. It's their fight, but you're in the middle, a nut caught in the jaws of the biggest nutcracker ever made. When those big shining jaws came together, they would crack your shoulder blades and the bones of your arms and the bones of your hands, until you couldn't wash them of anything, and the bones of your thighs and legs and ribs, and then the jaws would slide up to your skull and slowly, surely, with a loud crunching sound, they would crack the bony white walls of your skull and suddenly the walls would cave in, crunching into sharp white splinters....

Damn!

Red got up and got a bottle and drank until he was so tight he could think of nothing. Nothing.

Chapter 6

Red ascended the high stoop of the brownstone and pressed the bell button and a woman appeared. She was tall, hatchet-faced, about fifty.

"Is Miss Porter in?" Red asked.

"I don't allow men to visit my female roomers," the woman said.

"This isn't a visit. I'm taking her to the hospital."

Her eyes, born suspicious, noted the russet-brown suit, snappy as leaves on a tree in November, and the green hat. "You ain't a doctor."

"No. I'm from the *Courier*."

Red showed her his press card, but that meant nothing. She said, "I don't allow men to visit my female roomers."

Red said, "You got a rooming house license?"

"Of course I have."

"Keep me out and you'll lose it. I cover City Hall. I can kill it just like that."

"I don't believe it," she said, but she spoke without conviction. There was fear on her face.

"Don't you?" Red turned as if to go.

She said hastily, "Miss Porter's on the fourth floor. Last room to the right."

He tipped the green hat, ironically, as he walked in.

He went up a narrow stairway with steps that slanted, so many feet had walked them and worn them, and he had to go slowly. He climbed to the fourth floor and went to the room that was last on the left and knocked and a woman's voice, young, said, "Who is it?" and he said, "My name's Norton. I'm from the *Courier*," and she said, "Oh." He heard her heels come clicking and stop clicking, but the door remained shut. "You're early," she said. She had a nice way of talking, refined, with a slight roll to her *r*'s that had never come out of the Second Ward.

"I guess I am," he said. She said, "You'll have to wait. I haven't finished packing." He said, "I'll help you." She said, "But Mrs. Johnston—" He said, "I know. She keeps a respectable house and she doesn't allow men to meet her female roomers." That got a laugh out of her, soft and light, nice as the way she spoke. "She made me an exception," he added. "The power of the press."

She said, "Couldn't you wait downstairs?"

He could, but he wanted to see what kind of a dump she lived in. It would make a good contrast to the room they would give her at the Medical Center. He supposed he could get a verbal description of it, but he'd rather see it with his own eyes. He had good reporter's eyes.

He said, "If you don't mind, I'd like to come in."

"All right," she said. She opened the door.

She was small, not more than five two and slim and delicate-boned and she wore a neat blue suit that made her even more slender. She was pretty, in a quiet way. Her face was a white oval and her eyes were dark blue, no, not exactly blue, but violet, and her nose was short and cleanly carved. Her face was oddly devoid of expression. But that might have been a mask against a stranger.

He wondered just how much she had been told. She didn't look the kind who wanted to get her name and face splashed all over a newspaper. He said, "They told you what this is all about?"

"Yes. You're going to write me up in the *Courier*." He noticed now that her voice was a monotone. The door had hidden that. Her voice was like her face. No life in it.

He looked around. When he was a kid he had lived in a railroad flat and some of the rooms were like this, but others were big and no matter what size they were, there were enough of them to give you elbow room. You could move and breathe, even if what you breathed was the smell of cabbage cooking and the smell of bedbugs and the smell of dirty underwear and the smell of the bathroom that always smelled as if someone had just come out of it. This room was like a cell in the old city jail, before the Mayor had built a new one. There was just room enough for a single bed, a dresser and a window that offered a fine view of someone's brick wall that had a sign painted on it advertising a personal loan company that loaned money at the lowest rates, with only your signature, that's all. There was light in this room but it came out of a bulb. It was a fine room, not to live in or breathe in but choke in. Cough in. She was coughing now. Not a big cough, but a low one that she covered quickly with her hand, turning away from him as she did so. She wiped her lips with a handkerchief, then went over to the bed on which lay an open valise with clothes beside it; a nightgown or two, a couple of slips, toothbrush, toothpaste, cold cream, powder, women's junk.

She shut the valise and snapped the lock and came over to him and said, "Excuse me" and slipped past him. She had a nice clean odor and her body slipping past him, her face not far from his, the front of her brushing the front of him, gave him a tingle. The feeling apparently wasn't mutual. She acted as though he didn't exist. Or as if she didn't exist. There was no life in her.

She opened the closet and took out a coat, a thin blue topper, and he helped her into it and she said, "Thank you." She put on her hat in front of a cracked mirror. He picked up the suitcase. "Got everything?"

"Yes."

She started for the door and he went after her. She stopped, so suddenly he almost bumped into her. He said, "What's the matter?"

She opened her purse, fast, and looked into it, then looked in her pockets. For the first time her face had expression. She looked worried. She said, "I'm sorry, but we'll have to open the suitcase."

"Anything important?"

"Yes. Very." Her voice, for the first time, had tone and color.

"Money?"

"No. A receipt." She didn't explain what kind of receipt. He put the suitcase on the bed and she opened it and emptied it, quickly, almost frantically. There were papers at the bottom of the suitcase and she went through them very carefully.

Squeezing past her, he pulled open the bureau drawers. They were all empty. He got down on his knees, banging his head against the bureau in the process, and cursed, but under his breath. He looked under the bureau and saw a small piece of paper. Maybe that was it. He had to bend like a contortionist to reach it. Unbending, he rose to his feet and looked at it.

It was a receipt issued by an outfit called the Memorial Lake Cemetery Corporation. Beneath the company's name was the company's slogan: "Give Your Loved Ones a Resting Place Beside a Lovely Lake." Under that was a penned notation to the effect that Miss Ann Porter, of 430 South 15th Street, Crescent City, had paid $50 as a down payment for a burial plot.

Red looked up. The girl was rummaging around in the closet. He said, "This what you're looking for?"

She turned. Her face lighted up. "Yes. Where did you find it?"

"Under the bureau."

She took it and put it in her purse. She was still smiling.

Red asked, "Is the plot for your parents?"

"I have no parents, Mr. Norton. It's for me."

"Oh."

She put her things back in the suitcase and they went downstairs. The landlady stuck her hatchet face out of a doorway and said with phony cheeriness, "Goodbye, dearie. I'll have your room all nice and clean for you when you get back," and the girl said, "Thank you, Mrs. Johnston," and the landlady said, "Good luck," and the girl said, "Thank you," and she and Red went out into the sunlight.

They got into the convertible. The convertible impressed most dames but not her. He started the car. He said, "You're pretty young to be worrying about burial plots, aren't you?"

"Am I?" She seemed genuinely surprised.

"I'm half a dozen years older than you, but you won't catch me buying burial plots."

"But you should," she said. "It's just as important as a house. Even more important. A burial plot isn't a house you live in twenty or thirty years. You live in it the rest—the rest of your death. That's a long time, Mr. Norton."

"I guess it is," Red said.

Chapter 7

There was a smooth highway leading to the hospital, but Red took Elm Street instead. It offered a more dramatic view of the hospital. Elm was three miles long and very narrow. Once elm trees had grown there but now all that grew there were kids. The homes were the homes of workmen who had broken away from the slum flats of the Second and Third Wards to buy slums of their own. They worked in the mills and came home from the mills and had their stew and then went out and had their beer and had their big fat wives, fat with the starchy junk the poor got fat on, and they had more children and a harder time meeting the taxes, but when spring came they had their gardens to putter in, a piece of dirt five feet by five feet, and on Sundays when they went to church in their best suits, they were bigshots, rich, above those who lived in the Second and Third Wards, because they were landowners. Sixty years ago the homes they lived in were new, but now they were rotting.

At the point where the two long lines of rotting workingmen's houses converged stood the main hospital of the Medical Center. It seemed to leap out of the ground.

Red glanced at the girl. She was gazing ahead toward the hospital but he had the feeling she wasn't looking at it. She was looking beyond the hospital, perhaps toward her grave that had the fifty-dollar down payment on it and was situated on a green hill beside a blue lake. *You have to live there the rest of your death.* It was the queerest thing Red had ever heard anyone say. He wondered how it would be living there, with a pine roof or a mahogany one over your head, low over your face and darkly shining, and above the roof earth and above the earth grass and all through the grass and earth, worms, and not far from you the murmur of water that could not be heard, and over everything the night wind blowing but unheard.

He shivered. He had, as a police reporter, seen a good deal of death in some of its worst forms; a chopped-up mass of mincemeat spread half a mile over a railroad track and the wheels of the locomotive shining with the grease of the meat; the bodies of a tenement fire, Negroes turned white by the flames, and the most terrible bodies of all, the floaters, so terrible that even the river, which could stomach almost anything—garbage, the chemicals of the mills, sewage—even the river spewed up the floater. The floater was beyond humanness, bloated with gas, the color of slate with eyes that were holes through which eels found passage and with an odor that haunted you for weeks. The odor of the floater seeped into your clothing and when you went to the toilet, that odor became the odor of the floater. Red had seen nothing of death to love. They could keep it. It was for the birds, the worms, the eels. Anyone who saw good in death, even rest, must be off her rocker. Or very sick. He had never been very sick. He pitied her. She was only a kid. Not bad looking, either. He liked her style. He had never had much truck with the quiet ones; he was always chasing the obvious ones. The quiet ones drew him and repelled him. Their quietness was a kind of purity, nun-like. It intrigued him. Their nun-like hood of quiet, whipped off, might reveal any number of interesting things.

He wondered if the girl had ever had anyone make a pass at her. They said girls with TB burned with love. A lot of tripe, probably. The only warmth in this girl, and you couldn't call it warmth, but a hunger, a want, was not for a man but for bed, not for a bed with a man in it but a dark wooden bed with peace in it. Peace be with you, baby.

He felt like a louse, thinking that. She looked like a scared kid now. They were swinging into the big driveway of the TB hospital. That dark wooden bed didn't look so enticing now. He said, "Take it easy. You're getting the best room in the joint. And there isn't a hotel that'll give you better food. And there's a big solarium where you can lay in the sun all day."

"I don't like hospitals," she said. "I hate them."

"Maybe you like that hole in the wall at Mrs. Johnston's better."

She flared a little at that. "At least it doesn't smell of ether. And there's no one there to—to tear you open."

"You won't feel it."

"Suppose they don't give me enough ether?"

"They've got it down to a science. You get exactly the right amount and no more."

"I wouldn't care much if they gave me an overdose. I—I'd just sleep then. But if there wasn't enough, I'd feel the knife—twisting in me."

He said, "Where do you get these nutty ideas, anyway?"

"I had laughing gas once. I was only fourteen. I had a bad tooth but I was scared to get it pulled and my mother said, all right, take laughing gas. First, they stuck a clamp in my mouth, to hold my jaws open. Then they gave me the gas and said to breathe deep and to count and I counted and counted and everything grew black, like a tunnel, but at the far end of the tunnel was a small light, that never went out, and I felt everything."

"You felt him pull the tooth?"

"Yes. And I couldn't do anything about it. All I could do was yell, down the tunnel, toward the little light."

"He didn't give you enough gas."

"Suppose they don't give me enough ether?"

"This isn't a two-bit dentist's office. This is the best hospital in the U.S.A."

"They still make mistakes—"

"Look. I'll make sure you get enough ether. Even if I have to give it to you myself."

She smiled. She had a nice smile.

In the marble-walled lobby of the hospital was a bronze plaque on which were engraved the words HEALTH ALONE IS VICTORY and under that MEDICAL CENTER TUBERCULOSIS HOSPITAL, ERECTED 1952 A.D. DURING THE ADMINISTRATION OF THE HONORABLE JOHN J. GOWAN, MAYOR OF CRESCENT CITY and under that an engraving of the Mayor's face, without wrinkles. Even without wrinkles, it was stern and cold. The engraving had been made from a photograph in which the Mayor looked right at you so that whether you moved to the right or the left, the Mayor's eyes followed you.

Red led the girl to the information desk and showed the nurse there his press card. "Dr. Winston's expecting you," she said. "Room three-three-five."

"Winston's chief surgeon of the hospital," Red told the girl as they headed for the elevators. "He operates on all the bigshots. He's operating on you, too."

She didn't seem to give a rap who Winston was. She had withdrawn into her shell again.

Red knocked on the door of 335 and Winston said, "Come in," and Red and the girl went in. Winston was seated at his desk and Heinie, the *Courier's* star photographer, short, wizened and bald, was seated beside him, sampling a glass of the doctor's liquor. Winston was a tall beefy man with a florid face that was running to jowl but that was still handsome. He had thick black hair, worn in a pompadour, with a dash of gray at each temple. He had a quick smile that Red suspected he could turn on and off as one turns a faucet. He had large hands, not slender, like a surgeon in the movies, but wide and long and strong-looking. Red had met him twice before, at the ceremony at which the Medical Center was officially opened and at a cocktail party in the Mayor's flat. The women at the party had made a big fuss over him. He was distinguished, impressive, very sure of himself.

Winston rose to his feet, but Heinie stayed put in his chair, giving the girl a slow up and down, not because he was interested in her as a woman but because he was a cameraman and she was his subject. He was a damn good cameraman, too. He had a great knack for realism, and for catching people off guard. His pictures had copped half a dozen prizes.

After making the introductions, Winston asked the girl how she felt and she said, "All right, thank you." Winston hadn't impressed her and he knew it. He gave her the Winston smile and asked if she minded posing for photographs and she said no. Heinie got up and picked up his camera and in his gruff way told her to sit down. A thousand other photographers would have told her to cross her legs—she had good legs—and would have shot her from the floor, but not Heinie. There was a time for cheesecake and this was not the time.

She sat down, straight-backed, hands in her lap, her thin, ivory-colored fingers lacing and unlacing, her face stiff, her eyes large with fear, and that was the way Heinie shot her. He shot her from five different angles.

Winston said, "Don't you think you ought to get her smiling?"

"I want her just like she is," Heinie said. "This ain't a beauty contest."

Winston shut up.

Heinie shot her once more, put a new plate in the camera and turned to

Winston. "It's your turn now." He leveled the camera. "Smile for the birdie, Doc."

Winston gave Heinie a dirty look, then erased it for a smile.

Heinie took a picture of Winston and said, "Now I'll take a shot of you both."

Just then the girl started coughing. A real fit. Hack. Hack. Hack. Her face turned a violent red.

Heinie changed his plates, lightning fast, and started to shoot her as she coughed, but Winston snapped, "That's enough. Cut it out."

Heinie looked at Red for advice and Red shook his head and Heinie put the camera down.

The girl was coughing like mad. Winston jerked open a drawer and took out a box of tissues and handed them to her and she grabbed a handful and pressed them to her mouth and coughed into them. Hack. Hack. Hack. Winston went to the water cooler and filled a paper cup and brought it to her. She drank some, thanked him, then leaned back her head and closed her eyes. She looked tired, very tired. The redness had left her face and now it was dead-white.

Red said, "Okay if I come back this afternoon?"

"No," Winston said curtly. "Make it tomorrow." Suddenly he remembered who he was talking to. A newspaperman, close to the Mayor. He turned on the smile. "I'm sorry, old man," he said, "but you understand?"

"Of course. Come on, Heinie."

Out in the corridor, Heinie said, "I don't know why you stopped me. That would have made a swell picture, her coughin'."

"There's such a thing, Heinie, as being too realistic."

Heinle grouched about it all the way down to the lobby. He sure was a bug on realism.

Red said, "Want a lift?"

"I've got my own car. Goin' to the office?"

"No. The Hall."

They passed the bronze plaque and the eyes of the Mayor trailed Red out.

Chapter 8

As usual, Murphy was on the phone when Red entered the Mayor's office. Red said, "Where's the Mayor?" and Murphy looked up and said, "He'll be here any minute. Olaf showed up late."

Olaf was the big Swede who gave the Mayor his daily massage. Olaf was courting another Swede who lived in Roxford, sixty miles away. Whenever he went to see Hilda, he stayed overnight at her parents' home and invariably he arrived late next morning at the Mayor's place. That made the Mayor late to work. Generally he was very punctual. The Mayor told Olaf to drop the Swede in Roxford and fall in love with someone in Crescent City, but Olaf said nothing doing. The Mayor could have hired plenty of other masseurs, but he stuck to Olaf. He said Olaf's massage made him feel ten years younger. When the Mayor went south in the winter he always took Olaf with him. This past winter, though, Olaf didn't go, because of the girl in Roxford. The Mayor even offered to stake *her* a trip south, but she wanted to stay with her folks. The Mayor had to get another masseur during the winter.

The Mayor sure had it soft, Red thought. An expensive Swede masseur to bring his skin to a glow, a gorgeous apartment with twelve rooms in it, a Filipino butler, a house on the lake in summer and the best house on Biscayne Bay in the winter. The house on Biscayne Bay had a toilet large enough to hold a convention, and beautiful enough to live in. Shea was always making cracks about it in his street-corner speeches. He'd say, "When I was a kid and we had to go, we went into a cold hall and stood there in line and waited our turn, and God help any tenant who stayed in there more than three minutes. They'd open the door and throw him out. There was no lock, you see. It was pretty awful. But you ought to see where your Mayor goes, when he has to go. Marble walls and a marble tub and faucets made of pure gold and a Rembrandt, a genuine Rembrandt, on the wall, and a bookcase full of first editions. Not that the Mayor ever reads them. I doubt if he ever read anything outside his bank account."

Whenever Shea went into his spiel about the Mayor's john, the crowd roared with laughter. Bitter laughter. Red had never seen so many people so bitter. What was it Bernie had said? *The city's changing, stirring. All Gowan needs is a shove. And when he goes down, you'll go down.*

Red's jaw hardened. Something had to be done about Bernie.

The door opened, the Mayor came in, looking like a million bucks. "See the girl?" he asked.

"Yes. But I didn't get much out of her. She had a coughing spell and I won't be able to interview her until tomorrow."

"She a local girl?"

"I don't know."

The Mayor was a great one for local people. The whole town was that way. It was a big town but a hick town. Even when it came to a thing like murder, no jury ever sent a convicted killer to the electric chair if he was a local boy. There was only one exception to the rule. That was the time a Negro holdup man killed a cop.

"I don't suppose you found out how she votes?"

"I didn't get a chance to ask her."

"It'll be a good angle if she's Fusion," the Mayor said. "Show how fair we are. The hell with race or creed. The Medical Center takes 'em all, irregardless how they vote."

Something's got to be done about Bernie.

Go ahead. Spill it.

Red said, "Who do you think I saw last night?"

"I'll bite. Who?"

There was a sudden welling of saliva in Red's mouth, as though he were about to get nauseous. He swallowed hard. The Mayor stared at him. Don't say it. Shove it back down your throat. Swallow it, bury it in your stomach, drown it in saliva, in the juices of your stomach. Keep it down.

"Who did you see last night?" the Mayor said.

"Bernstein." There. It was out. Beyond retrieving.

"Bernstein!" The Mayor bellowed the word. Murphy got up from his desk and came over.

Red nodded. He couldn't speak. His mouth was full of water.

"How come you saw him?"

Red swallowed again. "He was outside the house, waiting, when I said goodbye to you."

"Go on," said the Mayor.

"I asked him to come up for a drink," Red said.

"You should of tossed him out on his ear," said Murphy.

"Only a jerk would do that." Now that the thing was out, beyond recalling, Red was getting a grip on himself. "I played it the only way it should have been played. He had a reason for coming, an important reason, and I wanted to find out what it was, so I played it friendly. To the hilt."

Murphy said, "You should of—"

"For Chrissake, Murphy, shut up!" said the Mayor. He said to Red, "Go ahead, Red." His voice was down now, normal. "What was the reason?"

"His paper's going to start a crusade," Red said. "They're going after you."

The Mayor's voice was calm, dangerously calm. "And where do you come in?"

"He wanted me to feed the *Post*. He wanted a reporter who was on the inside."

"You should of brained the—" began Murphy.

"If you had any brains, Murphy, you'd shut your trap and keep it shut," said the Mayor. "Sometimes I wonder what I pay you for. You used your skull, Red. That's what I like about you. You got a head on your shoulders. Take Murph now. If Murph had been there, he'd of called Bern-

stein every kind of Jew in the calendar and we'd never know what was going on until that son-of-a-bitchen paper started blastin' me. Did you take
his proposition?"

"I stalled. After all I wanted to talk to you first. But of course," Red added
with a grin, "I didn't tell him that."

"If you had," said the Mayor, "that would have put you in Murphy's
class. If there's anything thicker than a thick donkey, I'd like to meet it....
When does this crusade start?"

"He didn't say and I didn't want to pump him or he might have gotten
suspicious. But I think it's going to be soon. I'm to tell him whether I accept or not by the end of the week."

"You'll tell him when I say to tell him," said the Mayor. "Stall him as
long as you can. Until we get a plan worked out. What would he do if you
turned him down flat?"

"Go on with the crusade anyway. He's probably got a reporter or two
nosing around here already."

The Mayor nodded thoughtfully. He took out his leather cigar case and
took out a cigar and bit off the end and stuck the cigar in his mouth and
Murphy produced a lighter and lit it for him and the Mayor took a long
puff and eyed the cigar with satisfaction. He said, still eyeing the cigar, "You
saw Bernstein right after we dropped you at the house?"

"Right."

"Around midnight, wasn't it?"

"Just about."

"Then why the hell did you wait until now to tell me?" The Mayor's voice
had the quality of a bullwhip cracking.

"I— I—"

"You could of phoned me at my flat."

"I— I figured I'd tell you when I saw you."

Through the blue cigar smoke, the Mayor's black eyes drilled him.
"How much did he offer you?"

"Two-fifty a week."

The Mayor whistled. "Not bad."

"I'll tell you why he didn't phone you," Murphy said, a nasty smile on
his face. "He wanted to think it over. Two-fifty a week ain't hay."

Red was sweating now. He could feel it oozing down his neck. "Look.
If I was going to pull a double cross, if I even thought about pulling it, I'd
never have told you I saw Bernstein. Never." He added, with feigned bitterness, "Maybe I shouldn't have told you. I give you a hot tip and what
happens. I get a third degree."

The Mayor smiled. His voice was smooth as butter. "Now don't get sore,
Red. All I'm tryin' to point out is that in a thing like this time can be im-

portant. You wasted hours. Hours. All you had to do was pick up the phone. A ten-cent phone call."

"I'm sorry, Boss," Red said.

The Mayor put a fatherly hand on his shoulder. "Forget it. After all, you finally did tell me." He turned to Murphy. "The first place Bernstein will send reporters to is Fusion Headquarters. Call Inspector Kelly and have him put some men on a twenty-four-hour plant outside the joint. Any new faces around there, I want 'em tailed."

"Oke," said Murphy. He scurried to his desk.

"Call Rosenthal, too. Tell him to come down to the Hall right away." Rosenthal was the Mayor's mouthpiece, smart as they came.

Murphy started working the phones.

The Mayor walked Red to the door. "Thanks for the tip, Red. Even if it did come a bit late."

Red smiled. "You needn't rub it in, Boss. It won't happen again."

"It better not," said the Mayor.

Chapter 9

The press room was empty when Red got there, but Giotti had left a note, saying he and Dawson were covering a meeting of the City Planning Commission and would give him the story when it was over. The note also said that Standish, editor and publisher of the *Courier*, had left word for Red to go to the *Courier* the moment he arrived at the Hall.

Red drove up to Courier Square. The Courier Building was a handsome four-storied structure made of a green stone so smooth and polished it looked like a stone from which jewels could be carved. There were many windows, all huge, and the sun glancing off the east side of the building was a blinding flash. The style of the building was ultra-modern. Standish had intended to build it in the Colonial fashion, red brick and white trim and two graceful columns before the entrance but the architect said no, it wouldn't go with the rest of the Square. Standish never could stand the new building. He was a bug on old Colonial. He wrote a column which was supposed to be about Crescent City but which was mostly about a lot of hick towns back East. He wrote of them lovingly, their quaint Cape Cods and salt boxes and the sprawling white mansions on their outskirts. He lived in such a mansion now. It had cost him $70,000 just to build the joint.

Red went through the city room to Standish's office. Standish was alone, in his shirtsleeves, pecking away at his typewriter with his forefingers. He was a tall, stooped, ungainly man. There was something Abe Lincolnish about his rugged face and his kindly eyes and the slow way he had of moving and talking. You'd never think the bastard had been a blackmailer. But that was what he'd been. He'd come to Crescent from a hick town downstate, with twenty bucks in his jeans and that kindly, rugged Honest-Abe way of his and slow-talked a banker into staking him to a weekly that was about to go under, and he went to town. He did all the legwork, writing, reporting. His staff consisted of three fast-talkers imported from a Wall Street boiler room. They got on the phone and called a lot of business men and politicians and asked them to place an ad in the paper and if they didn't place an ad, Christ help them. Standish could really sling vitriol. And if there was a breath of scandal involved he blew it up from a breath to a gale, and still stayed clear of libel. In two years, he turned the *Courier* into a daily.

That was twenty-three years ago.

He quickly came to an understanding with the politicos then in power. Two years later, when Gowan was striving to become Mayor, he blasted Gowan's head off, but all the vitriol and all the near-libel failed to stop John Gowan. The day after election, old Honest Abe Standish was down at the Hall, shaking the Mayor's hand with his strong honest handclasp. He got a fat job-printing contract and a juicy piece of the city's legal advertising and later a $20,000-a-year job as State Statistician. The only time he ever showed up at the State Statistician's office was to pick up his check. And some people thought country boys were jerks.

Standish nodded at Red and told him to sit down and resumed his pecking for a couple of minutes. Then he stopped and lit his pipe. "Heinie got some good pictures of that girl."

"He's a swell photographer."

"Tell me about her."

Red told what he knew and Standish shook his head sympathetically. "The trouble," he said, "is these damned cities. You don't breathe air. You breathe smoke, gasoline, filth. It's a wonder we all don't have TB. She doesn't need a hospital. Give her some good country air, fresh eggs, milk warm from the cow, and she'd be a new woman."

Yes, Red thought, and give her a nice Early American mansion to chase herself around in, instead of that rat hole on 15th Street, and some nice Late American greenbacks, so she wouldn't have to work. That would fix her up pretty. The trouble with Ann Porter was that she wasn't a blackmailer. Be a blackmailer and your lungs stay strong.

Standish said, "I think you'd better start knocking out a promotion piece. Just two or three paragraphs, enough for a two-column box. Don't tell too much. Tease 'em."

"Okay, Mr. Standish."

"Here. Use my machine."

Red knocked out a teaser and handed it to Standish who bluepencilled one sentence and handed it back. "This is fine. Give it to Fox on your way out."

Red went into the city room and dropped the teaser on the city desk. He chewed the fat with Fox awhile and then one of the city desk phones rang. Fox answered it and looked up and said, "It's for you."

"Who is it?"

"Someone named Frankie Collins."

"I'll take it in a booth."

Red went into one of the booths and picked up the phone. "Hello, Frankie."

"Hiya, Red," Frank said softly. "We had quite a time last night, didn't we?"

"We sure did."

"I always get a kick out of the Wyandotte. Not only the food, but meetin' old friends, talkin' over old times."

"Yeah," said Red. Even a strongarm had his sentimental moments.

"I wonder if you could help me out."

Sentiment, my eye. The guy was looking for a touch. "I'll do what I can," said Red.

"I'm throwin' a little party tonight. I got four girls lined up—honeys— and four guys, but one guy calls up and says he has to go out of town, so here I am stuck with three guys and four girls. Seein' that them tomatoes are costin' me two hundred each, I didn't want to waste one, so I phoned you."

Two hundred each. Call girls. From out-of-town, of course. No call girl, no street-walker, could set up shop in Crescent City. The Mayor could have made a sweet piece of change out of the racket, but it was one racket he didn't dare touch. The church crowd would have howled to high heaven. Some of them did enough howling as it was.

Red asked, "Can't you cancel the extra dame?"

"The pimp gets paid, whether you cancel or not. That's the way he does business."

"I see."

"They're terrific, Red, just like show girls. And you can have your pick. There's a juicy blonde and a tall brunette and a short brunette and one with hair as red as yours. And it's on me!"

"Okay, Frankie. What's the address?"

"Two thirty eight Harmon Boulevard. Go up to the penthouse."

"A penthouse, eh?"

"There's a terrace'll knock your eye out. A real garden, up in the sky."

"Sounds swell."

"There's only one trouble. The guy who owns the apartment—"

"I thought it was yours."

"I'm doin' all right, Red—but not that good. Like I was sayin', there's only one thing wrong. The terrace wall is too low. One of these days someone with a load on is gonna take a look at the view and drop. Twenty-two stories."

"You'd think the guy would put up a higher wall."

"He says a higher wall would spoil the view. I told him he oughta put guards up, but said them steel guards they make look like hell. He said, just stay sober and nothin' will happen. So remember that, Red."

"I'll remember."

Frankie laughed softly.

Chapter 10

There was a switchboard in the lobby with a Negro seated at it. He was in a purple uniform. He stopped Red and spoke in the limey accent of a West Indian. "Whom do you wish to see?" he asked.

Whom.

"Mr. Collins. Tell him it's Red Norton."

The switchboard man stuck a plug into the board and said into his phone, "Mr. Collins? Mr. Norton wishes to see you. Very well." He whipped out the plug. "Please take the private elevator, Mr. Norton." He nodded toward a door across the lobby.

Red went to it. It was a self-service job. Under the button was a white name plate and the name on it leaped slowly out, getting big as an eight-column headline. The name was: *Mike Calitorcio.*

Mike ran the waterfront rackets. He hired the city's hoods.

The elevator glided upward and came to a stop so gentle that for a moment Red wasn't even aware that it had stopped. The gate slid open and he stepped off. He was in a small room made entirely of steel; probably bullet-proof. There was a door and a bell button and he went to it and pressed the button and a little later a peephole in the door opened and an eye stared at him and Frankie's voice said, "Hi, Red." A lock slid softly and the door opened and he stepped through the doorway, into night.

He was on the terrace, flagstoned, with tables here and there. No one was at the tables. It was a bit cool for sitting around.

He saw the low wall. It was low, all right.

"Nice, huh?" said Frankie.

"Terrific."

"I got somethin' even better to show you."

"The girls here yet?"

"They're here."

"This is Calitorcio's joint, isn't it?"

"Yeah. Know him?"

"Just to say hello."

"He's my boss."

"He giving the party?"

"I am. He lends me the place every now and then, just as long as my friends don't start bustin' the furniture, or try doin' cartwheels on top of that wall." Frankie nodded at the wall. "You wouldn't believe it but we actually had a drunk climb on it and start walkin' on his hands. He was an acrobat, but I wouldn't even trust an acrobat when he's fried. I grabbed him and hauled him off and flattened him. If he ever fell off, it would have been my last party up here. Mike don't stand for nonsense."

They entered the apartment. It was like a Hollywood set, big, dazzling with mirrors.

There were two girls in the living room, if you could all a room as fancy as that a living room. One was mixing drinks and the other was seated. The one mixing drinks was a sultry-looking little dish, very dark, rather thin, Italian. The one that was seated was big, blonde, breasty, creamy. She reminded Red of a glass of cream. Frankie introduced Red. The little dame's name was Carmen, and the glass of cream was called Eileen. Red would have liked to have given her a belt in a field in the country, in a bale of hay.

Carmen said, "What do you drink?" and Red said, "A martini. Dry."

There was an arched doorway leading to the next room and two people came through it, a red-haired woman with a tight black dress on and breasts shoved hard against the dress, and a man, Captain Hartung, the Mayor's bodyguard. He had an arm around the redhead and his hand, white and repulsive, the rat-killing hand, was cupped over one of her breasts. The redhead was handsome, with slanting eyebrows and a smile that was a challenge.

"Alice," said Frankie, addressing her, "meet Red."

She said, "Hello, Red."

Red said, "Hello, Red."

"His hair is just like mine, isn't it?" she said.

Carmen said, "Yes. Only it does not come out of a bottle."

Alice freed herself from Hartung and took hold of Red's hand. "Come here." She led him over to one of the wall mirrors and stood very close to him and pressed her face sideward against his. Her cheek was soft and her perfume was exciting. She studied the reflection of their two red heads in the glass. Their heads were so close the hair seemed to merge.

"Exactly the same shade," she said. "People'd take you for my brother."

"You wouldn't want me for a brother, would you?" Red asked, breathing hard.

"No," she said. "Not for a brother."

Hartung came over. His little eyes were mean. He had obviously started drinking early. He glared at her. "Say, who are you with—him or me?"

The girl studied Hartung's reflection in the mirror, a half-smile on her lips. Frankie said, "She's with Red, Hartung."

"Oh, yeah—?"

Frankie said softly, "I said she's with Red."

Hartung wheeled. His eyes studied Frankie a moment, then dropped to Frankie's fists. Hartung was strong as a bull but you could see he had a lot of respect for Frankie's fists. He said, "Ain't she got something to say about this?"

"I guess she has," Frankie said.

She was still looking in the glass. She said, "Beat it, Hartung. You annoy me."

Hartung looked as if he'd murder then and there. Frankie said, "Be nice, Rudy. You know Mike don't like people brawlin' in his apartment."

Hartung grunted and turned to Carmen. "Gimme a whiskey double."

She gave him one. He sat down, pulled her into his lap. A philosopher, thought Red.

Frankie paired off with the glass of cream and Red sat down on a divan with Alice. Frankie touched a switch, lowering the light.

Alice said, low-voiced, "You know why I picked you?"

"Sure. We've got the same hair."

"Loving you will be like loving myself." She laughed. He kissed her laughing mouth. Her lips were bought lips but after awhile they caught fire.

Between kisses they drank.

She said, "Let's go outside."

She was no ordinary prostie. An ordinary prostie would have led him right into the nearest bedroom. Get it over with. Not her. She was giving it a buildup. She was stringing it out. She was an artist. She ought to be. Two hundred bucks.

They went out on the terrace. They went over to the wall. The city lay sprawled beneath them. The moon showed up its good points and skipped the bad and the city was breathtaking.

She put her hands on the wall and leaned forward and looked straight down. He looked straight down. Far below, narrow with distance, lay the gray sidewalk.

"I wonder how it would feel?" she said.

"What?"

"Falling through space."

"It's all according to whether you've got a parachute."

"I mean from here. Just falling."

"It's fun," said Red. "Try it sometime."

"Do you think you'd stay conscious all the way down?"

"Some people do. I've covered leapers who screamed till they hit. But let's not get morbid." He slipped an arm around her waist.

There was a sudden pound of footsteps behind him and the girl slipped out of his grasp to one side. He turned. Frankie and Hartung were coming toward him, fast. Too fast for him to do anything, except get away from the wall. They got hold of him.

"You drunken bastards," said Red, struggling and laughing although he didn't exactly feel like laughing.

Their hands closed on his arms like steel clamps. Their teeth flashed, either in grins or in the exertion of holding him quiet.

He said, "What is it—a new parlor game?"

They turned him around so that he faced the wall and a hand closed on his neck and slowly forced him forward to the wall. The hand forced him downward.

The sidewalk seesawed.

"How do you like the view?" asked Hartung.

There was a beating of drums, rising, as blood raced into his head. Red was almost jackknifed over the wall. He tried to say something but the height below, that distant sidewalk, a gray strip, sent the words choking back down his throat. He heard the girl's laughter, sweet and derisive and high, high as twenty-two stories.

"How do you like the view?" Hartung asked again.

Red managed somehow to talk. "Won—der—ful," he gasped. "I—I'll take a two year lease." He'd give that redhead something to laugh at.

"You know," said Frankie. "I actually think he likes it."

"Since he loves it so much," said Hartung, "we'll let him see some more."

Arms slid around Red's legs, tightened. He was heaved upward. A huge gust of air that might have been a cry tore from his mouth, his throat, the bottom of his lungs, as he hurtled out into space, over the wall and out. The arms around his legs held him fast, but in the fragment of time in which he hurtled outward it was like the beginning of a plunge that could end only on the sidewalk. He went out, then swung down and the brick wall of the building came rushing toward him and he thought his face would smash against it, but his outflung hands took the blow.

He was now upside down. He was now looking *up* at the sidewalk. He was lying flat against the building. The building wall was a sidewalk and he was lying on it but there was a pull, a pull, from upward, from the sidewalk, as though the center of gravity had shifted from down to up. It was pulling him up toward the sidewalk, hard, but the arms held fast to his legs.

The drumming in his head rose and became the rush of a locomotive. His blood was a long locomotive rushing through his head.

A crazy thought came riding on the loco. Kick the son of-a-bitch in the chin. Just get one of your feet free and kick him in the chin.

Sure. Kick him and you go flying up. When he lets go you catapult, up to the roof of the sky. The roof is made of gray cement and maybe you tear a hole through it and maybe you don't, but the roof won't mind. The roof would feel no pain. Would you? Is there any pain in you when you tear into a cement roof twenty-two stories above you? There must be all the pain of the world, all the pain you had ever known and all the pain you had never known, the tearing rending pain that women must feel in childbirth and the sickening pain of a heavy toe slamming into your crotch and all the pain of a man being ripped apart by dynamite, into a million pieces— all that would be concentrated in the big smash against the sidewalk.

How long would the pain last?

A second. A piece of a second. A piece so small you couldn't see it with a microscope. But it would seem the age of the world.

Does a man stay conscious falling through space? If not, how many floors must he fall to lose consciousness, to slide into darkness that would save him pain, the short but concentrated pain, the world of pain capsuled into a pill of time, that would come of smashing against the sidewalk?

No, they didn't lose consciousness. He had covered many a leaper. Even those who had sought death, had thought it beautiful, went down screaming.

I won't scream. She's laughing. I won't give her the satisfaction.

His head pounded as though his heart had dropped into it. His misplaced heart suddenly burst, like a blown-up bladder, and black blood gushed from it and blinded his eyes and darkened his consciousness.

The grasp on his legs ended.

He went plunging, tumbling, toward a gray sidewalk he could no longer see, toward the big smashup, the big wet splatter, while high above his falling body hung a thin, derisive thread of laughter....

He opened his eyes. He was seated at the wheel of an automobile. The thought struck him: I must have dropped through the roof of a car. MIRACULOUS ESCAPE BY REPORTER: PLUNGES 22 STORIES, CAR ROOF BREAKS FALL. He raised his eyes. No hole in the roof. No roof. He was in a convertible, his convertible. His car hadn't been parked anywhere near the sidewalk toward which he had plunged. He hadn't plunged. The grasp had never left his legs. His legs had simply lost feeling and he had passed out. Then Frankie and Hartung had pulled him back and carried him down to the car.

That dame. He could still hear her laughing. He'd like to kick her in the teeth. And not just for laughing. She had been more than a spectator. She had been the come-on, the lure to get him out on the terrace, near the wall. Everything had been planned. Everything but Hartung's getting drunk. That had almost thrown a crimp into things. But Frankie had gotten him under control and from there on the party had gone through without a hitch. A little party tendered by Mayor John J. Gowan in honor of Mr. Red Norton to teach Mr. Norton to phone the Mayor immediately, next time someone propositioned him.

Red swore. He had a good mind to take Bernie up on that deal.

Yeah. Sure. And the next time they swung him over a rooftop, it would be rockabye baby, over the hills and far away....

Chapter 11

Red said, "How's the patient?"

"She needs building up, of course," said Winston, "and her mental attitude leaves much to be desired. She is—how did Keats put it—'half in love with easeful death.' But she'll get over it. A few strokes of the scalpel and she'll be a new woman, physically and mentally."

"When are you going to operate?"

"A week from Saturday."

"What time?"

"Two P.M."

"Can you give me some details of the operation?"

"Of course." The surgeon opened a drawer and took out a sheet of paper. He produced a fountain pen and drew an oval on the paper. "This is the left lung." He divided the oval with a horizontal line. "These are the two lobes. If this were the right lung, there would be three. A portion of this lobe—" he tapped the oval with the pen "—is infected. I cut into it, apply clamps to the major blood vessel, and slice away the contaminated area. Quite simple."

"Then she's in no real danger?"

"There is an element of danger in any operation. But I'm sure she'll pull through."

"No chance of her dying?"

Winston sighed. "I suppose it would make good copy if I said the operation was extremely hazardous—"

"It would."

Winston shrugged. "Say what you like. Only don't quote me. And don't lay it on too thick."

"Can I see her now?"

"Certainly. But don't third-degree her. A little at a time."

Red nodded and got up. "What room is she in?"

"Five-seventeen."

There was a knock and Winston asked who it was and low voice said, "Karsch," and Winston said, "Come in."

A pale man in a gray suit entered. He was one of the most colorless men Red had ever met. He had pale blue eyes behind rimless spectacles and his eyebrows were so light you could barely see them. He had thin blonde hair, small features and practically no chin.

Winston said, "Dr. Karsch, my assistant. Mr. Norton of the *Courier*."

Karsch's face reddened. He gave Red a quick, shy handclasp.

Winston said, "Norton's the reporter who is going to do the series on Miss Porter."

A flicker of interest showed in the pale eyes. "Oh, yes?"

Winston said, "I almost forgot. You'd better wear a mask, Norton."

"I can just see myself asking questions through a mask. Forget it, Doc."

Winston shrugged.

Chapter 12

She lay with her back to him, facing a picture window that ran almost the length of the room. The huge Venetian blind was drawn down about half way. Outside the window was a terrace with a wall, but a high wall, sensible, not like the wall at Calitorcio's. They couldn't take a chance having a low wall on a hospital terrace. Some patients got ideas, even patients who could afford a room like this. It was a beauty, everything painted a soft rich gray. Even the TV set, operated by a control switch attached to the bed, was painted gray. The switch was on the other side of the bed and Red couldn't see it, but he knew it was there. When the Mayor had been operated on for appendicitis, he had had a room just like this. A beauty. The only thing wrong was the bed. It was a bed like any other hospital bed, with cranks and ratchets, built for use, not looks.

Red said, "Hello, Miss Porter," but there was no answer. He went over to the bed. She was sleeping. Her face was rosy, warm-looking, like a baby's, only this warmth and rosiness came from disease. Her lips were very red. They were parted slightly and moist. She stirred and turned so that she lay face up and her moist red lips moved. She was talking in her sleep. He was tempted to lean close to her to hear what she was saying, but she was a TB. He didn't care to get that close.

She smiled in her sleep.

What was she dreaming?

— That she was healthy again, cured.

— That she had 500 bucks on a 100 to 1 shot and that the 100 to 1 shot had won.

— That she was in her little green plot, beside a lovely lake.

— That she was in bed with a guy, maybe me, and not a high narrow bed, hard to the back, with cranks and ratchets, but very broad and very long and very soft, with a cover made of polar bear furs or the fur of ermine that you could roll in to your heart's content and over the bed a ceiling made of mirrored glass so she could see herself and the guy beside her, me.

Her eyes opened. She saw him. "Oh. It's you."

"How are you?"

"All right."

"Your dream must have been all right, too."

"Why?"

"You were smiling."

She smiled again, not at him, but beyond him, at a memory.

"What did you dream about? Did you hit on the Sweepstakes?"

"I dreamed I was on the sea, floating."

"Well, as long as you didn't drown—"

"It was beautiful. Warm and sunny—like green gold. I lay there floating and then I turned and looked down and somehow it looked even nicer down there. Darker, cooler. The warmness and sun were nice, but suddenly I wanted to be down there, so I let myself slide down. I slid through layer after layer, each a little darker than the one above it. Like the layers of different liquors you see in one of those fancy drinks."

"What do you know about fancy drinks?"

"Not much. I saw one in a movie once. That was the way that water was—striped, each stripe darker than the one above it, until the bottom stripe was midnight blue, almost black. When I reached it I felt sand against me. It wasn't as soft as it was floating on top, but it was nice. Solid. I felt safe. I felt as though I had come home."

"And that's what made you smile?"

"I suppose. It was heavenly."

"Some people have a weird idea of heaven."

"I wouldn't exactly call it heaven but it was nice. When I die, that's the way I'd like—"

"Let's talk about living. It's more fun."

"Is it?" She had that *beyond* look again.

"Let's talk about you. After all, that's why I'm here."

"All right. Only there isn't much to talk about, Mr. Norton,"

"Red."

"Red."

She was right about there not being much to talk about. Born in Crescent City. Reared in Crescent City. Public school, high school and then college, but just before she was to start college, her parents were killed in an auto accident. She had to go to work. Her people left no money to speak of but judging by the neighborhood they had lived in, Red gathered they had been of a pretty good class. A good, solid, Clean Government neighborhood. Clean Government had tied up with the rebels in the Party and that was how Fusion had started. Red asked the girl if her father voted Clean Government and she gave him a look and asked, "Does it matter?"

"Don't be scared," Red said. "It's okay, no matter how he voted."

"I thought maybe—"

"A lot of people think that to get anything in Crescent City you have to vote the Party, but that's bunk. How did he vote?"

"Clean Government."

"And how did you vote? And don't kid me, because I can check it with the Board of Elections."

"I never voted, Mr.—"

"Red."

"Red."

"Why didn't you vote?"

She shrugged. "I never really cared." She wasn't kidding. All she'd ever vote for was a long slide through blueness, or a plot with a hole in it six feet deep.

"Have you got a boy friend?"

She flushed. "No."

"Stop kidding."

"I'm not kidding."

"A good-looker like you—"

"I've got TB. Remember?"

"I'd never let a thing like that stop me."

"No?"

"No."

"Well, *they* did."

"Who's they?"

"Fellows I met. We'd get along fine, and then I'd tell them, and they'd drop me—like a hot penny."

"Jerks."

"No. They were right. After all, why risk—"

"Jerks," said Red. "Yellow jerks."

"I don't know," she said. "Maybe I'd do the same thing, if it was the other way around."

"But you're not hopelessly sick. The doctor said when he got through with you, you'd be good as new."

"I don't know as I'd want to be good as new. Maybe if they'd just let me alone—"

Red put his hand on hers. "You're going to get well, whether you like it or not. So you might as well resign yourself."

She looked at his hand, so large it blotted hers from sight. He thought she was going to pull her hand away, but she didn't. Her bosom under the white bed jacket began rising, falling. Suddenly she raised her eyes and her gaze met his. The collision had a jolt in it. Her fingers, quiet at first, closed on his, tight, very tight. Her eyes had the oddest look. There was fear in them, as though she felt that by leaving her hand in his, by looking straight into his eyes, she was going too far, and there was a challenge, not to him, but to herself, to keep looking into his eyes, to keep holding his hand, tight. Red had heretofore regarded holding hands with a girl as something akin to spin-the-bottle, but now he was getting a charge out of it. Probably because she was getting such a charge out of it.

"Well!" someone exclaimed.

The girl and Red turned and the girl jerked her hand away. There was a nurse in the doorway, a plump little woman with a mick face and iron-gray hair and a grin on her puss a mile wide.

The nurse came over and Ann, her face averted, said, "Mr. Norton—Mrs. O'Brien."

"Sure and I'm happy to meet you, Mr. Norton," Mrs. O'Brien said. She sure had a brogue. "Where's Miss Ann been hidin' you?"

"I didn't hide him," Ann replied. "He's the newspaperman I told you about."

"Newspaperman, is it? From the way he was actin' I thought he was your boy friend." Mrs. O'Brien gazed at Red with undisguised admiration. "Look at the mop on him. Like a blaze of fire. I'll bet if you touched it, your hands would be blistered for a week." She turned to Ann. "You should of done what I told you, Miss Ann, and not wear that crummy jacket that looks like a laundry sack—"

"It will do, Mrs. O'Brien," the girl replied coldly.

Mrs. O'Brien shrugged. "In my day, when a girl was receivin' a male visitor, even if she was in a sick bed, she tried to look her best." She slipped a thermometer into Ann's mouth and sat beside the bed and held the girl's wrist. She drew out the thermometer and studied it. "You're a bad influence, Mr. Norton. Her temperature's up two degrees and her pulse is goin' sixty miles an hour."

"I don't think it had anything to do with me—"

"You needn't apologize, young man. Sometimes it's good for a girl to have her heart beat fast."

"Mrs. O'Brien!" the girl exclaimed. "I would deeply appreciate it if you would kindly refrain from making—"

"Okay, okay, Your Royal Highness," Mrs. O'Brien said huffily. "Sure and she's like the Queen of England herself, isn't she, Mr. Norton?"

Red grinned. "I better beat it. Glad to meet you, Mrs. O'Brien."

"Glad to meet *you*, Mr. Norton," Mrs. O'Brien said with enthusiasm.

The girl said, "Mr. Norton?"

"Yes?"

"You—you're coming back?"

"Sure."

"When?"

"Tomorrow."

"What time?"

"Sometime in the morning."

"Goodbye, Mr. Norton."

"Red."

The girl smiled. "Red."

Chapter 13

Red flipped his cigarette at the statue of General Grant, high on his horse, his hand tucked into his coat like Napoleon, his stone hat white with pigeon droppings. The butt hit Ulysses right on the nose. Red grinned and mounted the City Hall steps three at a time. He couldn't figure out why, but he was feeling great. He felt as though he had just had a long drink of something very smooth and very strong. He supposed it was the weather. The day was perfect.

Up in the press room, Dawson was his usual bastardly self, trying to needle Red about Bernie but Red ignored him. Red was feeling too good to get sore. Dawson gave him a short piece on a City Commission meeting— he shared the news only because he feared reprisal if he didn't give Red the story—and Red phoned it to the *Courier*. Then Red went down to the Mayor's office. The feeling of wellbeing, ease of mind, left him.

The Mayor greeted him with a sly smile. "Hello, Red. Lookin' kind of pale, aren't you?"

"I shouldn't wonder," Red said. "You'd look pretty gray yourself after hanging by the legs twenty-two stories high."

The Mayor and Murphy played it deadpan. They were both great actors.

Murphy said, "What's this about twenty-two stories?"

"Skip it," said Red.

"How did you make out with the girl?" the Mayor asked.

"Fine. Her old man wasn't Fusion but he was the next thing to it—Clean Government. Just the angle you wanted."

"Play it to the hilt, Red. The Medical Center helps everyone, irregardless of color or creed. When will you start on it?"

"I'll bat something out tonight. Home. I work better there."

"Don't forget to save me a carbon."

Red nodded. "Anything doing?"

"Yes. I'm going to the ball park this afternoon. Want to come along?"

"Sure."

"We'll leave right after lunch. Meet me outside the Oyster Bar at 1:30."

"Right."

"Who do you think's gonna cop the pennant?"

Red knew damn well who'd win the pennant. The Crescent Comets. They hadn't lost a pennant in ten years. That was because the club never hesitated to spend big money for players. The Comets were rolling in dough and not simply because they led the league. They had coined money even when they were in the second division. They became a gold mine the minute the Mayor secretly purchased a piece of the club. From then on, every job-holder receiving over three hundred a month, and every merchant who got favors from the Hall, had to buy a ticket to the ball park at least once a week, whether they went to the ball game or not.

Whenever the Mayor asked you what team you thought would win the pennant, you were supposed to say the Ajax Jays or the Bridgetown Bears, any team but the Comets. Then the Mayor would challenge you to a twenty dollar bet. And because you had a soft racket at the Hall or needed the Mayor's help in getting a building or street contract, you took the bet, even though you knew from the start you were going to lose. Even Red, who sometimes gave Murphy chills, the way he talked back to the Mayor, always bet the way the Mayor wanted. It gave the old boy a kick to win on the Comets. It wasn't the dough. He'd bet as low as half a buck on the Comets. It was just the fun of thinking he'd picked the winning team and everyone else hadn't.

But Red didn't feel like humoring him this time. Red said, "The Comets are going to win. In fact, I'll give you twenty to ten on them."

The Mayor growled, "Big-hearted, aren't you?"

Red smiled and waved. "See you at 1:30.... Oh. Before I forget. Give my regards to Hartung and Frankie Collins. Thank them for not letting go of me, up on that roof."

"What's he ravin' about?" Murphy asked.

"You know," said Red, "and the Mayor knows and so do I."

The Mayor smiled sourly. "You got a head on your shoulders, Red."

"And a nose on your face," said Murphy. "From now on, keep it clean."

Chapter 14

They arrived at the ball park ten minutes before game time. Ball games were the sole event at which the Mayor arrived early. As was his custom he led his party to the clubhouse, then through the long passageway that the Comets used to get to their dugout. He shook hands with the manager and the players and talked baseball. In his youth he had played shortstop on a semi-pro team and they said he was pretty good at it, but not as good as he liked people to believe. According to him, he had received an offer from the Giants, no less, to go to New York for a tryout, but had turned the offer down because he was more interested in politics.

Just before game time he and his party walked out on the field and slowly headed for his box. This was usually the signal for a cheer from the crowd. There was a cheer—and something else. A fan in the grandstand not far behind the box yelled, in a high clear voice, vaguely familiar:

"We came to see the game, Mayor—not you!"

There was a ripple of laughter in the stands. When the Mayor got to his box, he said to Murphy, "Who was that son-of-a-bitch?"

"I dunno."

The anthem was played. The Mayor looked fine as he stood there in the sunlight, tall, well built, a fine figure of a man, his face patriotically solemn, his hat held over his heart.

The first three men in the lineup of the visiting team, the Bears, went out on strikes. The leadoff man for the Comets rapped out a sharp single. He was a fast man and easily stole second.

"Nice stealing!" the fan with the clear voice yelled. "You're almost as good as Gowan!"

There was another ripple of laughter, louder than before.

Red said, "He's got a trenchcoat on. I think it's Shea."

The Mayor said through his teeth, "Hartung. Go up there and sit down beside that bum and when he makes another crack tell him to shut up. Start a fight. Smash him. Smash his face in."

"If it's Shea, there'll be a riot," Red warned.

"Smash him for me, Hartung. Smash him."

Hartung knew his stuff. He stayed put in his seat for fully two minutes, then he rose and entered the passage that took you under the grandstand,

to the frankfurter and beer stand. He could have gone directly up to where
the man in the trenchcoat sat but that would have been too obvious. He
was going to come at Mr. Trenchcoat from behind.

Murphy whispered, "Don't watch Hartung, Red. Watch the game."

Red watched it. He saw, without the suspense he would ordinarily have
felt, the windup and the throw and the swing of the batter and the ball
bouncing back to the pitcher and the throw to first and the man sliding at
third. One out. The next man struck out. The third man flied out and the
man on third, who was such a good stealer like Mayor Gowan, died there.

He heard Hartung saying, "He beat it, Mayor. He was gone before I got
there. Yaller."

"Was it Shea?" the Mayor asked, watching the Comets toss the ball
around.

"So they said."

"He's not yellow. Call him anything you like, but not yellow."

"Well," said Hartung, sitting down, "he scrammed."

"I don't blame him. If he kept that stuff up much longer, the crowd would
have torn him to ribbons. Sure they laughed. But it wasn't much of a laugh.
I got friends here. This place is full of them."

"Then why didn't they do something?" said Hartung.

The Mayor smiled. He was relaxed, now that Shea was gone. "They're
at a ball game. They're full of peanuts and beer and soda pop and they're
all excited over who's gonna win. They're not interested in politics. A crowd
like that takes time to get sore. But if he kept it up, they'd tear him limb
by limb." … The Mayor cupped his hands around his mouth and yelled,
"C'mon, Wilson. Let's see that old screwball!"

"A good sharp curve, Wilson!" someone else called. "Just like the curves
Gowan's been pitching at this town for twenty years!"

Hartung sighed. "Shea's back again."

"Where?" said Murphy.

"Christ knows."

"He don't know when to stop," said the Mayor. "He don't know when
to leave well enough alone. They'll murder him."

"If they murder him," said Hartung, "then you won't need me, I guess."

"You go out there and find him and throw him out of the park. We got
to do it for his own protection. If he puts up a fight, then can you help it
if you have to hit him? Hit him good, Hartung."

"First," said Hartung wearily, "I gotta find him."

"You'll find him," said the Mayor. "Just keep your eyes open."

"Suppose he stops hecklin'?"

"He won't. Not Shea."

A full inning went by but the only catcalls were directed against the players, the umpires. Then, in the third, the home team came to bat. The score was 0-0 and the old, old chant of fans at a scoreless ball game began rising from the stadium, low-voiced, slow-cadenced.

We want a run. We want a run. We want a run.

Accompanying it was a low rhythmic clapping.

The Mayor joined it, partly because he wanted the Comets to get across a run and partly because he got a kick out of being part of a crowd. The only time he ever merged with a crowd, in act, in spirit, was at a ball game.

We want a run. We want a run. We want a run.

The Mayor had once told Red that the best way to rattle an opposing pitcher was to give him the slow, low chant, steady, and the low steady handclap. In the old days the coaches would sometimes go out in front of the stands and lead the chant.

After a moment Red frowned. There was something wrong. He couldn't put his finger on it, but something was out of place. The chant. It had the same tempo, slow and low, but something in it had changed.

The words.

There was no longer one chant but two, and the second one was getting louder and spreading and finally it topped the other.

Throw Gowan out. Throw Gowan out. Throw Gowan out.

The Bears' pitcher rubbed the ball with his hands and looked up into the stands. The batter turned around and looked into the stands, too.

Throw Gowan out. Throw Gowan out. Throw Gowan out.

All Red could see was thousands of mouths, chanting the same refrain. There was something weird about it. He had heard defiance shouted, but never this deadly, monotonous chant. It seemed to creep into you and fill you up.

An umpire's voice knifed through it. "Play ball!"

The pitcher went into his windup, the ball shot over the plate, the batter missed it.

Throw Gowan out. Throw Gowan out.

A heavy whiskey voice rose above it. "Hooray for Mayor Gowan! Down with Fusion!"

Throw Gowan out. Throw Gowan out.

"You'll never throw Gowan out as Mayor!" the whiskey voice bellowed. "He's been Mayor twenty years and he'll be Mayor twenty years more!"

Throw Gowan out. Throw Gowan out.

Red stole a glance at the Mayor. The Mayor was standing, his hand clutching the box rail. His face had the look of a corpse, and the skin of his hand was tight-drawn and white. His eyes could not believe what his ears were hearing.

Throw Gowan out. Throw Gowan out.

"C'mon," the Mayor said.

Red and Hartung got up but Murphy stayed put, like a man dazed. "C'-mon," said the Mayor. The word grated as though he were grinding it between his teeth. Murphy snapped out of it and rose to his feet.

They went out, not to the field, but to the passage under the stands, into its welcome darkness, toward the welcome light of its exit.

Throw Gowan out. Throw Gowan out. The chant grew softer and softer. Suddenly, just as the Mayor was getting into his car, the chant stopped.

"There must of been hundreds of Party men in them stands," said Murphy, as Hartung started the car, "but not one let out a peep."

"One did," said Hartung. "He told 'em off."

"He was drunk," the Mayor said dully.

"All I got to say," said Murphy, "is when your own jobholders, who by rights should be out shovelin' manure, instead of holdin' down easy, good-payin' desk jobs, don't stand up for you, it's gonna be a tough election."

"The miserable scum," said the Mayor. Red had never seen him so bitter. "They were too surprised to act. Too stupid. You got to lay everything out for them. Plan, days beforehand. Tell 'em what to do—coach 'em—and they're fine. But let somethin' happen that ain't on the program, and they're lost, up the creek."

Murphy shook his head. "It looks bad, Boss. Bad."

"Shut up, Murphy."

"I was only—"

The Mayor suddenly raised his fist and brought it down hard, like a club, on Murphy's head. Murphy cried out and cowered in his corner of the seat.

"You talk too goddam much," said the Mayor.

He sat riding in silence, looking out the window.

Chapter 15

Red opened his bedroom closet and picked up twenty or so books of copy paper and his portable typewriter and went into the kitchen. The portable was a beauty. It was the most expensive job on the market. The Mayor had given it to him for Christmas. On it, in neat gold lettering, were the words, "To Red Norton from John Gowan."

He plugged in the electric coffee pot. He would have preferred whiskey, but contrary to the notion that newspapermen functioned best on liquor, he found the stuff threw off his thinking. When he had a load on, or even half a load, and wrote a piece, it looked like a million bucks, sparkling and original, but when he was sober, it generally looked like hell. He had heard of newspapermen who wrote well while drunk, but he had never met any of them.

He shoved a book into the machine and pecked out a lead. He wrote anything that came into his head. He was what was known in the business as a false starter. They wrote anything that came into their heads, then read it, then, generally, threw it away. Bernie seldom threw his first book away. He never wrote the first thing that came into his head. He thought it out, beforehand, every word. Red had to see words first, in black and white, before he could work with them.

The story called for a sob, but the lead sobbed so much Red had to laugh. He tossed it away and tried another and still another and finally he hit on something. He started at the start, without embellishment; the visit to Ann Porter's room, the cubbyhole with walls crowding in; her goal in life, another cubbyhole, six feet under but not without beauty, in a plot covered with flowers on a green hill, beside still water. Once he got the right angle, the story poured.

He read it and liked it. He might have trouble getting it past Standish, because it wasn't a run-of-the-mill sob story and Standish, like most newspaper editors, doted on what was ordinary because what was ordinary was quickly understood by the pinheads who read newspapers. This story was strange. The girl was strange. Her hankering for death, for the peace of nothingness, for the soft soft quiet of one's body crumbling slowly to powder sounded almost weird. And yet people would understand it. Especially the bitter, the lonely, the ignored, the sick, all those whom life in one way or another had given a boot in the pants. And there were plenty of them. Red was not one of them, but he knew of their existence. Without them there would be no police blotter, and little news. They dived off bridges and roofs and turned on gas jets and raised pistols to their temples or mouths and pulled the triggers. And sometimes they just waited. They didn't have the guts, or despair, to kill themselves. They waited for time to kill them. The Second Ward was full of them, women worn from hard work, torn up from child-bearing, torn up so much they no longer enjoyed going to bed with a man, and men, hard laborers, worn out before they were fifty, from heaving cargo at the dock, from swinging picks, from operating pneumatic drills that his father, who had operated one, said would shake loose your teeth and fill your ears with a din that took hours to die. Even the Mayor, sick with what happened to him at the ball park, would understand. Red himself had only vaguely understood—until now, when he saw it before him, in black and white.

That dame Ann Porter was having an effect on him. He'd better watch out.

Baloney. She was a story, that's all. A story.

Chapter 16

It was nine in the morning when he awakened, but very dark. It was raining, teeming. The rain swept down in sheets of dark silver. Every now and then a wind would race through it; you could mark the pat of the wind by the almost horizontal gusts of rain, a lighter, shinier silver, that slammed through the downpour that was slamming into the garden, bending the saplings and tearing off the new weak leaves of spring and whipping the lawns into brown rich mud.

The phone rang. It was Murphy. "Better see the girl this afternoon. We're havin' a City Commission meetin' this morning."

"So what? It's worth two paragraphs. I can pick it up—"

"Not this you can't. This is front page stuff. You be there." Murphy hung up.

Red phoned the Medical Center and was connected with Ann's room. She answered the phone.

"I'm sorry, Ann," he said, "but I can't make it this morning."

"You can't?"

"No. I've got an important story to cover. But I'll be over in the afternoon."

"No. I have to take some tests this afternoon."

"Okay. Tomorrow."

"What—what about tonight?"

Tonight. He had a date tonight. That waitress down at the City Hall Bar.

"Of course," she said coldly, "if you have a date—"

"I did have a business appointment, but I guess I can postpone it an hour or so."

"Don't let me inconvenience you. If you'd rather not come tonight, don't. I don't care—"

"I'll be there tonight."

"If you—"

"Look. You said tonight. I'm saying tonight."

"Do you know the visiting hours?"

"I don't have to know them. I can visit any time. I'm a newspaperman, remember?"

He hung up, baffled at himself. Why had he given her that baloney about a business appointment? That was the kind of stall you gave a dame you were going with, you were interested in.

No. That wasn't why he had given her the stall. He had given it to her because she was a woman and no woman liked to be told that a guy, even a guy she hardly knew, couldn't see her because he had a date with another broad.

Red put on his hat and raincoat and went out. The rain was warm on his face. He slopped along the gravel path to the garage, got into the convertible, raised the top, drove out. It sure was raining. It made a steady thump on the car top.

There was a lightning flash and a low explosion of thunder. Summer wasn't far off. He wondered what this summer would be like, if he would still be covering the Hall for the *Courier*, if everything would be as it had been, the Party still in power, the Mayor taking life easy down at his summer place on the shore, Red visiting him weekends, enjoying the long white-sanded private beach and the long cold drinks and the rides on the Mayor's cabin cruiser. The Mayor had always wanted a yacht, but hadn't dared buy one. He had risked buying the mansion on Biscayne Bay with its hoity-toity toilet and now he regretted it, but he had never dared risk the yacht. That would have been too much. Even the people in the Organization would have squawked. It was the one thing the Mayor couldn't have, and it burned him up.

"You could buy one when you retire," Red had once told him.

"Retire?" the Mayor had laughed. "I'll never retire—not till I'm dead."

"Don't you ever get tired of politics?"

"Do you ever get tired of women? It's like havin' a woman, Red. Even better. There's nothin' in the whole wide world more excitin' than sittin' down and plannin' some scheme to fix your enemy's wagon. You work out the scheme, carefully, enjoying every minute of it, and then you start the scheme going. It's wonderful, watching a scheme work. And there's the power. The people all yellin' your name, listenin' to every word you say, obeyin' every order you give. I tell you, Red, once it gets in your blood, you can't get rid of it till your blood freezes."

If he ever lost his power, he would die. That was why, when the crowd at the ball park gave him the chant, the razzberry, he had looked so much like a corpse. He had died then and there. But just for a while. He was a tough man to kill.

The Commission meeting proved that. The meeting, as Murphy had predicted, turned out to be a hell of a story. Shea was present, of course, all set to go into his usual song and dance about lower taxes, slum clearance, etc., when the Mayor yanked the rug from under him. He called upon Finance Commissioner Barton to speak and Barton rose, a mimeographed statement in his hand, and started reading it aloud.

The statement was a resolution to reduce the real estate tax rate, a prime issue of the campaign, by $15 per $1,000. This was a terrific chop. Even Shea himself had demanded no more than a cut of $10 per $1,000. Barton explained that the reduction had been made possible through a "long planned economy program promulgated by Mayor John J. Gowan." A number of city employees would be laid off as a result, he said, but they had to be sacrificed, he added piously, for the greater good of the community.

A long planned economy program. Red knew damn well how long it had been planned. Less than twenty-four hours. The Mayor had started working on the scheme directly he had recovered from the shock of the reception they gave him at the ball park. The $15 cut in the tax rate was his answer to the low chant that had left him dazed, humiliated, and as close to a sense of impending defeat as he had probably ever experienced.

The answer was devastating. The Commission chambers were packed to overflow with people, many of them Shea supporters, but there wasn't a boo throughout the entire reading of the resolution. When Barton finished, the chambers resounded with applause.

Shea made a frantic effort to turn the tide. He shouted that the move was nothing more than a desperate bid for votes, which it was, and warned that after Election Day the ward heelers would come flocking back to their jobs and the tax rate would shoot up again. But it all sounded like sour grapes, and when the meeting was over, the Mayor was almost mobbed by back-slappers.

The reporters dashed out to call their papers.

Later, they went down to the Mayor's office. All the Commissioners were there. Drinks were being served. There was a lot of chatter. It was like the hour of victory, just after the returns had come in on Election Night. Everyone was making a big fuss over the Mayor.

In the Mayor's waste basket lay a folded newspaper, with a black stripe of a headline. Red recognized the type as that of the *Ajax Post* and unobtrusively fished the paper out. The headline said: MAYOR GOWAN GETS RAZZBERRY AT BALL GAME. Bernie had started his dirty work.

Red dropped the paper back in the basket. Murphy came over and gave him a drink. Red stared at him. He was smoking one of his secret cigars. "You better get rid of that stogie," whispered Red, solemnly. "If the Mayor notices it, you'll be tossed out on your can."

"Holy Christ," said Murphy, whipping the cigar out of his mouth. He got rid of it fast.

After awhile the room emptied. The Mayor said, "Well, Red, how did we do?"

"Terrific. You really gave Shea the works." Red handed him a sheaf of copy. "Here's the first story on that girl. I thought you'd like a look at it."

"Sure. Sure." The Mayor sat down and read it. He read it thoroughly, then looked up. "This is okay, Red, okay. She sounds kind of wacky though, all that harpin' on croakin'."

"Do you want me to cut it out?"

"Hell, no." The Mayor handed the story back. "The more hopeless things look for her now, the better the story will be when she's cured."

"I got a feeling Standish is going to yelp."

"You tell Standish to print it as is. Tell him I said so." The Mayor's gaze drifted toward the waste basket, then snapped back to Red. "If more newspapers printed this kind of story, Red, it would be a better world, a lot better. People read this stuff, a sick girl dyin', a great hospital savin' her, they feel better. They gain confidence in those who govern them. Without that confidence, that faith, this country will go to hell, Red. Right to hell. There's too much freedom in the United States." His glance shot momentarily back to the waste basket again. "The newspapers, they got too much power. I know, I know, they got the Constitution behind them, but maybe it wouldn't be a bad idea if the Constitution was amended. Or better yet, scrapped. This country is like a 1953 car on a 1776 engine. Just because some old jerks who have been dead a couple of hundred years said it was all right, any stewbum who can get his hands on a printin' press can come out and say anything he pleases. It ain't right, Red. It ain't."

"Too bad he don't run for President, eh, Red?" said Murphy. "There'd be some changes then. Boy, would there be changes."

Chapter 17

Red ate that night in a spaghetti joint in Little Italy. The rain poured in buckets but when he went out into it, he barely felt it, because of the spicy food warming him and the thick red wine. He wasn't high. Just warm.

When he reached the hospital, it was still pouring. It was only a short run to the entrance but he was drenched by the time he got to it. The rain had poured down his coat collar and under his shirt. He felt steamy with rain, with sweat.

The girl at the reception desk started to tell him visiting hours were over, but he flashed his press card and that was that. He opened his coat to air himself out. He boarded an elevator. A couple of nurses boarded it, too. They were cute, in spotless white. They looked as if they must smell of soap, but he couldn't smell them because all he could smell was himself, steamy with wine sweat, with rainwater. For fear they would smell him, he buttoned his coat again.

He got off at the fifth floor and heard them giggling behind him and thought: if I had one of you alone on that elevator, you'd giggle on the other side of your mouth.

Room 517. He opened the door.

The room was pitch dark. He couldn't see a damn thing. "Ann? You up?"

"Red?"

"Yeah."

"Come in."

"What's the matter? You trying to save the city money?"

"Save the city money?" Her voice sounded odd, strained.

"On electricity."

"Oh."

There was suddenly a flash of lightning whose glow seemed to fill the room. Just before thunder cracked, Red heard his own breath, sucked in, sharply.

The girl on the bed was nude.

He stood there motionless in the darkness, breathing hard, hearing his breath above the sound of rain, his eyelids blinking, his eyes straining to recapture what they had just seen.

Her voice came to him, low, hungry, filled with hunger. "Here, Red. Here."

He strode swiftly to the bed, finding it with no trouble, as though the lightning, like the tiny amount of light that was all that was required to imprint a scene on the film of a camera, had imprinted the bed and what lay on it upon his brain.

He stopped, looming over her. He could see her now, no details, but enough, enough; the pale slim curves of her legs and the rounder curves of her thighs and hips and the small white roundness of her belly and the small white mounds of her bosom and the sharp-planed whiteness of her face and shadows where her eyes and mouth were. Her pale arms curved through the darkness and he felt her fingers in his hair. "Kiss me, Red. Kiss me."

He bent down, but her hands tightened on his hair. "Not on the mouth," she whispered. "Here. Here."

His lips, at her hands' direction, touched one of her breasts and powerful quivers rippled through her. The fingers entwined in his hair twisted and jerked convulsively. Outside the night flamed and thundered.

"We're nuts."

"Why, Red?"

"Leaving that door unlocked. If anyone came in—"

"But no one did."

"I must have been out of my head."

"We both were."

"I feel like a first class heel."

"Why?"

"Taking advantage of you. You're only a kid."

"I'm a woman now, Red. And you didn't take advantage of me. It was the other way around. Red, the storm's stopped."

"It's still raining."

"But the worst part is over. It's so nice now. Peaceful."

"Maybe you better go to sleep."

"You worried about that—business appointment?"

"No. Why?"

"I don't know. You sounded as if you wanted to get rid of me."

"I never want to get rid of you."

"Do you mean that?"

"I mean it."

"I've got TB, Red."

"You'll beat it."

"Suppose I don't?"

"I still wouldn't want to get rid of you."

"You don't have to say that, Red."

"I'm not saying it because I have to. I'm saying it because I want to."

"You're sweet."

"Damn."

"What's the matter?"

"I—it just hit me."

"What?"

"You—you might become a mother."

"*A mother!*"

"Yeah."

"Wonderful!"

"I don't think Doc Winston would consider it wonderful."

"Who cares what Winston thinks?"

"It could mean your life."

"Don't be silly, Red. A woman with tuberculosis can have a child."

"You sound like an authority on the subject."

"I'm something of an authority on TB. I've read a lot about it."

"I still say I shouldn't have taken the chance."

"Please forget it, Red. You're free to do anything you like. No obligations whatever. In fact I wouldn't think of marrying you, burdening you—"

"You're no burden, baby…. Better get some sleep."

"Red?"

"Yes?"

"Lock the door."

"Now look—"

"Lock the door."

"It's too dangerous, Ann. In your condition—"

"I'll tell you my condition. I'm hungry, Red. Hungry. Before it was another hunger. To do something I had never before dared. To do it because there was no longer anything to lose and because time was so short. One last fling before the funeral."

"And now?"

"Now I'm just hungry to live. Lock the door."

It had stopped raining. There was a big dark cloud overhead, but it was moving rapidly, disclosing stars. It looked like a big bug with a silver tail. The pavements had the glisten of patent leather. He got into the car. He was tired, very tired. He had never known a girl like her. She had given everything and taken everything. He had never made love, or been loved, so completely. The hunger she had spoken of had swallowed him up. But there was more to it than her hunger. There was his hunger. It was not the same hunger he had known when he was with other women. It had more depth, more importance.

Would she be cured? She had to be. She just had to be. Then what?

He smiled ruefully. There was no getting away from it, he was hooked. Even if she didn't find herself knitting baby clothes in the next few months, he was hooked. This was it. He had often wondered how love was, whether he would even know it when he saw it. He didn't have to wonder anymore. This was it.

He wished it had come to him some other time, though. The time now was bad. Things were all bolixed up. Damn Bernie. He spoiled it. The mere thought of him spoiled it. If he hadn't gotten that job in Ajax or hadn't thought up that crusade of his, things would have been perfect. Then Red could think exclusively of her, having her again, and not in a lousy hospital room with a high bed hard as nails but in their own bed, their own home. On his salary he could give her a home, a knockout. Rest was everything to someone recovering from TB, and the kind of home he could give her, she could rest all day. Everything automatic, buttons and levers. And when she got tired of pressing buttons, all she'd have to do was yell for the maid. In one year she'd be fat as a tub. But there was Bernie. There was always something. Everytime something good came to you, a stinker followed it. Damn Bernie. Damn the Mayor. Damn Shea. Damn politics. Damn everything. Forget everything, everything but her. Just keep concentrating.

Tomorrow's the day I'm supposed to call Bernie. What are they cooking up, the Mayor and Rosenthal? How will it all end?

You forgot to forget everything. Concentrate... concentrate....

How will it all end?

Chapter 18

"We got it all lined up," the Mayor said.

"What?" said Red.

"The rug we're gonna pull from under Bernstein."

"Go ahead."

"First, Red, you phone him and say you'll play ball with him. Then you feed him two, maybe three, stories on gamblin'. But that's the come-on, the bait."

"And what's the hook?"

"I'll come to that. We'll take the gamblin' first. You start off by writin' that bookmakin' is a big racket in Crescent City—"

"Bernstein knows that."

"In a general way, yes. But you're gonna name names."

The Mayor opened a drawer of his desk and took out a folded sheet of paper and handed it to Red. "This is a list of eighty horse joints—addresses, who runs 'em, how much business they do, the daily play."

"Does it say how much of a take your three bagmen pick up?"

"You get around, Red. A lot more than I thought."

"I guess I do."

"We'll skip the part about the bagmen."

"Bernstein won't. He'll want to know about the take."

"We got that angle covered. But you don't say anything about bagmen, see?"

"Okay."

"You say that the horse joints are bein' protected by corrupt members of the plainclothes squad. We'll even see to it that two plainclothesmen pick up the ice so Bernstein's photographers can snap their picture."

"You're framing them?"

"I never frame a friend. Those two cops are gonna know the whole setup from start to finish. When your story and the photograph come out in the *Post*, I get indignant as hell. I shake up the plainclothes squad. We indict the boys spotted takin' the ice."

Red nodded. "And then after election the indictments get quashed."

"You catch on fast."

"A lot of people will still think you're the one getting the ice."

"Let 'em. Let 'em think all they want. They like me for it. The people want gamblin'. Otherwise every horse parlor in town would be out of business. They want it and they want to know that if they make a killin' on a horse, they'll be paid off. I guarantee that. No bookie in this town reneges on a bet. You can even hint that in your stories. Yessir, the people can *think* all they want about me—just as long as they don't *know*. And they're not gonna know because you don't mention my bagmen. The rap falls on the plainclothes squad. Get it?"

"I get it. Now what about the hook?"

"After you got Bernstein convinced that you know more about Crescent City than anyone but maybe myself, you write a story that you have learned exclusively that Mrs. John Gowan has started suit for divorce in State Supreme Court. You say that because of my influence, the case has been kept hush-hush. You say that nevertheless you managed to get a look at the divorce papers and found out that my wife and a flock of private eyes raided a room at the Davenport Hotel and caught me with a blonde."

Red stared, stricken momentarily dumb. The Mayor had always enjoyed a fine reputation as a family man. His devotion to his wife was the talk of the whole city. She was a sweet, motherly woman who busied herself with half a dozen charities, and not because she wanted to get her picture in the paper. Even Shea had reportedly confided to friends that the one regret he would have, if he ever succeeded in overthrowing the machine, was that Mrs. Gowan would be a victim.

The Mayor said, "The story, of course, is a complete phony—"

"So you hit Bernstein with a libel suit."

The Mayor nodded.

"But it takes weeks, months, sometimes before a libel suit goes to trial. Meantime, you've been tarred up and down the state."

"You're jumpin' ahead of the story, Red. We know how long you got to wait for a trial. We ain't waitin' for a trial. The day after the story comes out, Rosenthal and I go up to the *Post* and see the publisher. We make a deal. He prints a retraction, calls off the crusade—fires Bernstein—we drop the suit."

"He won't do that unless you can prove, immediately, that the story's a phony."

"That's easy. They check the blonde and find out, yes, there was such a blonde, but she died a couple of years ago. They check the time of the raid on the room at the Davenport and they find that exactly at that hour I was down in Miami, addressin' a big union convention. I'll even have to show the film that they took when they televised the speech. I got it home right now."

"You've got every angle covered, all right."

"You bet I have. It's gonna be the most devastatin' retraction ever printed. Anyone reads that, has to believe it. The dead blonde. Me not bein' in Crescent City when I was supposed to. Air-tight."

"What about me?"

"You got nothin' to worry about. When Bernstein asks you what the hell happened, you just say that you can't understand it, because the source that gave it to you was strictly reliable and never let you down before. All Bernstein can do is fire you."

"Suppose, when I send in the story, Bernstein decides to check the court to see if the suit's filed."

"He'll get the brushoff. He won't be told the story's phony. The clerk will simply tell him he ain't sayin' a word. That will tie up nice with your story about the suit bein' a deep secret. He'll bite, don't worry about that."

"Have you got the dope?"

"Rosenthal is preparin' the charges now. The lingo's so legal I almost believed it myself." The Mayor grinned. "Legal but sexy. I never thought I was such a wolf."

"Have you told Mrs. Gowan about it yet?"

The Mayor's face clouded. "Yeah. At first she wouldn't stand for it, not even for a fake story, but she came around finally, after I convinced her it was a matter of life and death."

"Is it?"

"It is, Red. It is. I thought I had Shea boxed in pretty with that tax rate cut but now I'm not so sure. This morning, less than twenty-four hours after he warned that the cut was a trick, I got twenty telegrams from crackpots, denouncin' me, I still think a lot of suckers will go for the tax cut gag, but where I thought it was in the bag, Shea made it an uncertainty. This election, Red, is like a guy on a tight wire. One little touch—a crusade by the *Post*—and it drops. Bop. And now suppose you get on the phone and call Mister Bernstein."

Red got up. He felt trapped. He said, "I'm going to give him double-talk, I'm even going to hide my voice. The idea is to make it look like I'm scared one of your boys is listening in."

"Good. I like that. Nothin' like a touch of realism. Here." The Mayor picked up one of the phones on his desk and handed it to Red. Then the Mayor picked up another phone, an extension. Murphy did likewise. Red stuffed a handkerchief against his mouthpiece, and the Mayor smilingly winked at Murphy.

Red dialed Information and got the number of the *Post*. He dialed the number. A girl said, "Ajax *City Post*, good morning," and Red said, "Give me the City Desk" and a man's voice came on, but it wasn't Bernstein's. It was deep, resonant. The man said, "City Desk." Red said, "Mr. Bernstein, please."

Deep-voice said, "Who is this?"

"Never mind who this is. Give me Bernstein."

"But my dear sir—"

"Don't dear sir me." The guy was only doing what any assistant city editor was supposed to do, but Red was all on edge. "Give me Bernstein. He's
expecting this call."

The deep voice hardened. "Give me your name first."

"I can't, stupid. I can't."

"Then you don't speak to Mr. Bernstein."

"Okay, okay, if that's the way you want it. But don't blame me if you get
a pink slip in your next pay envelope. And that's what you're going to get.
You'll be fired so fast you won't know what happened to you."

"Just a minute."

A few moments later Bernstein's voice came on. "Hello?"

"Hello," said Red. "This is a friend of yours. You went to see him the
other night. Tuesday night. Remember?"

Bernie's voice warmed right up. "I remember."

"You made him a proposition."

"Right."

"It's a deal."

"Great. Can you get over here?"

"I can't take the chance. If I got spotted, my name would be mud."

"Can't we meet somewhere else?"

"I'd rather not."

"Okay."

"When does the big story start?"

"Wednesday. We've got six articles written already. I'd hoped you'd look
them over and tell me what you thought of them. After all, the reporter
who dug up the stuff isn't on the ground floor."

Red looked at the Mayor for instructions. The Mayor nodded.

"Tell you what," said Red. "Mail the carbons special delivery."

"To your home?"

"Hell, no. I'll rent a post office box out of town. I'll phone you the box
number in an hour. We'll use that for a drop."

"Very well."

"And the next time I phone I'll use the name McBride. You tell that to
your assistant, will you?"

Bernie laughed. "Don't mind him. Fletcher's really a nice guy. But he's
new here and he wasn't taking any chances."

"He's forgiven. Tell him I'm sorry the way I talked to him."

"I'll tell him…. I'll hear from you in about an hour?"

"Right."

Red hung up.

Murphy said, "Double talk. Post office box. Why all the cloak and dagger crap?"

The Mayor said, "It's just what a newspaperman would do if this was on the level, isn't it, Red?"

Red said wearily, "It is."

"Well, now, Red," the Mayor said, "you're gonna have two series of articles runnin' next week. One all about what a louse I am and the other what a great humanitarian I am." He slapped his thigh. "That's rich. Rich. I'll bet no other newspaperman in the whole U.S.A. ever did a thing like that."

"I'll bet," said Red.

There's only one way out, Red thought as he headed for the pressroom. Leave town. Leave and never come back. You can't. Leave town and you leave *her.*

Damn. Why did she have to pull that stunt last night? Crazy. All nude there in the lightning. Crazy.

No. Desperate. Trying to snatch a handful of life just before she went down, under the clods of earth.

He was the one that was crazy. He shouldn't have touched her.

But he had wanted to. He had wanted to even before he had entered that room. He had wanted her all along. He hadn't realized it, but he realized it now. He could have gotten out of seeing her last night. Easy. All he had had to do was stick to his excuse about a "business appointment." But he hadn't. He had wanted to see her. He hadn't expected to find her waiting for him, without a stitch of clothes on, but it wasn't disappointing.

Funny. You knew a dozen broads, intimately, some for years, like Mrs. Kelty, and then along came a dame you knew just three or four days, a stranger, and bop, you fell.

What the hell. There was nothing to do but make the best of things. He was double-crossing Bernie, but in a mess like this, someone had to be double-crossed. You couldn't be a piece of rope in a tug-of-war forever. Someone had to lose. And it might just as well be Bernie. He'd asked for it. It wasn't as if Red had gone to him and lured him into a double-cross. Bernie had begged for it.

I don't know why the Christ I'm letting him get me down, Red thought. He's no knight in shining armor. He's doing this to get circulation. Do-re-mi. Make himself a bigshot. And because he wants to be a bigshot, I'm supposed to stick my neck out.

Nuts to him.

Chapter 19

The door to Room 517 was locked. He rapped on it. "Just a minute," someone called. It was Mrs. O'Brien. Red could tell her brogue a mile away.

She opened the door about two inches. "It's the redhead, is it? And with a big bouquet of red roses, too. How nice."

"Can I come in?"

"You'll have to be waitin' your turn, Mr. Norton. Miss Porter is entertainin' another gentleman."

"She—she is?"

"Someone very close to her heart."

"Yeah? Who?"

"Dr. Winston. He's checkin' her heart with a stethoscope."

"Oh."

"Sure, and you weren't gettin' jealous, were you?"

"A little."

"Wait here like a good boy. As soon as the doctor's through with her, you can go in."

"Okay."

He felt like a jerk standing out there with the roses. Every nurse who passed, grinned.

Presently Winston came out, followed by Mrs. O'Brien.

"How's Miss Porter?" Red asked.

"Amazing," said Winston.

"What's amazing?"

"Her attitude. She's a changed woman, Norton. A changed woman. It's wonderful what cheerful surroundings and good food and excellent care can do for a person."

"Yes," said Red, "it's wonderful."

"Those are handsome roses, Norton."

"For a handsome girl," said Mrs. O'Brien.

Winston smiled and he and Mrs. O'Brien walked off. Red went into the room. Ann wasn't wearing the bed jacket she had worn yesterday. She was wearing a nightgown, soft and filmy, not sexy but okay. She sure was pretty.

"Red!" she cried, when she saw the bouquet. "How lovely!"

He handed it to her and she buried her face in the flowers. Her face was almost as rosy as they were. He wished it wasn't.

She said, "Well, have you recovered?"

"From what?"

"Me. Last night. Things look so different in the morning."

"No," said Red. "I haven't recovered. Have you?"

She shook her head. Her face above the roses was like the face of a girl he had seen when he was a boy, on an old-fashioned calendar, sweet beyond measure. It seemed incredible to him that this was the same face that only a matter of hours before, disclosed by lightning, had twisted in the agony of sex, writhed back its lips and uttered sounds no lady on an old-fashioned calendar would think of uttering. The contradiction charmed him. He sensed it would charm him a long time.

He heard Mrs. O'Brien bustle in and quickly drew out pencil and paper. She said, taking the roses from the girl, "You needn't git busy on my account, Mr. Norton."

Ann laughed, full-throated.

"Sure, darlin', and it's good to hear you laugh like that. She's gettin' better, Mr. Norton—and it ain't the food or the hospital that's doin' it, no matter what the Doctor said."

"No?" said Red.

"No," said Mrs. O'Brien.

"Do—do you think they might not have to operate?" Ann asked.

"Now don't be gettin' false hopes. TB isn't a cold. If Dr. Winston says you have to be operated on, then you have to be operated on. And they ain't changed their plans yet."

"But I thought maybe—"

"Sometimes a patient gets better all by himself. As though, suddenly, the long finger of God came down and touched him. But don't count on it, dearie. You tell yourself you're goin' to be operated on and then, if they wheel you into the O.R., you won't be disappointed. It isn't as bad as it sounds, Miss Porter. Especially with you havin' one of the best surgeons money can buy."

"But I know I can get better. If they'd only leave me alone. I—"

Whatever the girl would have said died in a low choking sound. She coughed, violently. Mrs. O'Brien grabbed the box of cotton on the table beside the bed and pulled out a wad and handed it to the girl and she pressed it to her lips. On it was a trace of blood.

Chapter 20

Next day Red drove over to Garville, where he had rented a post office box to receive Bernie's mail, and found a bulging envelope waiting for him. He opened it in the car. It contained carbon copies of the first week's stories of the *Post* expose. There was also a note from Bernie which listed the *Post*'s deadlines and informed Red that he would get his first pay check the following Friday.

"The enclosed stories were turned in by Jim Wentworth, a good, solid reporter," Bernstein wrote. "But you may be able to improve on them. If so, call me at my home. The number is Ajax 2-3849. By the way, only three persons know the contents of the stories—Wentworth, myself and you."

Red looked them over. First of all there was a character study of the Mayor. It was tops, witty, full of sting. Then there was a two-piece job on the horse room racket. It was vague, just as the Mayor had predicted. There were three other stories, devoted to payroll padding. Much of the material was old hat, stuff campaign orators had fired and refired at the Mayor for years, but it was well put together. The new material, what there was of it, was all right. One paragraph in particular gave Red a laugh. This was about the prisoners' vans at the city jail.

"There are four vans," Wentworth had written, "and fifty-six men assigned to drive them. That's all—drive them. On the basis of eight-hour work shifts, seven drivers must sit at the wheel of each van, all at once. Presumably they sit on one another's laps."

All in all Wentworth had done a pretty good job, considering that he wasn't on the inside.

It was Saturday and the Hall was closed, so Red drove to the Mayor's apartment. He got there just as the Filipino boy was serving the Mayor lunch. There was a soup tureen containing oyster bisque, a favorite of the Mayor's, and Red's mouth watered when he smelled it. That Filipino sure could cook up a meal.

"Sit down and have a bite, Red," the Mayor said, and Red sat down and the Filipino went out to get some plates. "What's new?"

"Bernstein mailed me those carbons on the crusade."

The Mayor put down his soup spoon. "Let's see them."

"Maybe you'd better wait till after lunch."

"Now."

Red handed them over and the Mayor leaned back and began reading them.

He did a slow burn. The character study. If there was one thing the Mayor hated, it was ridicule. He barely glanced at the other stories. He read the character study three times.

"Who wrote this goddam lyin' tripe?"

"A guy named Jim Wentworth."

"Know him?"

Red shook his head.

"Hear anything about him?"

"I've had Fusion Headquarters staked out day and night, but Kelly's men haven't picked up a thing. Evidently this rat Wentworth's too smart to hang around here." He handed the sheaf of paper back to Red.

The Filipino came in with a platter of baked ham and french fries. "You—you haven't eaten your soup," he said. He looked as if someone had just slapped him in the face.

"—— the soup," said the Mayor.

"I'll heat it."

The Mayor looked as if he wanted to throw the soup at the Filipino. But he didn't dare. The Filipino was a whiz of a cook. He didn't take much guff from the Mayor.

"—— the soup," the Mayor said again.

The Filipino shrugged and carried off the Mayor's cold soup. The Mayor picked up the carving knife and fork. "Of all the vicious, lyin', scurrilous stories I ever read, that one takes the cake."

"Forget it. In a week from now you'll fix their wagon good. That libel suit—"

"It ain't enough, Red. It ain't enough. I'd like to—"

The Mayor, unable to find words strong enough to express himself, let the sentence die and drove the carving knife down into the ham. He drove it down as though the knife were a dagger and the ham human, living flesh.

He hacked off several slices, dumped some on Red's plate and some on his own and proceeded to eat. His strong teeth chewed, tore and rended the flesh, not with appetite, but in hate.

He looked up after awhile. "What's the matter, Red? You ain't eatin'."

"I'm not hungry."

"Go ahead. Eat."

"I'll settle for a martini," said Red.

"Manuel!" yelled the Mayor. "Fix Mr. Norton a martini!"

Red lit a cigarette. He didn't look at the Mayor. But he could hear his teeth, champing into the thick flesh.

After lunch, at the Mayor's direction, Red went into the study and dialed Bernie. The Mayor listened in at his extension in the dining room. Red told Bernie he thought Wentworth had done a swell job until he hit the horse room racket and then the series had rolled over and died. Bernie agreed it wasn't any too strong and asked if Red had anything better and Red told him about the list of horse joints he had.

Bernie got all excited. "Don't bother writing anything. Just mail the list special delivery. I'll throw out Wentworth's gambling stories and have him do a rewrite."

"There's something else," Red said. "If you send a cameraman to 9982 Green Street at two o'clock Tuesday afternoon, he'll get some shots that'll knock your eye out."

"Shots of what?"

"Two crooked plainclothesmen in the act of collecting their ice."

"Ice?"

"I forgot," said Red. "You editors lead a sheltered life. Ice is protection money. The bookie will pass it to them on the back porch."

"You certainly work fast, kid. Where did you dig up all this stuff?"

"From what is known in the trade as an unimpeachable source. Don't ask me more."

"I won't. Nice going."

The Mayor came into the study. He was happy again. He said, "You doin' anything this afternoon?"

"I was going to the hospital."

"Skip the hospital and come down the shore with me. The wife's there, gettin' the place in shape for the summer—"

"And you want me to help take out the storm windows—"

The Mayor laughed. "Don't be a sap. I got servants for that."

"I know. A servant for each storm window."

"You gonna come?"

"I'd like to, Boss, but I've got to see Ann—"

"Ann?"

Red's face felt suddenly warm. "You know. The girl with TB."

"So it's Ann already, is it?"

"It is."

"As Bernstein says, you work fast, Red."

"When two people get thrown together—"

"Listen, Red." The Mayor's face was serious. "I know you're young, full of hell, and she's young and pretty, but you can't touch this one, Red. If it ever got around that anyone made a pass at one of my patients, right in the hospital, there'd be a mess. First thing you know Shea'd be sayin' it ain't safe for a woman to go to my hospital—"

"You don't think I'm going to rape her, do you?"

"I wouldn't put it past you, Red."

"Don't worry."

"Maybe she'd try to rape you. They say them TBs are hot-natured."

Resentment boiled up in Red. It showed in his face. The Mayor said, "Take it easy, Red. I was only kiddin'."

Red didn't say anything.

The Mayor said, "Like her, don't you?"

Red said, "I guess I do."

"Enough to marry her?"

"Enough."

"Make a good story. Reporter Weds Girl Patient He Wrote Up. The perfect ending for the hospital series. You could say I played Cupid—"

Red burst out laughing.

"What's so goddam funny?"

"You—with a bow and arrow in your hand—and not a stitch of clothes on."

The Mayor tossed a mock punch which Red easily ducked.

"I still say it's a hell of an ending to the hospital series. Every dame in town would eat it up. We'd get thousands of votes, thousands. Nothin' like a romance to catch the women's vote."

"Don't you ever think of anything but politics?"

"Never. When's she going to be operated on?"

"One week from today."

"Figurin' on another two weeks, even three, before she recovers, she could still be married before election. As a matter of fact, if it looks like her recuperation is gonna take longer, she could be married right in the hospital."

"Just a minute. I didn't tell *you* when or where to get married, did I?"

"You weren't around. And I'm not tellin' you anything, Red. I'm just suggestin'."

"Let's leave it to her."

"Sure we'll leave it to her. But you can ask her, can't you?"

"All right. I'll ask her."

"By the way, next article you do, make sure you give Winston a plug. You barely mentioned him. I meant to speak to you about it before but with all the other things on my mind, it slid by."

"Okay. I'll plug him."

"He's a wonderful surgeon, Red. He took my appendix out and it was a work of art. You can barely see the scar. You give him a good writeup. Remember, it ain't just him you're writin' up. It's me. When you say the TB hospital has a great surgeon, it reflects on me."

"I'll plug him."

Chapter 21

Red went to the *Courier* and looked up the chips on Winston. There were quite a few. He was not only a specialist in TB but a general surgeon as well, and everybody who was anybody in Crescent City and required a knife job called on him. Even Fusionists. He had lost some patients, but nevertheless his batting average was tops. Before he was appointed chief surgeon of the TB Hospital, he had been assistant to the chief surgeon at the City Hospital, which the Medical Center had superseded. According to one story, he had been a protégé of Doc Stevens, who was medical su-

perintendent of the City Hospital and now held down the same job at the
Medical Center. There were a few lines about the organizations Winston
belonged to, the County Medical Society, etc., and that was it. Most of the
clips were about the bigshots he had cut. There was very little biographi-
cal material. An interview should take care of that.

Red went to the hospital. As he approached Winston's office, he heard
voices, behind Winston's door, and it was clear the voices were having an
argument. Red looked up and down the corridor. There was no one
around, so Red pressed his ear to the door. Red was a newspaperman,
nosey as hell.

He recognized Winston's voice. "I can't, Karsch. It's utterly impossible!"

"You can and you will." Karsch looked like a mouse, but he didn't talk
like one. Not now anyhow.

"Just this once, Karsch. Just this once." Winston was actually pleading
with the guy.

"No. I've done it for the last time. Either you do as I ask—"

"You can't let me down. You—"

Whatever else Winston said was lost in the sound of footsteps descend-
ing stairs somewhere behind Red. Red stopped eavesdropping and rapped
on Winston's door.

Winston opened it. His face was haggard. Karsch's face behind him was
hard. The guy had almost sprouted a chin.

The Winston smile, which nothing could down, appeared. "Oh. Hello,
Norton. What can I do for you?"

"I'd like an interview—"

"I'm terribly busy right now," Winston said. "Could you drop around
later?"

"Sure. About an hour?"

"Fine."

The door closed. What had Karsch meant by saying he was going to walk
out? And why should Winston be so steamed up over it? Maybe Karsch
wanted more dough. A one-man strike. First thing you know he'd be outside with a picket sign. UNFAIR TO KARSCH.

When Red entered Ann's room, she was propped up in bed, watching
television. She was wearing pajamas. Some pajamas.

They were made of black silk and they had a plunging neckline. They
were the kind of pajamas a guy bought a dame so she would excite him.
You could see half her breasts. She had cute breasts. They were small but
round, firm.

Seeing Red, she switched off the television set and demanded, "Where
were you all morning?"

"Working. Where did you get those pajamas?"

"I had Mrs. O'Brien buy them. Like them?"

"I like them. I'll bet the orderlies like them, too."

She smiled. There was something shameless about the smile. It looked odd on her. Her face had a sweetness against which shamelessness looked strange. An angel with a trace of whore in her. Every dame had a little of the whore in her.

She said, "Aren't you going to kiss me?"

"Sure." He bent down and kissed her on the forehead. He heard a movement of silk.

When he drew back his head he saw that she had lowered her pajama coat from her shoulders and part of her breasts were exposed.

Red said through clenched teeth. "Cover up. You gone nuts or something?"

Her body strained upward toward him and the pajama top tightened over her breasts. She held her arms out to him longingly.

"I'm yours, Red." Her whisper was hoarse. "Kiss me. Hard. Hard. Hard."

Red said, "Cover up."

"You—you don't want to—?"

"Of course I want to. But it's broad daylight. Suppose Mrs. O'Brien came in? Or Doc Winston?"

"You could lock the door. Go ahead, Red." She strained forward.

"If I locked the door, the whole hospital would wonder what's going on. Cover up."

Tears welled in her eyes. She pulled up the shoulders of the pajama coat.

"You're hateful. Hateful. Get out. I don't want to ever see you again. Get out and stay out."

Red grinned and sat down at the foot of the bed. She kicked out under the cover and her little foot slammed against his thigh.

He laughed. Furious, she turned and dug her wet face into the pillow.

"Look," Red said, "if we ever got caught, you know what would happen? They'd throw you out of the hospital."

"Let them. I don't care. I hate this old hospital anyway."

"And I'd lose my job. A guy about to get married would be in an awful spot without a job, wouldn't he now?"

She turned slowly around. "*Are* we going to get married?"

"Soon as you get out of here. I was only telling the Mayor this morning—"

"You told him?"

"Why not?"

She reached out and took some tissues out of the box beside the bed and began drying her face. "What did he say?"

"He thought it was swell. In fact he'd like us to get married before election. He thought it would help get him a big women's vote."

She bridled. "He did, did he? What does he want to do—make a circus out of it?"

"I wouldn't call it that," Red said, dead-pan. "All he wants is a nice cozy little wedding on the steps of City Hall—with only four or five thousand people around—and television and movie cameramen—"

"Well, he's not going to have it," she said. "It's bad enough I agreed to go through with this hospital story."

"I hate to disappoint him," Red said.

"If Mr. Gowan thinks I'm going to make a spectacle of myself, just to get him votes, he'd better have his head examined."

"Tell you what. If you want a really quiet wedding, we could borrow his private plane and parachute down into Courier Square."

"Red—you're kidding!"

He laughed.

"Did he really suggest we marry before election?"

"He did. He thought it might even be a good idea to get married here. But just ignore it, Ann."

"I don't know. I think it's sort of cute. Only no matter when we do it or where, it's going to be quiet. Just the witnesses and the best man and the bridesmaid. No more."

"You're the boss."

"Red, look on the dresser and get me my compact. I must look a sight."

"You do."

She crinkled her nose at him.

He went to the dresser.

"Red, while you're there, get me a nightgown. In the second drawer. Something nice and demure."

He brought her the nightgown and compact. "Hold the powder," she said. "I'll change first."

She threw back the sheet and removed her pajama coat. She did it very slowly. Then she started on the trousers. She didn't bother unbuttoning them. She shoved her body upward and then slowly, slowly, worked the trousers down past her hips. She had cute white hips. She had a cute fig-ure. He felt like taking a bite out of it. When the trousers were down to her knees, she slowly drew out one leg. Then she pretended that the other leg had somehow gotten snarled up in the pants and made a big to-do to free it, squirming around, wriggling her little round hips. He wanted to take a bite out of her then and there. He had all he could do to hold himself back.

She was giving him the works, of course. A little payoff for what he had done to her, or rather what he hadn't done. If she was any other dame, he'd take that bite and throw himself on her, then and there. Any other dame but her. He couldn't risk it. Not now, or tonight, or any other night. Not until the night she was out of here. And then, God help her.

Chapter 22

That night Red tackled the typewriter again. He plugged Winston, as the Mayor had requested. It wasn't an easy job. There wasn't much material. Red's interview with the surgeon had been far from satisfactory. It wasn't easy to squeeze information out of a guy who was worried. And Winston was worried. "Either you do as I ask," Karsch had said behind the door, "or—" Or what? It sounded like a threat, an ultimatum. Where did Karsch get off, issuing ultimatums to the great Winston?

The phone rang. It was Mrs. Kelty. She was furious. "I've been sitting around two hours waitin' for you to call. What happened?"

"I'm busy."

"Too busy to call?"

"I couldn't help it, Mary. I'm all tied up."

"Yeah. All tied up with a woman."

"Don't be silly. I'm doing a job for the Mayor."

"You're a liar."

"Okay, I'm a liar."

"You *are* a liar."

"If you don't believe me, come up and see."

"That's exactly what I'm going to do."

"Now, look, Mary—"

"You said to come up, didn't you? Well, I'm coming up."

"Have it your own way. But I hope you don't mind company."

"Company?"

Red lowered his voice. "The Mayor's here."

She said, awed, "He is?"

"We're preparing a statement."

"Is—is he near you?"

"No. He's in the kitchen, having coffee."

"How long will he be over there?"

"I don't know. Hours, maybe. It takes time to prepare a statement. Everything's got to be perfect. You know him."

"Yes, I know."

"Then I'll expect you—"

"No, Red. I can't come if *he's* there."

"Why not?"

"You know damned well why not. I'm leader of the Second Ward Auxiliary. What would he think if the leader of an auxiliary—from his home ward—came up to your apartment?"

"That's right. I never thought of that."

"I got a reputation to maintain."

"Of course."

"I wish I could come up though," she said wistfully. "I'd love to see him at work."

She was crazy about the Mayor. Sometimes Red suspected that the reason she went to bed with him was that it was a sort of substitute for going to bed with the Mayor.

"Come on up then."

"I told you I can't. I got a reputation to maintain. How about tomorrow?"

"I'll be all tied up. Let's not set a date, Mary. Soon as I'm clear I'll call you."

"All right, Red. Good night."

"Good night."

Red wondered, as he returned to the typewriter, whether he shouldn't have dated her tonight after all. Ann, with that little strip tease of hers, had gotten him all hot and bothered and he could use a woman. But somehow he didn't want Mrs. Kelty. He wanted something young and fresh, like Ann. He wanted Ann, when you got right down to it. He had never wanted one particular woman before. Before, any haybag would do. He had half a mind to grab his hat and chase over to the hospital and surprise her. She wouldn't have to peel for him. He'd rip the clothes off himself. He'd rip them off and show his teeth—what big teeth you have, grandpa—and take a bite out of her. Not a big bite. Just a nip. Just enough to get the flavor of her.

No. He couldn't take the risk. Even with the door locked it was a risk. He didn't give a damn about himself, but he couldn't get her in a jam. He just couldn't. He was nuts about her.

He sighed and started hitting the keys again.

Chapter 23

On Monday, the first article in Red's hospital series hit the street and the reaction was almost immediate. The switchboards at the Medical Center, the *Courier* and City Hall were swamped with phone calls. Most of the callers said they were going to send Ann contributions and wanted to know where to send them. Some, who had had TB, wanted to give her advice.

Half a dozen crackpots proposed marriage.

The Mayor said exultingly that the reaction to the story topped even that of his first election to office. Ann was pleased and displeased. She hated the publicity. She was annoyed that people should regard her as an object of charity. And yet their offers to help touched her. And although she pretended to be amused by the marriage proposals, it was obvious they gave her quite a kick.

Red walked on air. Even Dawson, his old enemy, told him the story was one of the best he had seen in print. Next morning there was a note from Bernie.

"Your yarn on Ann Porter was a honey. If the rest of the stories are anywhere near as good, I'm afraid nobody in Crescent City is going to bother even reading the *Post* series. My only regret is that a guy with your ability should corrupt it in behalf of Gowan. But we'll fix that, Red. After the election, you'll be working on a real newspaper."

Red showed the note to the Mayor, in the hope that maybe he could talk him into dropping his libel suit scheme. After all, if the *Post* series should be overshadowed by the series on Ann, the libel gimmick might be unnecessary.

The Mayor didn't agree. "You can never tell what the people are gonna do, from one day to the next. They're fickle as a dame. Today you're a humanitarian; tomorrow you're a dirty grafter. No, Red, we gotta stop that exposé and do it fast. There's no tellin' what that Wentworth will dig up. And there's another thing. I don't wanna just stop the *Post*. I want Bernstein's hide. And I'm gonna get it. I'm gonna rip it off and hang it up on the flagpole, right under the Stars and Stripes. Old Glory's mighty pretty, but Bernstein's hide will be even prettier."

Red shrugged. "The most that'll happen is he'll lose his job. He'll get another."

"There's more to it than that. The guy's been dreaming, day and night, for two years, of one thing—to cut my throat. The dream is almost comin' true and then suddenly, bop, the libel suit. No more dream. No more nothin'. That'll be worse than losin' his job. Even worse."

Murphy stuck his head in the doorway. He and two of the office staff had set up shop in an adjoining room to count the money people were sending in for Ann. "Boss," he said, "you know how much them jerks sent in? Almost a thousand bucks. In nickels and dimes and dollar bills. And we ain't finished countin'." His head popped out of sight again.

"And that don't include the dough they're gettin' at the hospital," said the Mayor. "Red, you and that girl will have a nice little nest egg by the time you're hitched."

"She doesn't want it," said Red.

"That ain't no attitude to take—"

"She said she wants it to go to charity."

"Charity? Not a bad idea. Tell you what. We'll set up a fund to build a new surgery. We'll call it the Ann Porter Memorial Surgery."

Red winced. "Not Memorial. That means she's dead."

"Sorry, Red. I just said it because it sounded good."

Chapter 24

Wednesday the *Post* came out with the first article of its anti-Gowan campaign, the character study. All over town, in bars, restaurants, on the street, you saw people reading it and laughing over it. Even at the Hall there was laughter, but it was silent, guarded. "See that story in the *Post?*" one heeler would say to another, and the other would say, "Yeah. Pretty vicious, wasn't it?" But the way they looked at each other, you could see they had gotten a big bang out of it.

Thursday's story featured the list of horse room joints. The cops raided the joints and shut them and confiscated the paraphernalia and arrested the bookies, and told them, under the hat, not to worry, they could reopen as soon as the heat was off.

The picture of the plainclothesmen receiving their take appeared Friday. The Police Commissioner announced that the two men had been identified from the photograph and had been suspended from pay and duty pending departmental trial. He added that under direct orders from Mayor Gowan he was going to re-shuffle the entire plainclothes division. "We'll have no grafting cops in our city!" the Commissioner declared.

That afternoon the Mayor handed Red an envelope containing the dope on the phony divorce suit. "Unload it," the Mayor said.

Red phoned the *Post* city desk and the deep-voiced man, Fletcher, answered. Red asked for Bernie. "He's in Trent's office," said Fletcher.

"Then have me connected to Trent's office."

"Trent is the publisher."

"I don't care if he's Queen of the May. Connect me with Bernie."

"Something hot?"

"Hot as a five-alarm fire."

"Okay. But I'll probably get my head handed to me... wait a minute. We're in luck. Bernstein's coming back. Hold on."

Bernie said, "I just spoke to the publisher. He was wild over that picture of the two cops. He said to give you a fifty-dollar bonus."

"If that was worth fifty," said Red, "this is worth a million."

"What?"

"The Mayor is being sued for divorce. The charge is adultery."

"Wow!"

"I thought you'd like it."

"I love it. But how come nothing's come in on it over the wire?"

"They've been keeping it under the hat for a week. I've got the story exclusive."

"I see. Has the suit been filed in court?"

"Certainly. I saw the affidavits, everything."

"You say you've got it sewed up?"

"There's only two newspapermen know about it—you and me."

"Do you think we could sit on it a day without fear of anyone else getting it?"

"What do you want to do—check up on it?"

"I don't have to check anything *you* send. I want to break it in Sunday's paper, not tomorrow. Our Sunday circulation tops the daily by fifty thousand."

"Okay. You can sit on it."

"We won't run it as part of the series. We'll run it as a separate story, leading the paper, under an eight-column streamer."

"Right. Want to give me a rewrite man?"

"You've got one. This is one story I'm writing myself!"

Chapter 25

He parked near the square and walked to the square and bought a *Courier* and went into a restaurant and sat down at a table and ordered coffee and toast. He didn't feel like eating much. This was the day. This was the day. He unfolded the *Courier*. There was an editorial on page one, right next to his article on Ann.

"At two o'clock this afternoon," the editorial began, "a young woman in the Tuberculosis Hospital of the Crescent City Medical Center will undergo an operation for the removal of part of her left lung. A whole city, touched by the series of articles Red Norton of the *Courier* is currently writing, has its eyes on her. But it need have no anxiety. Ann Porter is in excellent hands.

"Although Miss Porter earned $35 a week as a stenographer, the care she has been receiving at the Medical Center and the surgical talent that will be placed at her disposal today are worthy of a millionaire. The case of Ann Porter is not unique—in Crescent City. Every man, woman and child who becomes a patient at the hospital that John J. Gowan built is assured precisely the same treatment—the very best.

"All his life Mayor Gowan has fought the fight of the common man and the Medical Center, by the equal treatment it metes out, to those who can afford to pay and those who cannot, symbolizes that fight. The Medical Center is more than a place where the sick go to be healed. It is democracy in action.

"The Medical Center is only part of the Gowan program to make our town a finer place to live in. Where once indecision and wishywashiness marked city government, we now have a strong hand, swift to act. Our highway system is the envy of the nation. Crime is at a minimum. No prostitute walks our streets. Our police force is without peer—despite the cloud now hanging over it. It isn't much of a cloud, really, no matter what the mud-gutter press says. Surely no person with an ounce of justice in his makeup will condemn 5,000 honest, courageous police officers for the depredations of a few. The grafters on the force are the exception that proves the rule. And the exception will not be with us long. The Mayor has already launched a sweeping shakeup, to root out the corrupt, and to get rid of those police officers who although they never actually participated in graft, winked at it.

"Space does not permit us to enumerate all the achievements of Mayor John J. Gowan. It is true—and we are the first to proclaim it—that there is a negative side to his administration. The city's tax bill has been a high one, although some welcome relief from the tax burden was voted by the City Commission this week. But one cannot have magnificent Medical Centers, filled with the latest equipment and staffed by brilliant personnel, without paying for it.

"To the average taxpayer, the bill may seem steep, but it is worth it. It is worth all the treasury of the world. One cannot stint on the Ann Porters. Our true treasury is our young women and young men.

"So next time you're tempted to gripe about the bill the city tax office sends you—just remember, part of that bill went to make Ann Porter a whole woman, to give her a place in the sun again."

Standish had slapped it on pretty heavy, and yet there was truth in what he said. A flock of lies, but one big truth. The Medical Center. Red supposed Ann could be operated on successfully in a million other hospitals, but he was glad it was going to be the Medical Center. No matter how many rackets, how many grafts, flourished in the Gowan organization, one thing stood immaculate. The hospital. Immaculate and perfect. They couldn't miss with that operation. They couldn't. Red had had his doubts. They had kept him awake half the night. But that was because he was in love with the dame. He couldn't think straight, thinking of her. Now he could think straight. He smiled wryly. Funny, a newspaperman actually believing what he read in his own newspaper. But you had to believe the truth, no matter who said it.

They were going to give her a place in the sun again. The phrase dripped with corn, and he knew it, but it got him just the same. She could use the sun. He remembered her room, the cubbyhole with the brick wall for a landscape, and he winced.

Just wait till she saw the place he got her. He'd get her a house, one of those shingle and fieldstone jobs with the huge picture windows the Whitney Construction Company was building, just outside the city, convenient, but with plenty of trees around, plenty of sun pouring into those picture windows. Whitney was soaking the suckers $20,000 apiece for them, but Red should be able to get one at cost. Very few people knew it, but Whitney Construction was John J. Gowan. The Mayor didn't like people to know about his investments. They'd start wondering how come he could go into all those big deals of his on a salary of $8,000 a year.

More power to the old bastard. He was a thief and a grafter and if you crossed him, you might hang by the legs from the roof of a twenty-two story building or wind up in concrete on the bed of the river, but when it came to the Medical Center, he was okay. He could have made a mint, giving Whitney the contract to build the hospital. But he didn't. When he said the Medical Center was going to be above politics, above graft, he meant it.

Chapter 26

She looked at the electric clock on the dresser. "It—it's almost time."

"Yeah," said Red.

"You'll—you'll wait till it's over?"

"Sure. As soon as it's over we're going to celebrate. Champagne and a steak dinner."

"Silly."

"Okay. We'll postpone it a couple of weeks. Any idea when they're going to let you out?"

"Maybe—maybe I'll never get out."

"Don't say that." He snapped the words at her as though the words were a whip.

"I'm sorry, Red."

"This is a pushover. Like getting a tooth pulled."

"Funny...."

"What?"

"Me being scared. A week ago I would have welcomed it."

"A week ago you were nuts."

"In a way I'm glad I'm scared. I—I've got something to lose now. Before there was nothing. Dying was just a fair exchange—one form of nothing for another."

"Let's can this talk about dying and being scared. Did you ever live in a house? I mean a house of your own?"

"No, Red. I never did."

"Neither did I. But we're going to. A ranch, everything on one floor, so you don't have to hike up and down stairs. I'm going to see the builder next week."

Her face turned suddenly away. She was having the weeps. That was good. Those tears were good. He rattled on as though he hadn't noticed.

"I haven't enough for the down payment but I know a guy who has. He'll get me a break on the price, too. That goes for the refrigerator and all the other junk. He's got his hand in everything. Of course, a house isn't like an apartment. Giotti—that's one of the reporters down at the Hall—he's got a house and he says it's work, work, work, all the time—work for him and work for the missus. But we'll hire a dame to do the housework."

Her hand fumbled in the tissue box but there were no more tissues. He whipped the handkerchief out of his breast pocket and gave it to her and she blew her nose in it.

She said, "Can you afford to hire a woman?"

"Of course."

"I'm still going to do the cooking."

"You any good at it?"

"Awful."

"Then why experiment on me?"

"Because I want to."

"Okay," he said resignedly. "Go ahead. My old lady used to say I had a stomach made of castiron."

The door opened and Mrs. O'Brien bustled in, followed by another nurse and a young guy who was probably an interne. "You better step outside, Mr. Norton," said Mrs. O'Brien. "We got to get her ready."

He waved at Ann. "Take it easy, kid."

In the corridor he took out a pack of cigarettes and tore the top open and tried to get hold of a butt and ripped the butt. He got the torn butt out and threw it away and got his fingers on another and pulled it and lit it. His hand, as he lit it, shook.

He took a long drag. A nurse, a middle-aged bat, a supervisor probably, very stern, came along and gave him a look. He glared back and she kept walking. She was going to tell him no smoking allowed. It was a good thing for her she hadn't. He'd have flipped the butt right down her throat.

He thought: I'm a fine one to be telling Ann to take it easy.

They wheeled her out finally. Her head was swathed in white and it was very small, like a kid's. She was all eyes, violet. She made a motion with her arm under the covers, as though she were going to give him her hand, but they had her all wrapped up like a mummy.

He walked beside her. They got into the elevator and rode upstairs and got off the elevator and then stopped in front of a door with two words on it. *Operating Room.* Mrs. O'Brien opened the door and they rolled Ann in. Red had a glimpse of Winston, masked, slipping his hands into rubber gloves. Red didn't like Winston, but he liked Winston's hands, strong and sure, with a great power in them, more powerful than the hands of a ditch digger or a truck driver or a longshoreman or a newspaperman with the power in his fingers to shape the minds of three, four hundred, thousand pinheads, or even the hands of a boss who could tell a newspaperman how to shape them. The boss had the power of death over men, but Winston's hands had the power of life. Her life.

The door closed until the hands were gone, Ann was gone, only Mrs. O'Brien's face remained. "Why don't you wait in her room?" she said. "I'll let you know as soon as it's over."

"Thanks."

The door shut completely.

Chapter 27

He was all alone. His watch and the electric clock were the only things in her room besides himself that lived, the low quick tick of the watch and the silent slow turning of the second hand of her clock. Jesus, it turned slowly. His watch wasn't going any faster but at least the damn thing sounded fast. The hand on the clock barely moved. He had a good mind to smash the window of the clock and grab the second hand and shove it around. Winston's hands had power but that second hand had power, too. It had the power to tear the guts out of you. A scalpel could do that, but that was no feat. A scalpel was sharp as a razor. And it had to be stuck into you. A clock hand could knife you without going near you.

He sat down and opened the *Courier*. He didn't look at page one; he turned to the sports section. Garner poled a homer with three on in the ninth and the Bears went out in front another game. Who cared? His gaze strayed back to the clock, its silent hand. It had barely knocked off a minute since he had looked at it last. It sure took its time turning....

His eyes blurred, and he lost the clock, lost everything in darkness and suddenly, as sudden as a flash of lightning, he saw her by sunlight brighter than lightning, bright on her and on a green hill behind her. She was coming toward him and there were flowers in her hands, violets, and she came to him and her face was no longer all red as it used to be but clear white with red where red should be, in the cheeks only, and her eyes were violets, two violets that had become detached somehow from the violets in her hands, and she said, "I've just complained to the Boss about the house," and he said, "Why?" and she said, "I didn't like the wall paper. The walls are papered with libel suits," and she added, "I've brought you something to eat," and held up the violets and he said, "I bet you baked them hard as a rock," and she laughed and he took the violets and took a mouthful and spat them out and said, "They're burnt," and she said, "Stop complaining. Look what I have to eat," and from nowhere she produced a long sword and put the point to her mouth and began pushing the sword down her throat, inch by inch, and he tried to stop her by grabbing one of her wrists and found the wrist was made of rubber, but strong as steel and she laughed up along the sword and the sword kept sinking into her and she said up along the sword, "This tastes delicious," and he heard a loud burst of applause and people shouting, "Vote for Ann! Vote for Ann!" and he said, "Take that sword out of her mouth and I'll vote for her," and she said, "Is that a promise?" and he said yes and she pulled out the sword and held it with the point to her breast and he said, "Don't, don't," and she said nothing but made a swift cutting motion with the sword, and her dress fell off and she was nude and she whirled and dropped the sword and ran toward the hill and he started after her, jumping over the naked blade of the sword, and her white legs flashed and her round buttocks shook a little with a movement that was at once comical and not comical, and he increased his speed and got closer and closer to her nakedness until he could see a bead of sweat, shining like a pearl, rolling down her back, and finally he caught her at the top of the hill and took her beaded nakedness in his arms and tightened his arms and she cried out, "Look out! Look out!" and her face was twisted with horror and he turned and saw what was on the other side of the hill, a black void, bottomless, but her nakedness was too much for him and he ignored the void and the horror in her face and squeezed her tighter, tighter, until the horror left her for a smile and then suddenly he lost his footing and she did too, tight-locked as she was in his arms, and they went tumbling down.

He woke up, yelling. He hoped nobody had heard him. Some dream.

He looked at the clock. Same old hand, turning the same old way, getting nowhere slowly.

He went to the sink and splattered his face with cold water and dried himself. He felt better after that. He'd feel still better yet if he had a drink. But he didn't dare leave the hospital. He had the feeling that if he left somehow he'd put a whammy on things.

He went over to the window and stared out, at the quiet street below. The minutes funeral-marched along.

He heard heavy steps and tensed and turned and saw the door open and saw Mrs. O'Brien come in. She stopped. She had a queer expression on her face. At the distance he couldn't tell whether she was about to laugh or cry.

He said, "Well?" His voice sounded strange to him, someone else's voice.

She said, "Mr. Norton—"

"Well? How is she?"

"She—she passed away on the operating table."

Chapter 28

This was a dream, too. Sure. He had only dreamed that he had awakened. Crazy, dreaming that you had been dreaming and had awakened and actually you hadn't awakened but only dreamed you had awakened. Crazy. And what Mrs. O'Brien had said was crazy, too. *She passed away on the operating table.* Not only crazy but lousy journalism. They'd never stand for that in a newspaper office. One of the first things the city editor of the *Courier* had told him was: "When you're writing an obit, never say *passed away.* Or *expired.* There's only one word allowed in this office or for that matter in any other newspaper office. *Died.* Short and to the point."

Someone was crying. The blur in Red's eyes cleared. It was Mrs. O'Brien. She was in the chair, swaying to and fro, crying.

It wasn't a dream.

Someone had pulled a fast one on him.

It wasn't a dream.

She had died.

Otherwise, what would Mrs. O'Brien be crying about? It was nice of her to cry for Ann. They were total strangers. It was good someone could cry for her. He couldn't. He never cried.

He said, "What happened?"

She didn't look at him. She looked at the floor. She said, "He never should have operated. He never should—" Suddenly, as though she had caught herself doing something she shouldn't, she looked up at Red, scared and clapped a hand over her mouth.

He strode to the chair. "Go ahead. Tell me. Why shouldn't he have operated?"

"I didn't say that, Mr. Norton. I—"

"You said it and I heard it. Now tell me why."

"I never said it. I swear by all the saints—"

"You said it."

She moaned. "You're hurtin' me, Mr. Norton." He looked down and saw that his hand was clutched tight on her arm. He let go of her and went out. He collided with an orderly, went on without apology. He reached the elevators and jammed the button and waited, waited. He looked up at the indicators. One elevator was at the top floor and wasn't moving and the other was at the second floor and was moving, but at a crawl. It would probably crawl up to the top, before it came down to him. He turned and half-ran to the stairway and hit the steps, three, four at a time.

He shouldn't have operated. He shouldn't have operated.

Red slammed his fist against Winston's door and Winston said, "Who is it?" and Red told him and Winston said, "Just a moment," and opened the door. He was still in surgeon's white. His face was haggard. He said, "Sit down. I've got the Mayor on the phone."

Red sat down. Winston talked into the phone. "I told you, Mayor, it couldn't be helped. I'd have given my life to save her." A high angry whine rose from the phone's earpiece. The Mayor must be lashing him. Red looked down. Something white near the waste basket had caught his eye, a crumpled little ball of paper. He bent to pick it up. He saw a name on it. Karsch. Karsch. He remembered the row Karsch had had yesterday with Winston. Maybe, somehow this was tied up with Ann.

Winston said, "I told the Mayor you just came in. He wants to talk to you."

Red stuck the ball of paper in his pocket and took the phone. Winston got up and went over to the window.

Red said, "Hello, Mayor."

"Winston just gave me the bad news," the Mayor said. "I feel awful, Red. I feel bad for you, most of all."

"Thanks." Red could hardly speak.

"But it's one of those things everyone has to go through, Red. It's a part of livin'."

"I know."

"You gonna phone the *Courier* or write it?"

"I'm phoning. The Sunday paper has an early deadline."

"Well, don't say she died on the operating table. Say she died half an hour later."

"What's the difference?"

"If she died on the table, she'd be under anesthetic, she couldn't talk. But if she died later, she could say something. I want you to have her say something."

Red said harshly, "What?"

"Don't get sore, Red. I know how you feel. But this is important. She died on us and we got to take the curse off it."

"Go ahead. How do you take the curse off it?"

"Tell the *Courier* that just before she died, she said it was no one's fault. The Medical Center was the most wonderful hospital in the world and if anyone could have saved her life, it was Dr. Winston. But it wasn't to be, that's all. Have her say that she thanked everyone who sent her contributions and she hoped they would keep on sending contributions to the Ann Porter Fund because she wanted the hospital to get that new reception room. Lou can also have her say—"

"Christ," said Red. "Hasn't she said enough?"

The Mayor said quietly, "I wouldn't take that from anyone but you, Red. I wouldn't even take it from you, if I didn't realize how upset you were."

"Go ahead," Red said. "What more do you want her to say?"

"That'll be enough."

"And you think that just because she makes a big deathbed speech, people will think your hospital is great?"

"The pinheads will eat it up. They don't think logically, Red. They think with their hearts. Give 'em corn, and they forget everything. You make it good and sad and we won't lose a vote."

"Good old votes," said Red.

"This was your idea, Red."

"It was mine, all right," Red said, bitterly.

"When you get through phonin' the *Courier*," the Mayor said, "come on down to the lake. And I don't mean for the weekend. A month, two months, long as you want. Couple of months of relaxation will make a new man outa you. What do you say?"

"Maybe."

"No maybes about it. You come down."

"I've got to take care of the funeral arrangements."

"I'll have Murphy do that. We'll give her the swellest funeral you ever saw. I'll even put her in my family plot—"

"No. She wanted to be buried—"

"Yeah, yeah, I remember now. I read it in your story. Okay. She'll be buried there. Hill. Grass. Lake. The works. I'll call Murphy right away. You're comin' down?"

"All right."

"And don't go on a bender. I know you want to get plastered, but lay off or you're liable to drive your car into a tree."

"All right. Goodbye."

Red hung up. He looked at Winston. Winston was still staring out the window. Red took the ball of paper out of his pocket and opened it. It said:

My Dear Winston:
You needn't expect me today. I'm through, and this time 1 mean it. 1 trust
the great Winston will be able to operate without me.
God help the girl!

Karsch.

Red got up and went over to Winston. Winston said, "I didn't know you
had a personal interest in Miss Porter. I hope you'll forgive me. But it could-
n't be helped—"

"Couldn't it?" Red thrust out the letter. "What about this?"

Winston's face went white. "Where did you get that?"

"On your floor. You meant it for the waste basket, but your aim was
lousy."

"You've got your nerve, reading my personal mail."

"What does it mean, Winston?"

"None of your damned—"

Red's hand shot out and clutched the top of Winston's white jacket and
twisted it. "What does it mean?"

Winston swung and his fist cracked against Red's jaw and Red let go of
the jacket and dropped the letter and rocked back until he felt the desk behind him. Winston came in to clip Red again but Red got out of the way.
Red was shorter than Winston but broader and younger and he had learned
fighting, not in college, but in the Second Ward. The next time Winston
threw one, Red ducked and slugged him, quite deliberately, in the groin and
Winston clutched himself there and looked sick. Red smashed him on the
chin and Winston went down. Red went over to him and drew back his
foot and aimed a kick at Winston's face but Winston managed to grab his
foot and twist it and Red joined him on the floor.

Winston climbed aboard him and slammed his fist against Red's mouth
and Red's teeth razored into his lower lip and he tasted blood. The fist came
down on his mouth again.

Red reached up, without altogether seeing just what he was reaching for,
and found Winston's neck and his thumbs found Winston's Adam's apple
and squeezed. Winston hit Red in the chin and Red knew a moment of
darkness but when he came out of it he was still squeezing that throat. Winston's tongue, thick and red with a touch of white coating on it, came out
toward him. His eyes stuck out, too.

Let's see his eyes drop out, Red said to himself.

Winston made gagging noises.

Red suddenly wrenched Winston's neck sideways and Winston heaved
off him sideways and Red got on top of him, still holding onto the throat.
Winston's fingernails tore thin red stripes in Red's wrist.

A big drop of blood from Red's mouth fell on Winston's face and flattened out. Red squeezed harder. Winston's hands left Red's wrists. Winston's hands began beating the rug.

Go ahead, beat it. Save the hospital a rug-beating bill.

Red suddenly relaxed the pressure and Winston's tongue went back where it belonged and Winston gulped air. The air rushed down his hungry throat. His eyes began getting back into their sockets.

"You going to tell me what that letter meant—or do I have to strangle you?"

Winston spoke, hoarsely. "All... right...."

Red got up. He picked up the letter and stuck it in his pocket. He took out a handkerchief and held it against his mouth.

Winston tried to get up but he was all pooped out. Red put the handkerchief back in his pocket and grabbed Winston under his arms and hauled him over to one of the chairs and pulled him to his feet. He stood there, swaying. Red gave him a little push and he fell back into the chair. Winston gasped. "Water...."

"Sure."

Red went to the water cooler and filled a paper cup. He went back to Winston. "Here."

He pitched the contents of the cup into Winston's face. "You'll get the water when you start talking. What did Karsch mean when he said he trusted you'd be able to operate without him?"

"He—he was being ironic...."

"I figured that out myself."

"He knew I couldn't operate—successfully."

"Why?"

"I—haven't performed an operation—in three years."

"What!"

"All my operations were performed by a ghost."

"A ghost?"

"There are ghost surgeons just as there are ghost writers—obscure doctors who perform operations for well-known surgeons with whom they split the fees."

"I've heard of the racket," Red said. "There was a story a few months ago about some national medical association starting a campaign against it. But they said only a few guys were pulling it."

"They didn't know Crescent City. The town's filthy with it."

"An airtight racket, too," Red said. "The ghost enters the operating room after the anesthetic's been administered and fades away before the patient comes to. He doesn't even know what happened."

Winston nodded. He was barely listening. He was looking at his right hand. He raised it slowly. It was no longer clean and strong but battered, swollen and crusted with dirt and blood. "You may not believe it, Norton, but there are at least thirty men and women walking the streets of this city today who would be dead now, if it were not for this hand. And now it's useless. Utterly useless."

"How did you get in the racket?"

"I was at the City Hospital then. I was tops, Norton. Tops. No operation, no matter how difficult, fazed me. I had the touch, the magic touch. Patients flocked to me. My practice naturally expanded. Eventually I had to refer the surplus to other surgeons. Then Stevens had a talk with me. You know Stevens?"

"I interviewed him when the boss appointed him superintendent of the Medical Center."

"He was superintendent of the City Hospital then. A very good friend of mine. In fact, it was he who gave me my start." Winston smiled crookedly. "And my finish. He took me aside one day and said he had heard I was sending patients to other doctors. He said I was a damned fool. I should use a ghost. I asked what he meant and he explained. I said it was unthinkable. He replied that several of my colleagues, including himself, employed ghosts. I replied I didn't give a damn what they did. I wasn't going to violate my oath. He said many people in Crescent City, judges, the prosecutor, the Mayor, violated their oaths every day. The town was rich with gravy and anyone who had a chance to get some and didn't, should have his head examined. He pointed out that I didn't have to use a ghost for the major operations. Just the easy ones, appendectomies, that sort of thing. I said it was a rotten business and would have no part of it."

"But in the end you did."

"I was trapped. By the atmosphere—and my own weakness. I should have pulled up stakes then and there. Or fought the racket. But I did neither. I tried to remain aloof to it. That was my big mistake. The racket was going on all about me and I knew it and because I knew it, I became a part of it. Once you condone rottenness, you become rotten yourself. One either fights it or joins it. I finally obtained a ghost. But at least—" Winston smiled wanly "—I had taste. Some surgeons chose anyone, men fresh from their internship. They didn't give a rap whether the patient lived or died, just as long as they collected their fees. I chose one of the best. Karsch."

"If Karsch was such a hot surgeon, why did he become a ghost?"

"A successful surgeon requires more than ability, Norton. Personality, presence—they count with patients even more than talent. Karsch lacked both. He was shy, retiring—almost afraid of people. One of the most brilliant men I know, but he would have starved if he hadn't become a ghost. Of course, not all ghost surgeons are shy. Their principal drawback is youth, inexperience."

Winston cleared his throat

"After Stevens made me his chief surgeon, at a very handsome salary, I grew lazy. I lost interest in my work. My pride of craftsmanship died. Corruption does that, you know. Slowly but surely it attacks every facet of you. I did less and less operating, Karsch did more and more. At last I stopped operating altogether. Why work? Everything was a racket. Only fools worked—"

"Was Karsch the one who removed the Mayor's appendix?"

Winston's smile was grim. "He was."

"Why didn't the bastard operate today?"

"Because he was fed up with being a ghost. He wanted more than money. Prestige. He demanded that the next time I was retained to operate on someone important, I announce that he was going to perform the operation. I wouldn't have to compromise myself, he said. All I would have to do was pretend to become ill at the last minute and call him in to do the operating. I agreed but it was only a stall. I didn't dare do what he asked. I was afraid to lose him. It might take months to find another ghost of his calibre. I kept stalling him. Then this case came up—Ann Porter. He renewed his demand for recognition. Again I put him off. We had several rows. The upshot of it all was that letter I so carelessly discarded. He had walked out on me, at the very last moment. I can't say I blame him. This operation, with all the publicity attending it, would have made him an instant success. Well, there I was. No ghost. I had one alternative—either get another ghost or operate myself. I suppose I might have called in one of the men my colleagues used, but most of them were butchers. And even the good ones would have difficulty, coming in at the very last minute. At least I had a thorough knowledge of the patient's ailment. Even if I hadn't operated in three years, I reasoned, I still had the touch. You couldn't lose the touch just like that. It was a gift that stayed with you forever." Winston sighed. "But I was wrong, Norton. Dreadfully wrong."

Red said, "Did she—?"

"Her death, Norton, was swift and painless."

"Sweet of you," said Red.

"I suppose you're going to tell the Mayor everything?"

"I don't know what I'm going to do."

"Go ahead. Tell him. I'll deny the whole damn thing. I don't care if you beat the life out of me. I'll deny everything. My word's as good as yours."

"You're right," said Red. "Your word's as good as mine. We both stink."

Chapter 29

He washed up in one of the lavatories. Aside from the swollen lip, he was unmarked.

When he emerged from the hospital, he turned and looked up, toward a fifth floor window. Her window. Where was she now? She was up there only a couple of hours ago. Where was she now?

He got into the convertible. He drove slowly, aimlessly. Who killed her? Winston, of course.

No. He was the knife that killed her.

The Mayor killed her. Not deliberately, but he killed her. His way of living killed her. His way was graft, the gravy, everybody hop on the old gravy train. That was what killed her. If Winston had stayed straight, she would be alive, but he fell for the gravy and now she was dead.

The Mayor did it. Every ward heeler in town did it. I killed her, too. Me.

We all killed her, everyone with a racket, a soft touch, our rottenness, our thirsty lapping of the gravy. Lap. Lap. Lap. He had a sudden vision, sharply clear against a crystal darkness, like the background of a dream, of thousands of faces, lapping, lapping, dipping their tongues into a sea of gravy, lapping, and when they stopped lapping, up from their mouths shot worms that grew, swiftly, into long wriggling columns.

He shut his eyes tight and gave his head a shake, to kill the vision.

There was only one thing to do. Smash them. Step on their tongues. Squash their worms. Squash 'em.

He could do it. He wasn't much, but he could do it.

He saw a drug store and parked in front of it. He went into the store and looked for a phone booth and found it and got in and dropped a coin in the box and dialed Ajax 2-3849.

There was no answer. Bernie wasn't home.

Don't hang up. Maybe he's in the bathroom. Maybe he's in the hay with Sylvia.

No answer.

Maybe he's at the *Post*. But he was off weekends. Maybe he'd gone there anyhow. Something important.

Red dialed the *Post*.

"*Ajax Post*, good afternoon."

"City desk."

Fletcher answered. Red didn't bother putting on the act of hiding his voice, his identity. "This is Red Norton. Is Bernstein there?"

"No. He's off."

"Do you know where I can get him?"

"He's gone away for the weekend. With friends."

"Who? It's important, Fletcher."

"I don't know who. He just mentioned something about going away for the weekend. Is there something I can do?"

"Yeah," Red said. "You know the story about the divorce suit against Gowan?"

"Do I know it? It's going to lead page one."

"It is, like hell. Kill it. Every line. Kill it."

"You gone crazy."

"I've just gone sane. It's a fake, a phony story from start to finish. Kill it or you'll be up to your ears in a libel suit. A million-dollar libel suit. Kill it."

"You needn't yell my ear off."

"Some guys, you have to yell. It's libel—"

"I heard you the first time, Red. I'll kill it."

"You still have time?"

"Sure. We don't hit the street until 7 p.m."

"Tell Bernie I'll be over the first thing Monday and explain everything."

"Right."

"Goodbye."

"Goodbye."

Red put the phone back on the hook. That was that. The first big squashing step.

Wait a minute. There was another phone call he had to make.

Ann's deathbed statement.

The mere thought of calling the office, sticking words into her mouth, made him want to puke.

An actual taste of vomit came into his mouth.

He plunged out of the booth, out of the store.

Across the street was a window with big lettering on it.

Gorham's Bar and Grill.

Hello, Mr. Gorham. Let's see if you can take the taste out of my mouth.

"A double rye."

"Soda?"

"A double rye, that's all."

He downed it. The taste stayed with him. He downed another. And another. And began losing count.

Well, the taste was gone.

But she wasn't. It would take a lot of rye to get rid of her. Where was she? Waiting.

She had a date with him to have steak dinner and champagne and if he hung around this dump, sopping up rye, he'd stand her up.

He reeled out.

Where was she?

She had stood him up.

Not many dames gave him a standup.

Find another dame. Someone who wouldn't stand him up. He started to go back in the bar but remembered there were no dames there and staggered on. He reached the corner and stood there swaying, and a neon sign down the side street caught his eye with its flashing and he went there and there were a couple of dames. One was with a guy and the other was alone, but you could have her. Red had a drink. Another. Another. Another. He hit another bar and there was a brunette, young, not bad, who smiled invitingly, and he joined her and got her a drink and got himself one and another and somewhere along the line he forgot her and remembered Ann, who had stood him up, by dying. She was dead, that's why she hadn't met him for champagne. She was in a drawer in a wall in the hospital morgue and in a couple of days she would slide into the ground, clods of earth falling on her, and when the sound of their falling stopped, there would be only the sound of the wind overhead and the sound of the water of the lake rippling and I wouldn't mind being there now enjoying a quiet evening beside her, until the worms came. When the worms came, you could have it. Death was for the birds. Death was for the worms.

Lips soft and moist touched his neck and the lips were like a pair of worms and he whirled and struck out, blindly, and the next thing he knew the brunette was sitting on the floor, holding her jaw, and calling him ten kinds of bastards and the bartender came and gave him the heaveho.

He drifted into another bar, not in search of dames, for there was only one dame and she was dead, and he drank and drank and suddenly he got sick and threw up, all over the floor, and got the heaveho again.

Getting sick sobered him up a bit.

It was getting dark. A vague uneasiness crept over him. He tried to put his finger on it, but couldn't. He'd better get a black coffee. That would snap him out of it, get his brain clear. He didn't know why but he sensed he needed a clear brain.

He hunted a restaurant and finally spotted a diner and went into it. He sat down at the counter. The guy next to him was reading a paper. Red said to the counterman, "Give me a black coffee," and the counterman poured one, a big thick cup of it and shoved it in front of Red and shoved a sugar bowl in front of him, but Red didn't bother with the sugar. He picked up the cup and swigged it. It was blazing hot and bitter as hell. It must have been brewing for a week. He felt the sweat leap out on his forehead. He sat back, waiting for it to cool. He looked around. His eye fell on the paper the guy next to him was reading.

It was the *Post* and across the top of page one were two black headlines that Red saw clearly for a moment and then saw in a crazy blur in which the letters of the headlines danced and reeled like drunken letters and then the blur faded and the letters sobered up and the double headline leaped up at him, filling his sight, blotting out everything:

"BOSS GOWAN AND BLONDE SURPRISED IN HOTEL RAID, MRS. GOWAN CHARGES IN SUIT FOR DIVORCE!"

Fletcher.

Instead of killing the divorce story, he had let it ride. He was a stooge for the Mayor.

The Mayor had eyes everywhere, everywhere.

Fletcher had done more than let the story ride. He had called the Mayor—he must have—and revealed what Red had done. Red had tried to kill the story the Mayor wanted in the *Ajax Post.*

Kill.

The next thing on the program to be killed was Red Norton.

Even now, the hoods must be looking for him.

He should have blown town, long ago. Right after he phoned the *Post.* That was what was eating him, making him uneasy. He should have blown town hours ago. Because even if Fletcher had been on the level and killed the story, Red was in a spot. The minute the *Post* hit the street, without that story in it, the Mayor would have suspected Red. At once. On general principles.

Should have scrammed hours ago.

Well, what's keeping you?

Red felt around his pocket for a quarter, found it, dropped it on the counter.

He went to the door but before he could open it, the door swung in and he stepped back. The man in the doorway was tall and slim and young. He looked like a bookie in clover. He had a long flowing jacket and a checked vest and a very narrow tie with red and blue stripes and a tiepin to make the knot stick out. He had black hair, worn long, that looked marcelled. He had a mouth soft as a dame's, but his eyes were hard, like black marbles. His left hand was in his jacket pocket and there was no doubt in Red's mind what he was.

A hood.

The hood said, "You Red Norton?"

Red's mind was like ice. All the confusion was gone.

Red belted him, with a looping overhand right that caught him on the nose. Red put everything in that right, all his weight. The bone of the nose cracked and gave and there was a thick gush of blood.

The hood staggered backward out of the doorway and fell.

Red ran past him, halted. There was a car parked outside the diner and indistinct forms of men were in it. He turned and ran for the corner. Someone yelled, "That's him!"

He heard a backfire.

That's not a backfire, Bud. That's a gun.

He whirled around the corner, saw an alley, plunged into it. A dog barked furiously. Ahead was a high fence. He hurled himself upward and caught the top of it.

Behind him, through the dog's yapping, was a sound of brakes.

He sweated like a pig as he tried to haul himself up. The dog was right below him now, barking its head off. He felt the dog's teeth sink into one of his legs. He slammed his leg against the fence and the dog squealed and let go. He hooked his foot around the fence top.

He heard feet pounding in the alley.

He pulled himself up and dropped on the other side of the fence.

He had dropped into a vacant lot. The moonlight cast a greasy shine on broken bottles, tin cans, discarded parts of machinery. Over to the left was a building wall and over to the right was a row of stores, the rear of the diner, and ahead was a street. He stumbled toward it. He heard a gun and saw a spot of dust kicked up in an ash heap a little ahead and to one side of him.

He got to the street and wheeled and ran down it.

His lungs felt ripped up. His legs felt as though they were sheathed in lead a foot thick.

Believe it or not, there was a taxi. He hailed it and the taxi stopped and he jumped in. "Go like hell," he gasped.

"Where?"

At a point near the vacant lot, flame made a quick yellow stab into the darkness.

"They shootin' at you?" the cabbie asked.

"Yes. Get going!"

The cabbie got going. It pursued a straight fast course for half a dozen blocks, then slowed down and started weaving through the streets.

"It's okay," Red said, still puffing. "We've shaken them."

"Who were they?"

"Heisters. They were trying to take my roll."

"You wanna go to a police station?"

"I'll report it later. Drop me off at Cornwall and Fifth."

Cornwall was heavily trafficked. Red could get a bus there. He had to make a switch. They'd check every cab company in town and they'd find this cabbie and he would tell everything he knew. That, or get his skull wrinkled.

Cornwall and Fifth. Red gave the driver a ten spot and told him to keep it and the driver thanked him and drove off.

Red took the first bus that came along. It was bound for Courier Square and was crowded with people, going to the movies, going to night clubs. He was glad of the crowd. Huddled in among them he was shielded from the bus windows, from the street. The people talked and laughed. He resented their laughter. He was jealous of it.

Five blocks from the square, he alighted. The square would be covered. Every hood in town, every available cop, would cover it.

What now?

Hit for Ajax. See Bernstein.

But they would cover the bridge to Ajax and they would be at the ferry terminal, too.

Hole up. Wait till the heat's off.

Hole up where?

A hotel? They'd check every hotel in town.

A furnished room. That was his only out. He thought instantly of *her* room, the cubbyhole with the brick wall confronting it. It drew him. To be where she had been, where she had lived, slept, yes, been unhappy in, lonely in, ill in, just as long as she had been there, it drew him with a tremendous pull.

But that would be a mistake. They'd go there, too. They'd go anywhere he'd want to go.

But they couldn't cover all the rooming houses. It would take weeks to cover them.

He found a place, a room with a two-burner gas range. He would have to eat in. He would have to stay in as much as possible, till the heat of the hunt cooled. He was lucky. He had about thirty dollars on him. The room cost him ten and he spent another ten, buying food at a neighborhood delicatessen. That should hold him till things cooled. He invested another five in a razor and a bottle of rye. He'd need both.

He bought a *Courier*. He wasn't surprised when he saw the story on Ann. It was all there, her phony death, in bed, not on the table, and her phony deathbed statement. Murphy must have called the *Courier* directly the Mayor had learned of Red's double-cross.

Red drank himself to sleep and the next day when he awakened he drank himself to sleep again. There wasn't much else to do, except sit around and listen to the couple next door argue or look outside and watch people going to church and radio cars going up and down. There seemed to be a lot of radio cars. It might have nothing to do with him, but Red thought it did.

When night came he slipped out of the building and went to a candy store up the block and phoned Bernstein's home, but there was still no answer. The guy must have gone somewhere for the weekend. Damn. Damn. Everything was going sour. Even the whiskey was running low.

Monday morning Red took a chance and went out in broad daylight. He called Bernstein's home again. Still no answer. He called the *Post*. The switchboard girl said no one was in the city room yet. When would Bernstein get in? Two o'clock.

At two o'clock Red went to the candy store. But he didn't go in. He stopped just in time, and stepped back. There was a cop in the store and he was talking to the store owner. Red was all for beating it, but he wanted to hear what they were saying.

He lit a cigaret and stood there, beside the open doorway, smoking, casual.

"I tell you, Farrell," the storekeeper was saying, "it's the same guy. Red hair, five feet nine, just like you said. He was in here this morning right after I opened up."

"Know where he lives?"

"How should I know? He's only been here twice before, to buy a paper and make a phone call, and he ain't talkative. But he must live around here somewheres."

"And he'll probably come back," Farrell said. "I better phone Headquarters. You don't mind if they plant some dicks here?"

"Of course I mind but what can I do? Only please, Farrell, tell them, don't make the arrest here. There's liable to be a fight and they'll wreck the store."

"Okay, Max. I'll tell them."

Red flipped the butt and walked fast. They were closing in.

He went past the rooming house. He walked until he came to a theater, some dump featuring Westerns. That would be as good a place as any to hole up in until nightfall. When nightfall came, he'd have to lam.

There was a line of five or six kids outside the cashier's booth and Red got into line and waited. Two of the kids clowned around, slapping each other, just sparring, but if they kept it up, sure as hell one would slap the other too hard and then there'd be a fist fight and it would draw a lot of attention and maybe it would even draw the cops.

"Cut it," Red snapped.

The two stopped slapping each other and glared at Red. One said, "Why don't you mind your —— business?"

Red said, "You want a punch in the snoot?"

The kid shut up. That was the only way to talk to kids like that. Snotty little bastards. They ought to be in school.

He finally got a ticket. He asked the ticket taker if there was a pay phone in the place and the ticket taker said yes, and told him where it was. It was on a wall in the back of the theater. It wasn't in a booth, but Red doubted if even a booth would have kept the noise out. The place was a bedlam. Every kid in the neighborhood must have been playing the hook.

Red hoped a newsreel would come on, because maybe it would show something nice and dull like some bigshot making a speech on the state of the nation, but instead of a newsreel a space ship serial came on and Red found a seat in the rear and sat down resignedly. Right after the serial there was a long string of cartoon shorts and more noise. The newsreel started, but the first thing on the program was a fashion show, full of beautiful models, and the theater filled with boyish wolf whistles. Then there was a boat race in which a couple of motorboats overturned and more yelling. No one came on and made a speech on the state of the nation. When the newsreel ended, another Western was flashed on the screen.

At last the show broke and there was an intermission and some of the mob went out and a lot of them stayed to see the show all over. A couple of candy butchers went through the audience, yelling "Candy! Ice cream," but Red figured he could take that. He went to the phone and called the *Post* and asked for the city desk.

"City desk, Lewis," someone said. Red hadn't expected to get Fletcher. Fletcher wouldn't dare stay on the *Post* after the stunt he pulled.

Red said, "Can I speak to Bernstein?"

"Who's this?"

"The guy who sent you the libelous story on Mayor Gowan."

Lewis' voice became hostile. "What do you want to do—send us another?"

"I want to take the *Post* off the hook."

"Oh."

"Let me talk to Bernstein."

"He's gone. He was just fired."

"Let me talk to Trent."

"Just a minute. I'll have you connected."

Red was connected with the publisher.

"This is Red Norton."

Trent's voice was icy. "Yes?"

"About that divorce story—"

"I've heard enough about it already."

"You've seen the Mayor?"

"And his attorney."

"That story was a deliberate fake, Trent. The Mayor gave it to me himself."

"You don't surprise me," Trent said wearily. "A clever man, Mayor

Gowan."

"Look. I'm prepared to sign an affidavit saying it was a fake. I'm even prepared to go into court and swear it."

"You're a bit late, Norton. The Mayor has agreed to drop the libel suit—"

"Sure, on condition that you drop the crusade and fire Bernstein. But you don't have to drop the crusade. You can hire Bernie back. You can tell the Mayor to go to hell. With my testimony—"

"Did it ever occur to you, Norton, that a jury might not accept the word of an admitted liar?"

"When they hear what I have to say, they'll believe me."

"Perhaps. But frankly I don't care to take the risk. The *Post* is an expensive property, Norton. He could put us right out of business—"

"Not if we put him out of business first. And we can do it. I've got enough information at my fingertips to wreck him."

"I'm no longer interested in wrecking him, or anyone else. I was never keen on crusading. The only reason I went into it was that your friend Bernstein sold me a bill of goods. I'm not buying anymore, Norton. Good day."

"But Mr. Trent—"

The kids started yelling again. Red talked into the phone, desperately, but could hear nothing. The yelling subsided and Red said, "Hello, hello," but no one replied. Trent had hung up.

He left after the second show. It was night. Clouds edged with silver raced across the sky. They raced across the face of the moon and the moon snapped off and on, irregularly, like an advertising sign that wasn't working right.

Which way should he go?

Eastward lay Ajax. But he was cut off from Ajax. The only way he could get there was swim. That went for the north, too. The river curved and the north was cut off, too.

South or west?

He fished a dime out of his pocket and flipped it. West.

He liked that. West had a good sound, a sound of newness, of beginnings. Then he smiled wryly. And of cowboys galloping after rustlers. Red Norton rides again.

He caught a local bus, going westward. It wound up at the city line, but there would be a reception committee waiting for him at the city line, so he got off half a mile from it. He had to keep away from the highway, until he was well out of the city. He cut south, until he was at least a mile from the highway, then went west again.

Ahead lay the meadowland, two miles of it. The sky over the meadows was huge. Off to the left he saw a cluster of low buildings, their lights, the silhouettes of young trees, and realized, with a tightening, as though a cold hand inside of him had closed on something vital, that those were the homes of the Whitney Construction Co. project. Twenty-two grand apiece. Nice. Fieldstone and shingle, and all on one floor, so a sick dame didn't have to hike up and down stairs. All on one floor.

He jerked his face away, fast. Ahead lay the meadows. They were all that counted now. Mud and weeds, two miles of it. Then he would cut to the highway. Then he would be safe. Mud and weeds. They were all that counted now.

He stood on a shoulder of the highway and mechanically waved his thumb. He'd been doing it for a couple of hours. Hunger had eaten a yawning hole in his belly and his legs felt ready to cave. A pair of headlights blazed into view and hope leaped in him, and then he saw the taillight and hope died. He had no kick coming. He'd shown his taillight to many a hitchhiker. Only time he'd ever stopped for a hitcher was if it was a dame. Now all the hitchers to whom he had ever shown his taillight were having their revenge. The road west was one long string of tiny red lights all saying, *Nuts to you, bud.*

And then the miracle happened. A long blue Packard went past him, slowed down and halted. That wasn't a taillight. It was a red bulb on a Christmas tree. Here I come, Santa Claus.

Hold it. How do you know who's in that car?

Might even be the Mayor himself. The Mayor had a Packard.

The car door opened and a face appeared. It was a big round face. It said, "Well, what are you waiting for?"

It wasn't the Mayor's face, but it might belong to a hood. Or a dick. He didn't know every dick on the force. "You want a ride or don't you?"

Red took a chance and went over to the car. The man at the wheel was fat and sloppy but his clothes were good. He said, "Get in."

"My shoes are kind of muddy," Red said. "You got something I can clean them with? I don't want to mess up your car."

The fat guy liked that. He reached in the back seat and handed Red a newspaper, and Red went to work on his shoes. Then he threw the paper away and got into the car.

"Where are you going?" the fat man asked.

"As far as you'll take me."

"You got a long ride, then," the fat man said, not without satisfaction. "I'm going to San Papete."

The West Coast. Red was in luck. The breaks were starting to come his way.

Unless this guy was a phony.

He wasn't. Instead of pulling a gun on Red, he talked Red's ears off. His name was Gelliston and he ran a big hardware store in San Papete, the biggest hardware store in town, and that was saying something, because San Papete was no whistle stop, but a real city, with ninety thousand people in it. He was on his way back now, from Ajax City, where the hardware merchants from all over the country had just held their annual convention. Ajax was a good town, a big town, yes, bigger than San Papete, but the climate stank. You couldn't beat San Papete's climate. Sunshine all the time.

"I guess I sound like a booster," he admitted, "but as I always told the boys back in the Chamber of Commerce, when you got a good thing, tell people about it. Never hide your light behind a bush. Just wait till you see this town. Well-paved streets, so clean you could eat lunch off them, and the lowest crime rate in the state. And our taxes. They'd make you laugh if I told you how low they were. Our Mayor's a nut on economy. Now you take that town behind us, Crescent City—" he paused, as if he felt he had said too much.

"You take it," Red said, "and keep it."

"You come from there?"

"No. But I've seen it."

"Awful dump, isn't it? But what can you expect? One of the men at the convention told me their Mayor makes a hundred thousand a year in graft. A hundred thousand a year."

Make it a million, Red thought, and you'll be closer.

"But they got a great hospital," Gelliston said. "You've got to hand it to him. He gave them a fine hospital."

"Yes," said Red. "I guess he did."

"We got nothing like that in San Papete, but then we don't need Medical Centers. No hospital in the world can beat that sunshine. You going to settle out west?"

"If I can get a job."

"What's your line?"

"I'm a newspaperman. You got any newspapers in San Papete?"

"Are you kidding? We've got two, the *Journal*—that comes out in the morning—and the *Pentagraph*, an afternoon paper. They're owned by the same company. Their combined circulation runs over thirty thousand. Real moneymakers. I know the advertising manager," Gelliston added. "If you want a job, I'll send you to him."

Red said, "Aren't you taking a chance? After all, I'm a total stranger. I might even crack the safe."

Gelliston smiled. "You can't kid me. I know character when I see it. You can't fool me on character."

He ought to compare notes with Bernie. Bernie could tell him about my character.

"Soon as we hit town," Gelliston said, "I'll send you over there. If there's a job open, you'll get it. The advertising manager and me are like that." He entwined two of his fingers.

"That's very kind of you."

"Any young man has the brains to want to settle in a town like San Papete deserves help."

"I'm damn near broke," said Red.

"I'll stake you," said Gelliston.

He was one in a million, Gelliston. He paid for Red's food and he paid Red's lodging at the motels they stopped at. Red said he'd pay him back soon as he got a job and Gelliston said he knew Red would. Gelliston knew character when he saw it.

They drove three days, with Red spelling Gelliston at the wheel. On the morning of the fourth day they came to a place called Mill City. Mill City was one big belch of smoke. It hazed the streets like a dark curtain. If there was a decent street in town, Red didn't see it. All he saw was factories, saloons, slums, political clubs.

The traffic signal flashed crimson and Red brought the car to a stop. Outside a tenement doorway, a dozen guys were shooting crap, rolling the dice against the building wall. On the sidewalk was a sizeable mound of bills. A cop came along. He walked past the crap game as though he were blind.

"I never saw that," Red said. "Not even in Crescent City."

"Crescent City may be a dump," said Gelliston, "but this joint takes the cake. Slums, whorehouses, gambling joints—wide open. And they don't even have a medical center. The administration is as crooked as they come. Someone ought to come here some night and put the torch to it and wipe it off the face of the earth."

"They got any newspapers here?"

"A daily paper that's just like that cop. Sees no evil, hears no evil. And a weekly that screams blue murder at the administration but that nobody pays any attention to. I think they got about two thousand circulation."

"What's the weekly called."

"The *Gazette*. Why?"

"Nothing. Just wondering."

The traffic signal flashed green and Red started the car and they rolled along. He saw something across the street and stopped.

Gelliston said, "What are you stopping for?"

"This is where I get off. Thanks for the ride."

"But I thought you were coming to San Papete?"

Red smiled. "I'm staying here."

He got out of the car and Gelliston squirmed behind the wheel. He held out a hand. "Good luck, son. I don't know why anyone would want to settle here, but if that's what you want go to it. Only don't say I didn't warn you,"

Red said, "I haven't forgotten that dough I owe you."

"I know you haven't. You know where to get in touch with me."

Red turned and crossed the street. In front of him was a store with no glass in its window. Instead of glass, there were boards. Above the boarded window was a sign, in faded gilt, "WEEKLY GAZETTE."

Red opened the door and went in. There were a couple of desks. Behind one sat a tall thin man with a big mop of iron-gray hair and steel-rimmed spectacles on his nose. He looked up.

Red said, "I'm looking for a job."

"You an ad man or a reporter?"

"A reporter."

"Then you'll have to learn how to sell ads. You have to do both on a weekly."

"I can learn."

"It's a rotten job, mister. Anyone who works here is crazy. I bet more reporters have walked out of here than any paper in the country."

"Why?"

"Simple. They want to live. As soon as a reporter around here gets nosey, he gets letters. Pretty letters, telling him what's going to happen if he doesn't catch wise. Well, if he doesn't catch wise they take him into an alley and give him a treatment. Had three or four men get treatments. If the letters didn't work, the treatment did. I been in the hospital twice myself. The outfit that runs Mill City plays rough, mister. They haven't killed anyone yet, but that don't mean there won't be a first time. Look at that goddam window."

"Someone heave a brick through it?"

"Yeah. And some day it's liable to be a pineapple. It don't pay to fight the people in power, mister. It just don't pay."

"Then why do you do it?"

"I'm crazy, that's why. If I was in my right senses, I'd pack up and go to some other city, a decent city, like San Papete, and open a print shop and make a lot of money and have a lot of friends. All I have now is bills—and threatening letters. If threatened men live long, I oughta live to two hundred."

"How much can you pay me?"

The shrewd eyes studied Red above the glasses. "Fifty a week."

"Make it seventy and you've got a deal."

"Let's split the difference. Sixty."

"Can anyone live on sixty a week?"

"You can do anything when you have a mind to. I'll tell you one way to cut expenses. Board at my place. Twenty a week for room and grub. Best grub you ever ate. My daughter can really cook up a meal. Her steaks are perfection and her lemon pie is out of this world. My big worry is some young squirt's gonna come along and marry her and it'll be goodbye lemon pie for me."

"Any guy makes a play for her, toss him but on his ear."

"I will. Don't worry about that." The old man became serious. "I almost forgot. I can't just hire any kind of reporter. I've got to have a man who knows politics."

Red grinned. "Do I know politics?"

The End

The End

The Man I Killed
by Shel Walker

Chapter One

I could give you a lot of reasons why I stood there that night on a gravel driveway, there in the cold red light of a king-size neon sign that said: CLUB MAÑANA. Maybe there'd be a little truth in each reason. Maybe they'd all be wrong. It's hard to know; it's hard to think clearly when you're thinking with your solar plexus, not your brain.

I could say I drifted here accidentally; I could say I came back because I had a conscience, or maybe I could say that I wanted to see if my conscience would bother me if I came back.

I could say that a murderer always returns to the scene of his crime.

So here was this neon sign and one part of it, a top hat and cane, kept blinking on and off several times each second, and that was the way my heart was beating. I stared at the sign for a while, then dropped my eyes to the main entrance, with its striped awning and uniformed doorman. The doorman hadn't seen me yet. There had been two or three other cars in the driveway and the taxi had let me off here, nearer the gate. I was in the shadow of the evergreens.

There hadn't been any evergreens and neon signs and certainly not a fancy doorman last time, I was thinking.

It was a cool, pleasant night. Nights are apt to be cool and pleasant in the Southwest. I'd forgotten about these clear nights with the sky so big you can't believe it and the stars clinging to the sky all the way down to the horizon. I'd forgotten the hushed sound in the canyon, here, just outside of town—a hush that was clear even through the music and talk and clatter of glasses that came from the club. Maybe I hadn't really forgotten; maybe this was part of what made me come back.

I told you I didn't really know.

I walked forward then, lighting a cigarette as I walked, and the doorman spotted me. He gave me an eye as cold as the onion in a cocktail. I finished lighting my cigarette, shook the match, tossed it away, and at the same time lifted my head slowly and exhaled a blue mist.

The doorman looked puzzled. He was jowly, tan, and the hair showed in his nostrils. I knew why he looked puzzled. I had on a leather jacket and needed a shave, and I could have been a worker from the new aircraft plant out here to spend some dough—or I could have been just off a freight that afternoon. The fact was, I was just off a bus that afternoon. You can get to need a shave on a bus. You can be too anxious to stop and take time for that shave in your hotel room.

He was blocking my way.

"Excuse me." I made to go past him.

"Just a minute, bud." I knew by his tone he had reached a verdict. The freight train.

Okay. I shouldn't get sore when people decide things like that about me. It's the face. It's a boxer's face—though I never stepped inside a ring, except perhaps in high school, and that was way, way back. The face came from a lot of things: the first break in the nose came from the end of a peavey swung by a guy who got sore at me in the woods in Washington state one time; I forget now what he was sore about. The second break came from a swinging loading boom in Duluth. The overhanging rock that is my forehead I was born with. The way my right ear is crumpled, that isn't a cauliflower ear, in fact it's a new one. An Army doctor gave it to me in New Guinea after I lost the original. Everybody says he did a fine job.

"Look, I want in," I said to the doorman. "You know what a customer is? A customer is a two-legged animal that spends dough. You know what happens to doormen who don't let dough into the joint?"

I could see he was uncertain. His eyes moved back and forth. He groped for something to say, found it, and it turned out to be, "Yeah?"

I put my hand into my pocket, took out a five dollar bill, lifted his hand, and smacked the five dollar bill into it and said, "Yeah."

He growled, "Okay, go on in."

I said thanks and went past him and thought of Little Audrey. If I had been Little Audrey I would have laughed and laughed, because the five dollar bill I had just given him was my last.

I ambled past the hatcheck girl without looking at her, although I could feel little cool patches on my cheek where she looked at me. Across from the hatcheck girl was a small switchboard and an operator, and I didn't remember anything like that from last time, either. I walked the length of the vestibule. The whole joint was divided into three parts, the first of which was inhabited by the barflies, the second the diners and dancers, and the third by those of sporting blood.

I couldn't see this third part all of the time, only when the door past the dance floor opened to let somebody in or out. Then I could glimpse people tense around tables and catch the flash of a dice hooker's stick.

"Yeah, there's a joint out in the canyon," the cab driver had said. "Only it ain't called Seely's any more. Some gamblers bought it. This whole town's gettin' wide open these days."

It was pretty clear where I would go. I didn't have dough for a drink, and the gambling room is one room where you can wander around without drinking and still not look out of place. Besides it was that room—if I remembered correctly—where the thing had happened ten years ago.

I crossed the dance floor and then, when I was only a few feet away from the door to the gambling room, it opened again to let somebody out, and I saw part of a man standing Inside. I only saw part of him because the door wasn't big enough to show all of him. The top of his head was cut off by the door. His hands were the size of catcher's mitts. He stopped somebody who tried to push inside, muttered something, and then let him go by.

Something told me Big Man wouldn't be letting me go by. Not in my leather jacket and two day beard, he wouldn't.

I glanced to the right and there, on the raised platform that partly sur-rounded the dance floor, was a table full of girls. I guess you would call the dresses they wore party dresses, only the way these were cut around the neck and bosom you knew right away what kind of a party. They sat all together, not talking to each other, and looking bored, and I knew they weren't free lance, but belonged here. What is it they call them? Hostesses.

With a hostess on my arm they'd let me in the gambling room, I would bet.

I walked up to the hostess nearest me, the one on the edge and said, "Hello."

Up and down went their eyes, up and down all of them, looking me over. None of them smiled. I wouldn't smile either if I had to sit there and look somebody like me over.

The orchestra was fidgeting to start another tune.

"Dance?" I said to the nearest one.

I couldn't see her too well in the dim light. She was little and dark, and that was all I saw right then. She was looking me up and down with the rest of them. Maybe my off-hand manner convinced her. Maybe she fig-ured that if I were really what I looked to be, Hairy-nose back there at the door wouldn't have let me in.

She said, "All right," and got up, still without smiling, and with a sug-gestion of a shrug.

The tune started. Rhumba, slow rhumba—my meat. I swung her out on the floor, gave her the beat by the slight pressure of my hand at her side for the first couple of steps, then swung back and left her free to sway. Her eyebrows rose and she looked at my face for the first time as if it were a face and not a blob in a crowd. I'd known that would do it.

"Like to rhumba?" I asked.

"Yeah," she said. She kept looking at me, thinking it over. All this time we kept dancing. Not Veloz and Yolanda, but still good. She looked at me for a few more steps and said, "Where'd you learn to rhumba?"

"Brazil," I said, "where Charlie's Aunt comes from."

I wasn't lying, but I could see she didn't believe me. Watching her not be-lieve me made me look at her a little more closely in general, and what I saw was surprising. Slightly, pleasantly surprising. The main thing was that she wasn't nearly as hard around the mouth and eyes as a girl in that kind of a party dress ought to be. Too much lipstick, of course, and big fake eyelashes—but not hard just the same. Her hair had looked dark at the table, but now the indirect lighting threw little copper glints into it as she turned and swirled. Her eyes were bright blue; they were large, and there was something odd about them that I couldn't put my finger on at first. It took me a moment or two, and then I got it. They were just slightly out of line, not really cockeyed, but just enough out of line to be interesting.

She answered my crack about Brazil and her voice sounded tired. "Another master of ceremonies," she said. "Everybody wants to be a master of ceremonies." She kept dancing but looked away.

So I was wrong. So I had thought she was the kind who would talk in smart cracks, and she was not the kind who would talk in smart cracks. "Wait a minute," I said. "I'm sorry. I didn't mean to be a wise guy." Just like that.

She looked at me again. "What's your name?"

"Lew Ross." That wasn't my name, but I'd been using it long enough to be used to it. "What's yours?"

"Kitty Fountain. You work in the aircraft factory?"

"Yeah."

"First time you've been out here?"

"Sure."

We danced around a little more.

"I'd like to look at the gambling room."

"Okay. If you say so."

"You'd rather dance?"

"Than eat. But I'll eat too if you'll buy me something to eat."

"Maybe later. First I want to ask a question."

"I'll ask it for you. What's a nice girl like me doing in a place like this?"

"That wasn't the question, but I'm glad you brought it up. Now answer it for me."

"I'd have to give you the story of my life."

"Okay."

"No. We won't be seeing each other that long."

"Won't we?"

"Be your age."

"My age is twenty-nine."

"Mine's twenty-five and I oughta know better. Come on, keep dancing."

We kept dancing and while we danced she kept looking at me in a funny way, studying me.

"I'm pretty, huh?" I said.

She frowned just a little. "Yeah, you are. In a beat-up sort of way. You know what?"

"What?"

"I like it. The way you aren't pretty."

"I'll bet you say that to all the boys."

"I'll bet I do, but I don't always mean it."

"Careful," I said. "Business before pleasure."

She looked up and said, "Business. I forgot." The orchestra stopped. "Business. Come on, you have to buy me a drink. I'll order scotch, but it's just bitters and soda. I get sick of the taste of bitters."

"Then have scotch some time."

She shook her head. "Marty doesn't allow it."

"Who's Marty?"

"Marty Evans. The big bad wolf. The manager of this joint."

I clucked my tongue. "Sweatshop conditions. Come on—let's have that drink in the gambling room."

She shrugged, slipped her arm in the crook of mine and said, "The customer is always right. Never give the customer an argument. God bless the customer."

The big man at the door hardly looked at me as I went in. I looked at him though. I had to bend back to do it. Seven feet? No, he wasn't quite that tall, but it would be better odds than the dice I heard clicking that he was over six foot six.

This is a funny thing: he looked soft and doughy and at the same time you knew he wasn't soft and doughy at all. Maybe that was because he was so pale. His black hair shone blue in the light and his skin against it was white as a nurse's cap. His nose was short and pugged and the nostrils were like two black holes in his face. He was dressed in a dark blue double-breasted that must have cost two hundred even without the extra three yards to make it his size.

"Who is the Jumbo shrimp?" I asked Kitty when we were past him.

"That's Wallace," she said.

"Henry Wallace?"

"No. Just Wallace."

I saw a table by a picture window past the crap and roulette and monte layouts and said, "Let's go over there."

"I thought you wanted to gamble."

"Later."

"Okay." She shrugged. We sat down and she leaned back. She closed her eyes just a moment. She didn't say anything, but as far as I was concerned she didn't have to say anything. She was a tired kid. Not sleepy, not tired so that her joints ached or anything—it was much more serious than that. She was tired of living.

I sat there and watched her and listened to the noises of the gambling room. The roulette wheel spun silently, but the little ball clicked softly and merrily in it; the dice tumbled, muted, over the green felt. The crowd murmured, buzzed, or gasped suddenly when somebody made a point or a number. The chips clicked. The dice-dealer's pitch, monotonous, yet inciting: "Bull's eye, next dice, try again, where she goes nobody knows, who'll play the field?, let's have a little field bet here...."

A waiter came and I ordered a scotch and soda for Kitty and a beer for me. I had enough change in my pocket to pay for the beer, maybe. All right, I thought, I'll wash dishes if that's what they really make you do.

Kitty said, "Look over there."

Over there was a door beyond the crap tables. A man had come out of it and was standing there, looking the room over for a moment. I had the feeling he always came out of a door that way, looking. He was evenly tanned and he had very dark eyes and white hair, soft, wavy white hair. A dresser. Not a crease out of place. He moved his hand and a finger glittered and at first I thought it might be a ring, but it wasn't, it was the polish on his fingernails.

"That's Marty Evans," she said.

"The big bad wolf?"

"The big bad wolf."

"Why don't you work somewhere where you don't have to play with wolves. Why don't you work for a cocker spaniel?"

"No cocker spaniel would hire me."

"Oh, I don't know," I said.

"That's right," she said. "You don't know."

I was still watching Marty Evans. He looked at me. He frowned. Then he crossed the room, weaving in and out of the tables, and went to Wallace at the door. Evans was tall but he had to look up to talk to Wallace. He talked to Wallace. Wallace looked at me. They both frowned.

Then I looked at Kitty again and saw that she hadn't been watching this performance but had been looking at me all the time, and she was frowning too, but in a different way. Her frown was very small and it was puzzled.

"Still think I'm pretty?" I asked.

She said, "What have you got? What have you got, you crazy goon? I'm supposed to be making you buy drinks and here I sit staring at you."

"Maybe you better tell me the story of your life after all."

"Here?"

I shook my head. "No. Not here. We could go to the zoo some afternoon."

"Are you kidding?"

"About the zoo maybe, but not about seeing you." Now I was lying to her. And to myself, too, because I didn't really mean to be in this town very long. Just long enough to come back to this road house in the canyon, to this room, which was now a gambling room, and look again....

Ten years ago, to the month if not the day, it had been. It hadn't been called the Club Mañana then, and it was just a cheap bar and dance floor, a beer joint, and the interior was done in bark and high school kids' initials. I was high; I was having a high old time. So was everybody else in the crowd. It was Saturday night. I had a dame with me. That was what I used to do every Saturday night, get a dame, a different one usually, and go out to Seely's, as it was called then, Seely's Canyon Rest. I would have done this week-day nights, too, but I made thirty-five a week as an attendant in a gas station and Saturday was all I could afford.

So how did the fight start?

I don't even remember whether or not the dame had anything to do with it. I don't remember how it started, that's the honest truth. The guy himself—I had the feeling he *wanted* to get into trouble. He was booze-flushed and full of fight, I remember that. I remember that he came out of the gambling room several times bumping into tables, people, pounding the bar, making himself generally obnoxious. Yes, there had been a gambling room in Seely's Canyon Rest—a two-by-four cubicle way in the back where only special friends of Seely's could lose a few bucks if they wanted to. Everybody knew about it, but the young crowd wasn't allowed in that room and in those days didn't care much anyway. Seems smarter to gamble, I guess, with a doorman and evergreens and a big rich neon sign. Maybe you kid yourself you have a chance of taking more from an outfit that seems to have more. I wouldn't know.

I know there was always talk around the town in those days about cleaning up the gambling—every election the party that didn't happen to be in would promise loudly to do it. But I never saw anything bigger than Seely's seedy crap game, and I got all around the place.

Well—the man I killed. You'd think you'd remember a thousand little things, little sharp things, about anyone you'd killed. I've got only a fuzzy impression. Women tell me they remember everything but the actual pain of childbirth: maybe the human mind doesn't take in the details of memories you know you won't be able to live with very long. Though what little I did remember was bad enough. This man: he was about my size, but a lot softer. He was stocky, I remember, and he looked huskier than he actually was.

Otherwise I wouldn't have hit him so hard.

I invited him outside, I remember that. Or we both agreed together to go outside. It was dim outside, under the pines, and there was nobody else around. I don't remember how many times I hit him, or which blow did the trick.

But I do remember that his eyes looked awfully funny rolled up under his lids as he lay there with his head on a large flat rock. And the blood looked dark in the moonlight. It trickled out of one ear.

I felt his pulse, listened to his chest. He was dead, all right.

I left. Fast. I crossed the mountain on foot that night and by dawn I came to the other highway and I put my thumb out and a car came and took me all the way to Oke City. Me expecting the cops to run us down any minute, or the guy on the radio to say something about it. But that didn't happen. I enlisted in the Army in Oke City. Later they gave me a yellow ribbon to show I'd been in before Pearl Harbor.

The war was a floating dream, sometimes a nightmare. After a while I stopped thinking I was going to be questioned about a murder every time the First Sergeant said the Lieutenant wanted to see me.

(Kitty was studying me: those off-center eyes of hers were fascinating, and I couldn't be sure which of my eyes she was looking into. Funny that I could notice this while I was thinking about all these other things. Funny that my mind could go over everything that had happened in just a few seconds like this. Funny, funny, funny. Maybe I would die laughing one of these days.)

And after the war I drifted.

I told you about the peavey in Washington state and the loading boom in Duluth. There were other things, other places. Sometimes I got hurt, and sometimes I did the hurting.

Because I couldn't stay away from hurting. Because every time I planted a solid right in someone's gut, every time I took a handful of knuckles on the chin I was punishing myself for what I'd done. Screwy? Nutsy talk? Ask a psychologist: he'll tell you the same thing, only in a lot bigger words.

I got a smattering of the stuff in the Army—there was a long convalescence in a North African hospital one time, and there weren't any western magazines around and I somehow got hold of this basic psychology book. For some reason the stuff interested me. I got more books on it. I talked to an Army psychologist once, and though I had the feeling he was even nuttier than his patients, I learned a lot from him. I mention all this to show you why I felt I had to come back—it was partly knowing a little about how these guilt feelings work, and it was partly instinct. It was the same thing drove little George Washington to tell his old man he'd chopped down that cherry tree.

Maybe I wanted to face the music, the clickety-snap of handcuffs on the wrist: maybe deep down I really wanted to give myself up and take whatever was coming. But how can a guy—even when he wants to—bring him-

self to come right out and do a thing like that?

Maybe now, coming back to the actual spot, I was doing the next best thing.

I'd made up my mind the day I saw a magazine article on the city, telling how there was a new aircraft plant here, and how wonderful the climate was, and how the city was busting at the seams. I started seeing the place all over again.

Only Seely's Canyon Rest—or the Club Mañana—was so changed around and made over now, I couldn't exactly remember where the bar had been, and the small gambling room—and how, outside, the body had lain....

"Listen," Kitty was saying, and she was leaning toward me, leaning against the edge of the table, "I live here, but you can't see me here. In a few days I'm getting out. I've got to. The breath of the big bad wolf is too hot on my neck."

"May I take a poke at the bum for you?"

"No, no." She laughed. "You wouldn't live long enough for a second poke. These boys play rough. They have big money behind them."

"Okay. Where will I see you?"

"I have a girl friend who'll know my address when I find a place. Irene Nolak, Five hundred Ridgeway Drive. Can you remember that?"

"Cinch."

She dipped her head. "Don't be too surprised at anything when you see Irene."

"What do you mean?"

"Well, in spite of anything you notice she still has a heart of gold, as they say. In fact she was the only one who was really decent to me when I blew into town. The others—oh, hell, forget it."

I wasn't really listening; I was still thinking about ten years ago.

She laughed suddenly. It was a hard laugh. "You won't be around. I'll never see you again."

"How do you know?"

She shrugged. "I just know."

Then I was going to answer her. I really was. I was going to come clean and tell her that I didn't even have dough to pay for her drink and that I would probably be nudged out of town by the management, but that just the same I'd had to come here, and she'd do me a favor not to ask me why.

But I didn't get a chance to say any of that because right then a big shadow fell across the table and I looked up. Wallace's white, doughy face was looking down at me.

Chapter Two

"Hello," said Wallace. He had a squeaky voice.

"Hello," I said.

He looked at Kitty. "Beat it."

She said, "What for?"

He said, "Beat it."

She shook her head.

I reached across the table and patted her hand. "Go on, kid. Don't get into trouble on account of me. Beat it. Wallace just wants to have a little talk with me. Isn't that right, Wallace?"

"You're smart," said Wallace. "You're intelligent."

Kitty said, "I don't know what the deal is, Lew, but—" she got up—"be careful." She had her eyes fastened on mine and I could see the slight cast in them clearly that way. I still liked it. I knew what she was saying with her eyes, too. She was saying not to turn my back on anybody in this joint unless there was a mirror I could look into.

"So long, baby-baby," I said. "It's all right."

She went off and Wallace stayed where he was, standing beside the table, looking down at me.

"Won't you sit down, Wallace?" I said.

"Who the hell are you?"

I shrugged. "Give me a name. I don't use my real one."

"The doorman says you gave him five bucks to get in. Why did you give him five bucks to get in?"

"Oh. That. Now it all comes clear. Wallace, you better sit down. Ever hear anybody say they can explain everything? That's what I now say to you, Wallace—I can explain everything."

Wallace frowned, moving the skin of his brows into rhinoceros-like folds. He didn't know whether I was kidding him or not. Neither did I, for that matter. He said, "What are you, a fresh guy?"

"Sit down, Wallace. Have a drink."

"Not on the job," he said.

"Then maybe you would be good enough to buy *me* a drink."

"Why the hell should I buy you a drink?"

"Because I haven't any money. Wait a minute. Correction." I looked at my change. "I have sixty cents. Will that pay for a scotch and a beer in a fine joint like this? No—I guess it won't."

It took a moment for Wallace to put all this together under that fat fore-head of his. When he finally did he said, "So that's it. A lousy deadbeat."

He took me by the shoulder. It hurt—he wasn't as doughy as he looked, not in the hands anyway, but I made myself keep a blank face.

"Wallace," I said quietly, "don't get rough with me. I tell you this as a favor. Don't get rough with me."

"Why you lousy deadbeat," he said, and then started to pull me up. I came faster than he thought I would. My shoulder came up first. He was bent over, and it caught him right under the chin. He grunted—it was a funny, high-pitched sound, almost a squeal—and then he grabbed for me with both big arms. Wanted to set me up for a haymaker, I suppose. He shouldn't have done that. He really shouldn't have started the whole thing in the first place.

I'll tell you something about bar room fighting. Science is good, but alone it's not enough. Experience is good, but not everything, either. Both, together, are very advantageous. The infantry gave me science and my natural sweet look gave me experience. People are always wanting to pick a fight with a face like mine.

Wallace looked up from the floor where I had dumped him and his brow was all in fat folds which meant he was still trying to figure out how I'd done it.

He came up again. Squealing and grunting. I was away from the table now. "Wallace, Wallace," I said. I hit him on the chin with everything; weight, pivot, back and leg muscles, everything. It would have given an ox a headache. All it did was rock Wallace off balance a little—I know it didn't hurt him, not in the way that you or I would be hurt.

He swung at me and I could have started a cigarette in the time he took to get the swing under way.

I hit him in the middle and my fist sank and I thought at first I'd hurt him when he said oof!, but he didn't even blink his eyes, let alone grab for his middle. He swung and missed me again.

Hitting. I could see, wasn't going to get me anywhere. Not in the time allotted, which was maybe ten seconds, because now I was being converged upon from several directions by men who would have looked big beside anybody but Wallace. I would have to put Wallace's own weight to work. I waited until he swung a third time. I ducked under it, put my right arm through his legs, my left arm over his neck, then straightened and lifted him. You can lift an awful lot of weight that way. I spun a few times, just to get him going, then dropped him on the table. The table broke. Wallace grunted. He was going to get up again; he was trying real hard.

Instead of hitting him this time I kicked him under the chin. That did it. Wallace closed his eyes.

I was grabbed from two sides. I felt something hit the back of my head, and I felt it in my twelve year molars. It didn't put me out, it just dazed me for a second. The daze fell away and I saw that at least three men were around me, holding me up. My legs were wobbly. I tried to jerk away and didn't have the strength. That had been a blackjack hitting me on the head; a blackjack does that to you.

"Now, tough guy," said a voice, and I never did know whose.

A big fist grew out of the air, covered my face, and when it went away again my nose was numb and there was sprayed blood on my shirt.

"Tough guy," said the same voice.

Another voice, a very smooth voice like a radio announcer's, said, "All right. Let him alone now. He's tame. Bring him into the office."

I blinked and things got a little clearer and I saw it was Marty Evans who had spoken. Marty Evans was standing a little apart from all of us—just out of reach, you might say—and he had one hand in his side coat pocket as if he were posing for a tailor's style book. It seemed to me that he was smiling, although I couldn't be sure.

They brought me to the office. They had to help me. I didn't want my legs to be wobbly now that my head was clear, but they were. Stay away from blackjacks.

"Sit down, young man," said Marty Evans' voice from behind a blond desk and that was the first time things were really clear.

The office was done in modern. It was very nice; it was really nice: without knowing much about such things you could tell it was a very superior interior decoration job. It had a desk and olive-colored leather chairs and a dark blue carpet with a nap up to your ankles and modern pictures on the walls, the kind that show a profile with two eyes.

There was a door on the far left wall that led, I would bet, to a private bath, or maybe a built-in yacht basin.

The only off-key touch was a corny, painted cast-iron statue on the desk in front of Marty Evans. It stood about a foot high and it was a babe, mostly nude, but wearing cards, aces, fore-and-aft, dice for brassiere and a roulette wheel for a hat. In a fancy script at the base was lettered *LADY LUCK*. I would bet somebody had won it putting a ball through a hoop at an amusement park.

So there I sat with Marty Evans and Lady Luck in front of me, and Wallace on one side of me, and a bruiser with crew-cut red hair on the other side. Wallace seemed to be recovered. I could only hope his jaw ached as much as my head did.

"All right, Wallace," said Evans, smiling, but not with his heart, "what's the trouble? What's this young man's trouble?"

"Deadbeat," said Wallace. "Comes in here and orders a beer and a scotch with sixty cents in his pocket."

"Is that all?"

"Ain't that enough?"

Evans looked at me. Funny, I almost liked the guy. You do that, you know, like or don't like some people right off the bat, and for no reason. There was something about Evans' smoothness and his almost phony beautiful voice—for all of it he got across the idea of being all man. That's hard to do. I like people who can do things that are hard to do. "This is interesting," Marty Evans said as he looked at me.

"Isn't it?" I said.

"Now, I could understand your coming in here and trying to beat us out of say, a hundred dollar check—or even ten dollars. But for a beer and scotch and soda. You must have something on your mind, young man." He picked up Lady Luck and held her in his lap and started to play with her.

"What does it cost, the beer and scotch?" I said. "A dollar and a half? I'll wash dishes for an hour. You can take the half dollar off for the slapping around these creeps of yours gave me."

"Fresh guy," said Wallace, looking down at me.

Evans held up his hand. "No, forget the dollar and a half. But I'm still interested. Just what is on your mind? What's your name?"

I said, "What's in a name? That's Shakespeare. Call me Shakespeare. No, hell, call me Bill." I knew I was being fresh and breezy, and that the fresh breeze was likely to stir up some trouble, I knew that, but I was still sore and maybe still a little dizzy from that clout on the head.

Evans got up and came around the desk. Not once did he change that half-smile of his. He came toward me easily and I thought he was going to offer me a cigarette or something, and that was what you would have thought, too.

He slapped me swiftly and viciously, backhand, across the cheek, and until I tasted the blood that trickled down into the corner of my mouth I didn't realize that he did wear a ring after all, a big one.

I tried to get up and Wallace and the red-head with the crew cut slammed me back into the chair again.

"Now what did you say your name was?" said Evans, and went back to his place behind the desk.

"Okay," I said. "Lew Ross."

"Nice to meet you, Lew. My name is Evans. This is Wallace, and on the other side of you is Varsity. Varsity went to college."

Wallace and the crew cut scowled at me and then at Evans, and then at me again. Evans shook just a little as though he were chuckling at them.

I couldn't think of anything else to say, so I said, "How do you do."

"Now, Lew," said Evans, smoothing back his white hair just over his ears, "I'm going to ask you a question and I would like a very truthful answer.

Do you think you could answer a question truthfully?"

"Ask it." I was through being fresh. I was beginning to wonder all over again why I had come here, and were there rocks in my head?

"Are you working for Ozzy Klein?"

I said, "Who's Ozzy Klein?"

Evans, still smiling, picked up the phone. He waited until a Donald Duck voice said something in the receiver. "Mildred," he said, "get me the La Plaza, and ask them to connect you with Mr. Klein's penthouse." Then he hung up again. "It certainly would be dangerous for you, Lew, if you happened to be working for Ozzy Klein. If Ozzy maybe sent you here to pretend you were just an aircraft worker or a fellow on a spree, so you could look around. I guess Ozzy's hoping to spot a crooked wheel, or something. Maybe he thinks he could put us out of business if he found a crooked wheel."

"Look, I don't know any Ozzy Klein. I just told you that. I don't work for anybody and I just blew in town this afternoon. I don't know why I came here and ordered drinks without any dough. Call it an impulse. Didn't you ever have an impulse?"

"Yes, lots of times," said Evans conversationally. He put Lady Luck back on the desk, then leaned back in his chair. "You know, you use bigger words than Varsity does, and he went to college. You wouldn't be a cop of some kind, would you? I know you're not from the City or County—we'd have heard about it a long time ago if you were. Maybe you're from the D.A.'s office. You aren't one of Torwell's new boys are you?"

I said, "I don't know who Torwell is."

"Mm," said Evans. Still studying me. "I guess we'd hear about it if Torwell sent you, too. And I don't think you're federal. As far as I know the federal heat isn't on. Yet you do use those big words. Did *you* ever go to college?"

"Only county schools," I said.

I could see a quick, passing light in his eyes—a light of interest. By county schools I meant county jails, of course, and the idea was to distinguish them from the federal pen, which graduates sometimes call their "college." It was like two infantrymen meeting and calling weapons "pieces" instead of "guns" or "rifles," and knowing right away that each talked the other's language.

"Very interesting," said Evans.

The phone rang.

He picked it up. "Hello, Ozzy. Marty Evans. How are you?"

I could hear the other voice, tinny but clear. "I'm fine, Marty, how are you?"

"Good. When are we going to get together for a little golf again?"

"Golf!" There was a laugh in Ozzy Klein's voice. "You chiseler. Next time you play golf with me I get a handicap. Ten bucks you take me for. Then just Sunday I learn from the pro you won State Amateurs back east. Marty, you don't have honest instincts."

"Okay, Ozzy. Next time we'll work out a handicap. Say, by the way, that kid of yours is here. You want him back?"

"Kid? What kid?"

"The kid you sent to smell around the joint. He told us how you sent him, and I'm letting him go this time. Only don't send any more, Ozzy. If you're looking for crooked wheels you won't find them; the percentage gives us plenty and we've got enough backing to take care of any runs."

"Marty, I don't know what you're talking about. What are you talking about, a kid?"

"Says his name is Lew Ross."

"Never heard of him."

"Wait a minute, I'll describe him." Evans kept his eye on me as he talked. "Looks like a boxer. Busted nose, and a bad ear. Not really bad looking though. Wears a leather jacket and I think he sleeps in it, too."

"He's a phony, Marty," said Ozzy, "whoever he is. I don't know any such person."

"Okay, Ozzy. Thanks." Evans gave me a short nod and I knew I'd passed. Only I still didn't know why it had to be, and what it was all about. Evans said, "How's your new place doing, Ozzy?"

"Terrif. How do you think a place of mine would do?"

"Well, you've got the experience, no question of that. You still don't want to sell the joint, huh?"

Ozzy laughed. "Why don't you stop, Marty? How many times does this make you've asked me to sell? And, Marty, you play pretty good golf, but otherwise you don't scare me; these little hints of yours don't scare me at all."

"Now, Ozzy, you know I wouldn't try to scare you." He glanced at Wallace and Varsity, and they grinned.

"Look, Marty," Ozzy said, "why don't you come over my place some night? I got an imported roulette wheel. From France. Inlaid. And not crooked either."

"Maybe I will. Maybe I will, at that."

"And if you're ever thinking of a change, I could use a good man."

"Sure," said Evans, "but a good man nowadays is hard to find."

Ozzy must have thought that was pretty funny. He laughed and kept laughing until Evans cut him short by saying, "Thanks again, Ozzy and good night." He hung up. He turned to me again. "Well, Lew, I'm glad you don't work for Ozzy. Ozzy's a nice fellow, but he's too ambitious. He'd like to own all the gambling in this town. Naturally, Boss and I don't see eye to eye with Ozzy."

I said, "Who's Boss?"

"You must be from out of town," said Evans, smiling. "Nobody asks that question here."

"Why not?"

"Let's put it this way. Let's just say Boss is shy."

I shrugged.

Evans said, "You know, I like you, Lew. I think you're all right."

I raised my eyebrows. "I'm supposed to say thank you?"

"Don't get fresh again, Lew. Don't get fresh again, because you've been doing very nicely. Wallace here is a good man. It's not many men can take Wallace."

Wallace, in his squeaky voice, said, "He didn't take me. He was just rassling and I tripped over the table. Everybody just come in too soon, that's all. I'd of took him."

Varsity looked at Wallace, grinned, and muttered a word.

Evans didn't pay any attention to either of them. He kept smiling at me and said, "If you're broke, Lew, you must need a job. Think you'd like a job?"

"Maybe," I said. "Would it have a future?"

"For an ambitious and conscientious young man," said Evans, "it would have a future. You'd work with Varsity and Wallace here. You would help keep the peace in the Club Mañana, and maybe once in a while you would do odd jobs on the side."

"It's the odd jobs that make me hesitate," I said.

And I didn't say it was also the firm I'd be working for. Mr. Marty Evans, you would have to admit, had a smell, actually: a smell of most expensive hand-blended shaving lotion out of a crystal bottle with twenty-two karat gold trimming, and his initials in Old English letters on the side. Mr. Evans had this kind of a smell. I did not like his smell.

"The salary," he said, "would be a hundred a week."

That didn't sound bad. I'd made a hundred a week before—I made a hundred and ten, once, logging—but you didn't pick a salary like that up every day.

Also, the work ought to be fairly easy. Even with the "odd jobs."

And I didn't have to stay with it if I really didn't like it.

And with a set-up like this there might be opportunities to pick up solid hunks of extra cash on the side.

And I was, after all, down to sixty cents at the moment.

I kept telling myself these things. I was talking myself into taking the job. And why? Picking a fight, maybe; finding a situation where the world and

I could hurt each other a little hit. Punishing myself again. What my friend, the Army psychologist, would have called "repeating a behavior pattern." You figure it out.

"A hundred a week," said Evans again.

"Throw in my bill tonight," I said—making a smart crack out of it to keep them from noticing how hard and fast I was trying to think—"and it's a deal."

Evans smiled. "That's a deal. You got anything to wear besides the Steve Canyon suit there?"

"All I have is this and a small bag in the Apache Hotel. Nothing clean."

"Well, that won't do," said Evans. He took a roll from his pocket. "Here. Two weeks' salary. Get a suit and some stuff. Dark—something that fades into a crowd."

I took it and said, "Thanks. When do I start?"

"Well, I'm short a man and I could use you tonight, but not in those clothes. Make it tomorrow night."

The way it had all happened—casually—I was just beginning to realize that I'd been hired. Yet I hadn't been shoved into it or anything; I could have said no. But I hadn't, and that meant some part of me wanted the job and wanted to stay in these parts for a while, in spite of the fact that somewhere in town there might be a man or woman who would recognize me and remember that I had killed a man. Crazy? Maybe it was a little crazy. I've read about people who get into accidents all the time, and about people who, deep down, want to be punished for something they've done, and they always manage to get themselves caught. *The criminal made one fatal mistake*—that's the phrase.

So was it that way with me? Was sticking around here going to be my one fatal mistake?

Or did I just want to see a girl with copper glints in her hair and bright blue eyes slightly out of line?

"There's one thing I think ought to be very clear," said Marty Evans.

"What?"

"The male employees in this place lay off the female employees."

"Sure."

"In your case you most especially lay off Kitty Fountain."

"I'll keep my love life outside."

"You don't understand, Lew," he went on quietly. "Inside, outside, anywhere. You lay off. Particularly you lay off Kitty."

I said, "Wait a minute. What do you care about outside working hours?"

"What do you think I care?"

I stared at him. Then got it. The big bad wolf, just like Kitty said. So I didn't commit myself, all I said was, "Sure, I understand. You saw her first."

And then Evans got up again and shook hands with me and so did Varsity and Wallace. Wallace tried to squeeze, but I limped-up on him and he couldn't do a thing. I smiled at Wallace. "No hard feelings, okay? About the lacing I gave you?"

He grunted. "You didn't give me no lacing."

"The hell he didn't," said Varsity.

I got to the office door and Evans said, "By the way, Lew—"

"Yeah?"

"I hope you've told the truth about everything. We'll be checking on you tomorrow."

"I'm not worried."

"Well, in case you are—" he was smiling, all this time—"and in case you're thinking of skipping town, I might as well tell you it won't do much good. Boss has connections all over. *All* over."

"Good for him," I said, and went out. Wallace came out behind me and watched me cross the dance floor again to the front door and get a taxi back to town. He just stared at me.

I knew, because I could feel it in the pores in the back of my neck.

Chapter Three

In the morning things looked different. In the morning I was feeling more foolish than ever about taking the job, and more than that, I was prickling all over with a kind of soft, electric scariness. I hadn't slept too well. There was only a thin door between my room and the next room and some heavy equipment salesmen and some girls were having a party all night.

I looked in the mirror as I shaved and the guy in the mirror kept moving his lips and saying, "You fool. You ought to have your head examined. You fool."

I had breakfast downstairs and I wondered if Kitty was having breakfast about now—with someone. With Marty Evans, perhaps. That's right, I was jealous. This and the electric scariness did not give me a sweet stomach. I ate in little picks.

I had a newspaper on the table, folded in quarters, and I didn't start looking at it until I was having coffee and a cigarette. Then I opened it idly and the first headlined word that caught my eye was GAMBLING. I looked more closely. The story had two columns on the right hand side of the page. NEW D.A. PROMISES CURB ON GAMBLING was the full headline.

So I read the story.

"Addressing a special session of the City Council and County Commissioners yesterday, Dean Torwell, newly elected District Attorney, promised 'full cooperation and concerted action' by his office in the current municipal and county fight against gambling. Speaking candidly, the young prosecutor admitted that gambling probably could never be completely eliminated, but added that in his opinion it could be 'curbed and curbed materially.'

"He called past police inefficiency and laxity the two main reasons for the year's influx of gambling here. 'The men who run gambling,' he said, 'are from the outside. They find our city, with its new population increase and prosperity, a fat plum, ripe for the picking. They find our policemen dazzled by freely spent graft, and perhaps even by their cheap notoriety. They reach into our very courts with their filthy fingers.'"

STATE OF SIEGE

"'Not the least of the danger,' said Torwell, 'is the internecine warfare these men wage on our streets, each seeking to eliminate his rivals and control all of the gambling. This puts the city in a virtual state of siege, endangering the lives of all decent, law-abiding citizens. This must be stopped. I am hiring new special investigators and conferring night and day with other law enforcement agencies in an effort to do so.'"

And so on. I folded the paper again and thought, well, good for you, Deany boy. We'll see that you get a merit badge. And I forgot Deany boy, and didn't dream I would pretty soon remember him again.

I went out, walked a block to the main street, and looked for a men's store. The place was busting at the seams, all right. New shops were going up in every available space, and the old ones were getting new chrome and plate glass. The sidewalks were crowded. The people were all open-faced and healthy, and they walked briskly, talked loudly, and laughed a lot. It wasn't at all like the city I had known ten years ago, which was sun-baked and sleepy and falling apart at the edges, but in a graceful way.

I bought a dark blue double-breasted suit with the lapel rolled down to the lower button. Sharp for me, but I figured the job called for it. I bought a couple of white broadcloth shirts and some hand-painted ties and a pair of cordovan shoes. The alterations would be finished on the suit late that afternoon.

I wandered after that, looking the old town over again once more. I didn't recognize much—the main hotels were in the same places and the Greek columns of the Masonic Temple hadn't changed, and City Hall was as ugly as ever—but for the most part I wouldn't have known the place. I passed

Police Headquarters in the back of City Hall and toyed with the idea of going in there and looking up my own case, my own unpunished murder, in the files. But that, I realized, would be going a little too far. That would be breaking a leg for a laugh.

Then I thought of one place where there would be details. I crossed to the other side of town and went to the editorial offices of the *Morning Times-Dispatch*. A pleasant, seedy old duck showed me into the library and showed me how the back numbers were filed and asked me if there was anything else I wanted. "Just solitude," I said, and he left.

My heart beat fast again as I turned to the old date. The pages were yellowish-brown around the edges. Old pages, old events, old lives… mummy pages, dry in my fingers. The stranger, the cardboard character that was myself when young. Ever get like that? Ever get crazy words you can't stop tumbling through your head?

Me, the stranger from the past. Just a boy, then; you wouldn't have known me from a hundred million. Raised in a country town in Colorado, rode broncs, played ball. The folks died, both in the same year. Drifted. Worked on ranches, worked the beet crop, fought, drank, lived and loved.

All this time I was turning the pages of that morning paper, that Monday morning after the deed. No story, no mention of the killing.

I frowned and went through it again and again, thinking I must have missed it. I read all the headlines, and all the sub-headlines. One story startled me with its similarity to the item about the D.A. I'd read this morning. Here, in this ten year old paper, a headline said:

MAYOR LAUDS
PROGRESS OF
VICE CRACKDOWN

The story went on to say that his honor, in a speech to the Chamber of Commerce, answered the critics who had been bitterly attacking him by saying that the crackdown he'd promised before election was already well under way. Several special investigators had been hired by the District Attorney's office. And so on. So even in those days—though I hadn't thought much about such things at the time—they put on little shows in the arena for the populace. Only today it seemed to be for real. For keeps.

I kept reading.

On page six I found something that for a brief moment I thought might be what I was looking for. *"Kansas City Man Found Dead,"* said the headline. But the Kansas City man—some creep who had a record of manslaughter and was thought to be in town looking for a job—had been fished out of the river, not lugged from under the trees at Seely's Canyon Rest.

I went through the next day's paper, and the day after that, and then the three days following. Maybe I had the date wrong; maybe my memory was wrong. I looked at papers *preceding* the original date. No.

I left the place and walked slowly, aimlessly down the street, frowning at the sidewalk. There was only one thing I could think of. Seely's Canyon Rest must have had pull with the newspaper. They must have had the whole thing hushed up so it wouldn't be bad for business. Either that, or—but no, he had been dead; I'd seen him lying there with the look of death, and then felt his pulse and listened to his heart, and he had been dead, all right.

I walked the streets till lunch time, and after lunch I took a nap in my room. The heavy equipment salesmen and their heavy dates had evidently checked out next door. At four o'clock I went and picked up my suit. I took a good long look in the triple mirrors at my newly-clad self. By gosh, she's right, I thought—I am pretty. If you can keep your eyes off my face I'm as pretty as can be.

No taxi extravagance this time; I took a bus out to the canyon and the Club Mañana. I went early—five o'clock. I told myself I'd like to have supper there just to see what it was like. But I didn't fool myself. I knew all along I was hoping I'd catch Kitty early, get a few words with her, get to study her eyes again.

The place looked smaller in daylight. Smaller and dirtier and a fish out of water, or a bomber on the ground. Out of place in daylight. Hairy-nose wasn't at the door. The switchboard wasn't being manned—or womaned, in this case. The bandstand in the dining room was empty, hollow. The tables were all set, but there was nobody eating. In the bar the bartender was slicing lemons. The door to the gambling room was closed and it looked locked. I went over and tried it and it was.

I went back to the bar. The bartender was heavy-set and had wide, flaring nostrils and a look that said: listen, bud, I've got troubles of my own.

"Marty around?" I asked.

He looked at me. He must have remembered me as the tough boy who had dumped Wallace on a table last night. The double-breasted drape had him stopped for a moment. "Oh, hello," he said finally. "It's you. You're workin' for us now, huh? No, Marty ain't around. I mean I ain't seen him. Maybe he's in his office the back way, but I haven't seen him."

"Okay," I said, "give me a beer. Today I can pay for it." He gave me a beer and I took a mouthful of foam and then said, "Seen Kitty Fountain?"

"She's around somewheres." He looked at his wrist watch. "She oughta be in here for her old-fashioned any minute. She always has an old-fashioned before she eats."

"Oh? No bitters and soda?"

He didn't laugh. He just turned away and started slicing lemons in the back of the bar. I kept sipping and by the time the glass was mostly full of rings Kitty came in.

She had her work clothes on; her party dress. She saw me, saw my suit, and said, "Well! Look at you!"

"Sit down, baby-baby. I'll buy your old-fashioned. I am no longer among the unemployed."

"So I heard." She sat down on the stool beside me. "You're a celebrity. Everybody's talking about you today. The way you threw Wallace on a table. Wallace isn't very happy about it. I'd watch Wallace if I were you."

"That's easy," I said. "You can't miss him."

The bartender was muddling her drink now. "Kitty—"

"Hm?"

"Look, it's none of my business, I guess, but I want to know. Call me nosy if you have to."

"What do you want to know?"

"You said you lived here. Here at the club."

"That's right. I have one of the cottages out back. They used to be tourist cabins but Marty had them made over into apartments."

"Any particular reason he did that?" I was looking at her steadily, and wondering how I was going to ask the rest of it if she didn't volunteer it.

"Not what you're thinking," she said. "Marty lives in one, and uses the others for guests once in a while, or to help out while one of the employees is looking for a place in town."

"Then—" and I had to moisten my lips—"it's not a—well, what I mean is, there's nothing ever went on between you and Marty?"

She looked at me full face. "If it did," she said slowly, "you wouldn't want to know. Isn't that right?"

"That's right," I said. My cheeks were hot. Me, the gentle maiden.

"And what difference would it make?" She was still speaking slowly.

"It wouldn't. I just had to ask. I just had to get it out of my craw. Kitty— ever since I met you last night, I—"

"No, Lew. Please. You don't know about me. You don't know what you'd be getting into."

The bartender brought her drink and I waited until he moved off again. "You don't know about me either," I said.

"I can guess you haven't been teaching Sunday School all your life," she said, "but with a man it's different."

"What's different?"

She took a good hard draw on the old-fashioned then looked into the mirror behind the bar and said, "Lew, I've been in prison. You'd better know that right now. I did five years in prison."

"Am I supposed to be horrified?"

"You don't know. You don't know what it means."

"It means nothing."

"It means I work in a place like this instead of a place where you work in the daytime and have steady hours and time off and decent people for company. It means I have to take things—from mugs like Wallace and heels like Evans. 'Miss Fountain, would you mind stepping in the office for a minute? I'd like to go over a few things.' He'd like to go over a few things, all right." Now she looked at me again. "It means if I ever had a couple of kids or anything their mother's jail sentence would always come up. Somebody would always find out and start talking—"

"How did it happen?"

She shrugged. "I was going around with a boy. He was wild. I guess I was wild, too. I guess I thought driving the car while he and his friends held up a movie was great fun."

There she was with her face turned toward me and her eyes moist, a little, and her lips just faintly parted and looking very soft, and the smell of her perfume, a light perfume it was, sweet in my nostrils. 1 put my hand on her arm. And then on her shoulder. I was thinking I had changed my mind about the lipstick and phony eyelashes: on anybody *else* they would have been too much. And then with just the slightest pressure I pulled her toward me. I said, "Baby-baby…."

Another voice, a little behind us, said, "Hello."

We both turned, startled. It was Marty Evans. He was standing there with his hand lightly in one pocket, lounging like a tailor's ad again. He had on chocolate brown slacks and a jacket that was somewhere between tan and mauve. We both said, "Hello," and looked at him.

"Did I interrupt something?" he asked. This was the trouble with Marty Evans: he always looked the same; he always wore that half-smile; you couldn't tell whether he was angry, pleased, indifferent, or what. He didn't wait for an answer to his question. "Kitty, I guess I have to talk to Lew. I guess you can take your old-fashioned with you."

"I'm finished," she said, and got off the stool. She paused in front of Marty before she left. "Lay off him, Marty."

"There's nothing to worry about, Kitty," he said.

"You mean that?"

He took her hand and patted it. "I mean just what I say. There's nothing to worry about."

She went off then. I watched Marty Evans. He smoothed back his white hair on the side. "Well, Lew, I've got a little special job for you this evening. A little errand before you start to work."

"Yeah?"

"I want you to go someplace and pick something up for me."

"Okay," I said, wondering why the elaborate build-up.

He turned to the bartender. "Vermouth over ice, Harry." Then to me again: "It's just a little package. Somebody will give it to you and you'll bring it back here. You'll have to go downtown to pick it up."

"Okay," I said again. He hires me for a hundred a week and then uses me for a messenger boy. He could get a messenger boy at Western Union.

"It's a little something Ozzy Klein in the La Plaza Hotel will have for you," he said.

I said, "Oh?"

His vermouth and ice came and he picked it up and said, "Maybe you'd better come back in the office to talk about it. Use the back door. Just go around the patio. I'll leave it open. Go ahead and finish your beer."

He walked off with his vermouth. I stared after him a moment and then I stared into my beer glass. I moved it in circles. I kept staring into it, as though it might be a crystal ball. Tell me, O Beer Glass, why does Marty Evans get a little package from a rival operator? Why does he send me? Is this a double-cross, or something, on the one called Boss, and he doesn't want any of his regulars to know about it? And why does he not even bat an eye about my smooching Kitty after that big fat warning of his last night?

The beer glass didn't know.

I emptied it, walked around back, and stepped into the office. Marty was adjusting his tie in a mirror at the other end. His vermouth was on the desk, as far as I could see, untouched. He smiled at me by way of the mirror and then turned around and smiled at me full-face. "You did very well by yourself," he said. "You look about two hundred percent better. Where did you get the suit?"

I told him the name of the men's store.

"Not bad," he said. "In fact, very fine for a custom made." He stepped over and felt the material of the lapel. It was about the best I'd ever had; but I didn't think it was *that* terrific. "Hm," said Evans. "Might get one myself. Here—let me try the jacket on." He peeled off his own jacket and draped it over the back of the chair. I peeled, and handed him mine. He stood before the mirror at least a minute, pulling, smoothing, hunching his shoulders, turning to look at the back. I thought: all right, so he likes clothes, and stood where I was, patiently.

Then he seemed to be done admiring himself in my coat and he started to take it off and nodded at the back door and said, "Close it, will you, Lew?"

I went over and closed it. He handed me my jacket back.

"Now sit down," he said; he nodded at the chair in front of the desk and went to his usual place behind the desk. "Well, Lew," he said, "I checked with Boss today and he made a few checks himself and you passed the test. But you understand you're still on probation, in a manner of speaking."

"Whatever you say," I said, with a shrug in my voice.

"Now before you start work this evening I want you to go down to the La Plaza Hotel, take the stairs without anybody noticing you, and go up to the penthouse, where Ozzy Klein lives."

"How many stories high is that?" I was thinking of the walk.

"Six," he said, and laughed. "You'll live through it. The important thing is not to be seen—don't ask me why, because I won't tell you. Varsity will wait downstairs for you. Mr. Klein will give you a little package and all you have to do is bring it back to me."

"I don't get it."

"You're not supposed to get it, Lew. You're not supposed to think about things. That's why I'm paying you a hundred a week. So you won't think about things."

"Okay," I said. "I just turned my brain off. Shall I go now, or shall I eat first?"

"You might as well eat," he said. He started to get up, then stopped himself. "By the way, do you have a gun?"

"No. They're dangerous. You have a gun, you get to shooting people. It's against the law."

"Can you use one?"

"The Army always thought so."

"Well, you'd better take one along. Just in case." He opened his desk drawer and took a small automatic in a holster from it and pushed it across the desk.

I took it out of the holster and looked at it. Smith and Wesson. Seemed large for a thirty-two. "It's not a thirty-eight, is it?"

"It's a thirty-five caliber. You don't see them very often. A little more shocking power than the thirty-two."

I started to shove it back in the holster.

"Just drop it in your pocket," said Evans. "I'll keep the holster here. Be sure to return that gun, too."

"Okay." I dropped the gun into my right hand pocket, where it made a bulge.

"Go ahead and eat now. I'll send Varsity to pick you up in about an hour. There'll be a taxi waiting."

"Mind if I ask a question?"

"No."

"Why the rod?"

"Somebody might try to take away the package Ozzy will give you."

I said, "I still don't get it."

Evans nodded. "Good. Don't try it. You'll be better off that way."

He had a point. I shrugged and left.

I ate in the bar room. While I ate I tried to think, and I had the feeling that there were answers somewhere, but finding them was like trying to get the first olive out of the bottle with your fingers.

Varsity came in and sat down while I was finishing coffee. "What do you say?" He had a friendly grin on his big, happy, stupid face.

"Hello, Varsity. Want some coffee?"

"Never touch it. You know what? Coffee is worse for you than alcohol even. That's a scientific fact. I always try to keep in shape."

"Good for you," I said.

"Yeah," he said, real earnest, nodding.

A taxi was waiting for us out front. Varsity said to the driver, "La Plaza Hotel," and then held the door open for me, and I got in, and he got in after me. The taxi headed for town. A few moments later we came to the mouth of the canyon, and now we could look down the long, straight road into town, ten miles of it. It was almost seven now and the sun was low and the town was clear but soft under the late afternoon light. It had a floating look, like a city in a fairy tale or the Arabian Nights. Now, from a distance, it didn't look as busy and bustling and full of growth and pride. It looked a little like the old city I had known. Made me feel funny—almost homesick. I got my cigarettes out.

"Want one?" I asked Varsity.

"I don't smoke," he said, "bad for the wind."

We passed tourist and trailer courts, the city limits, the residential section, and then the heights shopping section, and after that the University, and presently we were in the center of town. The taxi started to coast toward the front entrance of the La Plaza. "Not in front," said Varsity, leaning toward the driver. "Let us off here."

We got out and Varsity paid the fare. I didn't look closely at the driver—just enough to see that he had a square face and mouth turned down at the corners, like a barracuda. There were people here and there on the street, cars parked in odd places, and cars going by, but no one was paying any attention to us. The cab pulled off. "You're staying down here?" I asked Varsity.

"Yeah," he said. "Don't be long."

I said. "What's it all about? What's it really all about, Varsity?"

"Search me," he said.

So I left him and went into the lobby of the hotel. I looked around and finally spotted the stairs. The place was busy, people checking in and out, drifting into the grill room, the bar, using the elevators. It was a nice, clean small hotel, built in Southwest style with white-washed walls and carved beams across the ceilings. The stairs were around the corner of the desk, near the entrance to the bar.

I started up. Six floors. I wished I hadn't had that last cigarette. Bad for the wind, as Varsity said. I climbed, and the sound of my climbing was sharp and hollow in the empty stair well. I passed the second floor and then the third. I could hear the strains of the jukebox from the bar room downstairs diminishing gradually. As I passed the open door to the fourth floor a bellboy went by carrying cracked ice and mixer, but he didn't see me.

On the fifth floor landing I stopped and panted a while.

Then I took the home stretch. The sixth floor landing was like the others and after that narrow stairs led up to a metal door in a kind of housing. The metal door opened as I pushed it; I was on the roof. The penthouse was about twenty-five feet ahead; it had a big plate-glass picture window and a patio, filled with boxed cactus, in front. The front door was partly open. I went to it, looked for a bell, and there wasn't any. I knocked on the door jamb. No answer. I knocked again and waited, but there wasn't even a stir of noise inside.

Okay, I thought, the hell with it.

I turned to leave. And then I turned back again. Varsity or Wallace or even Marty Evans wouldn't have turned back. Varsity and Wallace because they were too dumb to be curious; Evans because he was too smart. I turned back out of curiosity and also from a hole in my head, and pushed the door all the way open just to see what Ozzy Klein's place would be like inside.

I didn't get a chance to look at the interior decoration. There was something else to look at. There was a little bald man in pajamas and a blue silk robe on the floor, and somehow I knew right away that this was Ozzy Klein.

He had bled quite a bit, but the thick, cream colored carpet had absorbed most of it.

Chapter Four

"Goodbye, Ozzy," I said, and closed the door again, quickly, shutting it all the way this time. I remembered reading stories or seeing movies where somebody walks in on a body, and the first thing they always do is walk over to it, stop, and sometimes check to see if it's really dead. Not me. Let somebody else find it and do all that and call the police and get his name in the papers.

I headed for the door to the stairs again. Now my mind was made up: as of this moment I was once more among the unemployed. I would go downstairs, give Varsity the pistol and tell him to take it back to Marty

Evans and thank him politely for me. The two weeks advance salary and the suit I figured I could keep—call it severance pay.

I was two steps from the metal door at that point.

The metal door opened and a cop in a blue uniform stood there and stared at me, surprised, the same way I stared at him.

"Looking for someone?" I finally managed to say.

The cop, instead of answering, drew his gun. He pointed it at me. Another cop came up the stairs behind him. And then I saw that there were two men in plainclothes behind the two cops.

"Get your hands up. Don't move," said the cop. He wasn't exactly scared, but he was wary. I would be like that too if I were a cop.

I said, "What's this all about?" That was what I figured a solid citizen, above suspicion, would have said. It didn't cost anything to make a try—

One of the plainclothesmen elbowed his way forward. He was big and oval-shaped and his face was as smooth as a Queen olive. His arms and legs were tapered, though, and his hands and feet small, so that for all his bulk he was graceful, like a dancer. He seemed to balance himself as he walked. When we spoke there was just a trace of accent, just enough to show that Mama and Papa had always talked Mexican at home.

"Frisk him, eh?" said this big man. "Frisk him good."

The first uniformed cop kept me covered and the second frisked me good. He brought what he found back to the big man, using a handkerchief on the thirty-five automatic. The automatic didn't surprise me. The sheaf of money that he took out of my inside coat pocket did.

"Hundred and twenty-five dollars," said the big man with the olive face, counting it. He turned to the other plainclothesman. This other one was small, thin, long-nosed and looked sleepy. "Sam, you go in the penthouse there and see if there is a dead man for sure, like they said on the telephone."

The thin man said, "Okay, Jose," and went.

I said, "What telephone? Who said what on the telephone?" I knew it was hopeless, but I was still trying to act surprised. Habit, or something.

Jose looked at me levelly. "Somebody stool-pigeoned on you, mister. Somebody told us you came up here to do a little robbery from Mr. Klein's strong box. Maybe your pal; maybe someone you know, eh?"

"I don't know what you're talking about."

"What's your name?"

"Lew Ross."

"Your real name?"

"You asked for a name. I gave you one."

"Okay. Now maybe you give me some other answers. What are you doing here?"

"Right now I'm waiting. I'm waiting for you to take me and book me and then let me use a phone. After I use the phone somebody'll probably get me a lawyer. And when I get the lawyer I'll answer questions, not before. So that's what I'm waiting for."

"Well, you are a smart cookie and a fresh guy, eh? One of these big city fellows laughing at the hick cops. Well, I tell you, Mr. Lew Ross, we have been getting a lot of experience with fellows like you. We know what to do."

Sam, the thin one, came back then. He looked up at Jose sleepily and said, "There's a dead man in there all right. He's about as dead as they come. Three bullet holes in him. The secretary's busted open, and a strong box is on it with the lid pried off. The box is empty."

"All right, Sam," said Jose. "You call headquarters and have them send a crew, eh?"

"Will do," said Sam, and went back into the penthouse.

Funny, until this point everything happened sharply and clearly. Maybe the shock was so big that it needed a minute or two to come along, maybe that was it. Anyway, everything now suddenly took on the feeling of a dream, dizzy and unreal, almost like being drunk, not high or tight, but really drunk, so that nothing, according to my senses, followed the way it ought to follow. There was a lot of palaver, I remember, and they all took turns going into the penthouse in various combinations and coming out again. Whoever didn't go into the penthouse would guard me. Jose, the big one—Lieutenant Garcia, one of the cops called him—he kept throwing questions at me from time to time, and I kept giving him the same answer about not talking without a lawyer. Though I didn't expect to get a lawyer, not really. I had a pretty good idea what would happen if and when I called Marty Evans. The brush-off. First the double-cross and then the brush-off. Reasons I didn't know; I only knew what had happened, what was happening....

A lot of others arrived and they all took turns going through the same routine: in the penthouse, out again, guard me, ask questions, back in the penthouse again. I was thinking: *Wait till they find out. Wait till they find out about the man I killed ten years ago, the one I really killed....*

Two cops and the detective called Sam took me back to City Hall. They used handcuffs. There wasn't any sign of Varsity on the street when we got there. They hustled me into a red car and gave me a free ride of exactly two blocks.

In City Hall they fingerprinted me, first thing.

That's it, I thought, that does it. They would surely have my fingerprints after that incident in Seely's Canyon Rest. It was just a matter of time now.

"Want a photo?" said the identification guy.

"No," said Sam. "We'll just wait until Jose gets back. It's Jose's baby."

They filled out a report of arrest, put my name in a book, noted the time, took my dough out of my pocket—my personal dough, that had been in my pants pocket—and gave me a receipt. They showed me to my room. My room was clean. I know it was clean because it had the most over-powering smell of creosote that you could imagine.

I sat on a board bed covered by a thin, hard mattress and smoked. They'd left me my cigarettes. I tried to think. My head was too thick to think. A cop in a blue shirt and pink arm bands passed at one point and looked in and I said, "Hey, how about using a phone?"

He said, "You wait until Lieutenant Garcia gets back."

And then a long time later—time enough to smoke three cigarettes with pauses in between—blue shirt and pink arm bands let me out of the cell, and he and a friend waltzed me back to the squad room and then into an office. Jose sat at a desk chair. There wasn't much else except a few chairs. A light on an adjustable cord hung from the middle of the ceiling and the light was big, five hundred watts, for a guess. I knew then that this was a cozy little nook set aside for interviews.

Sam, the thin detective, and a couple of others whom I couldn't see too clearly, stood behind Jose's desk, leaning against the wall. There was a chair across from Jose.

"Sit down," Jose said, and I did. He pushed a piece of typewritten pa-per across the desk. "A little story I'd like you to read."

The paper said:

I, Lew Ross, being of sound mind and body and not under duress, ei-ther mental or physical, do hereby freely and willingly confess to the mur-der of Oswald J. Klein in the premises known as "The Penthouse" at the La Plaza Hotel, this city, during the time and date herein noted.

There was a line for my signature and those of three witnesses.

I handed it back. "This is fiction, Lieutenant. I like true stories."

Jose seemed to sigh. He shifted his bulk a little. "Well, Lew," he said, "you like true stories. I tell you something, eh? In fiction detectives always do detective work, you know? The fingerprints and the ashes from the cigar and the test tubes and everything? But in true life there's a different way to get a confession. It takes a little longer, and we have to be real patient, but we can work in shifts, and we have all the time in the world. We do it all in this room, right here. You won't like it, Lew. After a while you're going to confess anyway—so why don't you do it now?"

I was scared, but I was hoping my voice wouldn't show it. It would be interesting, of course, to see how the local boys worked a beating that wouldn't show, that wouldn't leave any marks for the court to see, but not interesting enough to play chief patsy just to see it. I tried to keep my voice sincere, like a manly little fellow. "Now listen, Lieutenant. Listen, because this is the honest truth. I was sent to Klein's penthouse by Marty Evans from the Club Mañana. I just started working for Marty today. You can call Marty and check—you can save yourself a lot of trouble by doing that."

Jose, still looking at me, said, "Go ahead, Sam. Call his Marty Evans." Sam slipped out of the room. Jose said, "While we're waiting, suppose you tell us a little about yourself, Lew."

I told them a little about myself. I told them every main fact except that I had lived in this city before, and had once had a fight in Seely's Canyon Rest. Jose just kept looking at me, his face a plump olive, no expression on it whatsoever.

Then the door opened again and at first I thought it would be Sam coming back but it was another of those cops in blue shirts. He put something down in front of Jose. "Form Fourteen, Lieutenant." Jose examined it. He looked up at me. "What time did Marty Evans send you to Klein's, eh?"

"Just before you guys showed up. I got there a couple of minutes before you did. I saw the body, but—I'll be frank—I didn't want to get in a mess. I figured I'd just back out and let somebody else find it. That's the honest truth."

"Well, if it *is* the honest truth," said Jose, "then you didn't murder Mr. Klein. Because the doctor here—" he tapped the Form Fourteen—"says he died between noon and four in the afternoon."

I said, "Yeah," and that was to cover, not very successfully, my sigh of relief.

"Only," said Jose, "I don't think you *are* telling the honest truth."
Sam came back.
Jose looked up at him.

"Out there," said Sam, "out at that Club Mañana, they say they never heard of no such person as Lew Ross."

I'd expected it, of course—but just the same it was like a cold, wet fish across the face. I was dazed. I couldn't think clearly, but I could see the outlines of a frame well enough. I could make a few rough guesses. Marty Evans, I could guess, had been figuring on taking this Ozzy Klein out of the competition for some time, and I had breezed in just in time to be useful. Me, the innocent lamb. The *perfect* innocent lamb—no connections, broke, with all the earmarks of a mug, no dough for a lawyer. Other things fell into place. Like Marty handing me a pistol in a holster so his fingerprints wouldn't be on it. And trying on my coat—that was when he must have slipped the hundred and twenty-five dollars into it, so that it would seem I had dipped into Ozzy's strong box. One hundred twenty-five, plus the two hundred advance salary, that made three twenty-five altogether.

Bargain price for a murder and a fine, tight frame.

I started talking. There was a touch of panic in my voice now, but I didn't care. "Now, listen, Lieutenant. Use your head, please. Don't go off half-cocked. If I fired those bullets that killed Ozzy Klein, where are the empty shells? The automatic's full. I looked at it. I tell you Marty Evans gave it to me. I tell you I was in my hotel—the Apache—between noon and four this afternoon. And I *did* go out to the Club Mañana—about five. And I don't even know this Ozzy Klein, I never met him, the first I ever heard of him was last night when Evans talked to him on the phone. Why would I kill Ozzy Klein anyway?"

"The money; the strong box," said Jose wearily.

"All right, all right—then why aren't my fingerprints on the strong box? I know they aren't. How did I ever hear about Ozzy Klein in the first place? How did I know he had dough in his apartment? Lieutenant, there are a lot of things that don't jive in this case, and you know it."

"That's right, Lew. And I'm thinking maybe you are going to give us the answers this evening, and then everything will jive, eh?"

I stared back at him. Finally I shook my head.

"Your last chance, Lew," said Jose. "Your last chance to talk before we go to work."

I shook my head again.

"Okay, fellows," said Jose. "Let's go to work."

It was interesting, all right. They had some good ideas out here in this fine, growing Southwest city. Nothing you could publish in the *Police Journal*, though, because all the law enforcement officers all over the country who read the *Police Journal* would undoubtedly be shocked to know such things go on. Outside of their own departments, that is.

At first they didn't touch me. They brought the light down so that it glared into my eyes, and I couldn't see anything else in the room, and then they started firing questions. Just any questions.

"What's your name?"

"Lew Ross."

"Your real name?"

"Lew Ross. I told you."

"That's not your real name."

"Yes it is."

Different voices would snap the questions in turn—it had all the precision of Tinkers to Evers to Chance, and it was numbing in its effect. There, in the aching light, they began to sound like the things you hear under an anesthetic.

"How'd you come into town?"

"By bus."

"What bus?"

"The seven o'clock bus."

"What day?"

"Yesterday."

"What was the number of the bus?"

"I don't know."

"How much did your ticket cost?"

"Around fifteen bucks."

"Exactly?"

"No. Just around fifteen bucks."

"How much did it cost exactly?"

"I don't know."

"Why don't you?"

"I tell you, I don't remember."

"What's your real name?"

On and on, like that. Fast, without let-up. My eyes were sore and my throat was dry and I wanted a cigarette and a glass of water. More than anything in the world I wanted a cigarette and a glass of water.

They—the voices out there in the blackness beyond the glaring light—seemed to sense when I was ripe, when my resistance was about as low as it would get from mere questioning. The mere questioning stopped then. We went into phase two. They led up to it like this:

"Tell us about that taxi again."

"What taxi?" I couldn't think.

"The one you say you took from the Club Mañana to the La Plaza. What was the driver's name?"

"I don't know, I don't know. But there was a taxi. Why don't you check?"

"We did check. No report of any such ride. You're lying, aren't you, Lew?"

"No!" I tried to shout it.

A fist came out of the blackness. It smashed full into my face, jarring my head, bringing that stringent feeling, like swallowing too much chlorinated water, to my nose and throat. The blow knocked me over, chair and everything.

They picked me up, with chair, in a tender, considerate way and somebody said, "Why don't you tell the truth, Lew?"

"I am, I am! I am telling the truth!" My voice was hoarse.

A fist just like the first knocked me over again. They picked me up again.

"Stand up, Lew."

I stood up.

Somebody slapped me back and forth, hard, across the cheeks. I lost my balance and sat down again.

"Lew, we told you to stand up."

Once more, the fist in my face.

And this went on for a while. The same things, over and over again, with just slight variations, until it began to have the zany effect of a cheap burlesque routine. *"Who's on first base?" "No, Watt's on first base."* Like that.

I would have laughed and laughed, if I'd had any laughter in me.

Phase Three. They stripped me to the waist. Somebody brought wet towels. They started snapping the towels on my bare skin. They made a ring around me, and it was kind of a game to see that I didn't get out of the glaring circle of light in the middle of the room.

And the questions, the questions.

"Where did you get the gun?"

"It isn't mine. Evans gave it to me."

"Evans has a gun. It's registered."

"I don't care—he gave me this one."

Snap. A wet towel again. Stinging pain, and a red welt. The welt would be clear in a few hours of course, and there would be no internal injuries. As for the pain, I could have borne any one or two or three welts easily—it was the total effect that made me gasp and grind my teeth after a while.

After a while, too, doors seemed to open and shut and the voices seemed to change, but I couldn't be sure. They're working in shifts, I thought. Somebody kept going out to wet the towels when they were dry.

"Where did you box, Lew?"

"I never boxed."

Whap. A towel lashing out of the darkness. "You boxed somewhere. With a face and build like that you boxed somewhere. You got into trouble didn't you, Lew?"

"No, no, no, no, no!"

Another towel.

Then they let me sit down. I was panting. I started to sprawl back in the chair, grateful for it, grateful for even a hard wooden seat, and they yanked me to my feet again.

"Not yet, Lew. Not until you answer some questions truthfully."

"I'm telling the truth—damn you, I'm telling the truth!"

Whap. The towel again.

They gave me a glass of water and I started to drink it and they knocked it out of my hand. One of them blew tobacco smoke in my face.

"Damn you, damn you, damn you," I said. I struck out at somebody—anybody—and missed. I sprawled on the floor.

"As soon as you tell the truth we'll stop, Lew. As soon as you tell the truth."

I don't know when it ended. I didn't lose consciousness exactly, but I was tired, tired so that dying wouldn't have mattered much, and I was sore and numb and shot through with dull, relentless pain. I couldn't touch the skin of my own body—it burned to the touch. I couldn't even move without starting a new patch of pain somewhere. So I didn't go out cold, I went into a kind of dim red swirl of pain, and I don't remember how I got back to the cell, whether they carried me, or whether I walked.

I went to sleep with my throat burning and the rough blanket under me like a hair shirt against my back.

In the morning the first thing I was aware of was somebody putting a tin plate of rice and mouse-colored gravy in front of me and saying, "You got questioned last night, huh? You'll get over it." It was my friend with the pink arm bands. He turned and went out of the cell again.

I couldn't eat the tin plate full of slop. I wouldn't have been able to touch breast of guinea hen under glass.

My clothes were in the cell. Somebody had thoughtfully wedged them between the steel bars. I found my cigarettes. I drank water from the tap, and from the tin cup hanging near it. I couldn't put my shirt on just yet. I was raw.

After a while I could hear people coming down the corridor toward my cell and talking. I didn't know what time it was—ten, perhaps—and I could only tell it was morning because blue daylight came in from somewhere down the corridor.

Arm-bands started to unlock my cell and I looked up and saw a fat man behind him. This man was short, and had a schoolgirl complexion, and pursed, rosebud lips. He looked like a spoiled child. He wore a natty gabardine suit and bright, flowered tie, and two-tone shoes, brown and white.

"Want me to come in with you, Mr. Torwell?" asked the turnkey.

"No, no, that's all right. I want to talk to him alone." So Fat Boy was the new fire-eating District Attorney I'd read about; the one who was going to clean up all the gambling. Dean Torwell. Deany-boy. He had a prissy voice, but it was very positive, as if, no matter what he said, he couldn't possibly be wrong. He would tell you the moon was made of green cheese in that same positive voice. You might even believe him.

I got up as he came in.

"Good morning!" He was brisk, smiling. He held out his hand. "I'm Dean Torwell, the District Attorney. How do you feel, Lew?"

I didn't take his hand. "I feel great. Just great. What they do to you here—it's even better than a Turkish bath. Tones you up."

Torwell laughed, his stomach shaking. "Well, you still have your sense of humor, I see." His eyes, which were small and greenish, had an unnatural brightness to them. He sat on the stool, motioned to the hard bed, and said, "Sit down, Lew."

I accepted one of his cigarettes. "Now, Lew," he said, said old Uncle Fat Boy Torwell in words of one syllable so little Lewsie could understand it, "I know how you must feel after the boys got a little rough with you. They were only trying to do their jobs, you know. There was nothing personal in it; I'm sure you must understand that, Lew. Personally, I don't approve of methods like that, but in many ways my hands are tied. They have their office and I have mine. They see only one part of it, and they're anxious to get a confession for a murder—you would do the same thing in their shoes, you know."

"Not with talent, though," I said. "Not with their great talent for it. I didn't start out right. I never pulled wings off flies."

Torwell slapped his fat leg. He laughed again. "Lew, you're all right. You certainly have a sense of humor. I think we're going to get along. With just a little cooperation I think we'll get along fine." He shifted on the stool. There wasn't enough stool for what he used to sit with. "Now, then. You understand my main interest is not especially making it hard for you, Lew. Mainly, I want to break up gambling in this county, that's all I want to do. I'll be frank with you. The party will back me for governor if I make a good showing in this thing. And to do it, Lew, I don't mind helping you all I can. Do you follow me?"

"Not exactly."

"Well, now, let's examine what we've got here. Ozzy Klein, the owner of a big new casino, and an out of town gentleman with a record of gambling is killed. There appears to have been some attempt to make the motive look like robbery. This might fool some people, Lew, but it doesn't fool me. I think perhaps Ozzy was killed because he was getting too big for his britches. Now do you follow?"

"Sure. I can say it quicker. You think somebody hired me to knock Ozzy off. I rat, I cop a plea. Roger?"

"Ah-ha-ha, yes," said Deany-boy.

"Well, there's one small trouble, Mr. District Attorney, defender of the faith. I don't know who to rat on. The story I've been telling those police goons all night is true."

"Lew," said Torwell, shaking his head, so that his fat lips shook too, "you're *not* being cooperative. Definitely not."

"Listen," I said. I waggled my finger in his face. "Who do you think you're fooling? I know something about evidence. I've been in hot water before. You need a confession from me because, by golly, you haven't got enough evidence to convict me!"

"What makes you say that, Lew?" He was suddenly calm, and I didn't like it.

I started ticking points off on my fingers. "They found me near the body.

I had a gun in my pocket. I had some dough—nobody's proved it was Ozzy Klein's dough. I can't account for my whereabouts at the time of the murder, but then lots of people couldn't. Okay, I admit it looks bad, but it still isn't enough to convict. A good lawyer would tear it to pieces."

"Yes, you're right, Lew," said Torwell, smiling. Then he got up. "But there's one thing your good lawyer—if you had one—might not tear apart so easily."

"What?"

He scratched his dimple. "They found three bullets in Ozzy Klein. All thirty-five caliber. They put them on the compound microscope along with a test bullet they fired with your gun. I'm sorry, Lew, but the bullets that killed Ozzy came from your gun."

I stared. My face was suddenly a mud pack. I was sick again. I couldn't say anything; I just stared.

"Ready to do business now, Lew?" said the Boy District Attorney softly.

Chapter Five

I didn't like his look when he left. He smiled like a fat cat. I still wasn't ready to do business, of course, and I told him as much, but he just kept smiling and scratching his dimple and straightening his flowered tie. He said, "I'll see you again later today, Lew," as he left the cell.

He meant the hearing, I supposed. According to the good laws of this good land you're not supposed to be held beyond eleven o'clock the next morning without a hearing, but I was in no position to insist on my rights, or send a letter to my congressman. They didn't just have me over a barrel; they had me in one, and the lid was on.

I sat down and thought about it. Surely, I said to myself, they must be investigating further. Surely they'll uncover things. The bartender, for instance, at the Club Mañana. O'Rourke. He saw me there last night. Marty Evans, apparently, had sworn he'd never heard of me. If I could prove he had—if I could prove Marty lied—that would change things, that would start them off on a new tack anyway.

Only I was sure Marty would have every possibility covered. He wasn't the kind to build a frame with worm holes in it.

The morning dragged on. I sat and paced, drank water and smoked cigarettes. I tried to live with all my aches and bruises. After a while I managed to get my shirt on. And think. That's what I had to do, right now, keep my shirt on. And think.

I thought about the man called Boss, whom Marty had kept referring to. I wondered if Ozzy Klein's murder had been his or Marty's idea. Murder.

That made me think of what I'd done ten years ago. Why hadn't they found that out yet? Could it be that Jose Garcia and his boys weren't as much on the ball as they pretended to be? Maybe the records had been misplaced. It had been a sleepy city in those days, and of its citizens the blue cops, the cops of the law, were sleepiest....

My friend with the arm-bands came in with lunch. You guessed it: rice and mouse-colored gravy. There was some fat meat in the gravy, because this was lunch, not breakfast. Then, when I was mopping up the last of the gravy with a piece of stale bread he came back again and said, "Come on. Some people want to see you."

He took me again to the questioning room. I took a deep breath as I entered, wondering how long I'd be able to stand up under it this time. And then the minute I stepped inside I let the deep breath go again, because the first person I saw, directly across the room, was a dark-haired girl with big, bright blue eyes that were slightly out of line.

"Well." I stopped. "Hello, Kitty."

"Hello, Lew," she said.

"All right," said a firm, prissy voice from the desk. "Remove his handcuffs."

Arm-bands looked surprised. "You mean—*off* him?"

"Please," said the Boy District Attorney. He was sitting where Garcia had been sitting last night. Garcia and Sam were standing against the wall behind him.

The handcuffs were taken off. I held up my arms. "Can I use them?"

Torwell saw me glance at Kitty, beamed pinkly, and nodded.

I went over to Kitty and took as much of her as I could get into my arms, and kissed her. Evans really had interrupted something at the bar yesterday. The kissing was good. It was terrific. It was out of this world. It was being thrown into a swimming pool full of champagne and gardenias. "Baby-baby," I said, and kissed her again.

Torwell cleared his throat.

"Okay," I said, and we broke, and I went and sat down. I looked blank and waited. A hundred questions stamped through my head, but I held them back. Somebody shuffled a chair into place for Kitty and she sat down too.

Torwell leaned back and put his chubby fingers together. "You have a great deal to thank Miss Fountain for, Mr. Ross," he said.

Mr. Ross now, was it? I said, "Yes?" and looked at Kitty, and she smiled, but it was a tight and worried smile. She wasn't wearing her uniform, her party dress this afternoon. She had on a Navy blue suit and some crisp, ruffly things at her neck. Seeing her like that you would never dream of the party dress.

"They framed you, Lew," said Kitty. "It was a dirty frame—and I just couldn't take it."

I said, "Well!"

The Boy District Attorney said, quickly, "That doesn't mean you're entirely in the clear, yet, Lew—it just gives us a new line of attack."

"Suppose," I said, "I hear the whole story. Suppose somebody gives me the latest news, courtesy of your neighborhood D.A."

"Certainly," said Torwell. He leaned forward on the desk. "Miss Fountain read that you'd been picked up in the paper this morning. She read where you claimed to be an employee of the Club Mañana, and where Mr. Martin Evans, the manager, denied this. Miss Fountain came to us and corroborated your story. She said that you were also there at five o'clock last night."

"Marty know you came here?" I asked Kitty.

"I wouldn't be here if he'd known I was coming," she said.

"But this means you're out of a job now, doesn't it?"

She shrugged. "I didn't like the job much anyway."

"You understand, Lew," Torwell cut in, "that we'll have to get more than just Miss Fountain's word for it. This new development still doesn't account for your whereabouts between two and four yesterday afternoon."

"So that means?"

"I'll have to hold you a little longer. But I think we'll be able to discuss things more amicably now, hm?" He turned to Kitty. "That'll be all we'll need you for, Miss Fountain, right now."

She got up. "You mean I can go?"

"Yes. And thank you very much. Oh—one more thing. We may need additional statements from you from time to time, as we run into new developments. You won't leave town, will you?"

She crossed to the door and said, "Suppose I do."

"Well, if you did, I don't suppose we could do very much about it. But I'd like you to keep in mind that right now you're the only witness who can keep Mr. Ross out of trouble. Serious trouble."

"All right," she said in a flat, tired voice. "I'll stick around. I'll let you know my address as soon as I get one—as soon as it's—safe." She smiled once at me—a forced smile again—and then left.

I got up. "Hey! Wait a minute! You can't just let her go—not just like that!"

Torwell said, "Why not?"

"Those mugs—Evans—those gamblers—they'll try to kill her when they find out what she's done!"

"Oh, I think she'll be safe," said Torwell. "She's changing her address. They won't find her. This is getting to be a pretty big city these days."

"You mean to say you're not even assigning a man to protect her?"

Torwell laughed. "We aren't *that* big. I haven't got that many men."

"Torwell," I said quietly

"Yes?"

"If anything happens to Kitty do you know what I'll do? I'll kill you. I'll kill you if anything happens to her, Fat Boy."

His eyes got hard for a moment and all his chins got red. But he held himself in; he didn't move. "You shouldn't have said that, Lew. Not in front of Lieutenant Garcia and Sam here. They're witnesses. That constitutes a criminal threat. I may have to use it sometime, Lew."

I got up. My voice was unsteady. I spread my hands and shouted, "What do you want with me? What does everybody want? Why can't you let me alone? I don't care about your town, or your gambling, or anything else—all I want to do is go somewhere and raise chickens, or something. Why the hell can't I?"

"Easy, Lew, sit down," said Torwell. "We have to talk some more. That's why I sent Miss Fountain out."

I sat down again. "Go ahead. Talk."

He beamed and lit a cigarette and kept glancing at me throughout the operation. "Lew," he said, "we know more than we allowed Miss Fountain to believe. We checked her story very carefully. We managed to get a statement out of the bartender, O'Rourke, to corroborate hers. We also checked your hotel pretty thoroughly and managed to refresh a few memories around there. They seemed to remember that you went up to your room to sleep, just as you said, after dinner. And then we checked the men's store whose label is in your suit, and they said you were there at four o'-clock."

"Well, well," I said. "So I wasn't lying after all. Now everybody can say he's sorry. Now you can all kiss the sore places on my back and say you're sorry."

"Lew," said Torwell, "without that sharp tongue of yours you might not have gotten into all this trouble in the first place."

I said, "Okay. So now I'm out of trouble. Give me my money and I'll go. I forgive you, all of you, for you know not what you do. You haven't got the brains to know."

"Not so fast, Lew." Torwell leaned back again. He put his hands behind his head, making fat wings of his arms. "First I'd like you to do a little job for me."

"Job, job," I said. "Everybody in this town offers me jobs. I don't want a job. I'll go and not plant something and let the government support me. Why should I do a job for you?"

"I'm glad you asked that question. I'm glad you asked it exactly that way.

Because now I can tell you why you should do a job for me, and I can tell you why you will want to cooperate to the fullest."

"I don't like the way you say that."

"Didn't think you would. But you must remember Lew that I want very much to be the next governor. I'm willing to hurt people, if I have to, in order to achieve that. I think this may hurt you, Lew, what I am about to say."

"Say it, then, say it."

"Lew," he said, "I think you will do exactly as I ask because of a little thing that happened in Seely's Canyon Rest on a summer night ten years ago."

I didn't say anything for a long time. For a long, long time. As much as a full minute, I'd be willing to bet. I just sat there and stared at the fat boy and he kept smiling back at me. Behind him, Garcia and Sam fidgeted, that's how long and uncomfortable the moment was.

Finally I moistened my lips and took a chance on my voice. It was all right. It was understandable, anyway. "You knew about that all this time?"

"I did," said Torwell. "But Lieutenant Garcia and Sam here don't know about it. And most of the other people who ever knew have forgotten."

"You're smart," I said. "I don't like you, but you're smart."

"You're tough," he said. "I don't like you either, but I can use a man who is tough. Are we getting somewhere now?"

"We are getting somewhere," I said.

He turned to Garcia and Sam then. "Mind leaving us alone for a few minutes, boys?"

Garcia's dark little eyes went back and forth in his olive face. But he left, and Sam went along with him.

"Torwell," I said, "I've heard of some ambitious guys, and I've even been told that now and then there's such a thing as a crooked District Attorney. But I never thought I'd run into one who would keep a murder quiet just to force some poor slob to do something."

"If you don't care for the ethics involved, you can refuse to cooperate. You have a choice, you know."

I said, "I don't care to hang."

"We use the chair in this state now."

"I wouldn't like that either. Modern improvements mean nothing to me."

"Good," said Torwell. "A man of old-fashioned virtue. Exactly what I need. Lew, do you know what you're going to do for me?"

"Maybe if I did, I'd take the chair after all. What is it?"

"You're going to find out who Boss is."

"Boss?"

"You heard Evans mention him. That was your statement."

"Oh, sure," I said. "Boss. Find out who he is. Nothing to it. He's probably in the phone book."

"It won't be hard," said Torwell. "You won't have to put out much effort at all. In fact, all you'll have to do is go sit someplace, and I have an idea that Boss will come to you."

"Let's go over that again. Slowly."

He chuckled. He was enjoying himself. It must be fun to be brilliant. "Suppose I start at the beginning, Lew. We've heard of the man called Boss, whoever he is. Our guess is that he's from out of town and is anxious to control *all* the gambling in the State, here, and possibly some of the State itself. Now, I'm in a peculiar position. I belong to the party not in power in the capital at the moment. Therefore we aren't getting any rake-off from the gambling and we don't mind trying to break it up; we don't mind at all. In fact, we feel if we can do something spectacular like that we're pretty sure to get the governor's chair and a few other posts next time."

"Well, good for you. That's a noble motive."

He went right on as if I hadn't spoken. "If I can find out who Boss is, I can get him. I'll find ways to get him—I'm confident of that. But I must know his identity first. Boss is the big fish. Now the surest way to catch a fish is with bait, right? *You're* going to be the bait, Lew."

"Me?"

"Yes. I'm going to release you this afternoon. Boss will hear of this soon enough—he undoubtedly has men in the police department on his payroll. He'll be disturbed. He'll be very curious as to why you were released. He'll wonder who in this town, besides himself, can possibly have enough pull to get you released—and why anyone would want to do it. So you see how simple it is, Lew? All you have to do is go sit in the park or something and pretty soon they'll be along."

"Well, well, well," I said.

"Like it?" He beamed.

"Oh, it's just peachy-fine. I think it's simply dandy. And when they take me to Boss I can explain it was all just a mistake and he says oh, excuse me, and lets me go, and then I come to you and tell you who he is. Why, it's positively masterful."

"Well, it won't be *that* easy, of course. They may not even take you to Boss, himself—in which case I've gambled and lost."

"*You've* lost," I said.

"But if they take you to Boss we'll try to arrange it so that somebody like Jose Garcia follows you there. You really ought to take a good look at Lieutenant Garcia while you have a chance. He's that great rarity, an honest cop. He makes less, in a year's time, than most of the men under him."

"Good for him," I said. "Probably his honest face will help him follow us when the boys get to me. He'll just walk right along behind us and since he's so honest-looking they'll never dream he's a cop."

Torwell waved his chubby fingers. "Don't get me wrong, Lew. I'm not saying that everything will go according to plan. In fact, I think it's a long shot that this scheme of mine will get anywhere. But I'm willing to take that long shot. What have I got to lose?"

"I'm not worrying about that. I'm worrying about what I've got to lose."

"Your life, Lew," he said mildly. "Possibly your life. Boss and his boys may very well want to kill you. On the other hand, they may not. They may be very puzzled by you, and how you got out. I'm sure they'll want to know all about it. Now, you're a tough lad, Lew, you've demonstrated that. You may find a way to get word to me if Garcia doesn't come through."

"Sure. I'll send a carrier pigeon. I'll send two—a white pigeon for the original and a black for the carbon."

"Let me continue. I was about to say that on the other hand, if you don't care to go through with this, you stand an *excellent* chance of losing your life. Or spending the rest of it in jail, which I would say was worse."

There he sat, Fat Boy, with his bright green eyes set like jewels in his chubby face, and there he sat and beamed. Fat Boy, Bright Boy, the little fellow most likely to succeed. Step right up, folks, and see what you think. Is he man or beast or fish or fowl? The grand prize of one set of beautiful hand embroidered slapping towels to each and every one to guess correctly.

"Okay, let's get the show on the road," I said.

Chapter Six

It was funny to be free again. It didn't seem quite right in the first few moments when I stood there on the steps of City Hall and looked out at all the bright lights and garish neons. It didn't seem quite right that there were no gray walls, no cement floors, no overpowering smell of creosote. I have walked out of other jails and had this feeling.

And here I was alone in the city.

I went down the stone steps and crossed the little park in front of City Hall. It was eight-thirty, just dark and the arm-in-arm couples were starting to drift into the park. The cars were just beginning to turn their headlights on; some glowed only with parking lamps.

And somewhere in this new, young city was a girl with bright blue, off center eyes who didn't know yet I was out, and who was only sticking around because she thought she might be able to help me. There was where

I'd go first—wherever she was. Torwell's crazy scheme could wait until I found Kitty, and warned her.

I counted the dough in my pocket. They'd kept the money I claimed was planted on me, but I still had something from my advance salary, even after buying the suit. Forty-three bucks. What the hell, I was rich. I walked to the main street, turned left, and then headed for the taxi stand a couple of blocks away.

Halfway to it I remembered that I was supposed to have company, and I turned quickly and looked, to see if I could spot Garcia's form twinkling along behind me, but I couldn't.

All right, first things first. Find Kitty. According to Torwell Boss and his playmates had a few pipelines into the department, and would know that Kitty had been there, and they would be thinking along the same lines. Find Kitty. Only I knew something they didn't know. They didn't know the address—Irene's address. Kitty had murmured it to me in the gambling room when I'd made that cockeyed remark about going to the zoo. And I was a smart little boy, I was; I could stick my tongue out at those other, big fellows and chant: "*I* know something *you* don't know!"

Except for one thing.

I didn't realize it until the cab pulled up. I'd wanted a cab, of course, and doubtless I stood there at the curb just like a man wanting a cab. One came. Driver stuck his head out of the window. "Cab?"

"Yeah." I opened the back door. I started to give him the address—Irene's address—and it wouldn't come. I stood frozen in time and space and with an idiot's open mouth.

The driver said patiently, "Where to, bud?"

It was like getting a bucket of ice water poured over you, finding this out. I had thought all along I *knew* this address. I had been so sure I knew it that I didn't even try to recall it. And now—now that I stood there half in the cab, half out, I reached for it. I reached into all the colored gumballs of my memory with the grappling hooks of my mind.

Parkway—Parkway Boulevard. Something like that. And even number—one of those numbers you swear will be easy to remember, like thirteen or four-four-four. Only they weren't it.

Good God—what was it?

I remembered Irene's last name suddenly. Nolak—Irene Nolak. That ought to do it. Phone book. There was a drug store down the street. "Never mind," I told the cabbie, and he muttered something low and foul and drove off.

In the drug store I slapped at the pages of the phone book until I came to the N's. Nolan, Noolan, Northwood, Nottingham—

Nuts. Not a sign of Nolak.

I said "Damn," bought a pack of cigarettes and went out.

City Directory, maybe. My seedy old friend was still there, at the *Times-Dispatch* office. "Oh, hello, there!" he said. "You find what you wanted the other day?" he asked.

"Yes," I said. "Thanks. Got a City Directory here?"

"Sure thing. Say, what happened way back then all you fellows are lookin' for, anyway?"

I looked at him oddly. "Way back when?"

"'Bout ten years ago. Seen you lookin' in those files when you were in here. And then those other cops."

"What other cops?" I said tautly.

He looked a little alarmed then. "Well—nothing. Guess I was mistaken."

My first idea was to grab him and shake it out of him, whatever it was. Other cops. That meant he thought I was a detective. Or had thought so, until just a moment ago. And it meant Deany-boy, or someone other than Deany-boy, had been poking into the past also. Yet if I raised a fuss about it, I'd only raise more suspicion. And besides I was in a hurry to find Kitty.

"Better just let us operate our own way," I said cryptically to the nice old duck, and he said, "Yes, sir," and found the City Directory for me.

I fine-combed it. No prize. No Nolak.

I went out again. I didn't know what to do now. I had a First Sergeant once who said when you don't know what the hell to do, do something else. By that he meant forget your problem for a while and let your subconscious work on it. Good stuff, and easier to understand the way he said it than the way guys with a string of degrees and a vocabulary would say it.

Okay, what something else could I do?

I might check my room at the Apache Hotel. Carefully. I didn't doubt some of Marty Evans's boys might be looking for me there. The hotel was three blocks away from the newspaper office. I headed there.

The shopping crowd was at its height now, and the sidewalks were full of people. You had to thread your way in and out to move along. I felt lonely. I always feel lonelier in crowds than when I'm alone... maybe in crowds I crawl into myself a little further to keep from being noticed... and there's a vague and cockeyed notion somewhere that if I don't all the crowd will find out what happened beside a canyon roadhouse ten years ago. I have dreams where it happens.

Absent-mindedly I started to cross a street against the traffic light and the cop in the middle of the street scowled at me and waved me back. I'd forgotten that in this part of the country traffic lights were for pedestrians too. I stood at the curb with the rest of the crowd and waited.

Somebody came up alongside me and said pleasantly, "Hello, Lew."

I turned my head and saw Varsity. He was hatless as usual, and he had one hand thrust deep in a side coat pocket. "Hello, Varsity," I said. The light changed and we started across the street.

"Marty wants to see you," said Varsity.

"I don't want to see him," I said.

"Lew," said Varsity, "don't give me trouble."

"Don't ask for it then," I said.

"Look, Lew, I just work here. I just do what Marty tells me. I got nothing against you, fella; I don't give a damn about you one way or the other. But Marty said bring you in. Now it can all be nice and pleasant, and we don't neither of us get ourselves overheated. Okay?"

"You're talking through your hat," I said. "The one you don't wear. You wouldn't start any trouble out here on the street and you know it. I think Lieutenant Garcia might like having something on you—say, an assault charge. Tell me, did you ever have Lieutenant Garcia's wet towel treatment? Better than a Turkish bath."

"Lew, I thought you were a reasonable guy. Why, when I first saw you I figured you had brains, like me, and not like that big ape, Wallace. Now why don't you be sensible and come along?"

"And stick my head into another one of Marty Evans's little frames? Don't be silly, pal."

"Marty just wants to talk to you. That's what he said."

"You go back, Varsity, and tell Marty I said for you to tell him what he's full of."

Varsity sighed. "I'm just trying to save you trouble, fella."

"You touch me. Your big heart makes me weep with joy."

"You'll get to see Marty one way or the other," he said. "You come with me now, nice and easy, or pretty soon you get dragged there."

"Try it," I said. "Make a pass. Try something. Go ahead."

"Not here in the crowd," said Varsity, "just like you said. But sooner or later, chum. Sooner or later."

"Go away," I said. "I want to be alone."

"Uh-uh," said Varsity, shaking his head. "I'm stickin' with you."

"Want to bet?"

"Sure. How much?"

"I'll bet you my life."

Varsity laughed and said, "You sure got a sense of humor, all right. Only Wallace don't appreciate it much. I never seen anybody so mad as Wallace is at you. Some day he's going to bust a blood vessel, the way he gets mad like that. Now, me, I always take it easy. You know why? Your blood pressure stays down. That's a scientific fact."

"How come you left college in the first place, Varsity?"

"Busted my knee-cap. I'd be playing ball today if wasn't for that."

"And how did a guy like you ever get mixed up with a bunch of racketeers?"

Varsity looked at me blankly and said, "What racketeers?"

"Okay," I said. "Have it your way. Maybe it's all in the viewpoint."

"You're a crazy guy, some of the things you say," said Varsity.

I said, "I know."

We were near the entrance to the Apache Hotel now. Varsity said, "You make up your mind yet? You coming nice and easy?"

Not if I could help it, I wasn't. And my mind was going clickety-clack, clickety-clack trying to find some way to help it. Going up to my room was out of the question, now; there Varsity could take out the gun he undoubtedly carried and just hold me until Marty came. He wouldn't hesitate to use that gun in a room, either.

"I don't think I want to see Marty, just yet."

"Be sensible. What do you think you're going to do—walk up and down these streets all evening? I got all evening, too. Pretty soon the crowd disappears. Then I take you."

"Suppose we go sit in the lobby," I said.

Varsity shrugged. "You can't stay there forever. Sooner or later you've got to move."

"Maybe you'll fall asleep," I said.

He snorted.

"Got to get your sleep, you know, Varsity, if you're going to keep in condition. Eight hours sleep a night. That's a scientific fact."

"I take ten," he said. "And I can stay awake four days. I did it once."

We went into the lobby of the Apache Hotel. It was crowded. We sat down in a couple of facing armchairs underneath a big Navajo blanket on the wall. I lit a cigarette.

"You shouldn't smoke those things so much," said Varsity. "I was watching you before. You smoke like a chimney. If you got to smoke, you ought to limit yourself to one an hour."

"Oh, I don't know," I said conversationally. "I'm in pretty good shape for a dissipated character. Besides smoking gives me something to do. To pass the time away. We've got a lot of time to pass, Varsity, haven't we?"

"That don't bother me at all," he said. "Because I'm in shape and my nerves are steady. I don't always have to be doing something, like that Wallace, for instance. Why, if he ever finds himself with ten minutes on his hands he's got to play gin rummy, or something, to keep from going nuts. I tell you, the guy is just a bundle of nerves."

"No doubt," I said. And then something clicked in my mind. Something fell into place almost accidentally. It was one of those cockeyed trains of thought that sometimes come along.… Varsity mentioned gin rummy, and for no particular reason that made me think of five hundred rummy, and in the next instant I remembered the address Kitty had mentioned. Five Hundred. Five Hundred Ridgeway Drive—that was it.

"And his diet," said Varsity. "You should see what that guy lives on. Acid-forming starches—"

I wasn't listening. I *had* to get away from Varsity now. I was looking around the room, trying to get an idea—and at the same time trying to look as though I wasn't looking around at all.

And I didn't see anything unusual. You know what a medium-size hotel lobby's like. Well, that was the lobby of the Apache, with a Southwest touch here and there to remind you where you were. Two or three people doing business at the cashier's cage and the desk. The door of the manager's office open nearby and a couple of people working at desks in there. The bellboy helping an incoming party at the main door; baggage piled on a rack, waiting to be taken to rooms. A couple of other bellboys standing around waiting for business. An old geek in the most comfortable chair in the joint reading a paper and smelling of cigar smoke. Two cattlemen from Texas at the broad window, each with a boot hiked on to the low sill, as though at a hitching rail. Expensive, six-stitch boots. They were probably getting ready to play poker with the serial numbers on million dollar bills to pass the time away. And now a Navajo Indian in a velvet blouse selling cheap necklaces and buttons … a well-fed, tame Indian with a fat vapid look to his face and none of the fierce pride of his brothers out in the desert. One more touch: the girl so studiously and seriously drinking coffee in the little coffee shop just beyond the lobby… glancing around every once in a while, and turning a very special eye when she did to the two cattlemen. It would save the bellboy's cut if she could make a contact herself.

So there it was: Hotel, American, mid-twentieth century, the age of the wise guy. And no way to get away from the one called Varsity—

Unless—

I was looking at the baggage rack by the door again. And remembering something. I hadn't seen the hotel detective in this little scene. He must be around somewhere. I started to search for him.

"It's a fact," Varsity was saying. "Most people just dig their own graves with their teeth. You have any idea what's in white bread? Just plain white bread you eat every day?"

"What's in it, Varsity?" I asked.

He tapped my knee for emphasis. His face was all gripped with earnestness. He was so close, and so wrapped up in what he was saying that I was for a moment tempted to bring one up from the floor and try to knock him out right here and now. But it's a very difficult thing to knock a man out: I can never believe it when the hero in the movies goes—wham!—with one punch, and the guy he hits falls cold. You have to wear a man down before you can do that. And then your aim has to be good; you have to catch him in exactly the right place on the jaw so that the shock goes to his brain. So I didn't swing at Varsity. I had a better idea now.

There was a man leaning on the cigar and cigarette counter near the entrance to the coffee shop. He wore one of these light western hats with a narrow ribbon, not a ten gallon job, but the modern western city version of it. He had on a cheap suit and cowboy boots. He was about forty, broad in the chest and shoulders and probably tough. He smoked a cigar. He was doing two things at once; he was holding a conversation with the girl at the counter and idly turning the pages of a comic book spread in front of him. I would bet he would be the house dick—and I would take a chance on that.

"What do you think makes stomach ulcers?" Varsity was asking.

"Stomachs and ulcers," I said. I got up.

"Where you going?" He got up.

"Out to walk my ulcers. Coming?"

"Try and shake me, pal. Just try. Say," he added, "you really got ulcers?"

I half-circled through the lobby so that we walked past the man I was sure was the house dick. I paused at the cigar counter, long enough to lean forward a little and glance at his comic book. It was *Bat Man*. That annoyed him enough for him to look up and notice me. I stared at him blankly, almost belligerently, for half a second, and then walked on. I knew he'd be watching us.

We neared the front entrance. The baggage rack, where the suitcases of incoming guests were placed, was behind a pillar, slightly out of the house dick's line of sight. I stopped to light a new cigarette, and waited until I was sure none of the bellboys were watching.

"I think Marty has ulcers, you know?" said Varsity. "Anyway, he's always taking these pills."

I grabbed a bag from the rack and handed it to Varsity. I did it quickly and casually, knowing he'd hold the bag—as the saying goes—and wonder what in the devil to do with it.

He said, "Huh?"

"Put that down!" I yelled at the top of my voice. "Baggage thief! Where's a cop? Somebody call a policeman!"

"Huh?" said Varsity again.

The words didn't matter; it was the tune. I kept shouting, babbling—putting all the excitement in the world into my voice. The world converged on us. A good part of it anyway: besides the hotel dick with the western

hat there were at least three bellboys and several private citizens. A man
in shirt sleeves came dashing out of the manager's office.

"Don't let him steal it! Don't let him get away!" I yelled.

Varsity was catching on. He dropped the bag like a hot potato. A couple of bellboys tried to grab him. He shook them away angrily, then whirled
like a cornered buffalo to meet anybody else who wanted to play.

After that it was hassle, pure hassle.

Remember that all this happened in three or four seconds—less time than
it takes to tell about it. And the other people weren't yet absolutely sure
what was happening; they were just excited. In a dim way they realized Varsity was apparently some kind of crook and ought to be stopped. Although
I was doing all the yelling nobody paid much attention to me. And Varsity helped matters beautifully by reacting to the guys who were trying to
hold him and showing fight.

If I had had time I would have stayed long enough to tell Varsity he
should eat more fish; it's brain food, and that's a scientific fact—but I did-
n't hang around that long. I got out of the main door on the crest of the
uproar.

I looked up and down the street. Somebody would be tearing out after
me in a moment. I had to take the chance of attracting attention and run—
the main thing was to get far away from here.

Then a taxi pulled from the curb further down the street and coasted to
a stop in front of me. The driver—I had a passing impression it was the
same driver who had found me on the steps of the city hall—said, "Cab?"
and I said, "You bet. Railroad station. Fast. Got to make a train."

He wailed off in second gear, rocking me back against the cushions, and
just as we departed people came out of the hotel yelling and waving—Varsity among them.

The cab two-wheeled a corner and the hotel was out of sight.

"Okay," I told the driver. "Relax. I changed my mind about the station."

The driver said, "You don't want to go to the station?"

"No. Make it Five Hundred Ridgeway Drive instead." I could see his
shrug. Cab drivers must get awfully philosophical after a while.

I said, "You know where Five Hundred Ridgeway Drive is?"

"Sure," he said, and kept driving.

I had been wondering where it might be ever since I'd remembered the
address. There hadn't been any such street when I'd lived in the city ten
years ago, so I reasoned that it would be part of one of the new suburban
developments that had sprung up from dry mesa and sagebrush land. The
driver headed East, on the highway, climbing to the University section, and
then through that area we had always called Swank Hill. It was getting dark
now; the quick-falling dark of the desert and mountain country.

The driver turned left. In the rear view mirror I saw the headlights of another car turning left. I had the feeling that the car back there was following us. But my common sense slapped that feeling down. It didn't seem reasonable that Varsity would get out of his mix-up this quickly—and then find a car, and then know exactly where I had gone. On the other hand Wallace, or gosh-knew-who, might have been around keeping an eye on things, ready to tail me in case I *did* make a break. I turned, looked out of the rear window. The other car was still with us. The driver made a right turn. A few seconds later the other car came along on the same track.

I frowned. There was a tiny gnawing feeling in my stomach, and it wasn't one of the ulcers that so fascinated Varsity... it was plain old-fashioned fear. It was the feeling I always used to get in North Africa on infantry patrol. Did you know I was a coward in the war? I was so damned scared most of the time I didn't know whether I was coming or going. The only thing that helped was that nearly everybody else felt that way, too.

Only now there was nobody else. Just me.

Then it occurred to me that the car following us—if the car behind *was* following—didn't necessarily have to belong to any of Marty Evans's boys. It could be the cops. Jose, for instance. Jose Ramon Garcia, Lieutenant of Detectives. He had shown a suspicious eye all along and I was sure he thought I knew more than I'd told, even under the wet towel treatment. It was possible he'd been having me tailed ever since I got out. If that were so, and if I had known it, I would have shaken Varsity a long time ago. And if I had had a million bucks I would have bought a fish-tail Cadillac and given you a ride. If, if, if. Nuts. Things to be done.

What things?

The cab driver suddenly swung the car in another left turn—violently this time. It threw me against the seat arm.

"Hey," I said, "where's the rodeo?"

"Sorry, Mac," he said.

And in the next breath he slammed to the right, again sending me sprawling.

"What goes on here?"

"Nothin'. I'm just goin' the shortest way."

I turned and looked back. No more headlights. I wondered if Jose had lost us, by accident, on account of those sudden turns. He certainly wouldn't be expecting them. Or—

Or maybe not by accident.

"All right, Indianapolis," I said, "stop the car."

He turned around and said, "Huh?"

We went past a street light in that moment and I had a good look at his face. I couldn't swear I remembered it, but I did have the strong feeling that

I'd seen it before. It was square, covered with a blond stubble and the mouth was wide and turned down at the ends like the mouth of a barracuda. And where I thought I had seen it before was in this same taxi, sitting alongside of Varsity, and talking about his physical condition.

The cops hadn't found a record of that taxi ride. That meant Fish-mouth here would be on Boss's, or Evans's payroll. And I remembered now how he'd pulled up alongside when I was heading for the cab stand.

"You heard me, stop the car!" I said.

"Can't, bud. Sorry." He took another corner on two wheels. Now he was on a diagonal boulevard that headed back into the center of town. And there were no headlights behind us. The cab shot forward again like a rocket. I had been leaning forward to grab him and now I slammed back into the cushions.

I got my balance again. He made another turn, to the left, his tires wailing on the street, and I grabbed the back of the front seat. Then I grabbed him. In that moment he slammed on the brakes. I kept going and my face cracked into the back of his head.

I saw flashing things for a second. I shook my head viciously, and they went away. Fish-mouth, right there in front of me, had his hands up to shoulder level. "Okay, bud," he was saying, "I don't want no trouble. Go ahead, you beat it. I was supposed to bring you someplace, but you beat it quick, right now."

"No," I said, "we're going to have a little talk, you and me." *Something wrong here; this was all too easy.*

"Look, don't give me no trouble. I got kids at home. Please don't give me no trouble."

"Maybe I won't," I said. "Maybe if you give me the right answers I won't."

"I don't know anything, honest. All I know is a couple of guys stopped me on the street and give me ten bucks and said pick you up and drive you around a while and then bring you out to Kearny Park. That's all I know."

"And what did these two guys look like?"

"I didn't see. It was dark."

"You're lying."

"Honest I'm not, honest, I didn't see their faces at all."

"All right, we'll come back to that later. How come you didn't report taking me to the La Plaza? I had a lot of grief with the police on account of that. If you'd reported that ride I might have ducked some of that grief."

"La Plaza? I never took you to no La Plaza. I never seen you before in my life."

And this was the worst of it: *I wasn't sure; I wasn't absolutely sure.* Maybe he was counting on that. Maybe he was figuring that nobody ever looks real closely at waiters and taxi drivers.

"This is a nice little talk," I said. "Let's get out in the fresh air where we can continue."

"Look—don't slug me. Please don't slug me or anything—"

"Come on, get out." I got out the left side.

He came out of his front door on the same side, and I was going to give him another chance or two before I actually started slapping him around. Soft hearted. Well, you know what happens to soft-hearted guys don't you? That's right.

He came out of that door with a tire iron in his hand, and the first I saw of it, it was in mid-air, whistling toward me.

I remember thinking as I ducked: *I knew this was all too easy.*

I ducked to the left. That's a rule—if the blow comes from the right, duck to the left, outside of it. Only I didn't duck soon enough and I didn't duck far enough. The tire iron caught me on my right ear, my good one. I could hear the crack on my skull, and I could feel the hot pain of torn flesh.

Now the tire iron was past me; now Fish-mouth was off balance. I came up again, and I brought a punch with me. The tire iron threw me off. It missed.

The tire iron came up and around again, swishing, or maybe it didn't swish, but it seemed so at the time, and I put my left arm up to block the blow, and the blow came right on through. The edge of the thing caught me on the forehead. The world jiggled. Blood came into my eyes, blinding me.

I kept punching. I couldn't see what I was punching at, and most of the blows spent themselves in clear Western air, but one or two connected and I heard Fish-mouth grunt when they did.

Then he started swinging the tire iron in earnest. In panic, maybe. I felt it strike my head and shoulders and arms and I wanted to cry out with pain, but I knew I shouldn't waste energy doing that. Fish-mouth was calling me foul names now. I punched toward the sound of his voice. I got his face once—his cheek, it felt like—and he backed away: I rushed forward, following my advantage, if that was what you would call it, but it wasn't much of an advantage. The tire iron caught me flat, then, fair and square. I didn't realize it right away. I didn't realize anything. There was just blackness.

I heard a voice before I could see anything, and it came through a buzzing that had been going on in my ears for some time. It said, "Sam, we got to get him to a doctor, eh? That's the first thing we got to do; get him to a doctor."

I said, "To hell with the doctor, I've got work to do." It sounded vaguely like a staggering drunk insisting he can drive. I opened my eyes as I spoke.

I still couldn't see much. I imagined the big bulk over me was Lieutenant Garcia and the vague shadow behind him, Sam. I could feel the cool night air on my cheek. It's always cool at night in the high Southwest.

"No, Lew, the doctor first, I think," said Jose Garcia.

I was lying in a street, near the curb, and it was the same street where the taxi driver, Fish-mouth, and I had stopped to chat. I started to sit up. An excruciating pain shot through my rib cage and I gasped.

"Maybe something's broken, eh?" said Garcia, almost cheerfully.

I started to sob, then. I couldn't help it. It wasn't the pain—it was the rotten, stinking frustration of everything. I was half crazy with it.

"Can we get him in the car?" came Sam's sleepy voice, through the sobs.

"Sure. *Como no?* This boy needs to rest. He's had a tough time the last couple of days, you know?"

"I don't want to rest. God damn it, I don't want to rest!"

"Take it easy, kid," said Garcia.

The car was only a few feet away. Both of them started to lift me. I jerked, swiped at them—and that terrible pain howled through me again. Fishmouth must have kicked me a few times here and there while I was down. I wondered how long he'd had to do that before Garcia and Sam came along and scared him off. I gave up. They got me into the back seat, half sprawling, and Garcia got in with me, kneeling on the floor. Sam took the wheel.

The car was moving then, Sam taking it tenderly over all the bumps.

"Got a cigarette?" I asked Garcia. My voice was getting clearer.

"Sure." He stuck one in my mouth, lighted it.

"Where are we going?"

"My place. The doctor don't live far from there."

"Why your place?"

"Well, maybe somebody who is looking for you would find you in a hospital, eh? I don't know. I just think maybe."

"Okay. All right. Your place. But it's got to be quick. I've got a date."

"With this girl, this Kitty, eh?"

"Damn right."

"You know where she stays?"

"I know an address. Friend of hers. She may be there. The friend'll know where she is, anyway. I mean probably she will." Shuddering sigh.

Garcia lit a cigarette for himself. "You think this Marty Evans also knows about her friend and where she lives?"

"I don't think so. But the longer we take, the more time he has to find out." I closed my eyes then and tried to relax, thinking that might take some of the pain away. It did, but not much. "How long was I out, Jose?"

"Not long. Few minutes, maybe. We were cruising up and down looking for that taxi. At first we thought maybe *you* were thinking you would lose us. Then we found you in the street."

"You get the taxi's number?"

Garcia sighed. "No. I was not thinking to do that."

"No matter," I said. "I'll know him when I see him again. Fish-mouth. I'll know him. We have to finish our little talk sometime. That makes a lot of guys I owe a lacing to in this silly town." I opened my eyes. "Including you, Jose. Including you when this is all over."

He didn't say anything; he just looked at me thoughtfully from behind the red glow of his cigarette. It gave his oval, olive face and dark, slitted eyes a funny oriental look.

The car passed through a residential section where the houses weren't as close together as in some others, and where they were all of pueblo adobe design. It turned into a driveway, and then a low-walled patio. Sam stopped it. Jose opened the door, and I looked around and saw that a house formed two walls of the patio, and the windows threw rectangles of light down upon the red-stone flagging.

"Come on, Lew," said Jose. He and Sam helped me out of the car. I could move my feet when they held my arms and shoulders. The pain was terrific. I bit my lip and felt warm blood on my chin.

They started to guide me across the patio to what looked like a wing of the main house, a structure with portales shading two doors. Then the front door of the main house opened and a woman's voice called out, *"Jose—estas tu?"*

"It's me, Mama," said Jose.

"Oh." Relief in her voice. "I didn't know if was burglars, or something!" She had considerably more of Old Mexico in her voice than Jose. I could only see her in silhouette, and all that I could gather was that she was built something like a light bulb, hanging upside down.

"This your joint?" I asked Jose.

"My ranch." He couldn't quite keep the pride out of his words. He had maybe half an acre here and you could call the neighbors without raising your voice much, but just the same it was a ranch. "That is Mrs. Garcia," Jose added. "She is from Guadalajara."

I guess it was an honor, or something, to be from Guadalajara. That was the way he said it. I had been to Guadalajara, and all they have there is a song. "Look," I said, "you don't have to bring me here. There's too much to do—"

"You better rest, then we talk." He turned his head to Mama. *"Por favor, Mama, llame el doctor, eh?"*

"Sí, sí, horita. Pero que hay?"

"Mas tarde, mas tarde," said Garcia impatiently.

"That's right, Jose," I said. "Always let 'em wait for an explanation."

"You understand Spanish, eh?"

"Enough to find a meal or a woman in Mexico," I said, and then a sharp stab of pain hit me and I groaned.

The next thing I knew, I was in bed and Garcia was talking to somebody he kept calling "Doctor." I could see the room dimly. There was a beehive fireplace in one corner and there were colored ears of corn on the walls. There was Indian pottery. I knew, somehow, that this room wasn't connected with the main house, but had its own separate entrance.

I couldn't see much of the doctor. Just enough to know that he was tall and had a deep, gloomy voice. "Don't let him out of bed until I see him tomorrow," said the doctor. "I'll be along sometime in the evening."

"Anything serious?"

"Hard to say. He's probably all right, but it isn't good take chances with head injuries like that."

"Sure, I understand," said Jose's voice.

I floated off somewhere. I remember the snap of the light switch as somebody turned the lights out, and I remember feeling that I was very, very tired and nothing was really important any more; nothing was so important that it couldn't be taken care of *mas tarde... mañana....*

It was light when I awoke, and the light came from the high window. There were the opening noises of a summer day. Birds were cheeping. In the distance a rooster crowed. A cricket rubbed his legs not far away.

I realized that the opening of a door had awakened me. I turned my head and a girl stood in the doorway. She held a breakfast tray. "Morning," I said. "Who are you?"

She was tiny, and I would have thought her to be very young, except that her eyes were a little too devilish to be *very* young. So was the faint come-on smile at the edges of her bright lips. She had jet black hair that came all the way down to her shoulders in a wild tumble; she wore a small gold ring in one ear. Her blouse hung over one shoulder, and I could see all of that magnificent, tanned, tiny shoulder, and the plump beginnings of her breasts just over the top of the blouse.

"I'm Raquel," she said. "Want your breakfast now?" Her voice was husky.

"Sure." I kept staring at her. She knew it; she knew just where I was staring. She brought the tray to the bedside table and leaned over to put it down. I didn't look away. She knew that, too. "My name's Lew," I said

"Yes. I know. Lew Ross."

"Jose must have told you."

"Yes."

I was still staring at her. "Do *you* come with breakfast? I've heard of hospitality, but Jose's outdoing himself."

"What?" She couldn't follow that exactly.

"Never mind. What I want to know is whose little girl are you?"

"I am nobody's little girl."

"I mean do you belong here? Are you Jose's niece or grandmother or something?"

"No, I just live here." That was how she was looking at me. Those black, black, starry black eyes saying: well, how good are you? What do you know how to do? One part of me wanted to show her, and the other part wanted to take her over my knee, spank her, and then send her inside to wash that lipstick off.

I said, "You just live here."

She laughed. She tossed her head back, sending waves and ripples through her blueblack hair. "Jose will tell you all about me. Don't worry. He won't miss telling you about me." And then she turned and went to the door.

"Where's Jose?"

"Having breakfast with Mama. He's coming to see you when he finishes." She opened the door then and started to slip through it, and for just a brief second she looked at me again, smiling that faintly wicked smile, and then she was gone.

I shook my head and clucked my tongue, pulled the tray over to my lap and started breakfast. Orange juice, eggs and chile, ham and coffee. Delicious. And I felt better—a little sore here and there, and my scalp ached every time I moved my eyebrows—but on the whole, better. I was naked under the covers and there were bandage pads on my head, and some tape over my ribs on the left side. I thought of Fish-mouth again, and what I owed him. I'd find him sometime; I'd stick around town longer than I had to just to find him—

I had my fork halfway to my mouth in that moment. I stopped it there. I stared straight ahead with my mouth then.

Fish-mouth knew Irene Nolak's address—500 Ridgeway Drive—I'd given it to him—

I put the tray back on the bedside table. I swung from the bed, stood up and swayed for a moment until the dizziness went away. Then I looked around for my clothes. I had to get out of here; I had to get to 500 Ridgeway Drive.

Only my clothes weren't anywhere in the room.

Chapter Seven

The door opened, and I looked around, and there was Lieutenant of Detectives Jose Ramon Garcia. His dark eyes were motionless in his olive face.

"Hello, Jose. Where are my clothes?"

"You're supposed to stay in bed."

"I don't want to. I've got things to do."

"Yes, but just the same you better, eh? The doctor says you better. You know what, kid? You took one hell of a beating last night."

I said, "Damn it, I want my clothes, and I want my cigarettes. I want my cigarettes first."

He took a pack out of his pocket and gave it to me. I lit one. "All right, Jose, thanks. Thanks for the cigarettes. Thanks for picking me up off the street, and bringing me here, and getting a doctor, and thanks for breakfast. Now will you kindly get my clothes?"

"No."

"Jose, do I have to get rough with you, too? All I do is get rough with people."

He shook his head and smiled. "You won't get rough with me. I carry a blackjack. Want to see it?" He reached for his hip pocket.

"Never mind. Just tell me why I can't have my clothes?"

"I told you. The doctor. Besides, I want to have a little talk with you this morning."

"I don't feel like a little talk." I turned away from him, walked over to the bureau and there was a mirror over the bureau, and I saw myself. "My God," I said.

"Yes," said Jose amiably, "you are not in good shape."

I stared at the grimy, bewhiskered face in the mirror and at the two red little eyes peering out from Rocky Mountain caves. "The least you can do is get me a razor—"

"There's one in the drawer. And soap. And water in the pitcher."

He sat down heavily in a pigskin *equipale* and watched while I got ready to shave. It crossed my mind to give him Irene Nolak's address and ask him to go there and talk to her, but I couldn't quite make myself trust him to do it right. The memory of those wet towels was still in the way. The best thing now, I decided, was to find a way to get my clothes back, and then beat it the hell out of here.

"Now I want to ask some questions, Lew," said Garcia.

I made a bitter noise, almost a laugh. "You already asked me questions. You had quite a time night before last asking me questions. How do you expect to ask questions without a wet towel in your hand?"

In the mirror I could see him frown. "Lew, I'm sorry about that, eh? You don't have to believe me, but I'm sorry every time I have to do something like that. We get some pretty tough and some pretty nasty people in there sometimes, and these people would do a lot worse than hit you with a towel if they were asking the questions. If there is a better way to handle them, I guess we don't know it."

"Don't tell it to me. Tell it at Confession."

He sighed. "I always do." Then he got up, helped himself to one of his own cigarettes, sat down again and lit it. He smoked for a few seconds, making a great show of handling the cigarette, and blowing smoke. When his question came it was sudden and off-hand. And I was flat-footed.

"Lew," he said, "what kind of a deal is going on between you and the District Attorney, eh?"

"Hm?" I said. "What?" As if I hadn't heard. But of course he knew I'd heard, and now, looking at me levelly with his dark, placid eyes he knew that the question had startled me, and maybe even frightened me a little.

"What little thing happened," he said patiently, "in Seely's Canyon Rest on a summer night ten years ago?"

"Those are Torwell's exact words, Jose. You have a good memory."

"For things I am interested in, yes."

"Well, then, if you're so interested why don't you go find out what happened on a summer night ten years ago?"

"I tried to. I had two men look in every newspaper for June, July and August ten years ago. The librarian said someone answering your description was already there."

My heart was beating fast. It was incredible that Jose, suspicious, wouldn't find something, somewhere. I wondered if he were giving me a cat-and-mouse job; if he had really looked and found the incident in question in the police records. There would surely be a Report of Crime filed away for that date. I kept shaving, being careful to keep the same rhythm and to make my voice as even as possible. "What do you care, Jose? What business is it of yours?"

He settled back in the chair. "Well, I'll tell you, Lew. You know something? We take an oath when we join the police department. We put the hand on the Bible and take an oath. It's a Protestant bible, but that don't make no difference. Now, tell you something. A lot of fellows don't take that oath very seriously, but me, I'm kind of old-fashioned and I do. Now this oath says you are supposed to stop a crime whenever you see one or think maybe one is going on. I forget the fancy words, but that's what it says. And it doesn't say you should forget the oath just because a man happens to be District Attorney, eh?"

"So that's it. You're gunning for Torwell."

"I am gunning for nobody. I am not in their politics down there. All I know is, something is funny."

"Something's funny, all right. I've been laughing and laughing for two days."

"You better tell me about it, eh?"

"No."

"Maybe you better think about it a while, and then maybe you see it would be better to tell me about it."

"Listen, Jose," I said, "confession may be good for the soul, but I haven't got any soul left for confession to be good for."

I said it real tough and positive, as if that ended the matter, but I knew I was lying through my teeth, and that confession, or something like it, was exactly what I needed, because this thing, this memory, this guilt of killing another man, had been a festering sickness in me all this time, and I was just now beginning to crack a little, and one of these days I would crack all the way....

Jose got up. "Well, Lew, if you won't tell me anything I guess I'll go down and talk to Torwell. I think it might be interesting to see how his face looks when I start asking questions."

"Go ahead," I said unconcernedly. And my heart took another hurdle.

"You stay here, Lew. And don't you try to leave. You better get back in bed, eh? Mama or Raquel will bring your meals."

"That reminds me. Who *is* Raquel?"

For the first time since I had known Lieutenant of Detectives Jose Ramon Garcia his olive face broke into a warm, broad smile. His eyes became bright, excited. "What do you think of that little girl, eh? What do you think of her?"

I wasn't sure whether to tell him or not. He'd said he was old-fashioned. "Well," I said, "she's a pretty little thing."

"Yes." He nodded. "You should have seen her when she came here. Lew, I want to tell you she was a tiger. She was really a tiger when she came here!"

"Where did you get her, the zoo?"

"No, no, no, no. She was in the reformatory. I helped arrest her. The poor thing—just a kid. You know how old she is?"

"Old enough to—" I checked myself and said, "Nineteen?"

"Eighteen," said Jose. "Just a baby. Just a little baby. Her mother was dead. Her father was a burglar. He would climb into houses and rob them. The poor thing, he made her stand outside and watch while he did this. And then one night she didn't watch so well, and we got him."

"Kill him?"

Jose nodded. He frowned and stared back into the past for a moment. "I tried to shoot him in the leg, but it was dark. I didn't like to do that."

"So you took the kid over?" I still didn't get it.

"Well, Raquel was charged with accessory. Your friend, Torwell—he was Assistant D.A. then. He was crazy to send people to jail. Still is, eh? So he sent Raquel to the reformatory and I couldn't get him not to. That was a year she spent in the reformatory. And then Mama and I started thinking, we didn't have any kids, and we always wanted some kids. Well, Raquel was too old to adopt, but there was another way. I got her paroled out of that reformatory." He had a hundred watts in his face now. He spread his hands. "I had her paroled to *me!*"

"Just so you could—raise her?" I couldn't keep the suspicion out of my voice.

"Sure. By golly, we got her speaking good English and table manners and going to Mass and everything. She don't have her head full of men and boys any more—Mama and I see to that. It's just like she is our own daughter. I tell you, this thing is what Mama and I needed all the time."

I stared at him, believing him, and yet trying to make my belief fit in with what I knew, or thought I knew, about people. There he stood, a good man, a wholly good man, without a really nasty thought in his head, and there he stood proud of the little angel he thought he'd made out of Raquel. Only that sidewinding look of hers was anything but angelic. Probably Jose had never even noticed it. I don't know why it always surprises me to see good man, a wholly good man, being taken for a ride and made a sucker of. Maybe I keep hoping some time it won't happen....

"Well, Jose," I said, "that sure is a wonderful thing for you to do."

What the hell else could I say?

Jose, still grinning, waved kind of clumsily and said, "See you later, eh?"

"Sure," I said, and he went out.

So, I thought, would Raquel see me later. I knew now how I was going to get my clothes back.

So I went to bed, covered up, and waited for Raquel. I sat there smoking and thinking. The insurance companies say you should never smoke in bed. Some people say you should never think, either. They have a point. All I could do was keep thinking about myself, and what a fouled-up mess I was in, and what a fouled-up mess I had always been in, and what fouled-up messes I would probably get into again. This is called introspection.

I was introspecting very deeply when Raquel finally showed up again. It was, for a guess, near noon. She opened the door part way and slipped in, brushing the firm little points of her breasts against the door. That devilish half-smile was still on her lips.

"Mama sent me to get the tray if you're through with it," she said.

"Sure. Help yourself." I nodded at the bedside table. I didn't stare at her this time, I pretended to be uninterested.

She came across the room, bent to pick up the tray, and I said, "There's a drawstring around the top of your blouse, isn't there? Why don't you tighten it?"

This is called the surprise attack. She almost dropped the tray and she said, "*What?*"

I turned slowly to look at her. "There's a word for little girls like you," I said. "There's a word for little girls who get men all excited—and then would probably scream if somebody touched them."

Her eyes hardened. "Who do you think you are? Who do you think you are, anyway, talking to me like that?"

"I'm the Shadow," I said. "The Shadow knows."

She said, "What?"

"Stop saying that. You ought to pretend to understand, even if you don't."

"Jose said you were a fresh guy." She moved her hand, tossing some stray hair out of the way. "And you sure are."

"Then how come you're so interested?"

"I'm *not* interested! Not in *you!*"

"Sure you are. You're as interested as you can be to see a man who's human for a change after listening to Jose preach and tell you what a good girl you have to be all the time."

"You're crazy. You don't know what you're talking about."

"Come here."

"I will not." And she swayed toward me a little.

I took the tray out of her hands and put it back on the bedside table.

"What are you doing?"

"This." I took her arm and pulled her down and around to a sitting position on the bed, practically on my lap. She didn't object much, just enough to make me grip hard and pull a little. Then I got my arms around her bare shoulders, bent her back, and brought my own head forward and kissed her, right on those full, red lips. I kissed her hard. The lips, moist and warm, parted just enough to take the kiss and then began to do things on their own. Here was something Mama and Jose hadn't taught her. She was an expert.

We broke and she said, "You shouldn't ought to do that."

"Neither should you."

"I better get back."

"No hurry. You can't have as much fun with Mama as you can with me."

Raquel's look was like a slow fuse, then. So was her voice. Slow and quiet. "Mama's out. She's shopping."

"Well," I said. "Well, well."

Then Raquel grabbed me, and this time she kissed me. Know what I mean? I didn't have to do a thing. I didn't want to. Everything she'd evidently been holding in for a long, long time stirred and trembled in her strong young body, and I could feel it do so.

She backed away finally, and I waited until her eyes fluttered open again, and I tried to keep my stare from those wide, soft lips, slightly moist, slightly open, and I said, "Look, Raquel, I'm no angel. But some things shouldn't be done."

Her eyes became big. "You mean you are too sick?"

"'No, no." I tried not to laugh. "I'm just as spry as I ever was—in that way, anyhow. I mean, Raquel, hell, you're only a kid, and Jose's practically your Papa, and he's been pretty square with me. I mean—"

The slow fuse hit the powder. Only it was a different explosion than I'd expected. She stood up, looked down at me. Small, hot points of anger in her eyes. "You're just like the rest, no? You're like Jose and Papa and the man in the reformatory! You're so holy someone's going to make you a saint, maybe!"

"Whoa—hold it, Raquel—"

"All the time you want me—all of you—want me bad! But you lie about this! You lie even to yourself!"

"Raquel, look, that may be sort of true, but—"

"And you're thinking about yourselves, all the time! You're thinking *you* want something, but *you* are going to do this or that. Well, what about *me*? What about Raquel? You think I am a little child still?" She ran her hands up and down her chest and thighs. I did not think she was a little child still.

"Everybody wants to pat my head and maybe give me a lollypop! God damn it, Señor," she said, with a startling blend of Old Mexico and New Southwest, "I am a *woman!* I want what a *woman* can have! I want love—like a man loves a woman—don't you understand?"

This was something the Army psychologist hadn't told me about. Probably he would have patted her on the head and given her a lollypop, too. And found a big word for what was bothering her. For something was bothering her, bad; I could sense that without knowing any big words.... I could sense that just once she *needed* to be treated as a woman, a desirable woman, and loved in that way. She needed it to straighten her out, knock everything back into place so she could start all over again within herself. You don't think a woman needs this sometimes? Put it this way. It's just like the urge that makes a man, when things get all tightened up and unbearable, go out and get himself into a good fist fight. It's as simple—and as complicated—as that.

"Come here, Raquel," I said.

She moved toward the bed. I put my arm around her waist, and my hand in the small of her back where I could feel the compact, alive trembling of her body. I started to pull her toward me, and she resisted. "You don't want to love me like a woman. You just want me for your own pleasure. You don't care for me—nobody cares for me. Nobody at all." Her voice was low and steady enough, but seemed just about to break.

"Baby, you *are* in a bad way," I said. "But, then—so am I. Maybe everybody is. Come and kiss me again."

She hesitated. "I don't want you to kiss me like a little child."

"I won't."

"I—I never had real love. Not *real*. You know? I am not a virgin—but I never had real."

"I know," I said.

She put one knee on the edge of the bed and bent down, I saw her upper torso under the hanging off-the-shoulder blouse. She was about as far from being a child as a woman can get. And there was a warmth, a faint warmth all around her that besides being warmth was a kind of perfume. I put my hands on her cheeks and temples, held her head while I looked into her eyes for a moment and said, "Easy now, Raquel. Easy, baby. Take it nice and easy."

The first time I had kissed her, and the second time she had kissed me. This time we kissed each other. This time we both put everything we had into it.

I pulled the rest of her to me, and she clung to me as hard as she could, digging her fingernails into my shoulder blades and the back of my neck; I crushed her with all my strength. I guess we hurt each other. I don't think we noticed or cared.

Outside the bright sun climbed to mid-morning, and the rooster was quiet and the bird had stopped cheeping and the cricket wasn't rubbing his legs together any more. There was just the hot silence of a Southwest day. It helped us to feel alone....

We were lying there, laughing at things that ordinarily wouldn't be funny enough to laugh at. She bit my ear. What's funny about biting somebody's ear? She bit my ear and I laughed.

"Lew... *querido*," she said.

"Yes, baby?"

"I feel better."

"Sure."

"I don't hate everybody now. I love everybody. Well—most everybody. I love you."

"Don't fall in love with me, Raquel," I said. "Don't let yourself in for that."

She looked at me; all of me. "I don't think is so bad to fall in love with you, no?"

"No," I said.

"Lew," she said slowly, stretching with a wonderful cat motion while she spoke, "take me out of here." I sighed. I thought about it. For a moment I even half-wished I hadn't met Kitty first. And then, remembering Kitty, I remembered that I had to get out of here. I had to get my clothes.

"Baby," I said, "get me my clothes out of the main house, will you?"

"You are going to leave?"

"I've got business."

She got up on her knees, leaned her elbows on my bare chest and smiled at me in an impish way. "I don't want you to leave."

"Look, I want to get out of here before Jose gets back. Now get my clothes, huh?"

She shook her head slowly and said, "No."

"Come on. Do that for me. Just do that one little thing for me."

"Then you will go, and I never see you again."

"I'll come back and see you."

"I don't think so." Her eyebrows were up-pointed in a tiny frown. "I think you forget Raquel pretty quick. Lew—"

"Yes?"

"Do you love me?"

"No, baby. Not in the way you mean. Not—you know—big one-time, one-and-only love."

She said, "Thank you, Lew."

"What for?"

"For talking to me like a grown woman, not a child. Nobody else does that but you." She sprang from the bed suddenly, picked up her skirt and blouse and said, "I will get your clothes."

When she had slipped out of the door I propped myself up and lit a cigarette. I had the feeling of having had a narrow escape—both Raquel and I had had one. We'd known just enough of each other to let out some of the tensions, but not enough to start any ties. This was exactly the right place to break it all off, and she knew that. Maybe she couldn't say it this clearly, but in her bones she knew it. She was a smart kid, and a good kid, and I hoped she'd be calmer now.

And then I got to thinking how a lot of people are actually smart kids and good kids, a lot of people who don't have much in the way of facts and fancy words stuffed in their heads, but whose brains work just as well as those that have degrees and titles. I thought of the guy who had swung the peavey that broke my nose in Washington state... mine wasn't the first bone belonging to somebody else he had broken; he was crew foreman and he started so many fights, and finished so many, that everybody was afraid to get on his crew: he was, in a dozen ways, a louse and a heel and a no-goodnick—and yet I learned later that this same guy was supporting, absolutely voluntarily, the widow and kid of one of his crewmen who had been killed in a log chute. I thought of the quiet little shoe salesman—a private, first class—who had got up and led our squad when the lieutenant, and then the sergeant got killed. That was the time I picked up the Purple Heart in North Africa. The little shoe salesman had trembled more from fright, and had been the biggest griper all along. He got himself a Silver Star for what he did in fifteen minutes that afternoon. Because when our squad took that bunker, the company moved around the end, and that cleared the way for the battalion, and the regiment followed, and so on. And the little shoe clerk didn't know beans about military tactics, but in his bones he felt that one time what had to be done.

A hot ash from the cigarette fell on my bare stomach and I snapped it off with my finger.

1 thought about Lieutenant of Detectives Jose Ramon Garcia who could flog me with a wet towel one day and take me into his home, giving me shelter and sanctuary the next.

I thought about all the good people I'd ever known, and how none of them had ever been entirely good, and then I turned it upside down and thought of all the bad people who were never entirely bad. I wondered—as I had wondered so many times—how you could ever really know good from bad, especially in the hairline cases, and how you could ever really know when something you did was right, or when it was wrong. Or when it was neither.

And then I came right back to where I'd started and thought that you must know it in your bones, whoever you were, and that they could stuff you with all the philosophies and govern you with all the laws in the world, but your bones would still take care of the tough decisions when they came along.

So what about what I had done ten years ago? How did my bones really feel about that?

I was just about to latch on to an answer when Raquel came back.

She had my clothes; she tossed the pile on the bed and said, "Here."

"Turn your back," I said coyly, taking hold of the covers.

She turned, laughing.

I got out of bed, dressed, and she kept peeking over her shoulder. I was knotting my tie at the mirror when she said, "Lew—"

"What?"

"Jose will know I helped you get away."

I turned, frowning. "That's right. I hadn't thought of that. He'll give you a hard time, won't he?"

She came suddenly forward and clung to my shoulders. "I can't stand it again, Lew! I can't stand how he talks to me like a little child, and looks at me—all the time like I am bad, and he is good, and he is so good he forgives me for it! If maybe sometime he will beat me, that will be okay—but always his eyes telling me what a bad girl I am!" She began to cry. "I am not a bad girl! You know? I am *not!*"

I thought it over for a moment. I'd hoped Raquel had straightened herself out a little. Now, with Jose trying to be kind and actually making her feel guilty as hell, she'd get herself tangled up inside all over again. That wouldn't do. "Maybe I can fix things." I said quietly.

"What do you mean?"

"Maybe I can fix it so Jose doesn't dream you wanted to help me."

Her eyes widened. She must have guessed in that moment what I had in mind.

I made it as easy as I could. I pushed her gently away from me, setting her up, and then I swung fast—aiming as carefully as possible for the exact center of the jaw. I wanted her to go out the first time so I wouldn't have to slug her again. Out she went. Her eyes became glass and she fell slowly and quietly to the floor.

I went back to the mirror and finished knotting my tie. I looked at the fellow in the mirror and said, "You're a heel."

The fellow in the mirror said the same thing.

Chapter Eight

Five Hundred Ridgeway Drive was part of a new apartment development that looked exactly like a tourist court. There was a square U of long buildings, more or less ranch house style, and a sort of landscaped area in the middle. A directory near the entrance gave the numbers of the apartments and the names of the tenants. Nolak, Miss Irene, was 4-C.

I went to the door of 4-C and pressed the buzzer.

It was about noon. It was hot. As I remembered it, there was usually a breeze in this town, even in midsummer, but every once in a while the breeze would forget to blow and then you would know that you were fairly far south. Under my dark blue snappy drape the sweat trickled down my back.

The door opened and a blonde, chemical, with a huge mouse over one eye, looked out at me coldly. She wore a salmon-colored house coat. "I don't want anything today. No insurance, no magazines, nothing." And as she spoke the air was filled with the fruity stink of alcohol.

"You're Irene?"

She raised her eyebrows and tried to focus her eyes a little better, so I knew she was.

"I'm Lew Ross," I said. "Maybe Kitty spoke about me."

Then she dropped her voice very low and said, "Get. Get out of here."

"Hey—wait a minute—"

She slammed the door.

I didn't get this at all. I stood there and hung a puzzled look on the door. Have to think this over. I went and sat on the one step of her porch and lit a cigarette. A car drove into the court. It was a black business coupe and it pulled right up to where I was sitting and a jolly gentleman in rimless glasses stuck his head out of the window. "Hi!" he said. "Irene in?"

I asked who wanted to know.

He looked vaguely frightened then, and I realized what I must look like in this sharp suit, me and my broken nose. Move over, Raft; move over, Widmark. The man said, "I—I'm a regular customer. Irene knows me. She knows who I am."

"A regular customer for what?" I asked.

He got very uncomfortable. "You know. Irene. You know what I mean." Then he drew his head back. "Are you a detective?"

"No," I said, "I'm Irene's father."

"What?"

"Beat it, chum. Irene isn't feeling well today."

"Okay, okay. I just thought I'd drop around." He and the black coupe got off in a hurry.

I got up and went to Irene's door again. This time I knocked instead of using the bell. There was a short silence, then I heard her come to the door and then she called out, "Who is it?"

"Vice squad," I said, making my voice high and nasal. "Open up, Irene!"

She opened the door a crack. I opened it the rest of the way. That sent Irene sprawling to the floor. I got in, slammed the door behind me, and she got up, and without a word, sailed into me.

She went for the eyes with both sets of claws. They were long and red. I grabbed her wrists and she brought her high heel down on my instep. I yelled, "Ow!" She called me a name—the same name Raquel had called me earlier. Then I took my hand from her left wrist, turned it thumb down, and grabbed her right. I spun her around. That way I had her arm in the small of her back.

"Now, Irene," I said, "you behave or I'll break this little arm of yours. You won't be able to do much business with a broken arm. Or don't you use your arms anyway?"

She hiccuped and called me that name again.

"You're getting in a rut, Irene," I said.

I eased her into the living room. It was disordered; newspapers and magazines were all over the floor, and there were bottles and ash trays. The bottles had been emptied; the ash trays hadn't.

"All right, Irene, I'm going to let you go now and you're going to sit quietly over there on the sofa. And if you get up from the sofa, if you even get up from it two inches, I'm going to hang a mouse on your other eye to match the one you've got."

I let go of her arm, pushed her down, and she sat there rock still and stared up at me, as if paralyzed.

I sat down across from her. "Now, Irene, why did you tell me to get out of here?"

Her voice was thick and bitter. She hiccuped again. "You're not Lew Ross. It's another lousy trick."

"But I am Lew Ross. Didn't Kitty mention me?"

"Yes."

"Did she describe me?"

"Yes."

"How did she describe me?"

"Ugly as sin. Only she liked it."

"Well, look at me."

She squinted. "Yes, I guess you are," she said and hiccuped again.

"Now we're getting somewhere. Now maybe you can tell what you mean by 'another lousy trick'?"

"I need a drink first." She closed her eyes tightly, as with pain, shuddered, and opened them again.

"You're plastered now."

"I still need a drink."

"Okay, where is it?"

"Under your chair."

There was a bottle there, all right, green stamp bourbon, half-full. I had a large slug myself without being asked, and then passed it to her. She had a larger slug. She brought the bottle down and said, "I don't usually drink like this. I hardly ever drink at all."

She was one of those remarkable people who can be cooked to the gills, who can barely walk straight, but who can talk what appears to be perfect sense—until you thought it over. I said, "This must be a special occasion."

"Yes," she said. She shuddered again. "Yes, I'll say it is. It's not every day I become a rat."

"What?"

"Rat. R-A-T. A small brown animal with a long tail who likes cheese and can't keep his mouth shut." She took another drink. "That sounds like the dictionary, doesn't it? I'll bet it's got a Latin name, too. The rat, I mean, not the dictionary."

"Irene," I said. "Make sense. Concentrate. All I want to know is where Kitty is."

"Yes," she said dreamily, leaning back, closing her eyes again. "You and six other guys. All you want to know is where Kitty is—"

"What do you mean, six other guys?"

"You know what I was? I was Kitty's best friend. I was the only one'd help her out just because she'd done time in stir. Met her at the employment agency. Yeah, I was looking for a job then, myself, but I changed my mind. Anyway, I got Kitty her job at the Club Mañana. What a pal, what a pal. And what the hell did I care? I'll tell you what I cared. She didn't care what I was, and I didn't care where she'd been." Then she started crying.

"Irene, for God's sake," I said.

She kept crying.

I stepped over to her, took her hands away from her face gently, then slapped her hard, twice, once on each cheek. That brought her out of it.

"Where's Kitty, Irene? What's this about six other guys?"

There was sudden terror in her eyes. They switched back and forth over my face. "You'll kill me."

I started to say I'd never killed anybody in my life, and then remembered differently and said, "Don't be silly. Look, every minute you waste here may be dangerous. I've got to get to Kitty. She needs me. She doesn't know I'm out of jail or she'd be with me now."

"I need another drink," she said, and reached for the bottle.

I grabbed it. "Not until you talk and make sense."

"All right," she said. "All right." I sat down again with the bottle. She looked at the floor and started talking. "They've been here. They came in here last night, a great big guy and another guy, a red-head. They knew I knew Kitty. They said Marty Evans knew I knew Kitty, and he did because I got her the job at his place."

"*You didn't tell them. You didn't tell them where Kitty is—*"

"They asked where. I said I didn't know. Then the big one held me and the red-head, he socked me. That's how I got the black eye."

"*But you didn't tell them—*"

"Then they said they were going to do something else."

"What?"

She put her face in her hands and started sobbing again. I gave her the bottle. She took a long pull, and then she looked at me with dead eyes and said, "I told them. I told them where Kitty was. Then I tried to phone.

There isn't any phone—"

I said, very slowly and evenly, "I ought to kill you."

She just nodded.

"All right, where is she?"

"She's in the Mesa Courts on the highway, West. Number Eight."

"She *was* there," I said. I got up, shaking with rage, dizzy, sick. I went out and slammed the door. I walked over to the highway, found a gas station and called a taxi. I half-hoped the driver would be Fish-mouth. I had something in me that needed to be taken out on somebody.

The driver wasn't Fish-mouth. He was a long, tall john in a cowboy hat and he talked Texas. "Wheah to, mistuh?" I told him, and he put the taxi into a sleepy jog. "A buck for every minute under fifteen you make it in," I told him. We broke into a canter.

We passed through the center of town. I kept looking head, not seeing. I kept thinking: *it's my fault, it's my fault, too.* Kitty could have left town easily enough; I was sure she had the money, but she'd stayed to help save my neck, in case she had to. She did this knowing Evans and his gorillas would be looking for her, partly to teach her a lesson, partly to keep her from doing any more damage. That was guts in my book. So I had finally met a girl who was pretty *and* smart *and* had courage—and now if I ever saw her again it would probably be in a funeral parlor.

We came into the Mesa Courts on two wheels. "Twelve minutes," said Texas proudly, looking at his wrist watch. I paid the fare and gave him an extra three.

"You want me tuh wait?"

I nodded and ran toward Court Number Eight. It was a crummy place; it needed paint and it needed stucco and judging from the empty car ports it needed customers. Kitty must have picked it figuring they'd never dream of looking for her here. The sun was still beating down. The shadows were sharp, like dark paper cut out and pasted in place. I knocked loudly on the door of Number Eight. It seemed very quiet inside; the knock echoed. I tried the door and it was locked, and then I moved over to the window, looked inside and saw a dim, empty room. The bed wasn't made and a chair was overturned.

I tried the window. That was locked, too. But it was an old window with wooden frames, rickety in its tracks. I went back to Texas who was standing by the cab watching me with a long, blank face.

"Got a tire iron?"

"What are you studyin' on, mister—burglin' that place?"

"I sure am. If you don't want to see something against the law you can turn your back."

"I ain't so sure you ought to burgle that place, mister." His face was still blank.

I said, "A buck for every minute under ten it takes you to get that tire iron."

He thought that over for five seconds. Then he opened the door of the cab, reached under the seat, and handed me a tire iron. I gave him ten bucks. I went back to the window, stuck the tire iron in the crack and pried it open. I stepped inside.

I looked all around, on the floor, under the bed, under the covers, in the bureau drawers, in the cracks of the upholstered chair, everywhere, hoping desperately to find some kind of clue, anything. There were clothes in the drawers, and there were things like nail polish and bobby pins around, so it looked as though Kitty hadn't yet checked out officially. Maybe she'd only gone for a pack of cigarettes or something. Maybe they hadn't gotten to her yet. Maybe they didn't really intend to bother with her after all. These wild hopes kept galloping through me.

I went into the tiny bathroom. The first thing I saw was the handwriting on the mirror. It was red, a hurried scrawl, and it had been done with lipstick. All it said was:

ROOM 412, APACHE—KITTY.

I stared at it for several seconds while the dawn came up. Then I could begin to picture what might have happened. Somebody—Wallace and Varsity for a guess—out there in the other room, and Kitty saying she'd be right with them, but the least they could do would be to let her put a face on. And then this writing on the mirror, just in case. How she knew they were taking her to Room 412 in the Apache Hotel, I wasn't sure. But this was no time to let a small detail like that be bothersome.

I went back to the taxi and said to Texas, "This sure is your lucky day. Now you get a buck for every minute under ten you get me to the Apache Hotel."

"Hop in," he said, "we're already there."

A couple of other cabs were parked in front of the Apache and Texas pulled up behind them. I shoved money at him and ran into the lobby. The desk clerk was busy and I didn't recognize any of the bellboys. For all I knew they were still holding my room, on the second floor, open for me. My bag and two shirts and a toothbrush and one thing and another were probably still in it. No time now to find out.

I took the elevator up to the fourth floor.

I guess the itching in my palms and the prickling in my insteps first hit me as I was walking along the corridor toward Room 412. I guess until that moment I'd been too excited, too sick and miserable to smell a rat very quickly. But now, as I walked, I had this terrible, unaccountable feeling of danger. That writing on the mirror. How *could* Kitty have known where they were taking her? Why would they take a chance on letting her step into the bathroom alone to powder her nose? It didn't add up; it didn't add up at all.

There was a sudden clatter behind me and I jumped. I whirled, crouching.

It was only one of the chambermaids carrying a bucket and mop from the closet down the hall.

I got a bright idea.

I rose from my crouch and walked quickly toward the chambermaid. She was bone-thin, Spanish-American, and wore rimless glasses. She looked more like a schoolteacher than a chambermaid.

I dug into my dwindling supply of bucks, took a dollar bill and put it into her hand. She stared at it and said, "Huh?"

"I'm planning a surprise party," I said. "I want to make sure my friend is in Room 412. All you have to do is knock on the door and ask him if he wants his room cleaned. I think he'll say no. All I want to do is see if he's in."

It seemed to convince her. She didn't ask me why I didn't phone from downstairs or anything. She stuffed the dollar in her apron, didn't nod or answer, but limped on down the hall toward 412.

I pressed myself into the niche where the elevator doors were. I could see 412 from there. The chambermaid knocked timidly, and almost immediately the door opened and half a face came out. It looked disappointed when it saw the chambermaid.

"You want your room cleaned now, huh?"

"Hell, no. It's already been cleaned. Beat it." The door slammed.

I had recognized that half a face. It was square and the mouth was turned down at the corners, like the mouth of a barracuda. And now I was thinking a little more clearly. That door had opened very quickly: Fish-mouth had been expecting some one. Me, for a fine fat guess. And he wouldn't be alone there in 412—but at the same time it was odds Kitty wouldn't be with him. That writing on Kitty's mirror had been for *my* benefit. Hell, now that I thought of it, it hadn't looked like a woman's handwriting anyway. No, they just wanted to be sure I'd come to the Apache Hotel one way or the other; they probably had a bellboy or someone bribed to let them know when I asked for my key at the desk. That would mean they wouldn't be planning mayhem on my person right here in the hotel, too many connections, but that was no comfort—they could still take me wherever they wanted to do it.

The chambermaid came back. "Was that all right, huh?"

"Terrific," I said. "You ought to be in the movies."

She just stared at me blankly for a second and then went back to the closet. I lit a cigarette to give me something to do while I stood there and thought for another few seconds. One thing I could do; I could try to get Lieutenant Garcia and an army of cops. But that would take time, and there wasn't much time, and besides I owed Fish-mouth a little something that I didn't think Garcia would let me pay back. If I could just get into 412; if I could just have a drop of about two seconds on whoever was in there waiting.

I thought suddenly of my own room on the second floor. It was separated from the one next to it by a door—that's how the heavy equipment salesmen had kept me awake. I went to the chambermaid again. "Look, is there an adjoining room to 412?"

"Yes, 413."

"Door between the two?"

"There's doors between all the odd and even sets except sixes and sevens," she said.

I gave her five bucks this time. "Let me into 413, will you? And give me a key to 412."

She looked frightened. "I don't think I can. We're not supposed—"

I took the five bucks back. "All right, I'll think of some other joke to play on good old Charley."

She took the five bucks back. "I guess I can," she said.

She knew how to open a door without making the key rattle. I blew her a kiss as she stepped out into the hall again and closed the door of 413 behind me.

The door leading to 412 was just around the corner of a little square bathroom. It was an ordinary door, no more, no less, and I could hear a radio playing on the other side. Voices, too. I put my eye to the keyhole. There, handsomely framed, was a stuffed chair facing away from me, and just over the top of the stuffed chair was a closely-cropped red head. Varsity was the one who was talking. "You got to exercise," he was saying, "whether you got muscles or not. It don't make no difference. The exercise burns the poison off. That's a scientific fact."

"It's a lotta hooey," said Fish-mouth's voice. "You think these ath-a-letes like Joe Louis and all exercise all the time? Look, I drive these fighters and ball players around when they come to town. They exercise in night clubs."

"Just the same when they exercise they burn the poisons off," said Varsity. "They'd all last longer if they didn't take that poison. You know alcohol can kill a man? You put grain alcohol in a tube in a guy's nose, you'll kill him."

"He's crazy enough to drink it through his nose he ought to drop dead," said Fish-mouth. Then I heard his steps across the room. "You think that broken-nosed bum, Ross, is really gonna show up?"

"How do I know? All I know is Marty says to wait here."

"Okay. You wanna play some gin? Penny a point."

"I don't gamble," said Varsity. "The odds are against you."

"What do you mean? You got as good a chance to win as I have."

"Yeah, but once you start the gambling, you get the habit. You know what habits come from? Conditioned reflexes. You can take a white rat, see, and give him a shock every time he tries to eat—"

"Why don't you go back to college?" said Fish-mouth in a disgusted voice.

"I would," said Varsity, "if I hadn't banged my kneecap. If I didn't have a bum knee-cap I'd be playing fullback somewhere right now."

"Okay, fullback," said Fish-mouth. "You hold the fort while I go powder my nose."

I moved fast then. I stepped back to the desk of Room 413 and found what I hoped to find: a glass inkwell, round and solid. I took my shoe off, not bothering to unlace it. I took my sock off, too. I dropped the inkwell in the sock, knotted the sock just above the inkwell and let it dangle. I stepped back to the door and then, holding my breath until it hurt, turned the key in the lock. It clicked. It sounded as loud as a pistol shot to me, but I guess it wasn't. Or maybe the radio kept Varsity from hearing it. Anyway, when I opened the door, there was Varsity's cropped red head, at about the level of my chest, and in perfect position.

I swung the sock and the inkwell just as hard as I possibly could.

Chapter Nine

Varsity stiffened, rose an inch, and for an instant I thought I hadn't done any good. Then he fell back again and his head rolled loosely to one side. The water was running in the bathroom. The door was just partly open. I stepped quickly into the narrow little hall that ran between the bathroom and the closet, and I flattened myself against the wall next to the bathroom door.

Fish-mouth stepped out. I grabbed him immediately, spun him the other way, held my forearm against his Adam's apple, under his chin, and jammed my knuckle into the small of his back. "I've got a gun," I said, "so don't move. Don't even breathe."

He did breathe, but in gasps. I took my forearm away from his neck, patted his side pockets and found a lump. It turned out to be a short barreled thirty-two revolver. I took it. I shoved him into the middle of the room, pointing his own gun at him.

"Turn around," I said.

His eyes were wide, his face was a little gray. I said, "Now we're going to finish our little talk. What's your name, baby?"

"Smith. Wilbur A. Smith." Eyes still wide.

"All right, Smitty. It's crowded in here. See if you can lug Varsity into the other room."

It was hard work, and he grunted, and he was already sweating, but he managed to do it. I took the time to put my shoe back on. Then I locked the door on Varsity so he would sleep better. I turned to Smitty, "This time, no tire iron."

"What—what are you gonna do?"

I dropped the gun in my pocket. "Even-Stephen, Smitty. I won't use the gun, and you haven't got a tire iron."

Smitty started to cry. He dropped to his knees and said, "Please. Please, please—oh, please—"

For just another moment there was still hate in my blood, and I could feel it pumping thickly through my neck, half choking me, and for just another moment I wanted to beat Wilbur A. Smith into a bright red mash. And then it left. I felt only sick instead; I felt dirty and contaminated. I didn't want revenge any more. To hell with revenge. I wasn't playing that way any more. I was through with hate and revenge because they were only parts of fear, and I wasn't afraid any more. Of what wasn't I afraid? I didn't know exactly; none of it was clear in my mind yet. Later. Later I would think it out—if I lived that long.

I walked over to Smitty and slapped him several times across the head, hard, but without passion, with no feeling at all. I was just doing a job now. "All right, Smitty. Where's the girl? Where's Miss Fountain?"

"I don't know! I don't know!" He lifted his face and he had real tears on his cheeks.

I kicked him under the chin. He went over backward, cried, and covered his head with his arms; I yanked him up again, held him, and slapped him one-two, one-two, one-two just like that, on each cheek in turn, using the palm and the back of my hand. "Smitty," I said, "I think I'll kill you. I think I'll kill you with my hands."

"No, no! I'll tell—I'll tell."

"Tell, then. And hurry."

"She's at the Club Mañana. They got her in the private office there. They were waiting for Boss—he's outa town, but he ought to be in by now."

"Your cab in front, Smitty?"

He nodded.

"Give me the keys."

He gave them to me.

"Look at me, Smitty."

He had to lift his head to do that. I hit him and knocked him out.

I walked out of the room and locked the door. I went downstairs and threw the key on the desk as I passed. Outside I saw the two taxis standing there, and the driver was sitting in one, so I figured the other must be Smitty's. It was. I got in, drove off, and headed east.

I got out of the central business section just fast enough to make time but not fast enough to be stopped for reckless driving. As soon as I hit the long climb through the Heights and past the University section I stepped on it. I streaked through Swank Hill, missing people.

Now I was past the clustered lawns and houses and on the long stretch of open road lined by gas stations, hamburger stands and tourist courts. Here and there a factory warehouse of pumic block was going up. Auto sales lots; trailer courts. Far to my left, down in the valley, were the shining roofs of the new aircraft plant. There was smoke in the valley. There was dust, here on the heights—

Ten years ago the air had been clear. Ten years ago all this had been sagebrush plain, a long, sloping plain to the mountains. Sometimes here we'd take chuck wagon rides, and sometimes we'd take a Saturday afternoon off and go out and pot jackrabbits, or just walk. We'd run into bunches of cattle in those days; we'd see antelope galloping off in the distance. Sometimes we'd find a lone cowboy, his face weather-cracked and his hands rope-calloused, and he would always stop and visit a while, one leg over the saddle. There was time to visit a while in those days. So you would sit and talk, for maybe the space of one cigarette, and although the city, down in the shadowy valley, would always be in sight, you would feel that you were miles away in space and time. You would feel that big, unhurried, plenty-for-everybody feel of the west.

Maybe, I thought, *we've all killed somebody, or something; maybe that's why none of us can feel as we used to feel ten years ago, back in another era. Maybe we all need to take what's coming to us, and then we'll feel better.*

I shook my head and made myself stop thinking. The kind of a job I had ahead, thinking would only get in the way. I had no plan—except to be careful when I got there —but I did know one thing. I'd get Kitty out. Some way, somehow. If I had to stop six bullets, get my legs broken, and the top of my head blown away, I would get Kitty out of there.

I left the long, straight stretch of highway and entered the curving road through the canyon. I came over the rise some minutes later and saw the top of the Club Mañana with its neon sign, now unlit and naked, just ahead. I pulled the car over on the shoulder and stopped it in the concealment of rocks and junipers. I got out, and headed on foot through the scrub and cactus toward the Club Mañana.

There was a big, bright green Cadillac parked out in front, and it had a Florida license. Nothing else, nobody in sight. I moved in the shadows of the evergreens, looked into the Cadillac, and saw the ignition keys hanging in the dashboard. I looked past it, toward the building. Nobody in there, at least not in the entrance hall, where both the hatcheck closet and switchboard were bare. I took a couple of quick steps, got the keys from the Cadillac and dropped them into my pocket. This might, this just might turn into a getaway car....

I circled to the rear of the building, where the private entrance to Marty's office was. This was just a plain door, of weathered wood, with the paint chipped off in places, and it looked like the door to a tool shed, and that, I supposed, was the idea.

I took Smitty's revolver out of my pocket. I glanced at it, checking it. Only one thing to do now, a long chance that I would have to take. I would need several breaks, all in succession. First the door would have to be open, so that I could barge in quickly. Second, anybody in there would have to be surprised and stay surprised for several seconds. Third, I would have to shoot straight without much time for aim, and hit as many people as possible and be sure to miss Kitty.

Outside of that it was a cinch.

I took a deep breath and started for the door.

Somebody behind me said, "Drop that gun and keep your hands away from your sides and hold real, real still."

A moment later I knew I should have whirled and fired, but by that time I had already done what the man said.

I heard footsteps behind me, and then from the shrubbery on either side of me appeared two other people. I recognized one of the bouncers from the gambling room—a stocky man with sideburns and a mustache. He was on my right. On my left was a little, dark complected guy in a tight-waisted palm beach suit and a cocoanut straw hat with a band that looked like a municipal flag for Miami. The one behind stepped around in front and he was almost the twin of the one in the cocoanut straw except that he wore a lightweight felt. Not local talent, these boys. They looked Big City. They each carried long-barreled thirty-eight revolvers, the kind you use for target work.

"You know what?" said cocoanut straw. "I think this is the guy the college clown was supposed to bring."

"Doubtless," said lightweight felt. "Frisk him down."

"Hands up higher," said cocoanut straw pleasantly. He patted my sides, forearms and legs. He found the keys.

Lightweight felt stepped up to the door and knocked. It was Marty

Evans's voice that answered. "Yes? Who is it?"

"Gigi, Mr. Evans," said lightweight felt. "Can you step out here a minute?"

Marty Evans opened the door. His eyebrows went way up when he saw me, but he pulled them down again in a hurry and then his tan, smooth face in its frame of white hair was as tan and smooth as ever. "Well, if it isn't Lew," he said. "Just the man we want to see. I guess you better step inside, Lew—and keep your hands up there while you're at it."

I came forward.

"You want us to do anything, or anything, Mr. Evans?" asked Gigi.

Evans shook his head. "Not right now. Just stay outside there and wait for Mr. Haynes. And nice work, boys. How did you find him?"

"Snoopin' around. He comes up to the door here and pulls a rod." Gigi had retrieved the rod and he held it up.

Evans smiled at me. "Still the big hero; still the lone wolf, eh?"

I said, "I need a drink. Got one in there?"

"By all means," said Marty Evans. "Come in and have a drink. I guess, under the circumstances, that's the least we can do for you."

So I went in and the door was shut behind me.

Kitty was there, across the room. She got up and said, "Lew!"

Wallace was towering beside her. He said, "Shut up," and pushed her down again. That was when I first noticed that one side of her face was red and swollen. I started forward, then held myself, and stood there, trembling.

Then Marty's desk caught my eye. It was on my left. I turned and saw a stranger sitting behind it. The Mr. Haynes Marty had mentioned, for a guess. He was looking at me in a curious, quiet flat way. He was not exactly fat, but he was heavy and round and he sat in the chair so that only his shoulders and head were visible above the edge of the desk. Evans' cast-iron figurine, Lady Luck, almost hid him completely. He had his hands in his lap. He was beautifully, impeccably dressed; his gray suit had a cut and sheen that yelled money. It wasn't draped, and the shoulders were his own. His eyes were heavy-lidded, like the eyes of a tortoise, and behind a pair of heavy, horn-rimmed glasses, they bulged.

I knew this was Boss. Nobody had to tell me.

"So this is the young fellow," said Boss. He ticked off his words very carefully, in the way that people who learn about words late in life are apt to do. Just a little afraid he might mispronounce one. "So this is the young man who has been causing all the difficulty." The way he said it was "causing gall."

"The name's Lew Ross," I said.

"How do you do," said Boss. "My name is Carroll Haynes."

It rang a bell. Not a very loud bell, but enough for me to recall reading about this and that investigation over the years, where Carroll Haynes had been named one of the big lads of gambling, nationwide gambling. Progress had come to these parts. I looked at Evans and said, "Shall Boss and I shake hands?"

Kitty said, "Oh, Lew, you shouldn't have! You shouldn't have come!"

Evans said, "You just better sit down, Lew. Sit down and have a drink."

I sat down. Same chair I'd sat in when Evans had first offered me a job. Funny, I had a momentary feeling it was that other time, that it was happening all over again. But only momentary. Evans was across the room at his little liquor cabinet; he had swung the doors out and was saying: "Bourbon or scotch?"

"Whatever costs the most," I said.

The Boss chuckled softly, but kept staring at me.

I looked at Kitty again. She was as beautiful as ever. Her off-center eyes were as madly attractive as ever. And as bright as ever. Today she wore a gabardine suit and a black blouse, and in spite of the fact that I didn't think she'd been allowed to powder her nose, it looked powdered. She had a face on. A wonderful face. She smiled at me, too.

"Everybody's smiling," I said, and then looked at Wallace's doughy glare and added, "Except you, you big stoop."

Wallace took a step forward and Evans said, "Not now."

Wallace stepped back, his brows a thundercloud.

"Mr. Evans told me," said Boss in his slow, artificial diction, "that you were quite a wisecracker."

"Mr. Evans told me nothing about you, Boss, so your ugly puss comes to me as a complete surprise."

Boss chuckled again.

Wallace said, "You better be careful, punk, how you talk to Boss."

Boss waved his hand. It was soft and pudgy. "Don't worry, Wallace. He doesn't bother me." He was looking at me as he talked. "Although I must admit he gives me a worry or two. How did you get out of jail? I suppose Miss Fountain's statement helped. I suppose the police think now that our little organization had something to do with Mr. Klein's unfortunate death."

Wallace said, "Ha!" and I knew then who had pulled the trigger.

"This makes you and Miss Fountain important witnesses. So I must admit you give me a worry or two," said Boss.

"Hear that, Lew?" said Evans, stepping toward me and handing me a drink. "You worry us."

I leaned back and sipped the drink. It was bourbon. They all watched me. They all seemed to be putting something off, saving it, like dessert.

"You know something?" I said. "You guys are scared. What do you think of that? Every one of you guys is scared gutless."

Boss smiled, but Wallace growled. "Who's scared?" said Wallace.

"I'll tell you why you're all scared," I said, shifting in the chair. "You break your necks to find Kitty and me. A couple of unimportant people. You send lugs after us—Varsity and Smitty are both resting nicely in Room 412 at the Apache, by the way. You're probably going to kill both of us." I was watching Boss's eyes real closely, and I knew I'd made a good guess—though a fat lot of satisfaction that was. I said, "People don't kill unimportant people unless they're scared—real scared."

Boss folded his hands. "I'm afraid I disagree with you, young man. There's no feelings whatsoever connected with anything we might do. It's business. It was business to get rid of Ozzy Klein—he was a fresh fellow like you, you know?"

Wallace said, "I like to take care of fresh fellows."

Boss continued. "It's going to be hard enough for us to have operations here the way things are. With you and the young lady to talk, it might even be dangerous. So you see how it is, don't you, young man?"

I looked around the room quickly, measuring with my eye the distance from me to Wallace, from Wallace to Evans, who was standing by the liquor cabinet, and then from Evans to Boss at the desk. I got up, as if to fumble for a cigarette.

Boss said quietly, "I wouldn't."

"No," said Evans, "I wouldn't try anything. Even if you managed to jump Wallace, or the rest of us, you wouldn't get out of here. Gigi and the boys are outside. You couldn't even phone for help—because the switchboard isn't plugged in. And you'd never get to the switchboard without attracting Gigi's attention."

Wallace said, "Don't tell him nothin'. Let him try somethin'. Just let him."

"And mess up my office?" said Evans. "Nothing doing."

Boss was still looking at me. Now he spoke to Evans. "Marty," he said, "it certainly is funny. Back in bigger places where we operate we don't have to do this kind of thing for a long time. It even gets a little old fashioned. But out here in the desert, in the sticks, we run into a situation right off. Isn't that funny? Maybe it's because people out here don't know enough to be afraid. Maybe this will be a good thing; maybe it will teach some people what to be afraid of."

While he was talking I glanced at Kitty. In a way her face was perfectly blank, and yet in another way it wasn't. She seemed to be holding back an idea, a nod, a go-ahead. It's hard to describe. Maybe it was even some kind of mental telepathy. I don't know. But I could almost hear her voice in my head, saying: *"Take a chance, Lew. Jump them, Lew. Take a chance."*

Boss said, "Well, I guess we're wasting time. We'll let Gigi supervise. He's done it before." He started to get up. Standing, he was no more than five feet tall. It was something to look at. And everybody was looking at him— and that was what I wanted.

I did two things at once; I did them mighty fast. I threw my drink in Evans' face, and I took a good, hard-flying leap at Wallace. In a way, they'd outsmarted themselves on this one: they'd told me nice and smugly how I couldn't possibly do it, and so they very much weren't expecting me to do it. It was an even better surprise than if they had never thought about it.

Wallace was especially surprised. I saw his face explode with it as I hit him; I struck him in his huge, billowy chest with my shoulder, and at the same time brought my knee forward, fast. Evans was still spluttering with the drink in his face. Wallace teetered, and for a second I thought he wasn't going to go over. Kitty took care of that. She grabbed his coat and pulled him over. As soon as he hit the floor I kicked hard, putting my whole body behind it. The point of my shoe caught his chin, and my heel scraped along his face. These were my new cordovans; expensive shoes. They always put leather heels on expensive shoes. I jumped, then, and came down on his face. He made a horrible, choking sound and grabbed his face with his hands—

All of this took three seconds, possibly four. All this time I waited for the sound of a gun and the slam of a bullet in my back, because I'd taken a gamble that Boss, upstanding character that he was, wouldn't be packing a rod.

So far, no shot. I whirled to the left. Evans had wiped the drink from his eyes and was jumping to get to the desk. I could guess that there was a gun in a drawer, and he knew which one. I picked up the chair I'd been sitting on and threw it at him. He ducked—away from the desk. I moved toward him as his head came up, and I clipped it, brushing his jaw. Marty Evans wasn't built for rough stuff. That gentle breeze of a punch knocked him hard into the wall. I heard his head crack against the plaster.

Then I knew suddenly that Wallace was behind me—heard him, I guess—and instead of turning to face him I bent fast, and when I felt him hit me I grabbed him and threw him forward, over my head. His chest hit the desk. He slid. He crashed into Boss, who was trying to get from behind the desk and to the door.

Evans was trying to get up again, and couldn't quite make it. Kitty, behind and to the right, was moving, doing something—I couldn't see what. I jumped to the top of the desk. Wallace was on top of Boss and trying to remove himself.

My foot hit Lady Luck, the Goddess of Chance. I picked her up. Lady

Luck weighed maybe five pounds and the shape of her head and shoulders was just right for the hand. I swung Lady Luck down on Wallace's skull, and she broke in half, but Wallace didn't know that. Wallace fell hard, pinning Boss to the floor and keeping him there.

I spun around then, to see if Marty Evans had managed to get up yet. He hadn't, but it wouldn't have made any difference if he had, because Kitty had moved to the desk, opened the top left drawer and found the pistol Marty was looking for. It was a thirty-five, just like the one he'd given me. It looked very black and efficient in Kitty's hot little hand.

"Baby-baby, you're wonderful," I said. "If we ever get out of this, I'll marry you."

"If we leave any witnesses alive," she said, "I'll hold you to that."

Boss squeezed out from under Wallace and she pointed the gun at him and said, "Sit over there with Marty. You two will like it together."

Boss, with five-foot dignity, and holding his broken glasses, stepped over to the wall and sat down beside Evans.

I held out my hand and Kitty gave me the gun. "This is all very chummy," I said. "But now how *do* we get out of the joint?"

Kitty laughed.

"What are you laughing at?"

"How Marty Evans brought me in here one time when everything was closed up and made a pass at me."

"Did he do that? Shame on you, Marty." He blinked. He wasn't hearing or seeing very well. Then I said to Kitty, "So what?"

She said, "If he hadn't brought me in here I wouldn't have seen him make a call when the switchboard wasn't plugged in. I wouldn't have known that the operator always leaves an outside line through before she goes. That's why I looked at you that way, Lew—hoping you'd take a chance."

"You're wonderful." That was all I could think or say. "You're wonderful." I went over to the phone and got a dial tone. I dialed the operator. "What is it you're supposed to say? Oh, yes—" and then, as the operator answered, "I want a policeman. Better make it several."

Chapter Ten

I sat in Dean Torwell's office on the second floor of the County Courthouse. I could look diagonally across the park and see City Hall. It was a summer morning, cool in this high Southwest, as summer mornings usually are, and the sun was bright, and the leaves of the trees were sharply outlined. The sounds of cars and trucks and busses and the feeling of the city coming to life drifted through the open window. The birds were singing.

Dean Torwell had a funny smile on his fat, infantile face and his little green eyes were looking at me very closely. He had summoned me here. To coach me for the trial, I supposed—they had put them all on the same indictment for Ozzy Klein's murder, most of them as accessories: Boss, Evans, Wallace and Varsity. Gigi and his friend were on a separate slip for attempted murder and conspiracy. Gambling was being done very quietly and in very few places all of a sudden. The Club Mañana was padlocked. Garcia had met me on the way here, looking very pleased, and I thought it was the crime situation in general, until he said:

"You know that girl of mine, Raquel? Something happened to her all of a sudden. She's really on the ball. She wants to study to be a policewoman!"

I said, "Oh?" and let an eyebrow float.

"You know something?" Garcia went on. "I think it was that sock on the jaw you gave her, eh?"

"Yeah," I said, "it must have been that." And I had to wait until he turned away before I could let the sigh out.

But now I had other things on my mind. And in my craw. I resented being called here by Torwell.

"Well, Lew," said the Boy District Attorney jollily, "you did a wonderful job. Congratulations. I might even congratulate myself—I had a hunch you might swing it, you know."

"Listen, Torwell," I said, "I'll cooperate with you in the trials, but I don't have to like you. Have you got that in your chubby head?"

He looked like a wounded doe.

I tapped his desk. "If Kitty hadn't been in a mess I wouldn't have done anything. I wouldn't have gone through with that harebrained scheme of yours at all."

"I suppose not." His voice was sad.

"So now if you have any business, let's get to it. Kitty's waiting outside. We have a date across the street in City Hall, first floor. Where they sell marriage licenses."

"Oh? Congratulations."

"Thank you. But it won't be a fancy wedding. And no reception—and I guess, damn it, no honeymoon. Not even... not even part of a honeymoon."

Deany-boy said, "I beg your pardon?" He meant he didn't savvy.

"As soon as the wedding's over," I said wearily, "I'm going to turn myself in to Garcia. Then we'll take our chances on the future—the long future—Kitty and I."

"Turn yourself in? For what?"

"For killing a man ten years ago. I'm getting it off my mind, finally. I think

with luck—and in this state, where they don't seem to mind a fair fight—
I might get as little as five years for manslaughter. Whatever it is, I'm taking it without a squawk."

Torwell started laughing then.

"Very funny," I said. "You'll pardon me if I don't join in."

"Lew," he said, still laughing, "I have a wedding present for you. I really have, Lew. Or maybe I should call you Lester."

Lester.

I stiffened.

Lester was my real name....

Well, he'd know it, of course, from that incident ten years ago. He'd
known all about it, as he had all the time. I said, "If you're going to double-cross me and turn me in, do me one favor. Wait. Just wait until I finish over at City Hall."

"Lew," he said, "it wouldn't make any difference if I double-crossed you
or not. Because you're not going to be able to turn yourself in for anything.
At least you're going to have one hell of a time proving your own case
against yourself."

I said, "What?"

"You hit a man in Seely's Canyon Rest, didn't you? Got into a fight over
a girl or something. You invited him outside, and he slammed his head on
a rock when he fell. You saw he was dead, and ran away."

"You seem to know all about it."

"I do. And here's your wedding present. The man you hit died from
drowning."

"I don't get it."

"*Officially*, he died from drowning. We want it to stay that way."

"What in the hell are you talking about?"

"Lew, I hope you're going to be sensible about this. I was city attorney
when all this happened; not a regular, salaried job, but retained by the city.
Anyway, I knew most of what was going on. The mayor, you may remember, had been elected on his promises to clean up the vice in town—although compared with what we have now there was precious little vice.
The District Attorney's office—the D.A. was in the same party—had
hired some special investigators. One of these was a man from Kansas; I'd
forgotten his name, and I don't suppose it even matters now."

Mayor's vice campaign... man from Kansas... drowning. I remembered
the news items I'd read in the *Times-Dispatch* dated the morning after I'd
run away. The recollection must have shown in my face, because Torwell
paused. "Go on," I told him.

"The town was pretty old-fashioned in those days. Surprising what a lot
of difference ten years will make. We didn't have modern gadgets in our

police department, and we didn't bother to investigate people very closely. The man the D.A. hired for an investigator had a prison record, but more than that he was wanted for questioning about a murder in Kansas. Seemed he'd been a crooked private detective, always in a mess. We found all that out later."

"But who threw him in the crick? And how could anybody say he drowned when the blood was coming out of his ears?"

"Let me finish, Lew. This man—let's call him Smith—talked himself into an investigator's job with the D.A. He immediately started in to take graft from the few small gambling places around town, promising them they'd stay in business. A couple of the municipal administration fellows were actually in with him on this. The Chief of Police was one. So, that night, Seely himself discovered the body out there and called the Chief. Smith had just been demanding payments from Seely. Seely didn't want the scandal of a murder, or a manslaughter, connected with his place, and he told the Chief this in no uncertain terms. He said if the Chief didn't do something about it he'd squawk to the newspapers and blow the whole graft thing wide open. Can you guess what happened now?"

I spoke through a half-daze. "The cops came—removed Smith—dumped his body in the river, and then fished it out again. The death certificate said by accidental drowning—"

"That's it, more or less." Torwell leaned back in his chair and scratched his dimple. "And as I said, that's the way we want it. There's another election coming up, you know, and as much as I deplore this thing, it wouldn't look good for our party to drag it out into the open now."

"It stinks. It's rotten," I said.

"Yes," agreed Torwell amiably.

"It makes me feel like shouting the whole story out."

"But you won't. There's the manslaughter charge you'll face if you do. And believe me, Lew, I'll work awfully hard to make it stick."

"Maybe," I said slowly, "I want to face this charge. Maybe that's why I came back here in the first place."

"So you're turning yourself in, Lew?" Torwell gave me the clinical, objective look of a botanist examining a daisy. "Well just let me ask you this: how long ago did all this happen?"

"You know as well as I do—ten years."

"And what have you been doing in the meantime?" I had no swift sharp answer for him so I kept quiet. "I'll tell you, Lew. You've been running. And I'll tell you another thing: you aren't going to stop running now."

I looked up at the sun slanting through the window. I looked toward the corridor where Kitty was waiting for me; I knew exactly how her face looked at this moment, bright and shining, full of hope for the good things that had been so long in coming to her—that might never come.

And I knew Torwell had me licked.

"Okay, Lew?" he said. He squeezed out of his chair to usher me to the door.

"You'll hear from me in a day or so, Torwell," I said.

"Sure, sure, Lew. Glad to see you around any time."

In the corridor Kitty took my arm, squeezed it, and said, "That was quick." She looked wonderful this morning. I don't know what she wore exactly; something Navy blue, but it was wonderful.

"Quick and dirty," I said. "Want to hear a sad story? About a bad conscience? And a weakling?"

"Any sex in it?" she said.

I hugged her. Then I told her the story.

"I love you," was her comment.

"Let's get out of here," I said. We went out onto the courthouse steps, and started going down them. And with each step the thing she had just said was working in me.

Halfway down the steps I stopped. "Say that again—what you said after I told you my story."

Kitty's face was very serious now. She said it again—"I love you."

I turned around, facing her, and kissed her hard. Then I started walking back up the steps.

Torwell would still be in his office. I wanted him to hear me tell my story to the papers.

I had lived too long with a dirty conscience. She said she loved me. Maybe she would wait....

The End

House of Evil
by Clayre and Michel Lipman

For Gene, Leo, and Rosa

ONE

The girl at The Red Parrot was a slut.

The name she usually gave was Nina Valjean and she sat with a half-emptied glass of ginger ale before her on the bar. Tawny brown hair tumbled loosely around sweat-gleaming shoulders as she let her glance search again among the men in the place, and then turn nervously toward the doorway. Nina was not over thirty despite the centuries of weariness in her eyes; there was even a hint of dignity and breeding in her casual movements, the mechanical lifting of the glass to her lips, the deep drag at a cigarette, the sweep of an arm. She was wearing a flashy black dress covered with a scattering of rhinestones. Her only jewelry was a pair of rhinestone earrings.

Bennie moved to her end of the bar, polishing a glass. They both looked at the clock. Midnight.

"Quiet as hell this week," Bennie said. He had a genial face set with small black-button eyes.

"You said it, honey." Nina's voice was rich, sultry, tired.

"Always the same before elections." Bennie spoke with a professional heartiness.

"It's not the elections—it's the amateur competition."

"Yeah, or the lousy weather. You'd be better off like I say, kid. Get yourself lined up with a good house somewhere. You can make a hundred or more clear a week." His glance on Nina was calculating, property wise.

She looked at him, her pupils pinpoints in the gray-green irises. "It's not enough, Bennie."

He polished a martini glass carefully. "I been doin' what I can for you, kid. Hell, get what time it is. There'll be nothing doing any more tonight. You might's well go on home and get some sleep."

"Sleep? I've *got* to make it tonight, Bennie. No fix since noon yesterday.... My God, Bennie, I'm bending now, and that stinking Vernie won't carry me. Cash, he wants. Cash on the drumhead every time!"

"Take it easy, kid. Something might show yet. You figure maybe Smith'll be back again tonight?"

Nina shivered. "*That* guy! I hope I never, *never* see *him* again."

Bennie walked away. Nina wet her lips. The nerves along her spine began to burn, warning of horrors to come. The hand that lifted the cigarette was trembling. She knew the shallowness of Bennie's apparent sympathy. As long as he got his split. As long as Vernie got his dough for a fix. While there was still a buck to be squeezed from her.

Nina slipped from her stool, sought a tall, almost indistinguishable man in one of the back booths, slid to the seat beside him. "Vernie—listen—"

"You know better than to ask, kid. What's the matter? You been workin' this week."

"Yes, but what do I get out of it? After Bennie gets his cut and the doc takes his and I have to buy a dress for the one that got torn up, and I keep the rent paid in advance or get thrown out, what does it leave me?"

Vernie shrugged. "*I* got to pay cash."

Hunger that was not hunger dug deeper talons into her as the burning grew. "Twelve dollars, Vernie. Every cent I got. How about letting me make up the balance...."

"Naw. I got all the women I want." He mopped his face delicately with a green silk handkerchief. "Go on—you can promote something if you *really* want it."

"Some day some junkie's going to kill you, Vernie! You know that, don't you?"

"Maybe. I don't cross no bridges 'til I come to 'em."

Nina went back to the bar, pulled a crumpled dollar bill from her bag. "Double, Bennie."

He served the drink, shaking his head with phony earnestness. "Just this one. You can't afford to get no heat on now, kid."

She didn't answer. The whiskey helped a little. She set the glass down, warmth curling around and touching the corners of her stomach where the hungry gnawing was. She wasn't aware that the stranger had come in and stood beside her until he spoke in his curiously low, sardonic voice.

"Good evening, Miss Valjean."

Nina started. "Oh—it's you." The whiskey had given her courage. "I—I'm booked tonight."

"Fifty says you're not booked tonight."

Fifty. A fix was thirty-five. Fifty and twelve was sixty-two; almost enough for two fixes.... "Not for fifty, Mister. You play too rough."

The stranger smiled. At least Nina thought he was smiling; it was hard to tell in the dim light.

"Make it a hundred," she said, hoping he would go away. Then the hunger prodded her with cruel, nerve-jerking reminders. There wasn't much time. She knew what would happen to her soon. It had happened before. Once. Before she went to working nights. She'd been living with a musician out near Fisherman's Wharf and had graduated from reefers. Vernie had given her a few free shots. Then the bite. The shots began to cost real money. The dance band drummer cleared out, taking the last of her cash with him. She was alone in the one-room attic studio. She didn't know how bad it could get, how it could go on, hour after hour.... She'd tried to call Vernie and couldn't reach him. She lay across the bed, fingers clenched, biting the pillow. Screaming. Finally she reached Vernie and he'd come to her at once.

When she'd relaxed, sobbing with relief at the magic touch of the needle, he'd said, "Get this, Nina. *That's the last one on the house.* From now on, it's cash on the line."

Nina knew she was hooked. She knew she'd have to have a fix every day. And she knew the only way she could get money.

Nina toyed with her glass, waiting.

"A hundred says you're not booked tonight," the man said.

"Give it to me now. And wait just a minute. I have to see a man out back."

"I'll go get a couple of fifths up the street. Meet you out by the taxi stand. Okay?"

She nodded, no longer caring. She had the money for a fix in her hand. She got up and walked back to the booth.

Vernie said, "This'll cost you forty, kid. They upped my price. Inflation."

She didn't try to bargain. In the shadowy booth, she pushed the short sleeve further up on her arm. The needle pricked her flesh gently, and she sighed with relief. Even her fear of the stranger left her. After all, he was just a man like any other man. Well, not quite like any other man, either....

Nina went out into Grogan's Alley, carrying the cheap red cotton knitted stole over her arm. Warm sticky night touched her bare shoulders, chilling her. He was waiting at the corner—another shadow in the dark, his face a blur under the rim of his pulled down hat.

She got into the cab feeling as though she'd stepped into another world. The stranger was silent but she didn't mind that because the ride would be short.

She knew the apartment building; she'd been there before. The plushy feel of the carpet under her sandals. The hush of elevator doors—everything about this place was quiet, soundless, different from The Red Parrot and everything that went with it.

Walking down the hallway to 1215, she felt an odd sense of unreality. Everything seemed different tonight. Maybe the man would be different—a little kinder.

She wished to God she could manage to stick it out for a few days at a time without a fix. They said if you have the guts to stick it out you won't need it any more. The monkey's off your back. She wished to God she could get the monkey off her back. She wished she could tell this horrible man to go to hell.

A small metal plaque on the door of 1215 bore the engraved name: *Joyce Masters*. The man stood beside her as she looked in. A floor lamp was still burning. "Jesus," Nina said, "hasn't anyone cleaned this mess up since the last time?"

The man laughed, put his hand on her back and shoved her inside.

The click of the lock was sharp and sudden in the soundless room. She was alone with this man in a place of his choosing, on terms dictated by him. Until morning she must drink with him, carouse with him, serve his pleasures.

He chucked his hat viciously into a corner and she saw his features clearly for the first time that evening.

Many men had looked at her, but never quite the way this man was looking at her now. He was grinning, thin lips drawn back over glittering white teeth and for the first time in months she had the impulse to cover herself with something more than the shoddy dress that teased out and accentuated her body's soft curves.

"Well now, baby," the man said softly....

The heavy, passionate hours crawled alcohol failed to relieve her misery. The man was reaching for her again.

Nina began to cry. Not with tears. Just with sounds in her throat.

The man growled something, displeased.

She tried to stop. She tried to smile for him. He should be entitled to a smile for his hundred bucks....

"H-how about another little drink?" she asked. If she could get drunk enough the night would pass and the day would come again.

The man did not answer.

He was staring at her and there was something in his eyes that made her almost sorry for him. For a moment, at least. Something apart from his dark flushed skin, the blue vein beating in his forehead. A desperate, searching, lost-soul look. Hopelessness as deep as her own.

He had a hundred bucks and she had a monkey on her back. He passed for a man and she had the guise of a woman....

She let her body go limp and tried to blank out her mind so it would know no part of what was happening. Only now it was different. The sky outside was lighter; the night was ending and daybreak would soon be here.

Then the man chuckled. Nina had never heard him chuckle quite like that before. Nor sensed such desperation in him that was like ravening hunger—whetted, not satisfied.

She knew what was going to happen to her, and the man knew she knew. She tried to scream, but there was no strength in her throat. She tried to double and twist away from his body but fear had numbed her muscles. Her lips moved, as if praying.

The man sighed deeply, shuddering in his soul, and the sound was like a frightened child whimpering.

He stood for a moment, fatigue lapping in him. The tightness was beginning again. Thought was stirring. Vague thought without form or direction. He stared at Nina and rubbed his palms against his thighs.

Nina…. There was something about her. Something he ought to do but he could not think what it was.

He frowned slightly. His face, so recently swollen and dark with raging emotions, was still ugly in its pallor. He pulled down the blinds, slowly, carefully, as though to shield a sleeper from the morning sun.

TWO

Roman Laird finished shaving, stared at his face in the mirror, and frowned.

He was looking tired these days, and small wonder. Fatigue didn't improve his appearance. It wasn't much of an appearance by anyone's standards, he thought on the few occasions when he really looked at himself. As ordinary as raisin pudding, his mother used to say, and on that point he agreed. There was no doubting his prototype ran to the dozens and the hundreds on Montgomery Street every day, and in the offices of the factories and plants spreading out along Bayshore. Nice young man in a brown suit.

Almost everyone he knew liked him, a fact that continually surprised Roman, as did the embarrassing attention he got from exuberant mothers with unmarried daughters. You *must* get so tired of bachelor meals, Mr. Laird. I *do* want you to drop over and have a real home cooked dinner some evening soon.

That was before Joyce, of course. Most of the dinner invitations stopped then, the mothers casting their baits before other rising young executives. Not that he and Joyce were engaged, exactly. He wished they were. There was something sweetly solid about marriage. And about Joyce, too. She'd hit him hard. A girl both beautiful and intelligent, with a mind to match his own. And the kind of face and figure that might be expected of one of the city's most in-demand models. There was a lot of money in modeling— more than in using her Master's degree in psychology to teach school.

"You do meet more interesting people, darling," she'd explained once. "I met you—which never would have happened if I'd been explaining Pavlov's dog's reflexes to a group of sleepy high school freshmen."

He'd smiled. "I've got some reflexes that Pavlov never heard of. Or his dog, either."

"I know. And I have an idea that if I explained them to the high school freshmen, they'd no longer be sleepy."

"You're a smart girl, Joyce. Far too smart to remain single. Why don't you forget Pavlov *and* his dog and make an honest man of me?"

"I don't know you well enough, mister."

They'd gone along that way for almost a year. Until he sensed a change in her. She went home to Ohio to visit her mother for a few weeks and her leaving was as casual as everything else about her. "See you soon, darling— and don't get lonesome." But seeing her mother, leaving the city, was merely an excuse. They both knew it.

Everybody join hands and conjugate: *non amo, non amas, non amat...* especially *non alms*: you do not love.

The clock warned him. He'd have to hurry to get to the plant on time. He was tired, so tired he actually ached. The suit he'd worn yesterday was wrinkled and needed pressing. He left it over a chairback for his houseboy Wong to send out, and chose a tweed.

He'd feel better when he got a couple of cups of coffee into him.

Overwork. Thinking of the production problem at Crane Chemical almost every moment of the day and night. Crowding his mind so that even the recollection of Joyce did not cling as strongly. The process that worked so smoothly in the glass experimental model was not so easily expanded 50,000 times to bulk procedures. Not that he was doing it by himself. The others had their problems, too.

Young Bob Pilcher handled administration and that was a headache. Sonnichsen was in charge of construction, while Barton, acting for Crane, had a finger in every part of the operation and kept everyone in a state of confusion.

Roman had the prime responsibility, and he felt it. Conferences, altercations, arguments. Always, it was Roman's cool, precise logic that beat down their objections, their errors.

Roman had come to Crane Chemical with the ink still wet on his diploma. He'd studied the Crane operation and devised an ingenious manner of production using the plant's existing facilities. J. Stanley Crane had listened sleepily for thirty-seven minutes. Then he had said, "No good. But it shows you're willing to think and that's more important than being willing to work. I can hire a hundred competent men willing to work. You, uh—Laird's the name?—be here at eight tomorrow. Research."

Roman had gone up fast. Even faster than Bob Pilcher had done in administration, though he was a couple of years younger than Roman and had started later. It was through Pilcher he'd met Joyce. He had taken her away from Bob, in fact; not out of malice or intent, but because that was just the way it happened.

Roman thought of that while sitting at the conference table with the rest of the top brass that morning. He thought of Joyce and their years' association, while the rest of them in the air-conditioned room studied charts and figures and nodded silently. Once, Pilcher drew a slide rule, made some quick calculations and jotted formulae on a pad. Roman smiled quietly. If there had been an error, Pilcher would have found it.

All the others seemed satisfied, as one by one they initialed the plans. J. Stanley Crane looked inquiringly at Pilcher but said nothing. Minutes passed. Pilcher glanced at Roman, his face impassive but his eyes dark in his honest pink face. J. Stanley shuffled his feet. "Well, Bob?" he asked finally.

"They're all right, I guess." Gruffly, reluctantly.

J. Stanley said, "This is fine, Laird." From him, it was the equivalent of the Congressional Medal.

Barton, chewing the stem of his cold pipe, said, "This would be a good time to hit the boss for a raise, Roman."

"I'd rather hit him for a vacation—I think I could become practically human again with a couple of weeks in the woods or at sea."

J. Stanley nodded. "Whenever you're ready. Why don't you take off this afternoon. We'll carry on from here."

Roman returned to his own office, stared at his littered desk, then began sorting papers.

It was a little after eleven but the day was already soggy-hot. The kind of damply oppressive heat that depresses and irritates.

He'd noticed it in those around him. The supervisors belligerent, the assistants slow, inaccurate. Roman's own work continued as meticulous and careful as ever. For him there was never any letdown, any hint of his personal discomfort, of his feelings, or emotions. Control, Joyce said. Which it wouldn't hurt him to lose once in a while, she added.

The door behind him opened. Pilcher came in looking unhappy. Not that Pilcher had looked happy for a long time. A year. Ever since Roman had started dating Joyce. Too long to mope. After all, Joyce hadn't worn a ring, and if a man can't hang on to his woman, there's not much point fuming. Streetcars and women; there's always another along in a little while. A bit of philosophy he'd better be learning himself, Roman thought, if his suspicions were right.

"What's on your mind, Bob?" Roman tried to speak kindly, but the words sounded insincere.

Pilcher shrugged. "Heard from Joyce lately?"

"Had a letter yesterday. Her mother's quite a bit better. She said she'll be back Sunday at two." He didn't mention the other part of her letter. The elaborately casual sentence in which she thought she'd find a little cottage down the peninsula or over in Marin where she could have a cat, and give up the city apartment.

"I got a postcard last week," Pilcher said, thickly. "Akron zoo."

"I didn't know Akron had a zoo."

Pilcher wet his lips. His baby-pink face gleamed with sweat. Nervous sweat. "When are you and—and Joyce getting married?"

"I don't believe we are, ever," Roman said casually. "We don't feel that our friendship could survive the experience." He thought that was rather good, even though it lacked complete candor, and was immediately sorry. The kid was obviously near the boiling point.

Hatred spewed out in tight bitter words. "I'd like to kill you, Roman Laird."

Roman lit a cigarette, blew out the match. "I know. You ought to go down to a gym and beat hell out of the punching bag. This way you're eating yourself up. Hurting yourself. It's no good, Bob."

"Concerned, are you? *I* wanted to marry Joyce. You knew that."

Roman shook his head. "It was really her decision, I'd say. If you had her in a marrying mood she wouldn't have dropped you for me. *Would* she now? Be honest Bob."

He hadn't expected Bob's fist to swing up with such vicious speed. The blow stung, rocking him, but he kept his feet, as rage—violent, surging, murderous rage—struck him for the smallest fraction of time. Only his hands, clenching at his sides, moved, as his conscious mind forced back the tide of emotion. "That one's for free," he said coldly. "After this, remember to act like an adult."

He thought Pilcher was going to cry. The man's lips worked as if he were trying to say something, then he swung around and rushed from the room.

To hell with him, Roman thought, sinking into a chair. To hell with the plant. To hell with Joyce. To hell with the whole damned world.

THREE

It was the letter from Joyce that worried him. A longish letter; longer than she usually wrote. Most of it was gay inconsequential chatter—which wasn't entirely like Joyce, either. She could be gay and sparkling and often was, but he'd always known it was a spirit born of the moment. Underneath, she was a deep, serious person. Maybe she really meant what she said about getting out of the City to someplace where she could keep a cat. Moving out of the apartment he'd found for her. Moving away from him.

There'd been other signs. Little things. Little coolnesses that could have meant anything. The trouble was he didn't really know too much about women.

He couldn't understand how he went so hard for Joyce. All the others before had been experiences; she was an epoch. He wished he'd pushed harder for marriage in the beginning. Later, she'd refused. "Sex isn't enough, darling," she'd said, "if you want marriage to last over into the second year. It takes something else."

"I know. That's how I feel about it, too."

Evidently they hadn't meant the same things.

The weariness hit him again—almost as hard as yesterday. Getting sore at that fool Pilcher, that was it. That and the pressure—the heavy, constant pressure. Like last night, hurrying through Wong's dinner to get to work in his room. Testing the idea of a catalytic reaction taking place at the beginning instead of at the present point. Sitting there, pencilling notes, probing, proving.

He'd worked furiously on, oblivious to the demands of his mind and body for rest. Yet entwined in the smooth clear operation of his brain were vague thoughts. Curious, indefinite thoughts that finally resolved themselves into a feeling of someone in the room with him. He ignored it, dragging at his cigarette. He'd worked on covering white paper with curious squiggling figures.

It was as though he was not alone. Being watched. His cigarette, fallen into the ashtray, generated a tiny thread of smoke that climbed straight up. He'd moved his hand gently, and the smoke-thread wavered and broke. The air currents had not been disturbed as they would have been had someone, or something, come in silently. He looked around and saw nothing amiss, so he dismissed the notion from his mind and returned to his calculations.

He'd yawned and stretched finally, gathered his notes, clipped them together and placed them carefully in his brief case. He undressed, hung the trousers of his suit on a hanger, smoothed the coat over them and placed it on the rack in his closet.

The deal was finished. All wrapped up and ready for delivery. And right. He'd known it was right and found satisfaction in that.

He went to bed, but for a long time he couldn't sleep. He was still bothered by that vague uneasiness, *the feeling of being watched.*

FOUR

He woke from his reverie with a start. Blackness; then reality. Heart beating fast. Nerves. He was really pooped.

His watch said a quarter of one. He called Johnny Madros, his travel agent, and caught him returning from lunch. "Johnny? Roman Laird. How's about getting me passage to Vancouver or somewhere, to leave tonight or tomorrow?"

"On a ship? That's not easy, Roman. Everything's filled and people waiting. Why don't you fly?"

"No ocean breezes on a plane. Can't you dig up a broom closet or something for me, Johnny?"

"Well, let's see. *The Vancouver Merchant* is due to pull out Monday noon. There might be a cancelation, and if so, I'll use my influence. Is this just for yourself, or—"

Monday. Joyce would be back Sunday. He'd meet her, of course, and then find out what it was all about. If he read the signs correctly, and she was really brushing him off, he'd need to get away for a while. If she wasn't, it might do her good to do a bit of wondering and waiting for ten days or so until he got back. He spoke firmly, "Just for myself, Johnny."

A few days on the water would get him over this jumpiness. This sense of—*of being watched.*

He controlled the impulse to turn around; to catch it—because there wasn't anyone in his office. There couldn't be. Any more than there'd been someone in his apartment last night. No. He wouldn't look around.

He sat still, his fingers tightening around the arms of his chair.

Five minutes. Ten.

It was this heat. This never-ending, irritating, muggy, thick heat that pressed and bore on a man so that he wanted to spring and destroy to find relief.

There was a knock, but Roman did not answer. He sat tense, and watched while the knob turned. The door opened slowly. Pilcher.

Roman said nothing.

Pilcher swallowed, his long hands knotted and bunched at his sides. "Roman—"

Roman realized the cause of the struggle. Pilcher was trying to apologize, and he wanted to say: Forget it, but the words were slow in forming. Finally, "Forget it, Bob. Forget it."

"I—I'm sorry—"

The tension in Roman dissolved and the tightness in his throat left. "It's okay, Bob."

"The heat."

"Makes us all a little crazy."

"Joyce doesn't mean anything to—to me, anyway."

Roman knew that Bob was near the breaking point and renouncing Joyce with his words, though she was still fastened pretty deeply into his heart. He was still—well, a kid.

With women, you had to be able to take 'em or leave 'em alone. It was a nice theory except that Roman couldn't make it work, either. From the beginning, Joyce had been more to him than a mere temporary convenience. He thought he meant more to her, too. Maybe not. Joyce Masters was an odd girl. Never quite reacting according to pattern. She wouldn't have married Bob Pilcher. Roman was convinced of that. They talked about Bob once. Joyce said, "He might have been fun—for a while."

Roman said, "How about driving me uptown, Bob? There's nothing to keep you around here and you might as well go home and soak in a cold tub the rest of the day."

"Okay."

That was good. Keep the boy's mind off his problem. Getting Bob to do a favor might help. He cleared his desk and locked the drawers.

"Let's go. I have to pack." He didn't have to, yet, of course. It would be several days before Johnny Madros could get confirmation for his trip.

They drove up Mission, across Third, and over to California.

They were passing Joyce's place which was only a few blocks from his apartment house. Without thinking, Roman said, "Stop here a minute, Bob. I left my other suitcase—"

The car jerked to a dead stop, tires screaming. Pilcher's face was white, and too late Roman saw the mistake of his words. There was no unsaying them. The fury leveled at him was as potent as a blow.

"You're smart, Laird." Pilcher's voice was low, tight. "And me, the stupid son-of-a-bitch that thought you were halfway white. I should have known you were just waiting for a chance to rub it in."

"Bob, I didn't mean—"

"Don't spoil a great act, Laird. You knew Joyce wouldn't marry me, but you didn't have to marry her to get what you wanted. And it makes the joke even funnier when you can throw your big achievement in my face. Well, laugh, Laird. Laugh."

"When you learn to control yourself, Bob, you'll be a lot happier."

"I'm happy now. I can appreciate what a terrific guy you are, and what a fumbling ass I am. And I'll be happier. I'll laugh fit to split one of these days. You know when, Laird? When *I'm* twisting the knife in *you*. I figure it won't be as long as you think!"

"Maybe not, Bob. And thanks for the ride."

Roman watched the car roar off, rubber smoking. He hoped Bob wouldn't kill someone before he cooled off. He shrugged and went in.

The elevator stopped at the twelfth floor and he walked down the corridor to Joyce's apartment. The key turned in her lock with easy familiarity and he stepped inside.

The smell of stale cigarette smoke came even before he snapped on the light, and apprehension hit him.

Cigarette smoke and whiskey.

But the place had been empty for ten days. Vandals had broken in. Burglars enjoying a several-days party. A drunken brawl.

He walked through the living room, distaste growing in him at the rumpled rugs, the disarray, the liquor stains marring Joyce's expensive, polished blondwood furniture. She'd always kept the place like a little jewel box. Tidy, neat, perfect.

Who the hell had done this? How had they gotten in to the place?

There were only two keys and his hadn't been out of his possession since Joyce had given it to him. She *could* have loaned hers to a friend, but if she had—which Roman doubted—certainly not to people who would pull a deal like this!

The bedroom was a mess.

He pulled aside the drapes and raised the shades. Books on the floor, pillows, whiskey bottles, a gardenia with brown shriveled edges but still fragrant. Scraps of a black dress, the glitter of rhinestones.

Somehow Roman was not surprised at the sight of the girl on the floor.

She went with the shambles, the devastation. She was part of the madhouse scene. Part of the play—blending with the violence. Not stirring, even though her only decoration was a sheer nylon stocking wound tightly around her throat.

She was quite beautiful. And quite dead.

Roman had seen death before, during the war.

But this was murder. Personal, intimate murder. The girl on the rug was the end-result of someone's passion.

Roman sat before Joyce's dressing table until the waves of sickness passed.

An accident? The unexpected climax of a week-long orgy?

No. The nylon stocking had been knotted around the girl's throat. Deliberately. In an orgy of hate.

Hatred was everywhere.

In the smashed perfume and lotion bottles, broken bed lamps, torn clothes. Someone had been charged with inconceivable passion, for everywhere was evidence of uncontrolled viciousness.

Roman stood up, still nauseated, and wandered around the room, examining the debris. A black velvet bag, pieces of black taffeta and rhinestones. A red sandal of two thin straps and a black sole, its high heel broken off and its mate flung into a far corner. A single nylon stocking hung from a twisted lamp.

He took up the velvet bag and emptied it on the bed.

Handkerchief, crumpled. Lipstick. Pack of cigarettes. Some greenbacks.

Empty glass vial with a rubber cork. A key; not one that would fit Joyce's apartment. Half a chocolate bar. Three matchbooks. *The Red Parrot— Where Old Friends Meet.* An advertising postcard folded in quarters.

He opened the card carefully and saw a full length photo of a girl. Exotically posed. The words: *Sexational Nina Valjean... outstrips them all! Nightly at The Red Parrot.*

It looked to Roman like a man's crime, and he thought of Bob Pilcher, of the burden of rage Bob carried within him. But there was nothing to connect Bob up with this girl—or was there?

Bob had known that Joyce was going to visit with her mother, knew her apartment would be vacant.

Roman jerked around, the feeling of being watched strong within him again. There was no one in the room. No one but the girl on the floor.

There was only one other key to the apartment, and Joyce had it. Joyce was in a ranch in Ohio with her mother. Roman's mind groped for an answer. *How did he know Joyce was in Ohio?*

It was absurd, thinking like that.

Roman slipped the matchbooks and postcard into his pocket and shoved the other items back into the velvet bag.

The police—they would have to come into this.

He hadn't thought of them. They would probe and pry. Take pictures. Measurements. Fingerprints. Examine. Question. Suspect....

Him?

Roman refused to be panicked.

Slowly and carefully he walked about the room, striving to imprint each detail in his memory. He might need to remember later.

He forced himself to look again at the huddled girl on the floor. The girl on the advertising postcard. *Sexational Nina Valjean....*

Tawny brown hair, shoulder length. Age—hard to tell now. No rings. A rhinestone cluster clinging to one ear like a flag nailed to the mast. Tiny needle pricks still visible along the main vein of her left arm. Appendicitis scar.

He left her exactly as he'd found her.

Not that it would make any difference. They'd have his fingerprints anyway. They were all over the apartment. Of course, there was no telling the age of a fingerprint—whether they were made two weeks ago or last night.

They'd find out about the keys in a hurry.

Learn that Joyce, in Akron, had one. That Roman Laird, who lived a few blocks away, had the other.

If the police needed a red-hot suspect—and he felt sure they would—he was one ready-made and waiting.

FIVE

The man called Smith moved in shadow.

In the City's silent alleys he was almost anonymous—black shapelessness obscured by the night.

A gray man; seldom noticed, never remembered.

A gray mind, memory hidden by clouds that swirled and fumed and broke only rarely, revealing but a momentary glimpse of the past, a hint of the future. Showing him paths that he followed eagerly, only to become lost again in the purple-gray mist.

Hurry—hurry. It must be over this way—yes; he knew this building; that power pole; this litter of garbage cans and trash-filled boxes. Quickly, before it was forgotten again—quickly, before the fogs came and swathed his straining mind with blackness.

The hunger in him awoke and began to gnaw. Gripping his bowels with strong ivory teeth and shaking until he wanted to run to escape the pain. Never fed. Never satisfied completely. Not by food, nor liquor, nor flesh, nor any sin that could be bought with the power of money or the bribery of love or the terror of violence.

Northward, between great dark buildings, to the smaller sheds and warehouses of the produce district that even before dawn would waken to the busy bartering of commission merchants. Deserted now, but for a sleepy watchman or two shuffling between the empty cauliflower and cabbage crates.

The hunger gnawed and his urgency grew.

The place was cluttered with canvases. Hanging from the walls and piled in stacks.

A kitchen table held a milk bottle filled with brushes. There were many paint tubes—some unopened, others twisted and empty—bottles of turpentine and oil, rags, a palette. Beside the table stood an easel holding an unfinished canvas. Except for a stool and a sink in one corner, the room was bare.

Smith paid no attention to the paintings on the walls—eerie nightmarish daubs of red and black, of swirling grays and blobs of yellow. Scenes of Infernos, of weird half-people struggling with fearful destinies. He studied the canvas, then, quickly squeezing fresh blobs of paint onto his palette, he selected a brush and began to work with feverish absorption.

With bold, yet delicate strokes images formed and took on solidity... a row of men and women hanging head down from hooks—meat hooks.

Neat and naked as so many spring lambs. The butcher, thin and fish-belly white, at work on his block.

Against the heavy-shadowed background, a girl began to emerge. Lying across the block while the butcher began to prepare her for the vacant hook above him. Of all the shadowed, distorted figures, the girl alone seemed vivid and real. Tawny brown hair swirled around her shoulders and framed her pale face. Dark eyes stared up at the painter. Eyes with the weariness of centuries. The gray-green eyes of one who knew the worst of life and had learned to expect nothing else, and yet who dared—foolishly and piteously—to hope.

Sweat formed on his forehead, gathered at his temples and ran in sticky paths down his cheeks. His breath labored and he could feel the small muscles of his eyes tighten with weariness. He knew that with the passing of his creative frenzy he would have to sleep.

Sleep?

No; he didn't dare sleep. Not here. It was not meant for him to sleep here. Perhaps that was why there was no bed; no couch.

Pouring turpentine into a cup he washed his brushes. Sweat ran into his eyes and he wiped impatiently with his sleeve. All wrong. The something he was looking for with his brushes and paints wasn't there.

Fear joined the hot thick emotions in him. Perhaps he'd never find it....

He seized a pile of canvases and began digging, staring hungrily at each one in turn. A shadowy man devouring a snake seemed to writhe and turn. A woman, strangely distorted, writing in a great black book that dripped blood. The woman's bare feet rested on a new-born infant.

Smith's hands shook as he turned the pictures.

He thought he had captured it. Somewhere among the tortured paintings he must have found what he was seeking. But it was no longer there. It had escaped.

Sometimes he thought he'd almost been successful. Sometimes he contrived to capture a color, a moment, a bird, a woman, a thin musical note. But he was never quite able to possess that which he wanted most.

There were dozens of canvases; hundreds of them. He scowled and let them lay where he dropped them.

Nothing. After hours of slaving, nothing.

A sound like a sob came from his throat. A wild, inhuman sound.

Out on the bay, a freighter's deep groaning echoed him. His head came up and he listened, trying to remember. He knew he must hurry. Someone was waiting. Someone back in the mists, back in the fogged images of his brain.

He hurried. First locking the door carefully. Out into the alley filled with the obscene shapes that people only the dusk and the dawn.

The streets where the taller buildings stood were still dark. A single cable-car picked its way by the light of a feeble head lamp. A police prowler cruised around a corner and he kept close to the shadows until it had gone.

Hurry. Time was growing short.

Yet his steps were heavy, and he moved with reluctance in the alleys behind towering apartment houses and big solid residences. Hating them. Filled with people. Pigs. Fit only to hang on a fantastic butcher's hooks. Especially one of them. In his sleep-sodden mind an image evolved, a face, blurred, the features unclear. Someone he'd seen before but could not bring back into clear focus. The one who hated him. The one who wanted to destroy him.

He grinned.

Someday the blurred face would clear and he would recognize the face of his enemy and seek him out. He would destroy or be destroyed.

Either way, he would be at peace.

He plodded on until he came to the back entrance of one of the great square apartment buildings. Looking up and down the alley, he opened the door and went into the cool, dark basement.

SIX

The newspapers did not mention the murder of Nina Valjean.

Roman read every word carefully, over a late breakfast and was sure he hadn't missed an item.

They hadn't found the body, unless they were keeping quiet for a purpose. He didn't think they'd have a purpose. He wished he knew more about the police and their procedures. They'd find out he had the other key to Joyce's apartment, and their relationship. It wouldn't help his story.

The pity was, he didn't have a story. He had no way of telling when the girl was killed—except that the crime had a nocturnal look about it. All right, what had he been doing with his nights lately? Reading, working, sleeping.

Alone.

No alibi.

On the other hand, what was there to tie him to the girl; to the murder?

The best thing Roman could do now would be to sit tight. When the police came to question him, give simple, direct answers.

If they didn't believe him, let them prove his guilt. Of course he wouldn't mention having gone to the apartment and finding the girl. He wished now he'd called headquarters and reported it. Now it was too late. They'd want to know why he waited so long.

His real worry was Joyce.

She'd be back Sunday. She'd walk into her apartment—and the shock wouldn't be pleasant. There ought to be something he could do to spare her that. Perhaps an anonymous telephone tip to the police? Well, maybe. He didn't know how fast they could trace calls. Fast enough, probably.

He could head Joyce off before she went to her apartment, of course. But what would he say? *"Don't go up right now, darling, there's a corpse in your bedroom?"*

Almost involuntarily, his fingers found the matchbook in his shirt pocket. *The Red Parrot...* and the girl's full length photo.

Sexational Nina Valjean.

He studied the address. Nearby. An alley off Pine.

He ought to call Johnny Machos—maybe take a plane for Canada. If he did that, it would look bad. Too hard to explain he wasn't running away; that he'd really planned a trip before he knew of the murder.

Perhaps it would be best if he just lounged around town, loafing and resting. Drive out to the beach, or out into the country where there were cool, green forests, forgetting everything.

Roman didn't really intend to go to The Red Parrot, but he found himself idling in during the afternoon. When his eyes had accustomed themselves to the shadows, he looked around.

It was a big place, with a cheap, sleazy look. A few tables gave the floor an empty appearance. Booths lined the sides. There was a deserted orchestra platform at one end. A couple of bleary men dozed over beers and a lonely bartender glanced up from his comic book. A sign over the cash register identified him as: *Mixologist, Ed.*

"Tom Collins," Roman said.

"Yeah. Sure been hot ain't it?"

"Cooling a little, according to the papers."

"Man, it'll feel good to be human again."

"I know what you mean. You better have something cooling, too," Roman suggested, dropping five on the bar.

"Yeah; thanks." He poured a shot, added water, tossed it off quickly.

Roman pulled a cigarette from a pack, reached casually out and took a book of matches from the ashtray. He lighted, puffed, glanced at the inside of the folder—as if seeing the picture for the first time. He let smoke filter through his nostrils and inclined his head slightly. "Not bad. When does she do her stuff?"

"Oh, her? We don't have a show any more. We got the word to clean up or close up six-seven months ago. Well, y'can't make no clean show pay in a dump like this. So we closed the show."

"What's she doing now?" Roman asked, and immediately realized he'd said the wrong thing.

Ed's face seemed to harden around the eyes. "She's around, I guess. You got some special interest?"

Roman slipped a ten-dollar bill into the small pile of change on the bar. "Special is right. The gal has a diamond ring my company is after. Guy bought it for her a year ago, made a few payments, and hasn't been heard from since. I'm supposed to get the ring. Or the money. Or *else.*"

The ten-spot disappeared. "Yeah, I know how them companies are. Well, I'll tell ya. I never seen her with no diamond ring, that's for sure. She must of hocked it a long time ago. What with Bennie promotin' her on one side, and Vernie jackin' her up for snow on the other, about all she owns is the clothes she got on. And I ain't sure she owns them."

"How could I get to talk to her?"

"Well, she's around most any night late. If I was you, I wouldn't try to talk to her around the Parrot. Bennie—that's the boss—he's tough, mister. And smart. And Bennie he don't like what ain't regular."

"What about where she lives?"

"That's anyplace. If anybody knows, it's a kid name of Merrill. Sissie or Cecille or something. She lives on Alvaron, near Powell. Some kind of fancy-pants dancer. She might know where Nina hocked the ring."

"That's what I'm mainly interested in—where she hocked it. Tell me this, does she have some special guy she might have passed the ring to?"

"Naw, she don't have no special guy. She works pretty much by herself. Picks up what she can around here, or Bennie lines up some sucker for her."

"No—no repeat customers?"

Ed shook his head, and his tone was almost professorial. "Naw. You take a girl works in a house, or goes out on call, she can build up a nice little following. If she treats the guys right, that is. Now you take a dump like the Parrot, it's pretty near always one night stuff. Hardly any repeaters. One or two, maybe, but mostly nuts. Like this character Bennie says went with her a couple nights and gave her a bad time."

"I guess some of 'em get some real weird ideas." Roman restrained an impulse to ask more questions. It wouldn't do to arouse the man's suspicions.

Chances were Ed had told all he knew, anyway. The real information would have to come from Bennie. Or from the guy himself—if he could ever get either of them to talk.

Roman nodded his goodbye to the bartender and went out.

A brisk movement of air alerted his senses, the first hint of fog-cooled weather that was sweeping in from the Pacific. And with it, intruding into his thoughts again, was the disturbing feeling of being watched.

He stopped before a shop window, glancing at the display and reaching for a cigarette. Under cover of the first puff, he glanced sideways at the street back of him, and his heart missed a beat. There *was* a man strolling along, about a block back. Too far to be obvious, but close enough to keep Roman in sight. Of course, he couldn't be sure. The man might not be following him at all. It was a reasonably busy street—yet there was something in the way the man ambled along....

He flipped his match into the gutter and continued walking. A taxi came toward him, cruising. He waited until it was close, then flagged it.

"Van Ness Avenue," he told the driver, and as they rolled from the curb he could see the stranger on the sidewalk keeping his steady pace. No hint of surprise, of interest. Which didn't prove anything. If the following were intentional, the tail wouldn't give himself away so easily. The police? Roman doubted it. Who then?

"Turn here and drop me at the St. Francis," he told the driver. "I've changed my mind."

"Right, Mac."

As near as Roman could tell, there was no pursuit, so he paid off the driver at the hotel, walked through the side entrance, and out the front. It wasn't far from Union Square. He bought a newspaper, went to the natty park in the middle of the City where other people walked the paths enjoying the cooling air.

"Feed the pigeons, mister? On'y fi' cents a bag."

Roman handed over a nickel for a bag of bread crumbs and began feeding them to the strutting birds. He was able to glance around in every direction as he tossed his crumbs to the birds. There was no casual man in sight.

He crumbled the empty bag and tossed it into a waste receptacle. There was an empty bench near one of the fountains; he sat down and tried to think.

He decided to go to his apartment, soak—a warm tub, and have a long, strong drink. Then he remembered that he'd finished the last of his Old Adam a couple of days before. Well, he wasn't far from the alley where The Red Parrot was located. There was a liquor store on the next corner, he noticed, and walked in.

The clerk was fat, red-faced and affable. "Real nice day, turned out to be, eh?"

"Quite a relief," Roman agreed.

"Yes, real nice. Guess we don't get a hot spell like we've had once in ten years, maybe. No, must be more'n that. Last one I remember must of been 1938. Yes sir, that was a real stinker. Lasted four or five days and I mean things sizzled! All up and down Montgomery bankers and brokers going around in their shirt-sleeves. You sure don't see that very often here."

"I didn't suppose a banker ever took his coat off this side of hell."

The clerk laughed. "Right you are, mister." He wrapped a fifth, slipped it into a bag and deftly clutched Roman's ten. "Well, I guess these last few days give us an idea what temp'r'chur to expect." He counted the change, "Five seventy-five, six, and four is ten. Thanks. Come in again."

Roman walked slowly toward his apartment. He looked around cautiously, then went in.

Wong was just leaving. "You're early, Mr. Laird," he said, "but dinner is ready—warming in the oven."

"Thanks, Wong. Did anyone phone or—"

"No one, Mr. Laird. And no mail."

Roman went into the bathroom and started the water running in the tub. No mail. He hadn't really expected any, since Joyce was on the train, but she could have had a postcard mailed somewhere along the route. Or wired. He would have liked to hear from her.

It wasn't until half an hour later, when he'd thoroughly soaked in the tub, dried and dressed, that the feeling of unease, of something alien around him, penetrated into his mind. A strange creepiness that ran in little shivers along his spine and prickled the hair on the nape of his neck.

He searched the room with his eyes, as though to trace the source of the eerie feeling. Nothing was disturbed. Nothing was out of place.

He opened the wardrobe door carefully. Nothing. His suits—just back from the cleaners—hung where Wong had placed them.

Then he noticed a small manila envelope, attached to a button—the kind of envelope cleaners used to return items found in pockets. He opened it; inserted his fingers. Something hard and cold. He shook it out and stared at it in the palm of his hand, and the cold clamp of fear clutched deep inside him; he felt sweat break from his forehead and his body.

A tight cluster of rhinestones—a woman's earring.

SEVEN

Three A.M.

He stood flanked by giants whose bones were riveted steel and whose flesh was of concrete. Brooding giants, despising him.

He lifted his heavy head to return their contempt. Hatred was a smoking, stinking mass in his stomach. His hands gathered themselves into fists, striking his forehead until lights danced and for a moment new pain replaced the old, but the fogs did not vanish. There was still no memory of yesterday, no inkling of tomorrow.

There was only now.

Some night he would remember.

Some night he would follow and find those masters who hid from him even as they drove him on. Tear them from their secret places. Force out the truth. Shake and strangle and beat them until they gave up what they now withheld. Gave up what belonged to him.

Phantoms.

They must be people he'd known in his past. People he'd loved and hated and perhaps lived for and killed for. Now their essence had slipped away; there were only these amorphous husks; white and tenuous shapes that changed and failed when he tried to recognize them.

But wait!

There was one... his pulses beat faster... one that did not slip away as quickly as the others. He moved faster now, almost running. A girl. Yes; that was it. A girl.

A girl with darkly tumbled hair and richly sensuous mouth who once before had promised and he had risen and followed. Had he ever found her?

He wiped his face; it was salty-wet.

Remember, he demanded. Remember, she echoed. Just ahead of him, just out of sight, beckoning him.

Another trick? Another plot of those shapeless things in the night to lure him on and then send their tentacles to catch and trip and sting him again?

He paused in his desperate haste, listening for their laughter. His perceptions searched the night for mockery, for bitterness.

There was only the girl, and he followed....

Then the mists were once more sneaking in, and the girl was gone. He stopped again, listening, feeling for her. If he could only remember her name—where she lived—*find her again....*

And then, suddenly, recognition.

A familiar entranceway before him stimulated a response. Yes—this was where he'd been before. Where the girl had been. He struck a match, bending low to peer at the nameplates. *Mr. and Mrs. Casper Axelrod. Mr. J. Howard Parsons. Mrs. Emory Fansel. Mr. and Mrs. James Traverson. Miss Joyce Masters....*

The fire touched his fingers and went out as he began to shake.

Miss Joyce Masters. He remembered now. *He remembered!*

Hours when he had been flame and not flesh. Hours when his deepest hungers had been sated, his darkest passions gratified. Joyce Masters. The girl of the tumbled dark hair and richly sensuous mouth whose body had become a wild, throbbing altar to their terrible gods.

The key fitted smoothly, the door opened silently. The elevator. Without conscious thought his finger touched the twelfth floor button. A silent carpeted corridor, another door, another lock that yielded to his bit of magical brass.

He remembered the place, even in the dark. The divan where they'd fallen once, and he had not known if the roaring had been in his own throat, or only the rush of blood against his eardrums. The coffee table. He even remembered the thickness of the rug and how it had felt as he'd lain exhausted on the floor, yet charged with that inconceivable, driving torment, increased by the girl's whimpered protests.

Yes, he remembered, but the memory was in flashes and patches. *They* still held fast, and only these glimpses broke through to him. It was enough. Later, there would be more, but now he had won a victory and for once the sly tentacles had been unable to follow him.

She had led him here, but was *she* here? Perhaps after all it was only a trick.

He went into the bedroom and a sob of relief welled up from his chest. In the pale radiance of moonlight, he saw her.

She lay on the rug, with only a shaft of moonlight across her marbled thighs and softly rounded belly.

Joyce.

Why didn't you come sooner? I've been here, waiting, waiting…. Moonlight cast a deep velvet shadow in the valley of her breasts.

Joyce.

Here I am. Here.

He dropped to his knees beside her, reached for her.

You're cold.

I'm burning, I'm in fever, in heat, in flame….

So cold, Joyce. You're so still. So quiet. JOYCE!

She was toying with him, teasing him—and already he had waited too long. Red anger pushed into him. Rage at her obstinacy. Cold flesh, unmoving arms, silent lips.

He seized her roughly; began to shake her. She did not respond. He slapped her, remembering how that had moved her to frenzy before, how she had reacted even in exhaustion.

She didn't move. He cursed her, threatened. Weeping with frustration, he beat at her body with his fists.

I fooled you, didn't I? Eluded you again. You're lying! I have you right here. Own you, possess you….

You have nothing. The essence is gone. The spirit gone, the fire and the despair. All gone.

It was true. There was nothing here. She had won again. He groaned, stumbling to his feet, and switched on a bedside lamp.

Fear laid a sleazy tentacle across his heart; he stared at the girl on the rug. At the nylon stocking twisted and almost hidden in the swollen flesh of her throat.

Memories clustered and rang within his brain-mists. He listened, hating them, to the confusion of words. Memories of another time. Another woman. Another woman?

She is like you, yet different… who is she? Who?

I cannot tell.

She too is naked and lusting. Who is she?

I cannot tell.

She is silent. She will not speak to me. Who is she? I cannot tell, cannot tell, cannot tell….

He dropped to his knees beside her, wringing his hands, weeping. He spoke gently now, caressing her, pleading with her.

I didn't mean to hurt you. Don't be angry.

I hate you. Look what you've done. I HATE YOU….

No. I—I didn't mean it… you don't understand.

… hate you. Punish you… you'll see.

No.

Panic came to him and he stared wildly around the room, at the disorder. She was right. They would punish him, hate him, no matter where he went. They would find him and call out his guilt. They would shame and deride him. Destroy him.

Whimpering, he dragged the girl to the wardrobe. Inside, far back behind the dresses hanging there, behind the long velvet evening coat.

The bedroom, cluttered, devastated… they would come and see it like this, and they would know. They would find out he had been here.

Carefully he remade the ravished bed, straightened the objects on the night table. A gold-framed double photograph on the dresser caught his eye and he picked it up, frowning. The girl had dark tousled hair and a richly sensuous mouth. Smiling. Provocative eyes. Joyce. Surely Joyce, but not the Joyce crumpled behind the velvet coat. That was another girl. He ought to have known, remembered. If this was Joyce, who was the not-Joyce who'd failed to respond to his kisses or his beatings? Was it one of *Their* tricks?

He glared at the man. Youngish. Good-looking. A scrawled message, a signature, *Love, Roman.*

Roman… Roman… Roman….

One of Them. One of the persecutors, the judges, the trappers and the entanglers. He would remember the name.

He replaced the photos, then went through the bedroom, tidying the place carefully, crawling around the rug on his knees. Then the living room. Removing the empty bottles, the scraps of taffeta and torn nylon, washing and drying the glasses and putting them on their shelves. When They came there would be nothing to reproach him for. Clean and neat. Everything tidy, clean and neat.

Anxiously he went over the apartment once more, making sure that everything was in its place, everything spotless. Then he turned out the lights and left. No one in the corridor; no one in the street.

Wet grayness enveloped the city, the streets black and wet, and from the bay came the groans of foghorns.

From somewhere a girl's voice seemed to be calling him. He could almost hear her words and tried to answer. This way? Joyce? Joyce? Is it you? Where are you? Wait for me. JOYCE!

He began to run, awkwardly, as the fog closed around and its grayness became one with his.

EIGHT

Roman awoke on Sunday morning from a fitful sleep. A sudden awakening. For this was the day Joyce was to return. The Oakland mole at 2 o'clock.

He rubbed his scalp, yawning, stretching muscles that ached from lying too long in one position. He must have slept like the proverbial log. He got up and shucked off his pajamas as he headed for the shower. Needles of cold water on his flesh. He was anxious to talk to Joyce. To find out what was pulling her away from him.

He toweled briskly, wishing he could understand her. He knew she'd been fond of him—very fond of him. He knew there'd been no pretense when he'd held her in his arms and the urbane sophistication had melted away and her primitive woman-nature emerged. Afterwards he had begun to sense the fine threads of her annoyance. At him; at herself.

He pulled on robe and slippers. No use bedeviling himself about it. He'd know more when he talked to Joyce this afternoon. At least he hoped he would. The picture of Joyce—the glow and aura of her personality faded from his mind, as memories tugged insistently at the corners of his consciousness.

A rhinestone earring.

He recalled the ugly shock when he'd opened the presser's envelope attached to his brown suit, and found it there.

Someone had planted the tell-tale rhinestone cluster in his pocket. Who?

Not Wong. The boy had worked for him for five years. Wong was loyal. Wong had no motive. Wong couldn't know about the dead girl in Joyce's apartment.

Pilcher?

Could Pilcher have known? Could Pilcher have killed the girl, taken the earring, and planted it on him as they sat in his car on the way home from the office? It was a possibility.

Had Roman picked it up himself, unconsciously, and carried it off with him? He shuddered. He had been so cool, so careful during those terrible moments. He had memorized every detail, studied every angle, guarded each movement. Yet somehow one of Nina Valjean's rhinestone earrings had gotten into the pocket of his suit.

He opened the lower drawer of his desk where he kept his blueprints. Under the sketches he'd made of the house he'd hoped to build for Joyce someday. Yes, the envelope was still there, where he'd hidden it last night.

He closed the drawer. He knew he hadn't picked it up himself. Fantastic though it sounded, the real murderer had planted the earring expecting somehow to entrap Roman. Even so, it wasn't a logical sort of plant—this was no way to frame an innocent man.

Unless the glittering bauble was intended for some kind of warning....

Warning of what? Warning by whom?

By the same person who'd been watching him? Was he the mysterious man who'd gone with Nina to Joyce's apartment? Was he the man the bartender at The Red Parrot had mentioned? The man who'd had Nina several nights and given her the bad time?

His head was throbbing. He went to the sideboard and poured a jigger of Old Adam. Drinking before breakfast now. Well, who could blame him? He stared moodily at the bottle; at the fig-leafed couple on the label, and the snake leering down at them. The coiling snake—the length of nylon twisted around Nina Valjean's throat....

Roman poured another jigger of Old Adam and swallowed it.

Roman wasn't sure how long he sat in his easy chair, the empty whiskey glass in his hand. Five minutes; ten. Perhaps he even dozed off. He'd never done that before in the morning, but it wasn't impossible, considering how he'd been beating his brains out eighteen hours a day over the new plant operation.

He put the bottle of Old Adam away and went into the kitchen. Wong had left pancake batter and coffee in the pot before leaving for the day, but Roman didn't feel hungry enough for a big breakfast. He drank two cups of coffee, fried a couple of strips of bacon and scrambled a single egg, hardly tasting the food.

Today he wanted to drop in on the dancer who lived on Alvaron Street.

What was the name that barman had given him? Merrill. Cecille Merrill. A girl who had known Nina Valjean. Surely she'd be able to give some hint; throw some light on the shadowy man who seemed to be hidden in the obscurity of Nina Valjean's life.

He'd better hurry and get over to see this Merrill girl before she learned of the murder. She'd be less hesitant about talking.

He went to the bedroom to get his hat and coat—and stood staring at the floor.

A letter addressed to Roman Laird. Torn through the middle and lying there on the floor. Two screaming bits of pink.

He picked them up. Joyce's letter. The one he'd carried in his inside coat pocket to read and re-read.

Roman stood still, letting his eyes drift around to the window, the hang of the yellow drapes, the wardrobe door. Nothing, apparently, disturbed. Yet someone had been in the room. Someone had come in, taken Joyce's letter from his desk, torn it, and left it where it had fallen.

He moved to the wardrobe silently. His hand closed on the knob; his heart picked up a faster beat.

He jerked the door open and lunged inside.

No one.

He prowled the apartment, searching carefully. Front door, back door—locked.

Roman checked the apartment again. Nothing missing. His wallet secure. Wrist watch where he'd left it. Father's cuff-links, which Roman never wore, undisturbed.

Why?

That sense of being watched, the murder of Nina, the irrelevant items of the earring and the letter—a pattern? Was there some common denominator here? Joyce? Or were they independent happenings, unrelated?

Roman got his car and drove along Powell. Alvaron was half a block long—a dead end street. He examined the cards tacked on three shabby apartment house lobbies until he found what he was looking for.

C. Merrill.

He rang. A buzzer sounded, and he went up.

At the second level, the door of number seven was open and a girl stood there waiting.

She had an amazed, freckled face, extremely wide green eyes, and dark red hair put up most unattractively in metal curlers.

"My God," she said, "is there a guy in the world so ungentlemanly as to call on a lady this hour of a Sunday morning?"

"I'm sorry to break in on you so informally, Miss Merrill," Roman said. "Just a little business matter that—"

"I'm not buying anything, handsome, even if it's nothing down and nothing a week."

"I'm not selling anything, Red. All I want's a little information."

"Well—come in."

She wore a shapeless, colorless housecoat, and was evidently eating break-fast while her hair dried. "Tell me about it while I finish my coffee," she said, studying him with candid green eyes.

"Well, I don't know if you can help or not, but it's about a diamond ring Nina Valjean once had. It's not paid for, and my company isn't taking any more excuses from me. Well, I haven't been able to contact Miss Valjean, but one person I ran into said you might know how I could reach her."

"Mmm. I saw her—guess it was Tuesday. This week. She came over to touch me for a loan, but I was broke."

"Where does she live?"

"On Tuesday, it was the Sherry-Todd Hotel. They were kicking her out, not that it would matter much to you, mister, because I'm sure Nina does-n't have a diamond ring now. Not if it was worth more than a couple of bucks."

"This ring was, and my boss is worried that she may have passed it on to some guy; someone who'd fence it so we couldn't follow it." He was surprised at his glib story. It was unusually easy to talk to this funny little redhead with the curlers in her hair. "Does she have anyone steady that you know of?"

"Not Nina. Vernie wouldn't give a girl the time of day or a deed to the Bay Bridge. Neither would Bennie. Nina didn't have any steady cus-tomers, either—that I know of. Unless it would be a guy named Smith she mentioned."

"Smith? What was his first name?"

"Well—" Cecille lighted a cigarette and watched smoke drift. "It was just a mention. She never said anything about a first name. Just said 'Smith.' The guy seemed to have plenty of money, but he wasn't—well, what you call—regular. Lots of fellows aren't regular, but this guy was *really* off, ac-cording to Nina. She told me what he—he did to her. God! I don't see how the poor kid can stand that kind of life, no matter what money she makes at it. She never had a dime left over anyway."

Roman nodded, careful not to show his excitement. He had the name of the man who murdered Nina Valjean. Smith. A guy who wasn't—reg-ular.

Of course there were probably hundreds of Smiths in the City, and the name might be phony, but it was something—a beginning.

"You a store investigator or a cop?"

"Not a cop. Just a guy working for a living."

Roman let his attention wander around the curiously furnished apart-ment. Teakwood coffee table, rattan chairs and divan. Tacked to the walls were what appeared to be some kind of ceremonial costumes of brightly woven metallic cloth. "Been shopping at Gumps?"

"Further away than that." Cecy Merrill smiled. "Java. The East Indies. My former husband had business connections there. I'd always been interested in dancing, and I spent a lot of time studying the native forms. When we came here last year, I brought a few dancing costumes along—never thinking Pete and I would split up and that I'd use them to make my living."

He inspected the robes on the wall. "They look old."

"They are. Several hundred years. They were used for temple ceremonies, by dancers who were trained almost from infancy. Of course, the ones I use professionally are either modern, or copies. With a lot of the material left out!" She laughed. "Supper club and nightclub audiences don't like feminine entertainers to be overdressed."

Roman nodded, sipping the hot coffee she'd served him. "I shouldn't think temple ceremonies would be the sort of thing that a supper club—"

"It didn't take me long to find *that* out! When you're hungry, you learn fast. So I hotted up my Javanese routines with some of the numbers I'd learned in South America and Cuba."

"Ought to be very successful." Roman was amused and interested. There was a freshness and exuberance about this girl that he liked. An honesty one didn't often find. "How you making out?"

"Sometimes good, sometimes bad. Show biz is spotty. Like I starved around here for a month until I landed a job at the Cafe Noir et Rouge. Three hundred a week! Talk about clover. I paid up my bills, got square with my landlady—then the dump went bankrupt. Owing me a hundred and twenty bucks, I might add."

"Tough. Guess my troubles aren't so bad after all."

"Oh well, I shouldn't complain. I've got another job now. At The Pink Cat. The show is practically burlesque, but the boss's wife is a nut for Culture and keeps telling him he needs something authentic. So I give them a genuine authentic mixture of Javanese, Cuban, South American, with a sprinkling of Egyptian belly-waggle for good measure."

Her smile flashed suddenly. "You know something? I'm surprised at myself. Rambling along here, telling you my life history, practically. I've never done that before—and I don't even know your name!"

"It wouldn't mean a thing to you anyway," he said, feeling guilty at having thought of an alias. "I'm Roman Laird, and I haven't done a thing in my life that sounds nearly as interesting and exciting as what you've been doing. I'll certainly be around to The Pink Cat one of these nights soon to catch your act. Especially that belly-waggle."

Cecy Merrill laughed. "You'd have to order a dinner, which costs like

fury, and will undoubtedly give you ptomaine. I'll whip into my working
clothes and give you a quick run-down on the finer points. If you'll just
start that tape-recorder over by the window—really authentic Indonesian
music I picked up in Jakarta before we left."

Roman switched on the equipment as she disappeared.

The beat of a drum, joined by more drums, rolled sinuously out of the
speaker, stirring an odd response in him. Then she came back into the room
and for an instant he didn't realize it was the same girl.

Dark red hair in luxuriant waves. Small face grave except for a subtle
twinkle in green eyes, slim figure moving in heavy brocade, with oriental
poise and dignity. She bowed to Roman, as to a visiting emperor, and
dropped gracefully to a cross-legged position on the floor.

Roman watched as only her fingers moved to the drummer's cadence.
Amazingly flexible fingers. She spoke softly in a foreign tongue, then in English: "*I show you a small stream of water bubbling over rocks and pebbles....*"

He saw, in the skillful hand and finger movements, the stream of water
she described, heard the ripple and tumble and gurgling.

"*And here, Roman, a mossy bank, ferns....*" Hands and braceleted arms,
by some strange magic, brought the picture to his mind. "*And growing on
the mossy bank, a lotus flower... so....*" Through an alchemy of motion
she painted the picture vividly, colorfully: "*Clouds gather overhead, dark,
threatening... rains begin to fall... the petals of the lotus gather up and
close....*"

The drum-rhythm came faster; the girl rose slowly and effortlessly, describing the storm and its fury with all the eloquence of fingers, arms, head
and body. The drums died away to silence. Then a new beat began, syn-
copated, and the weird melody of a flute.

"So much for the authentic Javanese," Cecy said, "from here on it's
strictly Merrill."

The flute took off suddenly on a minor key, and some reed instrument
backed up a long, involved passage, seeming to shiver through the supple
dancer. Here was a new phase; primitive, earthy. The girl was really good,
Roman realized. She could be in big time show business. Probably would
be, some day.

When the music reached a crescendo, she laughed, threw back her head,
reached behind her and flung off the ornate and heavily embroidered costume. The glitter fell to the floor and what remained of her costume left
very little Cecille Merrill to the imagination.

If he had thought of her as a freckled-faced kid, he'd been mistaken. No
kid, but a slim and richly-rounded woman promising fulfillment of a man's
most intimate dreams. He watched closely as the music's rising excitement

seemed to possess her. Eyes half closed, lips parted, her body moved bonelessly, passionately, with each undulating passage.

Cymbals clashed toward the climax; with arms raised, breasts thrusting forward under their slight restraint, hips weaving in nervous motion, the girl was pure provocation.

Came the smash of drum and brass, and a silence that still seemed filled with the energy and violence of the dance.

Flushed, eyes sparkling, her breath coming in short gasps, she smiled at him and said, "See what I mean, Roman?"

He was breathing a little hard himself and he felt his own face flush as he spoke. "I certainly do. How do they let you get away with it? Even at The Pink Cat?"

She pulled a robe around her sweating body and laughed. "Well, let's just say I'm the kind of performer who responds well to the mood of her audience. Did you like it?"

"Who wouldn't? So you learned all this from the Javanese?"

"Just the beginning movements. The rest I picked up from natives in different places where we lived." She came to him, a slight smile on her red lips. "Am I boring you, Roman?"

"If you don't know what you're doing, you're very close to finding out," he said, reaching out and taking her shoulder. She came in against him, head back, lips parted.

"I liked you the minute I saw you," she whispered, before he stopped her mouth with his own.

She pulled away after a long moment, evading him as he reached for her. "A girl mustn't appear too eager, they say. Give me a cigarette, will you, Roman?"

He lit it for her, the flame trembling as it touched the tobacco. "Glad it isn't king-sized," he said. "They take a longer time to smoke."

"Roman—that's really your name, isn't it? It's not the sort you'd make up."

"No. As a child, I hated it. Afterwards, I guess it was just something I got used to."

"My husband's name was Peter. Peter Anthony Merrill." Her voice was as lazy as the cigarette smoke curling from her lips. "He was a truly handsome dog and I was crazy about him. So was every other bitch on five continents. Well—you can handle some of the competition some of the time, but—"

Roman wasn't listening very intently. The sound of her voice was smoothly exciting; the words seemed unimportant.

He'd been staring at the window as though at a picture. Through the thin curtains at the houses across the narrow street. At a doorway.

Leaning in the doorway, stood a man.

Squat, heavy-set, with a bland, hearty face and small button-black eyes. The man's right hand was thrust deep in his jacket pocket.

Roman turned to face Cecy. She was curled up on the divan, the robe dropped carelessly from her shoulder. The cigarette, only one third smoked, snubbed out in the ash tray before her. "Trouble outside," he said.

She bounded across the floor, bare feet soundless on the thin carpeting, and glanced through the curtained window. "Bennie," she said. "Who was this friend who said I knew where you could find Nina?"

"The day barman at The Red Parrot."

"Nina told me about him. Eddie. A no-good rat who was trying to put Nina on the market for himself. You talked to him and he talked to Bennie. I don't know what's up, but there's something. You'd better blow fast."

Roman pulled a cigarette, lighted it deliberately. Bennie would have no word yet of Nina's murder, but he might be suspicious of anyone asking questions about her. Unless he himself were the murderer. "This opens up some interesting possibilities," he said.

She stared at him. "You don't want to get tangled up with some of these characters, Roman."

"There's no reason to be frightened. But I would like to find a back exit at the moment."

She came to the door with him. "Go to the end of the hallway. Where the garbage chute is. Stairs go down. There's a narrow passage between two buildings that'll take you through to the other street."

"Thanks, honey."

She moved closer to him. Voice low. "Don't mention it, Roman. Stop by again some time—when you don't have a crowd of people following you."

NINE

He thought of Nina Valjean as he pulled the Jaguar out of his garage. Lying dead on the floor of Joyce's bedroom. The devastated apartment charged with outrage and powerful, unnatural lust, in such violent opposition to Joyce's neat, orderly, urbane life.

Roman hated to think of her entering that room. He wished now he'd dared that anonymous phone call to the police; at least they would have gotten in there and have everything cleaned up by now.

At the Embarcadero he parked and caught the ferry to the Oakland mole just a few moments before it pulled out.

The City of San Bruno was five minutes late coming in; he joined the scattered group of people waiting for the train. He saw Joyce first, and there was, as always, that funny little feeling of pride and surprise. She looked so completely lovely, standing there on the platform, train-case beside her. Cool, possessed, perfectly groomed in her light blue suit and tiny impertinent hat.

"Oh, there you are, darling!" She took his hand in both of hers. No kiss; not in public, anyway.

"You look completely beautiful."

She smiled. "Had a wonderful rest, which you apparently haven't. You've lost weight, Roman."

He picked up her bag and they started walking toward the ferry. "They've had me working on the double. Job's done now, though. J. Stanley gave me time off to recuperate. How was your mother?"

"Just fine. Dad, too. They haven't changed a bit."

"Now how about you? Are you tired? Does the inner woman crave food? A cocktail? An emerald? A bunch of violets?" He tried to speak brightly, aware that his words sounded false. Wondering if she sensed the falsity.

"Nothing, Roman; thanks. I just want to get home."

Home. The word loosed a small trickle of horror in him. Home, where a girl lay dead in the midst of carnage.

On the brief ferry ride, during the short walk to his car, they talked of trivial things. Hoping to fortify her, he said, "Let's stop and have a couple of martinis to celebrate your homecoming."

She shook her head. "Just drop me off at the apartment, and you can run along and have your drinks."

He slammed the powerful car into a hard turn, rubber churning and squealing. She had made the statement with deceptive casualness; but the firm dismissal was there. Okay, but before coping with that problem, he'd have to see her through the one that lay ahead; the more immediate problem.

He braked the long roadster to a stop in front of her place, jumped out and opened the door for her. "Thanks, darling. You were sweet to meet me. Don't bother to come up."

"No bother at all," he said firmly. "I'd like to get my suitcase. I won't be able to stay."

She glanced at him and he sensed her first uncertainty. She hadn't expected that. He was rather pleased with the small victory. "Going somewhere, darling?"

"A short cruise, if Johnny Madros can get me reservations," he said as they went up the elevator. "Need a rest. I'm beat."

She didn't answer, fitting her key to the lock.

She pushed the door open, and he followed close behind. She wouldn't faint or scream. Of that he was sure. But there'd be shock.

He wished he could have thought of some way to spare her.

It was dim inside; the shades were down. But when she snapped on the lights, the shock was his.

"Ah," Joyce said, "it's good to be back."

Roman felt the blood drain from his face; his sight wavered and blurred. He blinked hard, his mouth dry and throat constricted.

The apartment was as it had always been. Neat. Spotless.

No whiskey bottles. No shreds of black rhinestone-studded taffeta. No stockings or shoes or purse, no overturned coffee tables. Clean, precise, cool as lavender.

He kept control of himself. Turning—casually, he hoped—toward her bedroom door, it was open, and beyond he could see the big Hollywood bed. Not tumbled about as he had seen it last. Made up smoothly as ever.

On the floor... nothing. Deep gray carpeting. No body. No Nina Valjean.

Joyce said, "What's the matter, Roman?"

He tried weakly to smile, wondering if she noticed the sweat breaking from his forehead and upper lip. Wondering if he looked as green and dizzy as he felt. "Why—why, nothing."

"You look as if you'd met up with a corpse or something."

"My suitcase," he said. "Wasn't it in the hall closet?"

TEN

A lone light bulb cast a yellowish glare in the cluttered studio. The canvas was large. Against a background of dark clouds, two monstrous shapes seemed to hurtle through space, carrying a girl, white body almost luminescent against the somber, turgid forms.

The labored breath of the artist intensified the silence. Breath almost agonized as he touched his brush to the girl's figure again and again. Finally he stepped back to glare at his work, jaw-muscles knotting in rage.

The girl was there, but she wasn't. He had tried to capture her, to entangle her in the fine hairs of his brush, to draw her to him out of color. Yet after all his cunning, he had only pinioned her shadow. The living girl herself eluded him, mocking him.

Always, always she eluded him.

The aching, terrible emptiness within him became unbearable and he flung away his brush, pacing, cursing the pain, groaning.

If he could only remember....

He had seen her once. Clearly. But the gray fogs shrouded his memory, infuriated him.

She existed. He knew she existed, but he could not bring her to life on the canvas. Not in the captured mocking figure. But somewhere in the city she was herself. Made of flesh and soft warm lips and arms as hungry for love as his own. He knew he must find and capture and possess her as he himself was possessed.

He could find her if he kept on looking. Covering the canvas with a damp cloth, he pulled a hat low over his eyes and crept silently down the stairs and out into the alley.

The first place he stumbled upon was too brightly lighted; he avoided it. The next was smoky, dim and reasonably crowded. Music. Loud; atonal. Couples dancing as if glued together, swaying, locked hypnotically to the steady throb of the bass. Couples at the bar, heads touching. Mumble of voices, and once a scream of laughter.

She wasn't here. He would have known. His senses would have quickened and he would have recognized her. He turned and walked out.

One o'clock.

The gin-mills and taverns and clubs were thinning out, except those where late-show entertainers struggled to draw a final spate of cash customers.

Most night spots he avoided; there was a strange prickling of danger about them. But this one was in a remote section of North Beach, small, well-filled. Tables with candles. Silent-footed waiters in jackets and berets. Grotesque wall paintings—the Eiffel Tower, Arc de Triomphe, imitation Lautrecs.

A strange sense of familiarity flicked his memory.

He found a stool in the darkest corner of the bar and ordered a brandy.

"Yes, M'sieur. Staying for the floor show? Starts in just a few moments."

He shrugged, searching among the faces that floated above the bar—pale blobs that twittered and whispered and laughed softly, intimately. The brandy came, and he motioned the barman to leave the bottle. He tossed off the drink; poured another. Watched the dancing couples.

The music ended in a blast of sound. A spotlight hit the dance floor; the dancers melted back to their tables and the lush darkness.

A master of ceremonies wearing a straw hat, cane, and over-ripe accent announced the greatest floor show this side of Paree.

The man in the darkest corner poured another brandy; the long frozen pits within him had not begun to thaw; hunger pulled and drew at the veins of his body, drawing his substance. The MC's words seemed to whirl in space, clatter against ancient stones and drop down in small, glassy fragments. The orchestra burst out with the inevitable *Orpheus in the Underworld*; six can-can girls with fixed bright smiles kicked about and flounced their skirts. The MC sang a song which may have been French, and then "Mademoiselle Fifi Duclos, fresh from ze Folies Bergère," did a strip-tease to scattered shouts of *"Take it off!"*

Laughter and applause.

The MC took the spotlight, said, "I hope that if any members of the *gendarmerie* were present, they happened to be looking the other way. And if there were any minors, please to leave, because some of the entertainment to follow is a little—how do you say in America?—down to the bare facts, eh? *C'est bon, non?"*

The man in the darkest corner did not laugh or applaud with the others, but within him, excitement was growing. The show was something more than the prancing, wiggling girls. He was only half conscious of them. He lit a cigarette quickly, furtively. Words cracked and burst around about him, mostly without meaning, but excitement swelled and grew in his tissues, tightening across his chest.

As he watched, a girl in the spot was doing odd things with her hands, sitting cross-legged on a kind of teakwood stool. The music now was only a drum-beat.

He tossed a bill on the bar, ready to leave, then held back. The flute came wailing across the drum-beat; a strange and lonely cry, rising and rolling in minor cadenzas. He turned again, slowly, to watch the girl.

There was something about her—

She had risen from the teakwood stool, to begin another phase of her dance—a dance of sinuous, graceful movement. Barbaric... Oriental... ancient... primitive.

When the music changed she flung off the rich brocaded costume, leaving only narrow bands of figured gold and tan fabric to match the warm ivory of her molded flesh. Dark red hair swirled loose around her shoulders. Her eyes were closed as though dreaming of a lover's ardent embrace.

Heart pounding as though it would burst through his ribs, he watched until the storm-violent climax, every nerve alert to the dance. Yes. It had to be. The girl. *The girl....*

He slipped away quietly during the dance act that followed. And there in back of the night club was the alley. A couple of street lights over the rear entrance cast long velvet shadows. He flattened into the darkness and watched.

She came out after a while. A slight figure, muffled in a light green coat with collar turned up against the night-cold. He watched as she walked out of the alley mouth and started down the street.

He followed, a long distance behind. For five blocks; six. Turned into a narrow street, blinking in the moonlight. He thought he'd lost her. She wasn't there when he turned the corner. The street came to a blind end, and he stared, dazed. Then he noticed the light at the second story window of one of the shabby apartments.

A slender shadow crossed the translucent shade; recrossed again.

It was the girl. He couldn't see her, but he knew. Faintly, the sound of water running; the raising of the window.

The light went out.

He waited immobile, though he was shaking inside. Fifteen minutes. Half an hour. He studied the building. A drain-pipe. From there, a foothold over a bay window. Narrow ledge. Window....

He climbed quickly, silently. Lifting the window with infinite caution. Tight wood protested. He froze. Minutes passed. No sound inside. Curtains swayed in the slight air movement—nothing else.

Cautiously, excitement beating in him, he climbed in. No sound.

Moonlight flooded part of the room; the part where the daybed had been opened.

The girl with the expressive hands lay there. The girl in his painting... asleep... real.

Smelling, tasting, feeling reality. His hand touched a box-like instrument. Two reels—knobs. Instinctively he turned the knobs. An orange-red light glimmered. And sound—low, insistent. A drum, joined by other drums. Drums tapped with fingers, lightly, sinuously. The same music she'd danced to earlier, at the nightclub. Into which she'd blended and been absorbed.

He watched her face, framed in an aura of hair that was pale in the moon-glow; watched an uncertain frown crease her forehead as drums reached inward to caress her consciousness.

The girl stirred, making small sounds in her throat.

He crept forward, watching intensely, yet careful not to move into the thin moonlight. He saw her eyelashes flutter, her eyes open, and drew his breath sharply.

She saw the shadow darker than the rest of the room, a shadow that breathed and felt and sought and bulked above her. The muscles of her throat tightened, thickening as if to scream, but there was no scream. She must have realized he was too close; it came out as a whisper: "Who—are—you?"

He was slow to answer. The unfamiliar word-sounds came hard to his stiffened lips.

"Dance," he said. "Dance like you did."

Her mouth worked, but no words came. He watched her face, taut and pale with terror. The thin, silvery notes of a flute cut in above the solid beat beat beat of drums; she rose to one elbow, head moving disbelievingly, wide eyes straining into the darkness at him.

"Dance," he repeated, urgency jolting him. He reached an arm forward into the patch of moonlight, clutched the blankets and jerked them aside.

"Now," he said. "Now!"

She whimpered a little, but she seemed to understand. She had to understand, he thought desperately. He felt himself trembling as she rose slowly. In the faint moonlight her body had the look of marble.

She began to move to the music, hands molding thin oriental harmonies, white arms creating hills and forests and lovers meeting. Caught up by the rhythm, she was swayed and blown and tousled as by a lustful wind.

The cry of the lute and the wail of strings seemed to compel her to a change of tempo. Latin rhythms leaped and she responded as she always had; with sinuous movement of thighs and hips. Movements that had their origins in the primitive ceremonials of interior Africa and Cuba.

Her terror, he sensed, was not dispelled, but it was now mixed with something else. The terror and fear of the night and the stranger were there, and excitement, too. Growing. Charging her with life. With a passion and a hunger to match his own.

His chest hurt with the force of his breathing. The drum beat, tormented, throbbed in him with a solid, demanding cadence. He knew it was the same with her; the physical demands of the dance were thrusting aside protective layers of her conventions as he had thrust aside the protective blankets.

Muted cymbals clashed and a battery of faraway tom-toms murmured to a reluctant close. The dance ended; the girl's expression was one of stunned disbelief.

He reached out and drew her into the shadows.

She was panting hard; he could feel her heart leaping wildly. His arms tightened around her; hands drinking exultation from her.

For long moments her body remained stiff. Not resisting, but antagonistic. Then she slowly relaxed, became limp, heavy. He half held her while she slumped to the floor. He dropped to one knee beside her, the old sense of savagery and rage boiling up in him again.

Almost almost almost and she had fled again!

He ground his teeth with the pain, tears stinging his eyes and crawling on small wet feet down his cheeks. He grasped her roughly by the shoulders, shook mercilessly and she moaned. Let her go. His fingers, clutching at the rough-textured carpet, found something soft, silky.

A nylon stocking. Filmy as a spider's web. Strong as a rope.

She must have come out of her faint without his being aware. Perhaps the touch of the nylon, whispering around her throat. It was dark; he could not have noticed her eyes opening; he was too filled with his own anger to sense her terror, her breasts rising as she drew breath and strength.

Her scream startled him; the sudden push shoved him off balance, and when he recovered an instant later he caught only a bare ankle that tore from his grasp.

He was too slow; she had reached a door and opened it. Light from the corridor came in, and he caught a glimpse of her pounding at a door before he recoiled. Heard the frantic pounding of her fists, her hysterical screams. *"Mrs. Cardozo! Mrs. Cardozo! A man.... Let me in!"*

Sounds through the walls—people moving, doors slamming. Shouts. What's going on there... help... help... police....

Sounds that were waves engulfed him. Shrill screams were rusty knives in his brain. He turned and darted to the window.

The street still clear. Run; run. Lights flashing on in the apartment building. Shouting and calls and noise.

Somewhere behind a heavy voice called, *"Hey, you...."* He lowered his head and ran faster. Faster and faster into the dark streets, into the alleys, into the bowels of the city.

ELEVEN

The telephone rang.

"Roman?"

"Yes, Joyce. How are you, darling?"

"Roman!" There was hysteria in her voice. *"There—there's a dead woman in my closet!"*

His hand grew sweaty on the telephone. "Call the police. Right away, Joyce."

"Roman—she must have been there all night. I *slept* here—with her in the closet!"

"It doesn't sound possible. You're quite sure she's—"

"Of course." Her voice sounded more controlled now. "I wasn't dreaming or seeing things. She's there. And she's dead. And she's been—been dead quite a while."

"Don't let it throw you, honey. Call the police, and I'll come right over."

There was silence, then she said, "I wouldn't have bothered you, Roman, only—for a moment I couldn't think; didn't know what to do. There's no reason for you to—I mean—I suppose the police will take care of everything—whatever there is to take care of."

"It's bound to be a bit unpleasant. Maybe I can help."

Her voice was suddenly tired. "All right, Roman."

The police hadn't yet arrived when he got to Joyce's apartment. "Where is she?" he asked.

She motioned. "Still in the closet. At the back. Some of my evening dresses are hanging there, and of course it was dark, and I didn't notice anything last night, and Roman, the police won't think *I* did it, will they?"

"I don't see how, Joyce. What's to connect you with it—her? You were away until yesterday afternoon. Is she anyone you know?"

"I don't think so. I didn't really get a good look at her face, but—"

"It sounds crazy, but there must be some rational explanation. She might have been drinking, or was drugged or something, and wandered in here to die."

He caught the quick, questioning look in her eyes. "She's stark naked, Roman!"

"She could still have been wandering— You know how some women get when they've been drinking too much."

Her questioning look increased, he thought, as the doorbell rang. A signal for her lithe body. She almost leaped to answer, and opened the door for two men.

"Trumbull," one of them said, "Homicide. This is Inspector Davis. You the lady who called us?"

"Yes. I'm Joyce Masters. This is Mr. Laird. Roman Laird."

Trumbull looked at Roman impassively. "Lawyer?"

Roman answered firmly, "Fiancé."

Joyce said, "She—she's in there."

Trumbull walked through Joyce's bedroom, and into the wardrobe closet. He came out a few moments later and spoke to Davis. "Get the boys. We've got a job." He turned to Joyce. "We'll have fingerprint men and police photographers here in a few minutes. Meanwhile, if you don't mind answering some questions—"

Joyce explained that she'd been visiting her family in Ohio for the past two weeks, returned only yesterday afternoon. She was tired and went to bed early. This morning she'd gone to the closet and in straightening up, discovered the body. She had promptly called the police —and Mr. Laird. She was quite sure she'd never seen the woman before, and had no idea who might have put her there.

"Who used your apartment while you were away?"

"No one. At least, no one with my authorization. As far as I know, the place was vacant."

"If you had to prove you only got in yesterday afternoon, I suppose you'd have no trouble doing that, Miss Masters? Train ticket, conductor, and so on?"

"I'd have no trouble."

"I met her at the train at two," Roman offered. "We took the ferry, and returned here about three or thereabouts."

"I see. Is this woman a stranger to you too, Mr. Laird?"

"I don't know. I haven't seen her yet." He'd walked around *that* one easily enough.

Trumbull asked his address, occupation, and a few more questions. The other members of the homicide squad came. They took pictures and drew sketches and made notes while fingerprint men dusted and examined.

Presently they carried out the body of Nina Valjean. Trumbull pulled back the sheet for a moment. She wasn't pretty. Not with the stocking still around her throat. Roman felt Joyce's hand grip his. He shook his head. "I don't remember having ever seen her before."

Trumbull nodded. "I'd like to have you both keep in touch with us until after the inquest. You're not under arrest or anything like that, of course. Just that there'll probably be more questions when we know who she is."

"No objection if we move Miss Masters to a hotel tonight? I don't imagine she'll want to stay here."

"No objection, Mr. Laird. She can pack some things and leave now if she wants."

"Oh, no," Joyce said weakly. "I—I'm all right here. I—"

Roman said, "You're not thinking of *staying*, are you?"

She looked trapped. "I don't know what I was thinking. No; you're right, Roman. I'd better go to a hotel. The Bellevue-Carlton."

The officer said, "Okay; just so we know."

Joyce packed a bag and they left, with the homicide men still at work. He took her to the hotel where she registered and had her bag sent up. Then they went into the Red Room where Roman ordered a double shot for each of them. "Just what I needed," Joyce said, shakily. "I thought I was doing pretty well, but—"

"After-shock. A nasty experience. Let's hope it won't be too unpleasant in the future."

"Meaning?"

"Newspapers. You know what they'll do with a thing like this. Mystery Nude Found in Beautiful Model's Apartment."

She frowned. "I didn't think about the newspapers—"

"People forget quickly enough, though. The papers may whoop it up for a couple of days, but there'll be an ax-murder soon, or a big fire, or another crisis in Asia."

She nodded absently, and then her face alerted with thought.

"Who was she, Roman?"

"Who? I haven't any idea."

"What became of her clothes? She had to have them on when she came in."

"Probably whoever killed her took them away. Or hung them in your wardrobe among your things. I don't suppose you've checked to see—"

"No. I don't suppose it matters. Only—God, it must have been horrible for her, Roman. Like a bad dream that turns out to be real."

"Here, Joyce; stop it." Roman laid his hand on her arm. "You've got to toughen your mind to it, honey. You can't let yourself think about it. You've got to teach yourself to forget."

She closed her eyes for a moment. "I think I'm all right now, Roman."

He studied the perfect oval of her face, the straight, patrician nose, wide-set eyes, full sensuous lips. "Sure," he said. "You're all right now, Joyce."

Then he saw her face go white. "I—I'll have to go back there to pack."

"Pack?" His throat went dry, and he took a generous sip of his drink, as she glanced at him guardedly.

"Didn't I tell you? Tom Barton's agent found me a place over in Marin that sounds exactly right. I'd intended going over today to see it, only—"

"Barton? Crane Chemical's Tom Barton?"

"Of course." She drained her glass. "I mentioned to Bart I was looking for a place before I went to Ohio. He said he'd have his agent check around. I guess he did, because he phoned last night."

Blood pounded in his head, but he spoke coolly. "I thought you were going to move down the peninsula. In your letter—"

"I know, but I believe I'd like the other side of the bay. It's less crowded. More hills and trees. An ideal place to raise cats." Her smile was a little strained, he thought.

"How about raising a few Laird children? Guaranteed not to scratch."

"Not this year, thanks. Cats aren't as hard on the figure." Her eyes darted away nervously.

Suddenly a new and disturbing thought came into Roman's mind. His first instinct was to reject it as absurd. He lit a cigarette, reviewing quickly. It didn't seem possible, but now, in this moment of realization, he could see that the pattern of evidence went back a long time. Several weeks.

Joyce was afraid.

And her fear, though it may have been accentuated by the finding of Nina, was no new thing. Even before she'd gone to Ohio she'd been nervous and uneasy. He'd caught the expression in her eyes though her manners were as smoothly gracious as ever. He'd sensed that her conversation masked unspoken thoughts. There was something... someone.

Another man?

He tested cautiously. "Where in the big county of Marin is this cat's paradise located, Joyce?"

"I really don't know. Sausalito, Ross, Fairfax; one of those little towns, I imagine. Or in the hills around them."

"Well, if you're looking for seclusion, that's where you'll find it. Take a lot longer to commute, though. Will you take the bus, or drive?"

He caught the wariness in her voice. "I might not do either. Not work at all for the next few months."

"Won't you get bored?"

"Oh, I'll be busy. Don't laugh, Roman, because I'm really serious about this: I may write a book."

"Why would I laugh? Lots of people write books. Some quite successful."

"Mine will hardly be a best-seller, but it's one I've had in mind a long time. On the psycho-dynamics of the graphic arts. In other words, the relationships between artists and photographers on one hand, and their work on the other, and which is the product of which. An interesting field. I've made reams of notes on my observations already."

"And after you get the book done, and it's published?"

She met his eyes reluctantly. "I don't know." Then she said, "I think I'll go to my room and try to sleep a little. I'm awfully tired all of a sudden."

"A good idea. How about me coming by later and we'll have an early dinner?"

He caught the faint tremor of her hand as she lifted her glass. "All right. Say about five?"

"Five it is."

In the lobby, she touched her fingertips quickly to his cheek, smiling almost shyly. He thought she was on the point of saying something, but she didn't. He watched her to the elevator, then walked out into Geary Street. The afternoon papers were already on the stands.

BIZARRE GIRL KILLING REVEALED. MURDERED NUDE FOUND IN CLOSET.

He bought copies, turned into a bar, ordered a drink, and read the items. They didn't tell much. *The strangle-murder of a young woman, as yet unidentified, was revealed today by the return of a vacationing fashion model, Joyce Masters, 1001 Farallone Street, who discovered the nude body in her clothes closet... preliminary investigation disclosed she had been dead about three days, apparently strangled by a nylon stocking. An autopsy report is awaited.*

There was more; he read quickly through the puddle of words for the few essential facts. Then came the shock.

Police are attempting to link the slaying with an attempted assault late last night on Cecille Merrill, 27, a dancer residing at 79 Alvaron Street. According to the victim's story, she awakened at around 2 A.M. to find a prowler in her room. He compelled her to perform a weird moonlight dance before seizing her. Miss Merrill said she believes she fainted, and recovered a few moments later to find the man in the act of twisting a nylon stocking around her throat. She succeeded in fighting him off, and ran screaming down the hall to the apartment of the manager, Louisa Cardozo, who called police. At Doctor's Hospital, where she was being treated for shock, she was unable to give a coherent description of the intruder, except that he was about five feet ten, and of medium build....

Roman wiped his forehead with a handkerchief. It seemed incredible that he should be concerned with two such weird events. The murder of Nina Valjean; the assault on Cecille... was the elusive Smith involved in both?

Smith. The man who'd picked up Nina at The Red Parrot. Who must have taken her to Joyce's apartment. Was he the same man who had assaulted Cecille? Was there a link between Smith and Roman's own feeling of being watched? Did he have anything to do with the earring planted in Roman's pocket or the torn letter Roman had found on the floor in his apartment? Incredible. The whole thing was an absurdity. Even assuming that Smith was a madman, there was no way in which all the events could be tied into a cohesive pattern. There was, of course, such a thing as coincidence. The things—or some of them—might have happened without any connection whatever.

He finished his drink and went to the telephone booth. When Doctor's Hospital answered, he asked if Miss Merrill was still there. The cool voice was doubtful.

"Who's calling, please?"

"Roman Laird. A friend of Miss Merrill's."

"Just a moment, please."

There was a delay, and then he heard Cecille. "Hello, Roman." She sounded a little shaky. "I suppose you've been reading the papers."

"Just saw them. Nice people you pick up with! How are you?"

"Well," and there was a trickle of wry humor in her voice, "I've been better. I wasn't really hurt but that guy sure scared hell out of me!"

"I don't wonder. How long are they going to keep you?"

"The doctor said I could leave now if I liked, but he recommended that I stay overnight, and I think I will. They've given me sedatives, and what with talking to the police and all, I'm a little punchy. To tell the truth, I'm not too anxious to spend the night alone in the—the apartment."

"You ought to have a gun. How about me driving you home tomorrow, and we'll see about getting you one, along with a license?"

"I'd like a ride home, but I don't know about the gun. We can talk about it."

"About nine, then? I'm on vacation."

"That'll be wonderful, Roman."

It was two o'clock. He'd go on home, have a sandwich and milk, shower, and perhaps get a nap before returning to the hotel to meet Joyce. He felt tired; a vacuum-like feeling that seemed to suck at his bones with quiet, steady malevolence.

As he unlocked his apartment door, a prickling sense of uneasiness rose in him. He swung the door cautiously, stepping in without sound. He moved from living room, to bedroom to kitchen. Nothing had been disturbed that he could see. No one hidden in closets or corners.

Imagination.

He found some cold ham in the refrigerator, and a bottle of milk. He ate his sandwich absently, still obsessed with a curious sense of unease.

On impulse he walked across the living room and looked out. A man was idling along the sidewalk, half a block away, his back toward Roman. The figure was familiar. The walk, the movement of head, the tilt of hat.

Pilcher.

Roman's eyes narrowed. Bob Pilcher, vindictive, half-crazed by jealousy. Half-man, half-boy; undisciplined emotionally. Smith? *Could Pilcher be—*

A sudden, electrifying thought came to him. It opened up a new, if horrifying, avenue of reasoning. It still left gaps, but it might go far to explain the body in Joyce's wardrobe, as well as her fear.

Suppose that unknown to him, Joyce had, for some reason of her own, loaned the apartment to Nina Valjean while she was away? Suppose Smith had gone there *expecting to find Joyce—and had killed Nina in error?*

Sweat broke out on his forehead, sweat needled his body with queasy, damp fear.

There were holes in the theory. He was forgetting there had first been a wild party. Someone had been there with Nina, drinking and carousing. Smith? Or someone else? Had Smith come later, when the revelry was over, and found Nina there alone? Had he killed her then? Who had cleaned up afterwards and placed her body in the wardrobe?

The facts didn't jibe. There was some important element he hadn't yet found, or hadn't been able to see. But it was clear that Joyce's life was somehow tangled with Smith's.

It was equally clear that she had known of his existence for some weeks back—and was in deadly fear of him. Smith. A madman. A faceless creature of cruel lusts and strange powers.

Maybe he was still trying to find her. And if he found her, then what? *Would he try again to kill her?*

TWELVE

Roman took a taxi to Joyce's hotel, arriving only a few moments before five. He had waited impatiently enough, but he knew she'd be safe in the Bellevue-Carlton, and she never liked to be hurried by having anyone arrive earlier than expected.

The evening newspapers had done the murder up in somewhat juicier headlines; the *Times* had a picture of Cecille in one of her dancing costumes captioned DANCER IN MYSTERY ATTACK, and he smiled slightly, remembering his visit to her apartment. Perhaps, he thought, he shouldn't have left so hastily. Bennie could have waited.

He felt himself going tense as he approached the hotel desk. "Will you ring Miss Masters, please. Tell her Roman Laird is calling."

The clerk was bland, impassive. "Miss Masters checked out about two—two-thirty this afternoon."

"You must be mistaken!" Anger began to rise in him, but he added quietly enough, "Perhaps you have confused Miss Masters with someone else; she only registered around noon today."

"I'll check again, sir, but I did so just about half hour ago for another gentleman. Here's Miss Masters' registration card; it shows she paid her bill and checked out at two-thirty."

"You—you're *sure?*"

"No mistake, sir. I was on duty myself."

No doubt about it, then. She'd left the hotel after promising to meet him at five. He thought of Smith; of his fear for her safety. "Was Joyce—Miss Masters alone? I—I mean, was there anyone near who might have been with her?"

"She came to the desk alone, but there was a man waiting for her in the lobby, as I remember. She went over to meet him and they went out together. She seemed pleased to see him."

"What did he look like? Can you tell me—"

"I didn't really notice, sir."

"Did Miss Masters leave a forwarding address, or message for me?"

"No sir."

"Okay; thanks."

Roman walked out, questions burning in his mind. What had happened to change Joyce's mind? Where had he gone? Who was the man waiting for her in the lobby? Smith?

Joyce feared Smith, but she seemed pleased to see the man who'd waited for her in the lobby of the Bellevue-Carlton. He swallowed, trying to relieve the hard ache in his chest. The very ground seemed to be shifting under him as he walked. Things were happening that had no right to happen in an orderly, logical world.

Here was Joyce Masters, happily greeting a man of whom she appeared to be in growing terror. Assuming the man was Smith. But who else *could* he be?

A cop? Maybe. If not—

He walked quickly, with nervous energy. It would have been impossible to stand still; to sit still. The idea of Joyce in the hands of the brute who'd murdered Nina, who'd tried to—to rape Cecille—kill her....

The police, yes. But—

Roman shuddered. He'd be running his neck into a noose.

And if he was?

Well, Joyce would be safe. She might feel bad about him. And J. Stanley would be annoyed. But other than that, the life of Roman Laird was of singularly little importance to anyone.

Very well, then; the police had to be notified.

Inspector Trumbull drew little squares on a notepad, and filled in every other one with careful pencil strokes. "Okay; you didn't tell us the whole story this morning. So now what have you got for us?"

"I can tell you who she is, where she came from, and that she was moved by someone."

"And who killed her?"

"Maybe. You give; I give."

The inspector changed over to circles. He put a dot in the center of each. "What are we supposed to give?"

"Joyce Masters checked out of the Bellevue-Carlton at two-thirty this afternoon. She went away with a man who might be the killer. Give me your assurance you'll find her; make sure she's safe."

"We don't make any deals, Laird."

"Your job is to prevent crime as well as investigate, isn't it? Find Joyce Masters, and you may be preventing a crime."

The detective took a small pocketknife from his desk and sharpened the point of his pencil. "Tell us what you know and if it's good we'll act."

"Her name was Nina Valjean. She was a prostitute who hung around The Red Parrot. It's a dive on Grogan's Alley. She was on dope. The owner, a beefy brute named Bennie, peddled her. Her supplier is named Vernie. He hangs around there too."

"Go on."

"She'd had a repeat customer. Smith is all the name I could get for him. There was something strange about him. I think he took her to Joyce's apartment and killed her."

"Why Joyce's apartment? And what makes you think she's gone off with him, as you say?"

"I don't know, but I'm convinced Joyce has known Smith, or known about him, or there's been some connection for some time back. She's been scared. That's why I'm worried about her."

"Where'd you get this story?"

Roman managed a wry grin. "This, Inspector, is where the going gets rough. Mostly for me, I'm afraid. You see, Joyce wasn't the first one to find Nina's body. I did."

"When?"

"At noon Friday. I went up to Joyce's place to get a suitcase, because I was trying to book a vacation trip on a steamer to Vancouver. When I went inside, I found the place a mess. As if someone had had one hell of a party there. Well—she was on the floor in the bedroom."

"You knew her?"

"No; I found out who she was later." He tossed the match-cover on the desk. "This was in her purse."

"*Sexational Nina Valjean.* You took this from the scene of the crime, eh?"

"Yes."

"Why didn't you report it?"

"That's the embarrassing part, Inspector. I was reasonably sure you'd think I did it. Because—I can see that's your next question—there are only two keys to the apartment—as far as I know—and I have one of them. Joyce was in Ohio when I found the body."

"You don't have an alibi?"

"I don't know when she was killed, though I imagine it was Thursday night or Friday morning."

"Yeah. We figure it between midnight and five A.M. Friday morning. Where were you then?"

"Home in bed. Sleeping."

"Well, most people are, at those hours. Alone, I suppose?"

"Alone; yes."

"Okay. Go on."

"That's all." No need to mention Cecille. Or the earring. Or the torn letter. Or the strange, creepy atmosphere that seemed to be settling down, fog-like, over him. "I suppose now you usher me to the lock-up?"

Trumbull looked up from his doodling. "Why would we do that?"

"Why? Well, the keys, for one thing. And the fact that my fingerprints have been all over the place. I was there, and didn't tell you. And—"

"Did you kill her?"

"No."

"Did we say you did?"

"No—but—"

"The keys don't bother us. I'm not saying there isn't plenty about this case that *does* bother us. But the keys don't. It's no big deal for a guy who's handy with such things to try a waxed blank in the lock and file out for the tumblers. Or the former tenant might have had an extra. Or the janitor got a little careless with his pass-key. As it happens, the particular janitor in that building quit only last week, saying he was retiring back to the old country. Sweden. We got a request out to the Stockholm police to pick him up for questioning."

"I—I didn't know that."

"Didn't suppose you did. We knew she'd been moved after she was dead, too. Blood has a way of following gravity when the heart stops. Goes to the part nearest the floor, naturally. Causes discoloration. Well, she was half sitting up in that closet, but the discoloration was on her back."

Roman grinned. "I guess people don't give the police enough credit. And I'm not trying to talk myself into a murder trial, but isn't it a little suspicious, about me not saying anything after I found her?"

Trumbull put the pencil back in his pocket and shoved the pad aside. "That part is bad. You should have reported, and you sure as hell shouldn't have monkeyed around and suppressed evidence. We knew you were there, see, and the facts don't seem to tie with guilt. At least not yet they don't."

"You knew I was there?" He could have hit himself on the head for his stupidity. Of course! How could he have forgotten. "Pilcher! Bob Pilcher! Naturally he'd tell you after the crime came out in the papers. He happens to hate my guts."

"Regardless how we know, she wasn't killed at noon Friday when you went there. If you did kill her early in the morning, and went back later to remove evidence or something, you wouldn't likely have brought along a witness."

Roman wiped his forehead. "I believe you. Now what about Joyce?"

"I can tell you this much. You don't have to worry about her."

"You know where she is?"

"We told you both to keep in touch with us and don't go anywhere we didn't know about. Miss Masters is a smart girl. When she moved, she got in touch with us."

"Where did she go?"

Trumbull shook his head.

"How do you know the man she left with isn't Smith? The killer?"

"This guy had nothing to do with the murder. We checked him out. He's clean."

"Who is he?"

The detective shook his head again. "How come if you're her fiancé, like you said, she didn't tell you herself?"

"We— I guess she didn't care to."

"Washed up?"

Roman lifted his shoulders.

"Since when?"

He drew a deep breath. "Well, nothing's been said. Not definitely, that is. I—just recently began to get the idea."

"Yeah. Anything else you want to get off your chest?"

"That's all I can think of."

"Okay. Let me know if anything comes back to you; anything we ought to know. Even if it doesn't make sense."

"It—it's all right for me to leave now?"

"Why not? Only, Laird, no more of this junior G-man stuff. And *strictly* no more fooling with evidence. Because next time I'll toss you in the poky for sure."

He was drawing little men with targets for eyes as Roman left.

He should be relieved, Roman told himself as the taxi took him home-ward. But he was more confused; more bewildered. At least Joyce was safe. *But who was the man?* How was he involved? He must have been involved, or the police wouldn't have investigated him in the first place. They'd checked him out. He was clean.

He paid off the driver at the curb and started to put his key into the lock. *"Where is she?"*

A hand on his shoulder spun Roman around.

"Where is she, damn you?"

Pilcher.

He ducked the clumsy swing easily; pinned the engineer against the en-trance wall. "Ask the police, Bob. They know. After all, you're so chummy with them these days."

"Are you going to tell me where Joyce is?"

"In your present hysterical state, no. And, Bob, keep out of my way. I don't want to hurt you, but if you force me, I'll hurt you bad."

Pilcher's pink face turned red. "You wait!" he snarled, and wrenched free from Roman's grasp. "You wait, Laird!"

Roman's lips twisted. He'd wait. There really wasn't much else he could do.

He entered his apartment carefully, as before. Wong was busy in the kitchen. He had evidently given the place his customary Monday vacu-uming. The pleasant odor of beef stew came from the stove. Good. He was hungry as a wolf. Pleasant odor; pleasant memory.

He thought of Cecille, whom he'd promised to drive home from the hospital tomorrow. He was surprised to find himself looking forward to seeing the insouciant little red-head again.

THIRTEEN

The night was clear and crisp and dark. No moon. The stars pushed back into their velvet hiding-places by the city's hazy lights. The streets were quiet and empty.

In the labyrinths, near the waterfront where lights were few, where the pavement was rough and broken by the weight of trucks and trailers, where even work-brightened rails failed to reflect a glimmer, a man moved.

Quickly, with the sure step of one who had passed here many times.

He did not feel the cold, for a hot, wicked excitement jetted through his veins and arteries and flickered like tiny sparks along his nerves.

He was remembering... *remembering!*

Not everything. Not nearly everything, but remembering fragments of the past that he could cling to, portions of pictures that did not dissolve away. Hungrily he turned them in his mind, caressing and polishing the broken bits, fearful they might escape again. As precious as they were meaningless.

A letter floating in a cloud, a musky living scent.... Satiny fabrics and frothy lace and soft warm flesh... (hold it tightly; hold it firm)... a child's shoe and a yowling cat. Day and night tumbling together, like jaded lovers tossing on their sweat-soaked bed.

Yes, he was remembering. The empty, pale cells of his mind were filling again; life was returning to them, one by one, like the lights of a city long before dawn. But so few... so useless a pattern. None of it with meaning, nothing to show him the Enemies still hidden in the receding fog.

He chuckled. Never mind. He was gaining on them. He *had* recaptured these memories, these small, polished pebbles, and he held them close and snug against his straining eyes.

He would have to hurry. Perhaps tonight his mind would spin out still more fragments and they would merge and form a picture. Perhaps this very night he would *know*.

A voice from the dark sedan called, "Hold it a minute there, bud."

Police!

Fear jolted him into action. He leaped forward, running.

The car's motor roared, he hunched forward, covering his face as a searchlight glare swept over him the instant before he swung around the corner into a protecting alley. He was fast. He was desperate.

The police car turned clumsily into the alley but he was already a hundred yards beyond. He dodged behind packing cases, into doorways, out of the bouncing lightway.

A loud *crack!*

They were shooting at him, warning him to stop.

He grunted with relief; here was the narrow place between the buildings. Too narrow for the car.

With an animal's fierce cunning, he dodged and swerved, appeared and disappeared in the rays of their handlights. No target. He heard the boom of guns; the deadly whisper of bullets. A fire-escape.

A leap upward, fingers clawing for the cold steel. Up and up, moving fast, the lights of the pursuers probing, cutting the darkness, seeking him, as he made his way to the roof.

"*Up there, Clancy!* Jeez, the guy's a regular ape! Take it slow now and pick him off. I'll hold the light."

Sweat blinded him. He ran with a cat's sure footing, crouching low.

Lights were flashing on in buildings all around... there were shouts from all directions: "There he is!" "*Hey*—get him now!" "He's going that way! *Hurry....*"

He caught the gleam of glass of the skylight, opened it, and plunged through. Dark, but he sensed no one in the room. Boxes? Storage? A doorknob turned in his sweaty hand and he ran down a corridor, heart hammering as loudly as his shoes on the bare floor.

A stairwell ahead, dimly lighted. Man in a bathrobe, huge pistol in his fist. There was no stopping. He careened into the man, both plunging down a few stairs, his legs moving with a strength and knowledge of their own, carried him along. A door opened; light flooded out. The fleeting glimpse of a fat woman peering, screaming, "*Henry! What is*—" Kitchen. Backdoor. Porch. Stairs, and the cold, covering night!

The shouts were at a distance now. Down this alley he ran, this alley of familiar smells and shapes.

Here was the doorway. *Here.*

The door yielded and he was inside gulping air, gulping the taste of stale grease and dirty oil. Safe?

There were no more sounds of pursuit.

He climbed the stairs, knees shaking; climbed to the well-known room. Stumbling to the window, he crouched on the floor and peered carefully over the sill. No lights in the narrow street.

He wiped sweat with a shaking hand. Slowly his terror subsided, and his breath returned.

He was safe.

There was something he had to do. But the mind-impulse could do nothing against the lethargy of his weary flesh.

He was tired; so tired his senses trailed off into nothingness. But there was something that might help. Whiskey.

Whiskey had helped before. He found the cardboard carton under the sink without light. The quart was there, almost full. He unscrewed the stopper, drank greedily from the bottle, the liquor tingling and warming him. He put it away in the box and sat down. Resting; gathering his strength, and presently, sure the hunt had ended, he switched on the solitary light bulb.

The painting—shadowy, unfinished—plucked at his interest, and he studied the harsh, compelling lines, the leaping, dancing gargoyles, the blazing coffins, the girl poised as if to flee in terror, yet peering over her shoulder in morbid fascination.

He touched his brush in carmine, flicked it to the flames, to lips, to breasts. Still the distortion, still the wavering as of pebbles seen through churning, restless green water.

He must break through the shadows.

The grayness began to fill the room gathering in the corners and rolling outward like a gray and stealthy marsh-gas. Smothering him. "No. *No!*" he screamed. "*No—*"

The paint brush dropped from his fingers, and he clutched at his aching head, trying to hold his memory-fragments, but the flood of memory was too weak. One by one the exciting images disappeared. There was nothing but the great, empty, evil grayness.

FOURTEEN

Cecille was waiting for him when he called for her at Doctor's Hospital. Smiling, bright-eyed, and fresh looking in a soft green coat.

"Healthiest looking specimen I ever saw leaving a hospital," he said.

He flagged a cab at the curb; for some obscure reason he hadn't wanted to take the Jaguar. As they started moving away, he said, "I hate to tell you this now, but if I don't, you'll know soon enough anyway. It hit the papers the same time your story did."

"Something about Nina?"

"Yes."

She drew a deep breath. "I'm okay, Roman. Tell me."

"She's dead. She—she was found strangled in another girl's apartment. The nylon stocking was still twisted around her neck."

"God have mercy on her." White-faced, Cecille closed her eyes, her fingers straying to her own throat. She whispered, "Then—the man who climbed through my window—he must have been the same one."

"The police think so."

"Do you?"

"I think there are too many points of similarity for any doubt."

"You talk funny sometimes, Roman." She wrinkled her nose at him.

"I've been told there are a lot of funny things about me. It's probably very true, too."

"You're not married?"

"The last girl wouldn't have me."

"I didn't think you looked married." She fell silent, and he saw her smile had disappeared. He said nothing more until the cab unloaded them in Alvaron Street. "I'd better go up with you—just in case."

She nodded. "I wish you would."

He entered first, and searched the apartment carefully. Cecille followed him in; frowning at the unmade bed, the rumpled throw-rug. "Just as I left it. I would have thought the police would have—done something or other."

"They probably dusted for fingerprints."

"Poor Nina. Poor lost soul!" The tears started; he saw them glimmer in her eyes before she covered her face with her hands, and he held her, comforting, soothing, knowing she needed the relief of sorrow. He felt a final shudder and sigh run through her slim body, heard her voice muffled against his chest. "Why didn't she scream, Roman? *Why?*"

"Maybe she did," he said thickly. "Or maybe—"

She pushed away and looked at him, cheeks wet, eyes serious. "Roman, are there two kinds of men? I mean two kinds?"

"Two kinds?"

"There must be some who aren't—aren't really human. Animals. Brutes. Things that only look like men. Because, Roman, they never just rape a girl—they want to destroy her, too. *Why? Where is the soul God gave men?*"

Small hairs prickled at the back of his neck. Where, indeed? Blackened and burned away by lusts that grew increasingly vile? Leached out of them by some corrosive by-product of evil and corruption?

She shook her head doggedly. "That's enough of this. Go in the kitchen and make a pot of coffee, will you, Roman? I want to straighten up a little."

"Right." He found half a can of coffee and got busy. When Cecille came in she'd changed to a simple black skirt and green sweater that lent color to her dark red hair. Her eyes, a little puffed, were the shade of the sweater and her smile, warm and somehow tremulous, caught him by surprise.

"I'm sorry I went morbid on you. Won't do it again."

"You're okay, Cecy. You're doing fine. Most women would be shaking for a week after such an experience."

"I'm pretty rugged, I guess. You get that way when you're kicked around for a while. Anyway, I can't afford to build a production out of it." She picked up the cups and he followed her into the living room. "The show must go on, because when it doesn't, the paycheck stops."

"You—you're not thinking of dancing tonight!"

"Why not? Sure dance tonight. It's just plain old physical exertion, like digging ditches or driving railroad spikes."

Roman frowned, sipping his coffee. A question was forming in his mind; a question that grew and became solid, and spewed a family of smaller ones. "This man the other night; the papers said he forced you to dance for him? What did that mean?"

There was a tiny sound; the trembling of the cup and saucer in her hand. "Just… just that, Roman. It was like—waking up into a nightmare. I'd been sleeping. And then I was aware of music. My music… and I remember wondering if I could have left the tape recorder running. I opened my eyes and there was bright moonlight in the room. I didn't see *him* at first."

"He wasn't in the room?"

"Oh yes! But the moonlight only filled a small part—over there by the window. He was in shadow. For a moment I didn't realize it was a man and not a shadow. Until he moved. I started to scream but he was too close. I knew if I screamed then, it would be the end of me."

"But—what about the dance?"

"He said to dance. It was odd, now that I think back—what he said. *'Dance like you did.'*"

"Like you did?"

"Like I did at The Pink Cat. He must have seen me there and followed me home. Only I couldn't think coherently just then. So he reached over and pulled away the bedcovers and I nearly died right there. He was standing over me, looking about eight feet tall, and he—he was shaking all over. Awful. So I thought—I *think* I thought—that if I could stall a few minutes, I could hold him off. So I—I got up and began to dance. I think I was crying. But he made no attempt to touch me, and somehow I got the feeling that he wouldn't as long as I danced. Only—there wasn't any doubt in my mind about what he wanted. Well, I kept thinking if I could only change the routine, improvise something less exciting; but the music wouldn't let me. I had to go on, and here's the awful thing, Roman—"

He put an arm around her; the slight tremor touched him. "Don't talk about it, Cecille. It's upsetting you."

"No. I—I have to talk about it. Please—if you don't mind. I couldn't tell the police. I couldn't tell anyone. The terrible thing about it was this... that a part of my mind seemed to be standing off to one side, thinking what a tremendously dramatic dance-form could be evolved from the situation! And almost *wanting* the dance to end so that—so that....

"Then it *was* over, and he did take hold of me, and I was almost hypnotized, I guess. I couldn't think. Not for several moments. And then—I woke up and realized where I was and what he was doing—and I must have fainted. Maybe it was a good thing, because when I revived, I had my chance to escape, to scream. And believe me, I did!"

"You didn't get a good look at him?"

She shook her head. "It was dark in this room, except for the moonlight. He was just a blur and his voice almost a whisper. Low, husky-like. I don't know—somehow my impressions are all mixed up."

"You were terrified."

"Yes, but I was thinking hard, too. He wasn't a *person;* he was more like a *thing.* A horrible creature. That probably doesn't make sense, but that's the impression I got—and at the same time, Roman, I—I *pitied* him. Why, do you suppose?"

Strangely, the image of Pilcher flickered in his mind. "Because he was evidently suffering. The weaklings, I think, are driven too hard by their hungers or desires or needs. So they steal, or attack, or destroy. I guess it's the same with people as it is with nations. If they don't have self-control, or respect for law, they try to take what others have. I think it's been that way all through history; the have-nots and the barbarians nibbling at the fringes of civilization, waiting their chance to smash in for loot and plunder. It's that way today. They're still hungering, still looking for anodynes to quiet their pain."

"Yes. Yes, I think you're right. That's why we pity them. But it doesn't help when we're their victims, does it?"

"The thing is not to be a victim, Cecille," Roman said, and brought out the .25 caliber Beretta. "I picked this up in Italy. Keep it handy when you're alone."

She stared at the small automatic. "I don't know. Shooting someone—I doubt that I could, Roman."

"If you'd had this the other night, you might have stopped Nina's murderer, and your own would-be murderer. Maybe the killer of someone else he hasn't even gotten to yet."

She whitened. "That—that's true. But—"

"He could come back."

She walked to the window, twisting her hands. "Might he? Would I have to—to kill him?"

"I think you should. If you're squeamish, aim for a shoulder or leg. This little pea-shooter carries a mean sting, but it won't kill unless you hit him in a vital spot. Have you ever handled a gun?"

"We used to plink at bottles in the surf with a .22."

"Okay. Keep this under your pillow."

She took it silently, and put it away. Her shoulders drooped a little, he noticed, and her face was drawn.

"You'd better get some rest," he said gently. "You're more tired than you realize. I'll come by tonight and see that you get to The Pink Cat safely."

"I don't want to bother you—I'll be all right taking a cab."

"Well, perhaps. Suppose, then, I pick you up when you've finished with your last show?"

"Would you? I guess I'm not quite brave enough to walk in here alone at midnight. Not just yet, anyway."

"See you at The Pink Cat, then."

"Thanks, Roman...."

The Pink Cat Club was filled without being crowded. He sat at a side table, picking at what passed for dessert following an expensive and highly indigestible meal. He felt cranky and irritable, though he'd spent part of the afternoon walking in an effort to calm his growing annoyance. Once he'd spotted Pilcher, evidently following him in an effort to find Joyce. Luckily, the man hadn't come close. Roman couldn't have taken any more abuse from the young idiot. Why wasn't he at Crane Chemical working? Administration must be coasting. It seemed a long time—weeks—since he'd taken off for his so-called vacation, and he wondered how they were getting along.

Roman felt an odd nostalgia for the plant, for problems he could cope with. Logical problems without innuendos and overtones.

He wanted a cold glass of water, and the waiter was nowhere in sight. He wanted quiet, and a master of ceremonies was braying banalities into a microphone. He wanted a cigarette and his pack was empty.

He wanted Joyce, and she was gone.

The damned police knew where, and they wouldn't tell. He wondered who else knew where she was. Pilcher? Probably not. The fool was really out of control. Joyce hadn't thought much of him even when he did have all his marbles.

He felt his heart go faster. *Smith? Could Pilcher be Smith?* Had the kid really cracked? It was possible—entirely possible. Pilcher hated him. Would he then try to destroy everything, everyone Roman had or seemed to have?

Did Pilcher kill Nina, thinking somehow she was Joyce?

Thinking Joyce belonged to him?

Did he try to kill Cecille, thinking she too—

It was possible. Very possible. Yet the idea wasn't compelling. The possibility felt remote.

The character with the microphone continued his braying; something about the greatest show this side of Paris... some girls pranced into the spotlight, kicking enthusiastically.

He wished Cecille's act would come on; he wanted to get out of this place with its synthetic atmosphere and synthetic food and synthetic conviviality.

The line of girls pranced off again, still kicking, still enthusiastic. There was a dull comedian, and some dull songs, and finally Cecille was there.

Calm-faced, her limber arms and hands describing fantastic oriental mountains, lovely flowers and exotic cultures. A curious fantasy that somehow seemed to Roman more real, more earthy than anything else around him.

Where she had hotted up the routine, he could sense the tension in the room increase as each man responded to her alluring invitation.

Ten minutes later, when the floor show was over, Cecille came to his table, unrecognized by the other patrons in her simple tailored suit. He ordered a drink for her. "Tired?"

"Pretty much. Guess I'm shakier than I thought. I slept a little this afternoon but it didn't seem to help."

She refused a second drink, and they left The Pink Cat. A cab was waiting and Roman gave the Alvaron Street address. As they pulled from the curb, a long yellow convertible zoomed past, braked abruptly, and careened around the next corner. The taxi driver mumbled an automatic obscenity.

Cecille stared after it, frowning. "Bennie has a car like that."

"Think it was him?"

"There were two men, but I couldn't see them clearly. I don't know—"

"What if it was Bennie?"

"Bennie's bad, Roman. I don't think he liked the idea of your asking questions around his place. He might connect it up somehow with Nina's death. Nina made him a nice profit, you know."

He hadn't thought about that.

The cab slowed, swung around a corner into the narrow, unlighted street. "Here y'are folks," the driver said. "Thanksveymuchg'night."

Roman sensed Cecille's shiver beside him when they were alone.

"You'll come up for a minute, won't you?"

His answer was interrupted by a glimpse of movement in the darkness; he crouched, alert.

The blow grazed his temple, stunning him. He had been too slow. Now he staggered back, avoiding a second, shaking his head. Brass knuckles.

Nothing else would stun like that.

A shadow closed over Cecille; he caught a hoarse growl. "One peep out of you, baby, and you'll get a few bones broke too."

He caught one on his forearm; pain radiating, numbing. A coarse chuckle from the squat, blocky figure pushing forward on him. "Okay, wise guy. When I'm through with you, you'll know not to meddle."

Bennie. The bartender who didn't like questions. The guy who'd helped put Nina on heroin and then peddled her to men like Smith. The small irritations of the evening swelled into a mountainous tide of rage in Roman.

Bennie was strong as a bull. His fists, armed with several ounces of brass, carried a killing jolt, but he'd counted too much on smashing his victim into helplessness with the first attack. Now he came wading in to beat Roman under. His haymaker missed by the smallest fraction of an inch, and Roman's fast right jab exploded against his nose. Blood gushed from broken cartilage and the shock stalled his rush for an instant, and Roman put a sickening left into Bennie's solar plexus.

Bennie retched.

Roman, having the measure of his man, laughed, and smashed rights and lefts to the huge, bony head, and then to the man's softer midriff.

The man holding Cecille—Ed, the day man, he thought—called out in alarm. "Smash 'im, Boss! Smash the bastard!"

Bennie, giving ground under the impact of Roman's blows, cursed, struck wildly, impotently.

Roman chopped at Bennie with cold ferocity; whipping at his nerve-centers, hammering at his battered, bleeding face, smashing him against the wall of the apartment building and pounding him mercilessly.

"Hold 'm, Boss! I'm comin'! Hang on a second!"

Roman whirled and caught the arm drawn back to knock Cecille into insensibility. He twisted and heard the satisfying crack of bone, the howl of pain, saw the shadow fall away and run, cursing.

The respite had given Bennie courage. Roman couldn't turn in time to meet the new attack. Heavy brass knuckles smashed into his ribs, exploded lights in his head. He dropped to one knee; caught a kick on his shoulder, then lurched up again, carrying Bennie backwards.

Somewhere in the red haze of his anger, he could hear Cecille's cries for the police, could hear the scream of sirens, but he was conscious only of the target in front of him, the thud of his fists, the whimpering moans of his attacker. Dimly he knew Bennie had dropped; he pulled the man upright by his thick hair and smashed again and again at the soggy, bloody face. Even with the police there, holding him, he tried to lunge again, snarling, rage-swollen. "Take it easy, pal, *take it easy!* Leave us something to lock up!"

Roman slumped back, aching lungs sucking at air; great gobs of air to fill his chest, to leave him weak and exhausted. He rubbed his face with a shaking hand, staring at Cecille in the light of the squad-car headlamps. Two officers were examining the man on the pavement.

"He's hurt bad," one of them said. "Better call an ambulance."

"He jumped us," Roman said thickly. "He—"

"Okay, bud; we know. He wasn't wearing them brass knuckles to a Sunday School picnic. Only it looks like he mixed with a guy clear out of his class. You better come along and let the doc look at you."

Roman nodded. "If one of you fellows will check Miss Merrill's apartment. She's the girl—man tried to kill her night before last—may come back here—"

"Yeah. We've been keeping an eye on the place. Riley, you take a run up, will you? Shake the place down good. Okay, feller; let's get along."

At headquarters, the surgeon examined Roman carefully for possible concussion or fractures. "Nothing serious here," he said, "aside from some skinned knuckles and some bruises. That's more than I can say for your recent sparring partner. Looks like his skull's fractured."

Sergeant Winterhalter questioned Roman carefully, seemed satisfied with his answers. "There's a possibility this Bennie was the guy attacked Miss Merrill—and maybe killed the Valjean girl. At least, he's tied in somewhere. If he talks at all, he should tell us plenty."

"You sure took the steam out of that guy fast, Mr. Laird," one of the squad car officers said in an awed voice. "He must weigh two-twenty, and hard as a rock. You a pro, or something?"

"Strictly amateur," Roman said. "He got me mad."

The officer laughed. "I hope you never get mad at me. Brother! Doc says he hasn't come to yet!"

FIFTEEN

He struggled up through a thick, red sludge, gasping, head aching, the light painful against his swollen eyes. His jaw, his ribs sore… his dull misery stabbed by short blades of sound.

The telephone.

He stumbled out of bed, muttering. "Hello…."

"Laird? Inspector Trumbull. I hear you turned in quite a performance last night. Look, we can't locate the other guy—Ed. Ed Wellman, his name is. And The Red Parrot is locked up. Wellman's never been booked, at least under that name, and we don't have a description. Can you tell us anything about him?"

Roman rubbed his scalp, trying to awaken his senses. "Tell you— Well, I'd say Ed was about thirty-five or so. Five feet—about eight. On the skinny side. Maybe about one-forty—one-fifty. Thin brownish hair and a narrow, lined face. Big ears; I remember he had big ears and a big Adam's apple. That's about all, except the impression of his character, mainly rat-like. His big aim in life is to have a couple or so girls working for him."

"Yeah. Well, we'll try to pick him up. We've got a lot of questions to ask that bird because it don't look like we're going to get much out of Bennie for a while."

"He won't talk?"

"He can't talk. Basal skull fracture. Still unconscious."

A little worm of sickness uncurled in Roman's stomach. "I'm sorry to hear that, Inspector."

In the bathroom, Roman checked himself over. One eye slightly swollen and blue—nothing a pair of dark glasses wouldn't conceal. Some bruises on his body. Not much visible damage considering how he felt.

Could Bennie be Smith? Joyce would have the answer if he could only locate her.

It was almost eleven and he'd had a pretty good sleep. He made some strong coffee and while sipping it hot he reviewed his last conversation with her. Barton's agent had found a place that was just about perfect. Who was Barton's agent?

He dialed Crane Chemical. Barton was out of town but his secretary was able to give him the name of his agent. It was a Mrs. Friedenberg, of Patterson and Broad Street.

Roman called the real estate office. They expected Mrs. Friedenberg about five. Would he call again?

He would—or he'd drop in if he was downtown. He'd be downtown— Joyce held the key to the riddle. Or, more accurately, Joyce herself was the riddle. If he could find her a lot would be explained.

He poured a stiff shot of Old Adam, and gulped it down. One more. That was better. The liquor's mellow glow spread through him, desensitizing his aches.

But the old sense of uneasiness was back. The feeling of being watched; of being observed, malevolently; with hatred and loathing. The feeling was strong; uncanny.

"Imagination," he said aloud. "*Nerves!* Has to be nerves."

Carefully he went through the apartment to satisfy himself that he was really alone. Nerves. He thought of Cecille. She'd be worried; wondering what had happened to him. She had no phone; he'd have to go over. Maybe take her to lunch. Good idea; he was starving, and he didn't want to bother fixing anything himself. He missed Wong. He poured himself another double shot. This being alone wasn't doing him any good. And Cecille was both companionable and interesting.

He shook his head, trying to remember where he was. This bouncing....
He was in a taxi, of course. He leaned forward. "Driver, what was the address I gave you?"

"Seventy-nine Alvaron. That right?"

"Yes; I thought for a minute I'd said nineteen."

"Yeah; funny how you kin forget numbers. Half the time I don't even remember what cab I got and have to check it when I make my report."

Roman frowned. His head felt dull, but he wasn't drunk, at least he didn't think he was drunk. Though three stiff ones on an empty stomach for a man who didn't drink a lot anyway, was a pretty good load.

"Here y'are. Seventy-nine Alvaron."

Her green eyes grew wide as she opened the door to him. "Oh, Roman! I've been so worried about you! Are you all right?"

"Sure—sure I'm all right." He grinned reassuringly.

She was wearing a sarong of Javanese design, a white gardenia at her waist. Mahogany-red hair hung loose and lustrous around her bare shoulders and her green eyes managed somehow to look almost Oriental.

"I wonder where you could wear that costume to lunch without starting a minor riot, Cecille?"

"Right here," she said. "You name your dish, and if we haven't got it, you can run out and get some at the market around the corner. As for sarongs... I just happen to like them better than housecoats. More comfortable."

"And much more interesting! I thought we might have a bite at Marellie's."

"We'll stay here. Later on, I'll fix an omelet. I never eat lunch at noon." She moved to the record player and soon dreamy Latin music filled the room. Unlike Joyce the sophisticated, who shared her thoughts only when she wished to do so, Cecille appeared to have no more guile than a child.

How did you get to *really* know a woman, anyway?

Climb into bed with her, the wise ones said.

He suspected that even the wise ones were sometimes fooled. The method of analysis might be pleasant, but its accuracy was open to question.

Cecille pulled a crumpled letter from her pocket and tossed it on the table. "Damn it, I'm *mad!* On top of everything else *Pete* has to write. He's stopping over here on his way to Hong Kong and thought it would be nice if we spent the evening together for old times' sake."

"Who is Pete?"

"You might call him my former husband, though in spite of the license, he considered me the girl he happened to be sleeping with at the time." She sighed, mockingly. "I hope I get a chance to be a wife someday. A real wife, I mean."

He watched her as she lit a cigarette and snubbed out the match. "What happened to your marriage?"

"I tried hard, but Pete—well, he always seemed to believe that the next woman could give him some special thrill the last one didn't. Women spoiled him rotten. He never thought of resisting. Before marriage or after. The bastard tore me to pieces regularly, on the average of once a week. I'd pull myself together and come crawling back. For almost five years."

She snubbed out her cigarette viciously. "Now he's coming through the city and wants to spend the night with me!" She began to laugh; then stopped. "It's almost funny."

He nodded, not quite sure of her meaning. Peter Merrill must have been pretty much of a fool to let a girl like this get away from him. He said, "I think you're still in love with the man. I doubt if a person ever really gets over his first love."

She stared at him. "Such as—the girl who wouldn't have you? The girl you mentioned?"

He shrugged. "I was speaking in general terms."

"You're on the rebound. She got her little spiked heel into your heart and she's grinding it around and you think you hate her, but you don't hate her at all, Roman."

"Then you admit that people don't ever get over their first loves. Regardless of the way Pete treated you, you haven't gotten over him yet."

Abruptly, she said, "Are you hungry? Do you want an omelet?"

"No... no, I think I'll go along. Shall I call for you at The Pink Cat around midnight?"

"No. Pete will be waiting for me."

"Oh. Good luck, baby."

There was a tight little smile on her lips. "Thanks. Goodbye, darling."

He walked out, sensing that a door had closed in his face. A dizzying wave of anger rose like a bubble, up into his brain and exploded quietly. He forced himself to relax. After all, Laird, what did you expect? You were interested. The girl was interested. You bungled. Maybe you wanted to bungle. Maybe you didn't.

It was Joyce, of course, who had laid a spell on him.

Fanciful term but he could think of nothing more accurate. He'd been feeling useless and empty ever since he realized she was through with him.

And the feeling was growing. He felt like hell, to be truthful. If the remedy for one woman was another woman, he was too sick a man to take the cure. Or the cure wouldn't take him, which probably amounted to the same thing.

He needed a drink—bad. He was supposed to see that real estate woman at five, but she could wait. He found a bar and settled on a stool. "Shot of Old Adam and a glass of water."

"Haven't had Old Adam for over a year. What about some Ben Franklin? It's about the same."

Roman nodded. "That's okay."

He drank his drink. The image of Joyce seemed to grow around the bottle; and puzzlement came over him. The bottle had the Old Adam label after all: the embarrassed male, the prudishly naked Eve with the silly looking serpent wound around her neck, the familiar apple.

A queer, momentary flash of having been here before.

But no—he must have been dreaming. It wasn't Old Adam he was drinking at all. There wasn't any woman, any man on the label. Instead, an illustrative bronze of Ben Franklin, looking a little more severe than usual. He shook his head. There wasn't the slightest similarity in labels. How could his imagination have played such a peculiar trick? He frowned.

"Ain't it about the same, Mister?" the barman asked anxiously. "A good, hundred-proof whiskey, that is. Well aged. That's all good whiskey is; stuff that's been aged a long time in charred barrels."

"The whiskey's all right." Roman laid a bill on the bar and walked out. Damn his imagination. Damn Cecille. Damn just about everything he could think of.

Mrs. Friedenberg wasn't the confiding type. He sat in her office and answered her cold questioning with a glib fabrication. She was thin, elderly, and wore a hat that was surely designed by Mr. Fredericks in one of his madder moments. The effect wasn't bad; a combination of ruthless efficiency with dashing femininity. She said, "I really don't know if we have anything right now, Mr. Laird, that would meet your requirements. These quiet little spots in the country where you can raise your laboratory animals—rabbits, did you say?—just don't come in much to a downtown office like ours."

"Mr. Barton spoke so highly of the place you found for Miss Masters, that I just assumed—"

The woman looked a little startled. He must have said the wrong thing. "I would hardly think her place suitable for—ah, rabbits."

He agreed hastily. "Well, not exactly, but something like it, you know."

"Yes; well, perhaps. We have several two-bedroom houses in Glennside Park; about thirty minutes from town. Regular track homes. Hardwood floors; very nice."

"How about something around Miss Masters' place. Something nice and quiet."

"Yes, but—" She was politely puzzled.

In desperation, he tried to force the issue. "The place in Fairfax, I mean. Isn't that the one she decided to take?"

"Dear me, no! We have a house in Ross; fairly pretentious. Would you want to pay around $350 a month, Mr. Laird?"

"That's a little too much." Suddenly he saw why she was confused. Joyce wasn't out of town at all! "Now, I remember; it was the place at Hollyway and Forty-fourth. I must have been a bit confused."

"Indeed you must, Mr. Laird." Her exasperation was plain. "*That* place happens to be on La Paloma Way, just half a block from Vasco da Gama Circle, and we positively *don't* have another *thing* out there. If we did, I'm sure you would never be permitted to raise guinea pigs in the yard!"

"Rabbits," he said, rising. "Rabbits are what we're interested in. Thank you very much for your time and trouble."

"That's quite all right."

He left Mrs. Friedenberg with the definite impression that she'd also cautioned him not to let it happen again.

La Paloma. Half a block off Vasco da Gama Circle.

Joyce had lied. Joyce hadn't trusted him.

He stood on the sidewalk at Kearny and Market, wiping his forehead, realizing he was sweating in the effort to hold down his anger. Careful, boy, careful. Maybe there's an explanation. If so, he had to find out. He had to make sure she was safe. That was the important thing. She might have decided to drop him; that was okay. That was her right. But he had to warn her. She ought at least to know what he knew about Nina Valjean and Cecille and Smith.

The police didn't seem to be worried, but the police didn't know too much, either. They didn't know, for instance, that somewhere in Joyce's background was this shadow-person who seemed to be aware of everything, who remained in the darkness and laughed at them.

Certainly Joyce had to be warned.

He parked the Jaguar at the intersection of La Paloma Way and Vasco da Gama Circle. When he saw the opulence of the neighborhood Roman whistled, puzzlement increasing. He himself made good money, but he'd never be able to afford anything like this, and he knew Joyce spent as much as she made—considerably more, in fact.

First things first, however. The problem was to locate her place. Half a block on La Paloma Way might be any one of several spacious homes. He walked along, studying them. Every house had a three-car garage, and in each was at least one car.

One house, a little older, a little further back from the street and more secluded behind its high, unkempt hedge, had no car. Joyce didn't drive. Nor were there lights, except in two windows toward the back. He opened the gate, and walked to the front door, his heart beating uncomfortably.

He paused before touching the button; his hand reached out almost involuntarily and tried the knob.

The door opened. She shouldn't leave doors unlocked. Dangerous. Far too dangerous. Suppose it was Smith who'd traced her, who'd come here and tried the catch?

It was too dark to see how well the house was furnished, but he got the impression of luxury from the thick soft feel of the rug, the gleam of crystal and polished furniture, the high ceiling and satin drapes. His discomfort mounted as he went up the carpeted stairs. If this were not Joyce's place, he'd have to think of a pretty good explanation for his intrusion.

A narrow beam of light bisected the hallway. He approached quietly and found a door slightly ajar. Standing there, he could look into the room. Large, luxurious, with heavy velvet draperies. And on the oversized Hollywood bed—Joyce.

SIXTEEN

A queer, heavy drumming started low inside him. Joyce was reading, a box of chocolates on the spread beside her. She hadn't heard him; didn't look up from her book. She was wearing a man's silk pajama top, carelessly fastened with only one button, slim bare legs like carefully turned ivory in the softly subdued light.

The drumming in him grew; desire swelled. She moved, revealing more of her modeled perfection. His throat grew tight and he was shaking with the impact of the heavy beat within him.

He realized now, he'd never understood Joyce. Perhaps it hadn't mattered, once. Now, in a time of stress, it mattered greatly.

Roman felt lost. Unable to plan, unable to think logically.

He knew, with terrible certainty, that he would never really know her. And he knew Joyce would never—voluntarily—belong to him again.

It was too much. The vision of her blurred; black waves leaped high, engulfing his consciousness for a moment. He covered his face with his hands and tried to hold back the low cry that came from somewhere inside his chest—a moan of utter despair.

She looked up and he moved forward into the light; holding his heavy hands before him.

"Roman!"

Surprise? Annoyance? Fear? Resignation?

"Roman!" Joyce repeated. "How did you find me?"

"You were going to meet me yesterday at five," he said stonily.

She moved away from him, off the bed, and pulling a black velvet dressing robe around her. "I—I couldn't wait for you, darling. This—this thing about the house came up and I had to take it right away or lose my—my deposit."

"You were running away, Joyce. To hide. You're hiding now."

She laughed; a high, silvery laugh. "Oh, Roman, you've developed an imagination. I never thought you would."

"You're afraid of something or someone, Joyce. You've been afraid for quite a few weeks. Before you went to Ohio, if that's where you went."

She dropped her pretense of amusement and said sullenly, "Of course it was. You know it was, Roman. Why shouldn't I have gone to see my parents?"

He used the words as he would a whip. *"Who was the man you left the hotel with yesterday?"*

Her lips, darkly red against her pale face, moved, but no sound came out.

"Who was the man who came later, inquiring for you, Joyce?"

"I—I don't know."

He moved around the bed toward her and saw her fingers move, pulling the velvet robe snugly around her. "Joyce, you're in danger. I don't think you know—"

Eyes wide, dark, she whispered, "I think I know, Roman. I—think—I—know...."

"This—this fellow Smith. Maybe that isn't his name. No one knows. No one seems to have gotten a good look at him. No one except this man—the bartender, Bennie, from The Red Parrot—and he's unconscious with a fractured skull."

She waited warily, staring at him, silent. He had struck no responsive chord. He went on. "All we know is that Smith is youngish—maybe around thirty—medium build, and well dressed. A man with a pretty bad mental twist. *Who* is he, Joyce? *Who is—Smith? Where is he?"*

"I—I don't know! I don't know anyone like that, Roman. Why should I—what makes you think I know him—Smith?"

"You must. He's the man who got into your apartment, Joyce. He killed the girl you found there. *Maybe he thought she was you!"*

She shuddered, covered her face for a moment. "Oh no! Roman, he—he couldn't possibly!"

"Joyce, I want to help you. I—I've got to help you. I've got to help myself. This Smith—he's a real wrongo, Joyce. None of us will be safe until he's caught."

She picked up his words. "None of *us?* You mean you're in danger from him too?"

"More than anyone, I think," he said slowly. "I don't know why. Or how. But he's left definite proof that he's watching me—and waiting."

She was thinking—hard. New, puzzling thoughts. "You're sure?"

He almost laughed. "You know me, Joyce. You know I'm not given to wild statements. Now, I've been in the middle of this thing for quite a few days. I don't want to give you all the details, but it adds up. The sum is all cock-eyed, but it's there. Smith is there. He had to be. *And you know who he is, Joyce!*"

"I don't! I don't know, Roman!" She was tight against the wall, anguish in her eyes. "I swear I don't have any idea! Not the slightest. I—I never met a man named Smith. *Never!*"

"Did you know Nina Valjean?"

"*No!* I told you I never saw her, be—before."

"But you aren't sure about Smith?"

"*I never met a man named Smith!*"

"You're lying, Joyce."

"No, Roman; *no!*"

"Yes. Your actions prove you're lying. Leaving your apartment to hide away here. Raising cats! Writing books!"

Rage mixed and stirred with his desire, with a sense of growing panic.

"*Lie, then!*" he shouted. "Hide. You know what he'll do, this Smith? This killer? This—*this rapist you're protecting?*"

She was motionless, pleading with him silently.

"He'll trace you to this place, Joyce. He'll find you just as I did. That wasn't hard—and he'll open the door you so conveniently left unlocked."

"No," she whispered. "No, Roman."

"He'll come up the stairs. Silently, while you're reading here some night. He'll walk in here. *Just as I did, Joyce!* Screaming won't help you. This house is a little too isolated. No one will hear you. No one heard Nina, you know, and he—Smith—will treat you pretty much the same way as he treated her."

"*Don't say any more, Roman Laird!*"

Roman laughed harshly, brutally. "He'll strip you naked, Joyce. *Like this—*"

She cried out as he tried to tear off the silken pajama top. He saw her through a pulsing red haze; wanting her desperately; hating her. "He'll laugh at you—*like this....*"

"*Roman! Please!*"

Gasping, his belly aching after the deep, racking, uncontrolled laughter, he reached out for her. Slowly she backed away from him; she was trembling, her eyes deep pools of dark horror.

"And then, my dear, he'll take you—"

"Don't move, Laird, or you're a dead man." The voice was heavy with menace.

Roman's arms dropped away from Joyce and he whirled around.

"Barton!"

He was aware of Joyce sobbing. Hammers at his temples. Barton. Barton, her lover. This expensive, isolated house. This elaborate furniture. And he hadn't even suspected. Barton with a dull blue .38 pointing at him.

"Nothing would give me greater joy than killing you, Laird. But there'd be a little bit of embarrassment in explaining—the crime—afterwards. You'd better get out of here before I change my mind. It could change fast."

He looked around, dazed. It was clear enough. Everything was clear.

He turned, stumbling, almost falling down the stairs.

Outside it was cold and dark. That was something. No one would see him. It looked like hell to see a grown man crying....

SEVENTEEN

He sat brooding in his apartment, a bottle of Old Adam half empty before him. The liquor had dulled his senses, but the hurting still came through. It must be long after midnight; he didn't know.

Barton. The rich man's kid. The son of a bitch who had everything. Money, career, family, wife, children. And Joyce.

And the police, those clever fools, had checked Barton out. They'd said so. Barton had an alibi. So if he hadn't killed Nina, he wasn't Smith.

Barton wasn't the man Joyce feared.

Who *was* the man?

Joyce had sworn she didn't know and he believed her now. She'd lied about everything else. But finally he'd scourged her with terror until she could no longer evade and fabricate. He had stripped her body and her mind of every concealment. If she had known Smith, she would have told him. He'd been prepared for the revelation of a former lover, a former husband. Even an insane brother; any psychotic intimate.

Somehow the conclusion let him feel less hostile toward her. The present he could accept. She had left him for Barton. Understandable. Roman didn't like it, but he had no lasting claim on her. She was free to sleep with anyone she wished. Just as he was.

It was the past he didn't want violated. The short, intoxicated life they'd had together—the few months that had been a world of their own creation. In all his years, he'd never had such bitter-sweet happiness. The close, beautiful, unbelievable intimacy.

It was unthinkable that their relationship was sham; that she'd been acting a part, belonging to Smith, accepting his domination, acceding to his depraved and ghastly whims.

Roman took another drink.

Half a bottle, he thought, staring at the coy Eve, the gauche Adam, the improbably leering snake. And still sober. Almost sober enough to recognize his uneasiness.

He listened, reaching out with his senses, and the tendrils of his mind touched something cold and damp and evil. Near him—watching, waiting, smiling.

Roman Laird, I know you....

He leaped from the chair; swung around.

Nothing. *Nothing?*

Smith—whatever the hell you are—come out. Come out, damn you. No more cat-and-mousing. Come out; this mouse is ready for you. This mouse will fight. Come out, you yellow-bellied bastard!

Was that the last echo of laughter?

Or his own voice?

Prickling with horror, he plunged through the rooms, seeking his enemy. There was no one. Nothing made of bones to break, flesh to rend, blood to spill.

Here was only an obscene chuckle, a shadow, a nothing.

Weariness like a sea of sluggish gelatine surged up in him. Weariness that drew dark marrow from his bones and iron-red substance from his blood. Weariness that drained his skin and turned it gray and coarse and finally drew from his brain the thoughts and confusions and the awareness that was Roman Laird....

He seemed to be laughing softly to himself.

Why the hell would he be laughing?

He seemed to be seated in an automobile in motion. "We've had some bad luck, Laird," the voice was saying.

"Bad luck?"

"Yeah." Inspector Trumbull leaned back in the squad car and touched a lighter flame to the stub of his cigar. "Yeah. We picked up Vernie, but we couldn't get a damned thing out of him."

"No?" He glanced out. Sutter. They hadn't gone far from the apartment. He couldn't have been here more than a minute.

"Well, nothing that helps. Admits he saw Nina the last night anyone saw her alive. As late as midnight, hanging around The Red Parrot bar, waiting for business. Saw some guy with her, too, but he didn't pay any special attention. We scared him enough for him to tell the truth."

"If he saw the man, he must have an idea of what he looked like."

Trumbull shrugged. "Middle height. Hat pulled down. Gray suit, or it might have been brown, or any color. Face didn't make any impression. It was darkish in the bar and he was over in a booth sipping his root beer—yeah; can you beat that—and he wasn't paying attention."

"It helps a little. Gives you time and place, doesn't it?"

"Nothing we didn't already have. We'd really hoped to get something from Bennie."

"He still can't talk?"

"He won't ever talk. Bennie's dead."

Roman felt a cold sickness start in his stomach and flood up into his chest. He stared down at his still-bruised knuckles, shuddering. Then with guilty horror, he remembered the delicious outpouring of rage when he'd torn into Bennie. Self-defense? A jury might believe that, if the matter ever went so far. Roman knew it was more—a deep-buried viciousness, an atavistic cruelty that he recognized with loathing and self-contempt.

"I suppose, Inspector, you are going to charge me with Bennie's death now?"

"Don't think there'll be any charge, Laird. I had a talk with the district attorney. You couldn't let Bennie slaughter you; if he got his brains bashed out, it was just the risk he took. I'd say he depended a little too much on those brass knucks. No, we wanted you to make an identification. We picked up a guy we think is Ed."

"Oh." Relief. He glanced suspiciously at the Inspector. Apparently he'd noticed nothing wrong, and perhaps nothing was wrong. Merely a trick of the mind; a trick of his memory. He'd been drinking; and he wasn't usually a heavy drinker. Identification would be quick. He was anxious to get away from Trumbull. Those sleepy-looking eyes of his missed nothing.

Preparing the line-up took longer than he thought it would. "We know you're probably more accurate than most witnesses, Laird," Trumbull said, "but if we bring this guy to trial, his attorney will probably ask how identification was made, and if we don't say out of a lineup, it looks bad."

Roman nodded indifferently. Finally they permitted him to look at five men. He pointed to one. "That's the man from The Red Parrot."

"That's the guy we thought. Okay, boys, take 'im away."

"Right. Say, Inspector, there's a call-in from Marshall and Clancy. Want you to come to this address and see what they found. Think it might be a tie-in with the Valjean kill."

Trumbull glanced at the slip of paper. "All right. Come on, Laird; I was going to drive you back down town anyway. Let's have a look."

An officer was waiting at the back door of what seemed to be an unused garage when they pulled up. "Marshall's upstairs with 'em. Damndest things you ever saw, Inspector."

"Yeah?" They went single file up the narrow wooden stairs. "What is this joint?"

"Used to be a little auto repair shop downstairs with a couple of rooms topside. Vacant now. Well, Marshall here caught the door open, and we decided to stir around. In here."

Trumbull and Roman stared around at the disheveled room, at the stack of oil paintings, the table paint-spattered and messy with brushes, tubes and bottles.

"The fellow we chased the other night disappeared somewhere in this neighborhood—maybe the same guy who attacked the Merrill girl."

"Yeah?" Trumbull stared at the canvases.

"Yep. Now let me show you somethin' me and Marshall found." The officer pulled a painting from the pile. A scene in a butcher shop. A fantastic butcher shop, the row of men and women hanging head down from meat hooks. The emaciated, pale butcher hovering over the girl on the block. A brown-haired girl with haunting, gray-green eyes.

For a strangely eerie moment, Roman felt that he was in the painting, that he was a part of the grotesque scene; one with the butcher, the girl, the neat and naked people.

From a far-off, unreal world he heard the policeman's voice. "Recognize anyone here, Inspector?"

"Yeah. I think so. I think you got something here, Clancy."

"Nina Valjean, huh?"

"Well, there's sure a resemblance, all right. You know anything about art, Laird? About painting? What do you make of this?"

Roman pulled himself back into the room with an effort. "I don't know much about art, Inspector. Most of my drawing has been mechanical—with a draughtsman's pencil, but I'd say there's damned good talent here. Trained talent, I think. There's a tremendous vitality in the technique. You see what I mean, Inspector? The man's savagery comes bursting right out at you."

"Man? Couldn't it have been a woman who did these?"

"I don't think a woman would have the strength or brutality for this kind of work. I'm not talking about the subject matter now; just the painting itself."

"What about the subject matter?"

"You'd better talk to a psychiatrist about that, but I think this is Nina, all right."

The officers began a search of the room while Roman examined several other paintings. All were grotesque, all were frightening in their outrageous symbolism. *Symbols of what?*

Uneasy, reluctant, he turned up one of the larger canvases. A midnight scene, a clashing, violent saturnalia. Gargoyles leaping in agonized abandonment around a fire of blazing coffins. Another girl, taut body poised in delicate balance between soul-destroying fear and morbid attraction. Her head half-turned, indecision, horror, innocent sensuality in her face.

Despite the wavering, unreal quality, the distorted nightmarishness, Roman knew the girl in the painting.

Cecille Merrill. Undoubtedly Cecille. The attitude of flight he recognized; one of the quick phases of her dance he'd watched in her apartment and again at The Pink Cat Club. The mahogany-red hair and pert features and slim elegance of body. And there was more.

His flesh crawled. Here was the revelation of forbidden mysteries; here the rending of the final veil, the violation of the last secret.

He remembered Cecille's trembling, her confession after her weird experience with the shadowy man in her apartment. How she'd been compelled by the music to continue the passionate routine. How, though she knew what must follow, she'd actually wanted the dance to end.

This monstrous painter had somehow, during that wild scene, ravished Cecille's mind and soul. He had reached into her core and drawn out the turbulent, beating emotions and imprisoned them here on the abominable canvas.

With appalling discernment, Smith had captured her ambivalence of mood, and delineated it for anyone to see.

Rape was a physical ravishment. This was worse.

Hastily, Roman returned the picture to the pile; placed another on top of it. The police hadn't noticed. They had gone through the canvases hurriedly, their sensitivities unsharpened. A bunch of crackpot paintings; who looked for murder clues in a maniac's crazy forms and clashing colors?

Roman hoped he would get a chance to destroy Cecille's portrait. It could do nothing to help catch the murderer, and its existence was an indecency. Perhaps he could slip back here later, after the police had gone, and destroy it somehow.

He took up another canvas and was studying it disinterestedly when Clancy came back from the other room. They seemed to have completed their investigation of the premises. "Nothing here, Inspector," Clancy said. "Some junk that must have been stored when the repair shop operated. Couple of beat-up fenders, an old motor block and a few parts that look as if they came out of Jack Benny's Maxwell."

"Yeah; well, come here, Clancy, and see what you make of this."

Roman was aware of their lowered voices; aware of a startled glance from Marshall. He felt foolish and uncomfortable. And then, seemingly with hesitation, Trumbull came toward him, a painting in his hand. His face, Roman thought with a trickle of panic, looked a little grim.

"You told us, Laird, you never knew this Smith. Or at least gave us that impression. Do you, or don't you know him?"

Roman stared. "I don't know him. Of course I don't know him."

"Well, pal, I got news for you. *He* knows *you!*"

Slowly Inspector Trumbull turned the painting to Roman's gaze.

Roman saw a queer forest of bare, white trees. Raising their twisted branches of bleached bones. At their roots thick purple-brown fungi, and long black worms; a great beetle, product of filth, seemed to brood over the carrion-growth.

It was not that which caused the small sweat-beads to form on his forehead and lip.

A young girl's body lay in the foreground, beyond the beetle.

Dead, from the grayish color of her flesh.

Where one of her breasts should have been was a brightly striped child's ball.

Where her head should have been, was a child's fuzzy teddy bear, stuffing coming out of its split hide.

Above the girl stood a centaur-like creature, with a scaly body and thick, scaly tail which trailed down and was wrapped around the girl's waist. The creature had a man's torso, and had plunged a sword into its own belly and was twisting it in the wound. The monster's face, agonized, distorted, was recognizable as his own!

Roman Laird!

"Well, Laird?" Trumbull said.

"It—it looks like *me.*"

"Yeah. That's what we thought, Laird."

"It might be just a coincidental resemblance. I'm a pretty ordinary looking character."

"It's a damned funny coincidence. In fact, there are a lot of damned funny coincidences in this case. A woman murdered in a girl's apartment to which you have the key, Laird. Then Bennie lays for you and you beat him up and we find you in the company of another girl who was attacked and almost murdered by the same method. Then Bennie, the only person who can tell us what Smith looks like, ups and dies on us. Then we find all this crud-painting, which looks like Smith's work—and you're tied in here again."

Roman managed a wry smile. "I told you I was a suspicious character,

Inspector."

"You did, Laird. At this point, an understatement. I'm wondering whether to toss you in the clink as a material witness, or for your own protection, or as the murderer."

Roman pulled a cigarette from his pack, his fingers steadier than they'd been for a long time. "I'll be very curious as to your decision."

"When it's made, pal, you'll know it. If it wasn't for *habeas corpus*, you'd be in now."

"Not enough evidence? Just let me know what you need. I'll supply it if I can."

Trumbull glared at him suspiciously. "Turning into a wise guy, Laird?"

"No," he said earnestly. "Maybe it's just that I don't give a damn. Call it a personal problem."

The detective grinned a little. "Figure if you get a bigger problem, you'll forget the smaller ones, eh?"

"Something like that, I suppose. But—" He gestured toward the painting with his cigarette, "I can assure you I never sat for that particular portrait. Or any portrait, for that matter. I don't know when or where Smith—or whoever the artist is—might have seen me. Although—well, there's a possibility—my photograph was in the newspapers not so long ago. A story about a new process for synthesizing a hormone we developed at Crane Chemical. And there were stories and photos in our company magazine at least a couple of times. Anyone might have seen them."

"Why did the man paint you, Laird? What's behind Smith's *thinking?*"

"If we knew that, we'd have the key to the whole stinking mess, I believe. I get the funny feeling we're dealing with a mind that operates in some other dimension—something entirely beyond us."

Officer Marshall said, "Not so far beyond us we can't strap him into the gas chamber some day."

Trumbull glared at Marshall. "You kidding? You know as well as I do what'll happen. We'll get this crack-pot all wrapped up. Evidence, confession, the works. The jury'll find him guilty. Then the court-appointed psychiatrist will testify his mental condition is such that at the time of the crimes he didn't know right from wrong. And they'll cart him off to a nice quiet institution for treatment and loving care until his head is right again. Which usually doesn't take long. Policeman's lot, Laird. If you ever want to get *really* frustrated, try being a cop for a while."

"No thanks. I'm having enough trouble being a suspect."

Clancy asked, "What'll we do with this stuff?"

"Leave it where it is. Leave everything where it is."

"There's half a fifth under the sink, and it don't smell like anything bad. You don't suppose—"

"I said leave *everything.*"

There was no warning. Roman had been glancing through the paintings and thinking what a sensational show they would make—if any gallery had nerve enough to handle them.

And there it was.

Swirling dark clouds and hairy nameless monsters. A dwarf, fantastically employed, and an eager-eyed, straining stallion. Distorted phantoms, leering and lewd.

A girl's white body in startling contrast. On her wrist, a broken gold chain. In her hair, a blood-red spider. And at her throat, a gray coiled snake. And in her attitude and expression was furious and welcoming lust.

The girl was Joyce! Shock came to Roman in a series of small explosions within him, tearing nerves from their channels, so that night and day seemed to mix and tumble together.

Joyce—revealed in the fullness of her shame, her lies. Her face in the painting might be explained. Even the voluptuous delineation of her body might be explained.

But not the tiny crescent-shaped scar that even a scanty bathing suit hid. No painter could guess. And there was only one way in which he could have known.

From far away, he heard a man's voice. "Jeeze, Laird, you going to pass out? You better get out of here. These damned pictures are enough to make anybody sick to his stomach."

EIGHTEEN

Roman Laird sprawled exhausted in his favorite chair. He had opened the window wide to cool some of the fever. One whiskey bottle beside him was empty; another open and started. The alcohol had filtered into his blood, adding its heat to the turmoil within him.

She'd lied. Lied with her lips, her body, her mind.

Beauty turned loathsome. Integrity become dishonor. Honest passion revealed as venal concupiscence.

Somewhere in North Beach a church bell began to toll the hour of mass... great clapper swinging within the bronzy mouth, the sweet clangor spreading out to the far reaches of the city.

Roman had not been to church for years, but now the impulse to go was strong. To lose himself in the inspired beauty of the temple, to hear the murmur of prayers, to feel the gentle wind of the Infinite blowing against his cheek.

The impulse was choked off, as by a coarse hand laid across the sensitive grid of his nerves.

Not for you, Roman Laird. Not for the accursed. Not for the judged, the condemned, the lost. Here is the other side of Infinity. Here is where you may worship; here is where you may burn....

And the evil vision that came to him matched the debauchery in Smith's monstrous paintings. Here goats capered and black cats yowled, and a young girl lay bound over a great pile of brush and leaves to form an altar. Around it stood hot-eyed women, chanting blasphemies and gesturing with unlighted candles in their left hands. Behind them, hairy-flanked men joined the chant, chuckling, and pausing to throw salt into the air.

His stomach sickened, as it had at the picture of Joyce in the wide bed. He tried to turn, to flee, but there was no fleeing. And then, mercifully, the scene blurred, colors running together as though sponged with turpentine.

Through his windows he could see the first thrustings of morning into the blue-black sky above the bay. He was sick. The events of the night had hammered on him too savagely. The weeks of concentrated work at the plant, the emotional upheavals. He was feverish. He'd see how he felt later; perhaps call Doctor Perryston....

The room above the garage waited. Window closed; air mixed with the odor of oil and stale cigars and an indefinable scent of wary animal.

In the dark, the paintings seemed to vibrate with a life of their own. The violent scenes on the walls, the scattered piles on the floor surged and pulsed with brutal vitality.

Outside, a squad car cruised.

Two officers glanced upward. "He won't be back," one said.

"Hell, no. After we chased him last night he's probably still running. Don't worry, Clancy; you'll never see *that* son-of-a-bitch again."

"Well, we got to keep an eye on it, anyway, like the Inspector says."

"We will," the other yawned. "Now whyncha drive around to Pancho's, and we'll grab a couple of coffees before we knock off?"

Both bottles were empty. He should be drunk by now, he thought. Dirty foul stinking drunk, but he had been defrauded again. The senses were not dulled, the nerves unimpeded. His bloodstream pulsed hot and painful despite the kindly alcohol.

He could not halt the thoughts. He could not drive Joyce of the painting from his mind. Joyce-of-the-painting versus Joyce-of-the-dream.

A grayness swept his senses from time to time. Not the cool grayness of fog or mist, but the gray of a dust-cloud, hot and dry, parching and deadly.

And the image of the girl in the painting rose, unobscured by the choking grayness. The joy and the wonder was ripped away and the strumpet soul revealed. Leering and depraved.

The nights when their breaths had mingled as one, her thoughts had been of someone else. The summer evenings when he'd thought them so close in mind and spirit and body—she dreamed of her nameless lover. In every hour they'd had together, alone, or in the friendly harmony of others, this other one had dogged them from the shadows. Smith. The murderer. The twisted inhuman being.

The demon lover who knew her down to the crescent mark on her body, down to the rotted portions in her soul.

The choking gray cloud came up, and he reached for the bottle in his agony. Empty. And small help if it had been full. There was nothing to halt the corrosion within him. No chemical that would reverse the reaction and give him back his peace. No drug, he knew, that would erase the vast repulsion that had flowed from the painting and wrapped itself around his heart. No relief for the terrible rage that was tearing him apart.

He groaned. There had to be an end to this soon. You couldn't endure such thoughts as this, and remain whole. He sank back, let himself be pulled down into the swirling, blinding mist.

The blinding, suffocating gray began to break apart, like a nightfog parting suddenly to reveal a bloody moon.

He thought, in his blindness, in his grinding rage, that someone had thrust the picture at him again. For wasn't this Joyce he saw through the breaking cloud?

Her face and hair and figure?

Dimly, wavering—then more clearly? Standing before him in her characteristic attitude, a slight twisting at the waist, one foot close and a little ahead of the other?

Exactly as in the painting.

Now she wore something of green clinging wool and now there was no livid anticipation in her face. Were her lips moving?

He watched. Yes; surely they were.

He listened—and heard her voice. Joyce's voice; he was sure of it. So lifelike. So real.

But of course she couldn't be here in his apartment. She wanted no more of Roman Laird. She had another lover. Richer, older, with more social position. Never would she come to him.

How he hated Joyce now, after what she had done; after what she had revealed herself to be!

He heard her voice as a silver bell ringing, and smelled her perfume as a heady wine, and in his nerves already felt her flesh bruising in his hands.

"Tell me! How did you get in here?"

Oh, but if it were only she, here in his apartment! Ah, but she'd be a long time getting out!

He said, too aflame with his passions to be puzzled, "I've been here all along, of course."

"The doors were locked, Roman. So were the windows on the lower floor." Accusingly?

He looked around. This thickly, richly carpeted floor—this wasn't his living room. That opulent furniture and soft velvet draperies—not of his own spare and simple choice.

Joyce's new home. Barton's and hers. Their own snug establishment. Roman had come here and Joyce wanted to know how.

"It doesn't seem to matter," he said. Aware of the tension in him; a great clock-spring, winding tighter, tighter. *How easily that belt would tear away, how easily the sheer fabric rip, how the gossamer would first resist and then come loose from her soft, struggling body.*

Joyce said nervously, *"You'd better go, Roman."*

"Go?" He'd just come. In some curious fashion, in some sodden confusion, he'd come here. He said, trying hard to discipline his mind, control the savage crawling of his nerves, "I want the truth, Joyce."

He caught her glance at the clock above the fireplace; knew she was estimating the time before someone—Barton, no doubt—would return. Caught the increased pallor of her face. How could he speak so calmly? How could he hold himself in?

"You know everything I know, Roman. I've told you—you've seen everything."

He laughed; a sound he'd never heard before, and saw her cringe slightly. "I've seen everything, all right. Including Smith's studio, and that charming little nude study he did of you. He's really caught the full flavor and quality of you, too!"

"I don't know what you are talking about."

He came closer.

"Oh but you do, my love. A little alley in North Beach, my beautiful lost dream. Over a vacant repair shop—garage. A madman's studio. A nightmare studio. Everything twisted and perverse and wrong. You seemed to *belong* there, Joyce."

Her eyes were wide. Fingers moving nervously at her throat.

"Dozens of paintings. Full of evil. And there you were—his masterpiece!"

Roman laughed, and somewhere in his mind there were echoes of other laughter. "You, my clean, cool Joyce, with your filthy dwarf and your degraded stallion and the rest of your miserable creatures. Only you weren't clean. Or cool. Because Smith knows you as you really are. He turned you inside out, Joyce, and painted your steaming, twisted soul!"

"*Roman....*"

Her face blurred for a moment, blotted out in the sudden gathering of grotesque shapes, tumbling over one another. He forced them away. "You're remembering now, aren't you?" And then he told her what they were doing in the painting and saw the look of fascinated horror, saw the flush come into her face and creep down the long V of her throat. "Even the mark. The little crescent moon mark on you. He painted that too. He didn't miss a thing."

He'd shaken her, he saw with greedy exultation. He'd gotten under her defenses at last, and now his impulse was to strike again and again. "I see you're remembering."

She rubbed her forehead. "*No. Not what you think. I swear I don't know this—this painter.*"

"Liar!" Rage bursting through him in gusts; revulsion and the gray sickness rose again and in its midst a blurred and mocking figure. Come closer; come and be recognized, you bastard, you enemy....

"*Roman, you have me so confused. I don't know. I don't understand.*"

"Anyone would understand that picture. Maybe I can get it hung in some local gallery. You'd like that, wouldn't you? Nothing like some good notoriety to help a fashion model along. You might do even better than Barton, with enough men knowing you for what you are."

She seemed to shrink away, and a wicked joy rose in him. He'd hit her again, and it hurt.

"You know what, Joyce? I could make a gift of the painting to Barton's wife. I'm sure she'd know how to use it most effectively."

"*Roman—whatever I've done isn't enough for you to hate me so.*"

"*Do* I hate you?" Did he? The surge of emotion, rising and falling, rising and smashing at his reason, retreating to gather strength and assail him again—was this hate, or love, or some weird alloy of the two?

"*I think so.*" She moved over to the fireplace, staring into the cold ashes. "*I think you've hated me for a long time, Roman. Even when you made love to me. I didn't realize it then, even though I felt something wasn't quite—right. Maybe that's why I could never really love you without reservation. You hated me a little bit even from the beginning. And more and more as time went on.*"

He wanted to slap her with all his strength. The clever, lying strumpet. "Quite a theory, Joyce. Gives you a fine excuse, doesn't it?"

She didn't seem to hear him. She was calmer now and her calm infuriated him even more. "*I began to be afraid of you, Roman. Something terrible was growing in you. You demanded to know last night who it was I feared. IT WAS YOU!*"

He felt his lips grinning. "That's why you cut me off? That's why you ditched me at the hotel? That's why you've been running away? Do you think I'm a child? You were snuggling up with Barton! That's why!"

"Bart came later. I didn't plan it. Neither of us could help ourselves. Call it rotten, Roman. You're entitled to call me names. But I—neither of us are as bad as you think."

"What does it matter what I think? One guy knew—and he recorded it in oils on canvas. He's got you as you really are, Joyce. If you've never seen the completed job, you wouldn't know what I mean."

"If there is such a painting I've never seen it."

Laughter bubbled within him. Thin ribbons of scorching fog reached out to engulf him. He shook them off. "You should see it. I'd like to show it to you. It's something you'll remember for the rest of your days."

"I don't want to see it."

"Of course you don't." He was surprised at the intuitive knowledge that came to him. "Do you know why? Do you suspect why? Well, I'll tell you. Because the memory will come between you and every normal man you ever go to bed with. You'll find yourself sinking down. Down with Smith and his kind. Down to the ones who only look like men. Your kind, Joyce...."

She laughed and her laugh glistened with anger. *"How absurd can you get? Really, Roman—"*

"A few moments ago you didn't want to see the painting. Now you're trying to laugh it away. You're afraid."

"Am I? AM I? Where is this marvelous horror? I'll show you whether I'm frightened or not!"

"Then come. Right now."

She glanced at the clock once more, tossed her head in a small defiant gesture, and walked with him toward the door.

NINETEEN

The drive across town in the Jaguar roadster was not entirely clear to him.

He hadn't known he would be so greatly disturbed by her nearness, hadn't realized he would catch the fragrance of Joyce's perfume again; that it would cut into his consciousness like a scalpel into tissue.

Yet he was curiously calm. As though he'd reached the epicenter of his emotional storms. On all sides there was violence and danger, waiting for him. But this moment—this instant of time—he felt a degree of relief. He could almost shut his mind and believe that Joyce and he were off on some fun-flecked adventure as they had enjoyed in the past.

Though Roman knew it was a false and transient peace, he was for the moment, almost happy.

He breathed deeply, sensing well-being as he swung the powerful car around corners until his headlights picked out the narrow alley running back of the garage. He braked to a quick stop. "This is as far as we can drive," he said. "It's just a bit further along here."

He helped her out; her hand felt cold to his touch.

She leaned away from him, bracing against the car. "I—I don't want to go. Take me back, Roman."

As though her resistance had been the signal. Back came the rage; the sharp ache, the shivering in his bones and the rumbling, hurting need deep in his bowels.

"You're here now," he said gruffly, still holding himself calm. "You're here."

He led her to the door, moving with sure step through the darkness. Unlocked. Her breath sounding hard with fright as she followed him into the room. He found the switch and light flooded the studio, then watched her as she blinked; then stared around curiously.

"Surely it's not so unfamiliar, Joyce?" he jibed. She didn't answer. He walked back to the door, locked it, dropped the key into his pocket.

"Why—why did you do that, Roman?"

He shrugged. "Why not? You've been alone with me before."

"I know, but—" She looked at some of the paintings, askew on the grimy walls. "God, what stuff!"

He watched her expression, fascinated by her reaction. Shock was plain as her eyes moved to one horror after another. As though the savage brutality in each canvas throbbed with a life of its own. *As though each scene hurled itself upon and into her, possessed her violently, and cast her away.*

His own desire grew. He was in fever.

He wished now he hadn't brought Joyce here. It was too much to bear. *Control, Laird, control.* These weird, obscene paintings seemed to set up a kind of high frequency current, charging his nerves with their poisonous vitality.

Sweating, he fumbled for the door key in his pocket. For a single compassionate moment his impulse was to toss it to Joyce, tell her to go; to run.

She spoke too soon. "I—I don't want to see any more, Roman." Her voice was low; pleading. "Please; I—"

The confession of weakness stirred his frenzy, exploding small pockets of anger within him. She didn't want to see any more of the paintings... but *he* wanted her to see more. He wanted her to see what he had seen.

He said harshly, "Wait," and rummaged in one of the canvas stacks until he found the painting of the emaciated butcher at work in his shop. "The girl on the block is Nina Valjean, Joyce. The man who used this studio painted her and killed her in your apartment."

The compelling violence on the canvas seemed to take hold of Joyce, to shake and stun her. "Please put it away, Roman. I—I can't stand any more."

"Can't you?" The laugh was harsh. He picked out another canvas. "Here's a later study; quite recent, I'd say. Some of the colors are still wettish, sticky. This is Cecille Merrill. He got into her apartment and tried to kill her, too. She managed to escape him with nothing on but the nylon stocking around her throat."

Joyce's big eyes held a piteous appeal, but she said nothing.

"Here's another; scarcely anything that will interest you, Joyce. My own dull features worked into a rather surprising effect. I've been aware of Mr. Smith's scrutiny for some time. He evidently has me marked for slaughter. Jealousy, perhaps, because of our former intimacy, Joyce. I can't imagine any other reason, can you?" He let the painting drop.

She shook her head, shoulders sagging. She looked small and tired and suddenly vulnerable. His temples began throbbing unmercifully, and the grayness seemed to reach out hot streamers groping to engulf his mind. Within his body, deep inside, was an insistent drumming. The room itself snarled its anger and in the dark corners crept another, more evil presence.

Smith.

Smith, the lewdly snickering shadow; enjoying the display of his work, perhaps? Enjoying the fear and the repulsion he'd stirred in Joyce.

Roman was trembling as he lifted the last painting from the stack.

"The one I promised you, Joyce. The likeness you refused to believe." He stood the painting on the easel and stood beside her. "Was I wrong, Joyce? Was I?"

Joyce covered her eyes, finally, and her fingers curled until her hands had become small clenched fists pressed against her forehead. A strangled sound came from her throat, then another. She was sobbing and trying hard not to. "Do you truly believe I'm like—like that, Roman? Do you?"

"Aren't you, Joyce? The man who used this studio seems to have had pretty keen perception. This killer of women, this man who may someday find you—"

She wasn't listening. She was looking away to one side of the room, then she turned and stared at him. Horror filled her eyes. An unwilling realization of a monstrous truth.

"ROMAN!"

Her hoarse whisper prickled his skin. Her hands fluttered helplessly; frightened birds unable to escape. Her tearstained face was ashy-white and deep labored breathing moved high her agitated breasts. She looked as though she were staring at Death itself.

"What, Joyce?" he gasped. "Wh—what is it?"

"*You* were the one who used this room! *You killed that girl in my apartment. YOU ARE SMITH!*"

The hot gray fog folded over him. The hot, sticky flow of rage rose in him. The fury and the violence and the driving, all-compelling urge.

He remembered her face fading as though obscured by the thick rolling gray clouds.

He turned to the painting of Joyce. To the girl at her wild, licentious pleasures, at the morbid twisted creatures of a morbid twisted world.

A world that seemed to reach out and draw him in—into its lividly violent depths.

TWENTY

He seemed to be struggling upward in a thick, cloying sea, breath squeezed from him, needing breath, needing the air, needing light in the place of the gray blindness. And then at last the sun, brightly hopeful and shining.

The world steadied and became motionless under him. Space solidified under him. He was laying on rough plank flooring, his head aching as though it had been beaten, his body stiff and throbbing with pain. He lifted his heavy head and wiped his eyes with the back of his hand.

His hand came away wet.

He blinked in the yellow light trying to clear his vision.

There was something in his other hand; he stared. A scrap of torn green material.

Alarm set his heart to violent action. Joyce... she had been here... *where was she?*

He stumbled to his feet.

"Joyce!"

"*JOYCE!*"

The madly pictured walls mocked him. In panic he looked around.

She wasn't hard to find. She was lying across a scattered stack of canvases. Eyes open, staring. Arms outstretched, and one leg drawn up and motionless. The whiteness of her body spotted with bruises. Like Nina.

Around her throat a nylon stocking, tightly wound.

Smith, Roman thought, staring about him, fists knotted to kill and destroy his enemy. Smith. He'd come back here. Gotten in somehow and ravished and murdered Joyce while he, Roman, lay unconscious.

But there was laughter in the room. Derisive, hooting laughter.

Oh no, not Smith. Turn now and face the truth, Roman Laird. Open your foolish eyes, Roman Laird. See and know and feel and smell your damnation, Roman Laird....

"Shut up!" he cried, his legs trembling so he could hardly stand. "Shut up, liars, demons. I won't listen!"

They laughed louder then. They squealed in his ears and slipped into his brain, chortling and chattering.

Remember what you're trying to forget. Remember what Joyce said. Remember when she was collapsing with fright and cried out to you, accusing you? Remember? You were the one who used this studio! You painted those horrible pictures! YOU YOURSELF ARE SMITH!

"No!" he screamed. *"No!"*

But They wrenched his head and tugged his eyeballs until he looked—and saw what Joyce had seen.

The bottle of whiskey under the sink. The fifth of Old Adam that had revealed to her in an intuitive flash what lay deep-buried in her unconscious all the while.

He fell to his knees before the bottle. He knew there could be no coincidence. Few people knew the brand; fewer used it.

The vapid Eve with the snake around her neck. *Joyce-of-the-painting with the snake around her neck; Joyce-of-the-flesh with the nylon around her neck.* He seized the bottle and smashed it against the sink, splashing whiskey and glass shards, slicing open the palm of his hand. He felt nothing of the cuts in his greater anguish.

Remember? They danced in glee. That memory that always eluded you? Remember the clerk who wrapped your favorite brand of whiskey without your asking? How did he know, Roman? You thought you hadn't seen him before, but he'd seen you before. You came to the store as Smith. Several times, on your way to debaucheries with Nina. Remember?

Your other self, Laird. Your other side, your other personality. It was there all the time, and you didn't know!

Waves of sickness followed waves of knowledge.

The sense of being watched. No more than his Smith-self peering out of his mind, trying to slip past the iron control of his Laird-self.

Smith, who crept forward at night, when his conscious mind was dormant. Who seized Roman's body and rode it about on his vicious errands. Smith, who was no more than his own buried lusts and passions.

By day, a clever, forceful engineer. By night, the unconscious slave of his inner self. Growing and gaining strength with each dark act. A creature of evil instinct. An incubus wrestling silently with the guardian of his mind.

Projecting hatred by small, irrelevant acts. The rhinestone earring, the torn letter... the one tortured body answering two implacable masters.

YES, ROMAN, YES! It's true! Now you know.

The wall shook; the masonry crumbled. Great stones fell from their places. The mind of one crawled over into the mind of the other. Smith became Laird and Laird, Smith. The memory of one became the memory of the other.

He thought, how much better it would have been if God had first destroyed him and sent him to his deserved hell.

He stared at his hands... the offensive tools that had twisted life from two women, that had broken a man so that he too died.

Kneeling by the body of Joyce, he wept. "I didn't mean to, darling. I didn't know...."

A thin streak of dawnlight crept across the sky. It touched feebly at the dirt-covered window; it passed the shuddering room.

He lifted her, tugged at her, his tears falling on her cooling flesh. "Don't you see, it wasn't my doing. It was his. Smith's. I loved you. I wouldn't have harmed you, Joyce. You know that. Try to get up; try to awaken. Try to forgive me. I loved you.... I loved you.... You believe me, don't you, darling? You believe he did it, don't you?"

Even when daylight came and there was the sound of heavy footsteps on the stairs, and a heavy rapping on the door, and heavy voices calling out, he was pulling at Joyce, trying to get her up, to awaken her.

He lifted his wet, puffy face when they smashed at the door, and called to them when he saw their white faces through the broken panelling.

"*He* did it... *Smith*... you understand, don't you? You don't blame me? Because it was the other one... Smith... not me... *the other one.*"

The End

Kermit Jaediker Bibliography
(1911-1986)

Tall Dark and Dead (1947)
Hero's Lust (1953)

Kermit Jaediker was born on April 19, 1911 in New Jersey. He worked in comic books from 1941 – 1943 as a writer and colorist. After that, he wrote his first book, *Tall Dark and Dead*, published by Mystery House in 1947. His only other novel, *Hero's Lust*, was published by Lion Books in 1953. Besides writing stories and articles for some of the men's magazines, Jaediker worked as a staff writer for the *New York Daily News* in the 1940s, specializing in true crime cases. His final byline occurred in 1973, when he wrote about the Zodiac Killer for the *Sunday News*. Jaediker passed away in 1986.

Walter J. Sheldon Bibliography
(1917-1996)

Fiction
Troubling of a Star (as by "Walt Sheldon"; 1954)
The Man Who Paid His Way (as by "Walt Sheldon"; 1955)
Tour of Duty (1959)
The Key to Tokyo (1962)
The Blue Kimono Kill (as by "Walt Sheldon"; 1965)
The House of Happy Mayhem (as by "Walt Sheldon"; 1967)
The Devil's Box (as by "Walt Sheldon"; 1968)
Red Flower Kill (1971)
Gold Bait (as by "Walt Sheldon"; 1973)
The Yellow Music Kill (as by "Walt Sheldon"; 1974)
Beast (1980)
The Rites of Murder (1984)
Brink of Madness (2015)

As by Ellery Queen
Guess Who's Coming to Kill You (1968)

As by Shel Walker
The Man I Killed (1952)

As by Shelly Walters
The Dunes (1974)

Non-Fiction
Enjoy Japan (as by "Walt Sheldon"; 1961)
The Honorable Conquerors: the Occupation of Japan 1945-1952 (as by "Walt Sheldon"; 1965)
Hell or High Water: MacArthur's Landing at Inchon (as by "Walt Sheldon"; 1968)
Tigers in the Rice: The Story of Vietnam (1969)
Boating Without Going Broke (1975)

Shel Walker is the pseudonym of Walker J. Sheldon, born January 9, 1917 in Philadelphia, Pennsylvania. He began writing for the pulps in 1940, eventually authoring 13 thrillers and 5 non-fiction works, mostly histories of WWII. Writing under his real name, he wrote many science fiction stories in the 1950s. *The Man I Killed,* published in 1952, was his first novel and the only book written under the "Shel Walker" byline. Sheldon has also worked as a newspaper reporter, a TV producer and a psychological operations specialist for the overseas Dept. of Defense. He lived for many years in Japan before moving to Washington, where he passed away June 9, 1996.

Clayre & Michel Lipman Bibliography
(Clayre: 1903-1978; Michel: 1913-2010)

Play
The Night We Ate Aunt Minnie (3 acts; 1943)

Stories
"The Walking Corpse," *Ellery Queen's Mystery Magazine*, Sept 1950.
"My Last Book," *Twenty Great Tales of Murder*, ed. Helen McCloy &
   Brett Halliday, 1951
"The Dilemma of Grandpa Dubois," *Crooks' Tour*, 1953.
"The House on Judas Street," *Malcolm's*, May 1954; also as "A Slice of
   Miss Wittles."
"Man Out of Time," *Malcolm's*, March 1954.
"Priest Hole," *Verdict Crime Detection Magazine*, Nov 1956; *Giant
   Manhunt* #12, 1958.
"A Slice of Miss Wittles," *Ellery Queen's Mystery Magazine,* July 1961;
   Ellery Queen's Mystery Magazine (UK), Jan 1962; originally
   published as "The House on Judas Street."

Novel
House of Evil (1954)

Clayre Lipman (1903-1978) and her husband Michel Lipman (1913-
2010) were a writing team who lived in Marin County, California. They
co-authored at least one 3-act play, *The Night We Ate Aunt Minnie*, in
1943, and published the guide, *The Modern Key to Money
Management* in 1955. They also wrote several mystery stories together
which were published in *Ellery Queen's Mystery Magazine, Malcolm's*
and *Verdict Crime Detection,* and provided the stories for a few 1950s
TV teleplays as well. *House of Evil*, published in 1954, is their sole
novel. After Clayre's death at age 74, Michel continued to write
children's and young adult books.

Suspense Classics from the Godmother of Noir...

Elisabeth Sanxay Holding

Lady Killer / Miasma
978-0-9667848-7-9 $19.95

Murder is suspected aboard a cruise ship to the Caribbean, and a young doctor falls into a miasma of doubt when he agrees to become medical assistant in a house of mystery. "*Miasma* and *Lady Killer* provides an excellent introduction to her world."—Ed Gorman

The Death Wish / Net of Cobwebs
978-0-9667848-9-3 $19.95

Poor Mr. Delancey is pulled into a murderous affair when he comes to the aid of a friend, and a merchant seaman suffering from battle trauma becomes the first suspect when Aunt Evie is found murdered. "A whodunit of the first order."—*Boston Herald*

Strange Crime in Bermuda / Too Many Bottles
978-0-9749438-5-5 $19.95

An intriguing tale of a sudden disappearance on a Caribbean island, and a mysterious death by pills, which could have been accidental—or murder. "The dialog is pitch perfect and Holding writes inner conflict and confusion better than anyone." —Rick Ollerman, *Amazon.com*

The Old Battle Ax / Dark Power
978-1-933586-16-8 $19.95

Mrs. Herriott spins a web of deception when her sister is found dead on the sidewalk, and a woman's vision of a family reunion is quickly shattered by feelings of dread when she answers her uncle's invitation to visit. "A skillfully told tale with deep implications."—*Atlanta Journal*

The Unfinished Crime / The Girl Who Had to Die
978-1-933586-41-0 $19.95

Priggish Andrew Branscombe tries to control everyone around him with such a web of deceit that he is the one finally caught up in its tangled skein. Jocelyn is convinced she is going to be murdered, so naturally everyone suspects young Killian when she is pushed off the cruise ship.

Speak of the Devil / The Obstinate Murderer
978-1-933586-71-7 $17.95

Murder stalks the halls at a Caribbean resort hotel, and an aging alcoholic is called in to solve a murder that hasn't happened yet. "Strongly recommended."—*Baltimore Sun.* "Amazing deviltry."—*Saturday Review.* "As a baffler, it's excellent."—*Waterbury American.*

Two novels in each trade paperback edition from:

Stark House Press
1315 H Street, Eureka, CA 95501
griffinskye3@sbcglobal.net
www.StarkHousePress.com

Available from your local bookstore, or order direct with check or via our website.